Praise for the work of

jaci burton

"Brilliant . . . a fiery romance [and] a gratifying book to read. The love scenes were romantic and gratifyingly hot! [A] fabulous plot, and . . . lovable characters. I'll read this . . . over and over again and I am sure you will too."   —*Just Erotic Romance Reviews*

"Lively and funny . . . The sex is both intense and loving; you can feel the connection that both the hero and heroine want to deny in every word and touch between them. I cannot say enough good things about this book."   —*Road to Romance*

"Burton's book packs an amazing wallop! It's rich with passion, excitement, intense emotion, and a sense of love that's utterly palpable."

—*Romantic Times*

"[An] exhilarating novel . . . flaming-hot . . . This is one sweet and spicy romance."   —*Romance Junkies*

wild, wicked, & wanton

Jaci Burton

heat | new york

THE BERKLEY PUBLISHING GROUP
Published by the Penguin Group
Penguin Group (USA) Inc.
375 Hudson Street, New York, New York 10014, USA
Penguin Group (Canada), 90 Eglinton Avenue East, Suite 700, Toronto, Ontario M4P 2Y3, Canada
(a division of Pearson Penguin Canada Inc.)
Penguin Books Ltd., 80 Strand, London WC2R 0RL, England
Penguin Group Ireland, 25 St. Stephen's Green, Dublin 2, Ireland (a division of Penguin Books Ltd.)
Penguin Group (Australia), 250 Camberwell Road, Camberwell, Victoria 3124, Australia
(a division of Pearson Australia Group Pty. Ltd.)
Penguin Books India Pvt. Ltd., 11 Community Centre, Panchsheel Park, New Delhi—110 017, India
Penguin Group (NZ), 67 Apollo Drive, Mairangi Bay, Auckland 1311, New Zealand
(a division of Pearson New Zealand Ltd.)
Penguin Books (South Africa) (Pty.) Ltd., 24 Sturdee Avenue, Rosebank, Johannesburg 2196,
South Africa

Penguin Books Ltd., Registered Offices: 80 Strand, London WC2R 0RL, England

This is an original publication of The Berkley Publishing Group

First edition: May 2007

Library of Congress Cataloging-in-Publication Data

Burton, Jaci.
    Wild, wicked, & wanton / Jaci Burton.—1st ed.
        p.   cm.
    ISBN 978-0-425-21383-4
    I. Title. II. Title: Wild, wicked, and wanton.
    PS3602.U776W55 2007
    813'.6—dc22

                                                                          2006039374

PRINTED IN THE UNITED STATES OF AMERICA

10   9   8   7   6

To the women I'd most like to have margaritas with. My BB's—
Angie, Mandy, Mel, and Shan.

To my editor, Kate Seaver—thank you for your patience, your
guidance, and for loving the ladies of WWW.

To my agent, Deidre Knight—thanks for always being there to
talk me down off the ledge.

To Lora Leigh and Shelley Bradley/Shayla Black—two amazing
women I admire. You ladies write with such incredible heat, you
singe my eyeballs when I read. Yet you always manage to tie up
my heart and soul in your books, and that's what makes a great
erotic romance. Thank you for the inspiration and for the help
you've given me along the way.

And, as always, to my husband, Charlie—the man who makes all
my fantasies a reality. Without you, my dreams would be empty,
as would my heart.

wild

ABBY

one

abby lawson stood outside the door to dr. mike Nottingham's office and raised her hand to knock, then stopped.

Okay, dumb ass. He called you to his office for a reason. If you're going to make a decent veterinarian, you've got to stop quaking in your boots every time one of the docs wants to see you.

She should have had an orgasm this morning. Now she was a jumble of pent-up anxieties. Okay, she was always a jumble of pent-up anxieties, but today more than usual.

It was all her ex-husband's fault. If Chad hadn't been such a lying, cheating, whoring son of a bitch, she might be a satisfied, happy woman. Instead, she was embarking on her first career, scared shitless and perpetually horny because she had no man in her life, no prospects for a man, no time for a man, and no desire to ever repeat the mistakes she'd made in the past. Too bad her sex drive didn't understand the *no man* part. Her libido wanted a man in the worst way.

It wasn't going to get one. Right now she had to concentrate on her career, not sex. And career meant focusing on what Mike wanted to talk to her about.

It was time for end-of-semester evaluations. Maybe that's why he wanted to see her. The two semesters she'd spent at Silverwood Veterinary Hospital had been damn near perfect. Silverwood Vet Hospital was one of the best in Oklahoma. Hell, she'd love to work there permanently if she didn't have a driving ambition to set up her own practice after graduation.

Jumping the gun was a really bad idea. For all she knew, Mike was going to tell her she had no future as a vet when she stepped into his office.

Quit being such a baby, Abby. Did she leave her self-esteem at home today? If her friends Blair and Callie could hear her thoughts, they'd smack her.

That's what she needed right now. A good slap in the face from her two best pals. They were great at pumping up her ego when she needed a boost. And she sure needed one at the moment. Or a swift kick in the ass, anyway.

Knock on the freakin' door! She rapped lightly.

"Come on in," Mike called out.

She stepped in and closed the door behind her. Mike was on the phone and motioned her to one of the chairs in front of his desk. She slipped into the chair, and as Mike turned to the side, she admired his profile. He wore his black hair a little long, and it curled at the ends. Thick, she itched to grab hold of it and run her fingers through the shiny darkness. He was tall, about six two, she'd guess. Not overly bulky, but more like a runner, all lean muscle. He wore jeans and a polo shirt that showed off his well-toned pecs and arms. Always relaxed, casual, and smiling. And tan.

Maybe he laid naked by his pool and worked on beautifying his already gorgeous body. Her pussy twitched. *Great, Abby. Good idea to launch a fantasy while sitting in the boss's office. Might as well just slip your hands between your legs and start masturbating right now. I'm sure he won't notice. Ugh.*

Career, remember? Not men. And definitely not this *man.*

She occupied her wayward mind by looking around his expansive office. Pictures of dogs, cats, lizards, birds, and horses filled the wall space. Behind his desk was an aquarium overflowing with exotic fish. Abby was mesmerized watching the colorful fish dashing through coral and around undulating sea grass.

"Sorry. Thanks for waiting."

Turning her attention from the hypnotic aquarium, she folded her hands in her lap and looked at him.

He winked a steely blue eye at her, his smile comforting.

Okay, so he *was* smiling. A good sign. "Not a problem."

"You didn't start without me, did you?"

Abby half-turned in her seat. Mike's partner, Seth Jacobs, stepped through the doorway, closed the door behind him, and flopped down in the chair next to hers. Just as casual as Mike in jeans and polo shirt, Seth grinned and brushed a lock of sandy brown hair away from his face. Abby warmed at his smile. Like Mike, Seth always made her stomach churn, though he was completely different in looks. Where Mike was the epitome of tall, dark, and handsome, Seth radiated boyish charm. Just under six feet tall, Seth was solid muscle, built like a warrior, yet one of the most gentle men she'd ever met. And he cracked jokes all the time, making her laugh so hard she'd end up doubled over against the counter with tears streaming down her face.

"Your internship is almost finished, Abby," Mike said, capturing her attention.

"I know." She felt a momentary sense of loss. She loved this place, would miss it when she was gone.

"And we've decided that we should celebrate," Seth said. "After all, we're your last stop before graduation, aren't we?"

"Yes. Last stop. Uh, celebrate?"

"Yeah. You know. Like a party?" Seth cocked a brow.

"Oh, that's not necessary. You've both been wonderful enough as it is." Heat rose up her neck and headed toward her face as they both stared at her, then back at each other.

"Of course it's necessary. We thought we'd do it at the club this weekend," Mike said, looking at Seth.

Seth nodded. "Great idea."

"Huh?" What were they talking about? "What club?"

"Silverwood Country Club, of course," Seth said. "We'll throw a big party for your impending graduation. Invite the entire office staff. You can bring along a few of your friends."

Abby shook her head, horrified at the thought of any attention, especially by these two men. "I don't think so, but thanks." Blair and Callie would have a field day with this one. They'd never let her live it down. Partying with two of Silverwood's most eligible bachelors? Oh, God, the mere thought of it—

"Don't be ridiculous. We insist. We've been wanting to, ah, take you out, anyway," Mike said.

Abby's gaze shot to his, certain she hadn't heard his last sentence correctly. "Take me out?"

"That was subtle, dumb ass," Seth said, glaring at Mike. "Abby, let me explain. Mike and I are both . . . interested in you."

"Interested." She knew she sounded like an echo, but honestly, she wasn't really grasping what they were trying to say. Okay, she was grasping, but she wasn't believing it. Not for one damn second.

"And you said I wasn't subtle?" Mike rolled his eyes at Seth.

"Well, it's not the easiest damn subject, is it?" Seth replied.

Abby had entered an alternate universe. That had to be it, because her reality was never like this.

Mike skirted his desk and squatted in front of her, picking up her hand and cradling it between his. Only this time there were no instruments, vaccination vials, or file folders between them. Just skin. Warm skin. Her fingers rested on his wrist, his pulse beating rhythmically. Normal. Which was more than she could say for her own, which rushed along at breakneck speed every time she took in a breath. His body was like a heat blanket. She inhaled again—really, she couldn't help herself, because he smelled like he'd just stepped out of the shower. Clean, fresh, God, what kind of soap did the man use? Some kind of aphrodisiac for sure. Eau de Torture of Women.

You are in such bad shape, Abby. So she hadn't had sex in like four hundred years. So what? Okay, maybe two years. Two years. Two goddamn years. She was thirty-three years old. In her prime, sexually, and she should be having the best sex of her life right now. Instead, she was knee-deep in finishing up her internship in veterinary school and the only release she was getting came from the self-induced variety with her vibrator.

Pathetic.

"Abby, I'm sure you've noticed Seth and I both have an interest in you."

Okay, she was definitely having some kind of weird daydream. "Uh, no."

Mike cocked a brow. "You didn't?"

And now she was embarrassed at being so clueless. They were interested in her? Holy hell in a handbasket. Where had she been the past year? Oh sure, they teased her and joked with her and were personable and friendly and gorgeous and smelled good and she'd like to unzip their pants and grab their cocks and . . . oh, God. Where was she going with this thought process, anyway?

The way Mike looked at her now, his eyes darkening, she realized he had been paying a lot of attention to her the past several months. She turned her gaze to Seth and saw the same probing look in his warm eyes. Only it wasn't a hands-off, professional look. It was heat.

Desire. Much more than just *Hey, you work here, and we think you'll make a great veterinarian.* It was more like a *Hey, baby, we'd like to get you naked.*

Shit. She was way out of her league here.

"I'm sorry, Abby. We're making you uncomfortable," Mike said. He stood and backed away, giving her space.

"No, you're not. Really." Yes, he was, really, but it was uncomfortable in a good way. Two men wanted her. Wow.

"You really had no idea," Seth said.

"No. I didn't. I mean, God, this is so embarrassing, but no, I really didn't." Could she be more clueless? Such an unattractive quality. She brushed her hair away from her face with her fingers, trying not to blush. She wasn't exactly the most experienced flirt. The only man she'd ever been with was Chad, and she hadn't flirted since high school. That was almost fifteen years ago. She was rusty.

"Okay, since Mike butchered this so damn badly, let's start over." Seth stood and pulled Abby from her chair, keeping hold of her hands. "Abby, over the past year Mike and I have gotten to know you very well, not only professionally but personally. You're not only competent as an up-and-coming veterinarian but also warm, charming, gorgeous, and funny, and we found ourselves with one hell of a dilemma. First off, we didn't want to approach you during your internship, because that would have been unprofessional. Now that you're finished up here, there's no moral conflict, and we felt we could ask you if you'd like to . . . shit, I'm not doing this any better than Mike did. This sounds like a fucking job interview."

She fought back a grin at his obvious discomfort. Okay, admittedly, this was fun. "A dilemma?"

"Yeah. We both want to ask you out."

She couldn't help it. Her lips quirked. "And that's a dilemma?" She felt the old flirtatious surge, long dormant, spring to life. Creaky and not used in a long time, but it was still there.

"A big dilemma," Mike added, stepping beside Seth to take one of her hands in his. "I'm sorry we overwhelmed you with this. We kind of thought you knew."

A little shiver of delight skittered down her spine as she realized she was sandwiched between two incredibly sexy men. Now this she could get used to. "I guess I was focusing on work and wasn't paying attention." But she was sure as hell paying attention now. And enjoying every second of having Mike and Seth look at her as if they wanted to eat her alive. Her body flushed, but this time not from embarrassment. Heat seared her from the inside out. Her panties moistened, and her nipples hardened to the point she wanted to look down and see if they showed through her scrubs.

"Too much work and not enough play," Mike said with a wink. "You've been working your ass off the past few years. It's time to play a little. Let Seth and me take you out this weekend. Since we realized we were both interested in you and neither one of us was willing to back off, we figured we'd both take you out and let you decide."

"Decide?" She looked at both of them and swallowed hard, not even wanting to ponder the implications of that word.

"Okay, not really decide," Seth corrected. "Mike's an ass. There's no decision to make. We'll just have fun. We'll buy you dinner at the club. The entire office staff will attend, and you can bring your friends, making it completely safe. We'll dance and toast your impending graduation with a bottle of champagne. Or two," he finished with a wink. "Then if you're interested in either of us or maybe both of us . . . well, we'll go from there."

Holy shit. Could she do this? Go out with two men? At the same time? Her head was beginning to pound. Everything was happening much too fast. This morning her biggest concern was getting home so she could to feed her cat, do her grocery shopping, and be done in time to catch her favorite television show before she had to start her homework. Such was the excitement of her life.

This was a little bit more than she was used to. She needed Blair and Callie, and she needed them now. A powwow was in order.

"I need to think about this," she said, her gaze flitting to both of them. Actually, she didn't. She wanted to jump on it right now before they changed their minds. But she really needed to talk to Blair and Callie first and get their advice. The only man she'd ever dated was Chad. It wasn't like she was loaded with experience here.

"You do that," Mike said. "No pressure. God, I'm really sorry about this, Abby. We mangled this whole invitation pretty badly."

She stood and, despite wanting to end the conversation on a professional note, couldn't manage to shake the smile from her lips. "Actually, I think you both did a pretty good job of making my day. Quite possibly my entire year. Thanks."

"Oh, Abby. One more thing," Mike said.

She paused. "Yeah?"

He pulled a file from his desk and handed it to her. "I want you to do the Jackson spay tomorrow."

She grinned and took the file. "You got it."

"You're going to make a helluva vet, Abby."

"Thanks to both of you. I've really enjoyed my time here, and I've learned so much. You're really too good to me."

Before she embarrassed herself any further, she hurried out of their office. After finishing up her paperwork, she hightailed it out of there and called Blair and Callie from her cell phone, scheduling a lunch for the next day.

If ever there was a need for her best buddies, it was now.

Holy hell, what a day.

"great move, dickhead," mike said, watching abby's sweet ass sway back and forth as she walked to her car. He reluctantly turned from the window of his office and leveled a glare at Seth.

Seth leaned against the corner of Mike's desk and folded his arms. "Yeah, you were Mr. Suave yourself."

"Fuck off."

Mike grinned back at him. "Okay, so neither of us handled it well. Not the easiest subject anyway."

"If you'd just back off we wouldn't have this problem."

"Or you could back off." But neither of them would. Which was the problem they'd faced ever since they realized they both lusted after Abby. Not the first time they'd had this dilemma. Friends for over thirty years, they had grown up together, fought together, shared toys and battled over them, shared girls in high school and occasionally came to blows over them, too, but usually gave up on the girl before they let their friendship suffer.

This time it was different.

Abby was different.

Mike loved women. He mostly loved fucking women. He wanted to fuck Abby. Beyond that, who knew? But Abby didn't give him the time of day other than respect as a boss, and that intrigued the hell out of him. Usually women fell all over him.

Okay, so her nonchalance bruised his ego a little. He had to laugh at himself over that. Maybe he was used to the adoration. Seth always referred to him as the pretty one, because he was tall, with black hair, tanned skin, and blue eyes, and he worked out enough that his body was in prime shape. So he had good looks and a great body and an easygoing personality, and maybe he used those charms once in awhile. All right, he used them a lot.

Seth called him a "pussy magnet." It made him laugh, but damn if it wasn't true. Then again, after awhile he wasn't sure if it was his looks, his money, or his sizable cock that attracted the women. Maybe a combination of all three.

Funny, though, none of those seemed to interest Abby at all. And she'd been around the clinic long enough to hear all the rumors.

Yet she hadn't batted one eyelash at him in the entire time he'd known her.

Maybe that's why he was interested in her. He'd never had to chase a woman before.

"So what do you think?" Seth asked.

Mike shrugged. "It's up to her."

"We probably scared the shit out of her. Especially you. You're a little . . . much, sometimes, Mike."

"What? My dick?"

Seth snorted. "She hasn't been graced with the Nottingham Monster yet unless you've been waving it at her behind closed doors."

He rolled his eyes at Seth and tossed a file at him. "Right. You know better than that. I save the pussy pursuits for outside the clinic." A fact they'd both agreed to when they set up the partnership. Business was business. Fun was for after hours only. And it had worked well for them the past ten years. No personal pursuits at the clinic. No dating employees and absolutely no fucking at the clinic. No entanglements with clients, ever. A firm rule that neither of them had ever broken, much to the chagrin of many of their female clientele.

Of course they'd occasionally lost a client that way, but it had helped maintain their business and their friendship. When a client wanted more from them than just business, they had to say no.

But now they wanted Abby. Both of them.

And Mike was a pretty good judge of women. Abby might have been shocked, but she was also interested. He'd seen the flare of interest in her eyes when they talked about wanting her. And if anyone needed a man and a seriously good fuck, it was her.

"Are you thinking this'll be one on one or two on one?" Mike asked.

Seth shrugged. "It could go either way."

"Which way do you want it to go?"

Seth laughed. "I want her for myself, asshole."

"Selfish bastard," Mike said, then snickered. They were too close for Mike to be insulted. "Not if I can talk her into taking me first."

"I think Abby will get whatever Abby wants. And if she wants both of us, I doubt either of us will complain about that."

Seth was right. "We've never complained about ménage before. Just the thought of it makes my dick hard. So stop talking about it before I have to walk down the hallway with a hard-on."

Mike shook his head and brought out a couple folders for Seth to sign off on, but his mind stayed on the woman who'd captured their attention.

If Abby agreed, he'd see to it that she had a really good time this weekend. He was already anticipating their party at the club, wondering if she could handle both of them or if she'd choose just one. And if she did choose one of them, which would she pick?

"We'll see how it goes, then," Seth said, handing Mike the folders. "I'm heading to my office."

"I'm out for the day. See you tomorrow."

Seth sat down at his desk to finish up paperwork. He liked nights after everyone left. Typically he was the last one here. Mike always had a date. Or a fuck buddy, anyway. It wasn't often that he would go home without a woman in tow.

Seth was more selective these days. And lately, he'd had his eye on Abby.

From her first day at the hospital, she brought change with her. Divorced from one hell of a bitch on wheels, Seth was convinced that no woman, and he meant no woman, could ever make him look twice again. Maybe for a quick fuck, yeah, but more than that? Never again.

He'd looked more than twice at Abby, though. Granted, he wanted to fuck her. Hell yeah he wanted to fuck her. Up, down, sideways, on top, from behind, and every which way. God, his cock twitched just thinking about the ways he wanted to climb inside that woman.

With her chin-length blonde hair and sky blue eyes, her creamy skin and lithe body, she was a walking wet dream.

But he also found himself wanting to spend time with Abby outside the bedroom. She was totally and completely guileless, which intrigued him more than anything. She had no freaking idea how attractive she was, didn't know the first thing about using her beauty and knockout body to wrap a man around her little finger. Whip smart, funny as hell, and innocent, too. What man wouldn't want to get down on his knees and worship her?

Except Mike just wanted to fuck her. Okay, maybe Mike wanted more than that; he'd give his best buddy that. Mike was the smoldering sex god, though, and Seth was the one who used charm and persuasion to get the women into bed. He was their friend first. Mike just used his sex appeal. They were completely different in their approach to women, and maybe that was one of the reasons they had never seriously pursued the same woman before. Maybe that was why their friendship worked. But Seth had an idea they'd be competing over Abby or possibly sharing her, which opened up endless possibilities.

If she agreed to the party on Saturday night, this weekend could be really interesting.

two

when abby walked into torinos, her favorite mexican restaurant, she spied Blair at their usual booth in the corner of the bar. A margarita was already waiting for her. Blair waved her over, her wrists jingling with the tinkle of several silver charm bracelets.

"Where's Callie?" Abby shouted over the loud roar of driving music. She slid into the vinyl seat across from Blair. They all loved Torinos, mainly for the killer margaritas, but also because they could gossip to their hearts' content without anyone eavesdropping. It was always crowded, noisy, and nobody could hear what they were saying unless they were practically sitting on top of them.

"Running late. She had to find someone to cover lunch at the shop. She'll be here in a few." Blair took a sip of her margarita and grabbed a chip to nibble on. "So what's up?"

"I'll wait 'til Callie gets here. I don't want to have to say this twice."

Blair arched a perfectly shaped auburn brow. "Really. That good?"

"That . . . interesting." She took a long swallow of the margarita, wincing at the tequila burn. Her eyes watered, and she munched on a chip to soak up the alcohol.

Drumming her long nails on the lacquered tabletop, Blair said, "You're killing me here, Abby. You know I hate waiting. Give me a hint."

"Uh-uh. We're waiting for Callie."

"Who's late, but here. Sorry. Scoot over, Blair." Callie slid into Blair's side of the booth and grinned at Abby. "Casey was sick today, and she normally covers lunch, so I had to wait for Jolene to come in."

"We could have rescheduled, Callie," Abby said. "Your shop is important. You didn't need to leave."

Callie raised her hand to signal the bartender for a margarita, then turned back to Abby. "Are you kidding? *You're* important. When one of the ABCs calls a powwow, it's serious business."

"You got that right, honey," Blair said. "I canceled a bikini wax for you."

Abby rolled her eyes but grinned as she looked at Blair and Callie. Complete opposites, those two. Blair with all her flash and beautiful mane of auburn hair, Callie with her gorgeous mocha skin and raven hair. One all style, the other soft and subtle. Blair was an interior decorator and Callie owned a coffee shop. Her two best friends for the past twenty-eight years. Where would she be without them? Since kindergarten they'd been known as the ABCs—inseparable, sharing every joy, every pain, and every secret, and giving advice when needed. Right now she really needed it.

"I have a problem."

"Figured that," Blair said. "So spill it."

After a couple long swallows of her margarita for courage, she said, "You know the vets I work for?"

"Mike Nottingham and Seth Jacobs," Callie said.

"Aka Hot Stuff and Hotter Stuff," Blair added.

Abby nearly spewed her drink and launched into a coughing fit that brought tears to her eyes. Callie left her side of the booth and hurried over to Abby, patting her on the back until she could breathe again.

"You okay, honey?" she asked.

Abby nodded and used her napkin to clean up the mess on her face. "Fine," she croaked. "Jesus, Blair, give a girl some warning next time."

Blair quirked a brow. "What did I do?"

"Never mind." How was she ever going to get this out?

"Well?" Blair asked, once again tapping her nails.

"Okay." Taking a deep breath, Abby said, "I can't believe this happened, but they asked me out. Sort of."

"They asked you out," Blair repeated. The tapping stopped.

Callie moved back to the other side of the booth to grab her margarita and take a drink, her amber eyes wide as saucers. "Both of them?"

"At the same time?" Blair clarified.

"Yeah. Sort of. I think. I'm not really sure, but yeah, I really do think they did." She drained her margarita this time, then signaled the waitress for another round.

"When? How? I want a play-by-play of every word," Blair demanded, her eyes glittering with excitement.

Grateful for the noisy atmosphere and blaring music, Abby gave them a recap of her bizarre conversation with Mike and Seth.

"Holy shit," Callie said when Abby finished. "Girl, you might as well go buy a lottery ticket, because your ship has come in."

Abby shrugged. "I don't know. It's beyond bizarre. I mean, I wasn't even aware of their interest."

"How the hell could you be unaware that two hot men wanted in your panties?" Blair asked, leaning back when the waitress brought another round of 'ritas. "Honey, that's every woman's dream."

"Not mine." Abby picked up a drink and sipped. She really needed cocktails and lots of them. This had been one hell of a week. It had been one hell of a two-year period, actually. The past couple days had just been the topper. A pretty good topper.

"Bullshit. Two guys, two prominent, rich, successful, hot-as-hell and sexy-enough-to-melt-your-clothes-off guys tell you they want to take you out. And by 'take you out,' honey, they mean they want to undress you, lick you all over, and fuck you until your brains ooze out your ears. And you're telling me that's not something you fantasize about when you're patting the ol' pussy?"

Leave it to Blair to give it to her in graphic detail. "Okay, maybe I have fantasized about being screwed by more than one man. But that's fantasy. And beside the point, since Mike and Seth didn't say anything about a threesome anyway."

"They don't have to *say* anything about one," Callie said. "You know it's on their minds. I'll bet they wouldn't mind sharing."

"Oh, God." Abby laid her head in her hands. "I can't deal with this."

"You can, too. I'd love to be in your shoes. Wanna trade?"

Abby lifted her head and cast beseeching eyes on Blair. "Sure. You go instead."

Callie snickered. "She'd eat those two up and spit them out like she does all her men."

Blair grabbed a chip and waved it at Callie. "Yeah, but they thank me for it." She popped the chip in her mouth and grinned as she chewed.

Abby laughed.

"Seriously, Abby, what have you got to lose?" Callie asked. "It's been forever since you dated. And it's the country club. Isn't Chad a member?"

"Yes."

Blair laughed. "Even better. Wouldn't he just die to see you walking in there with Mike and Seth? I mean literally die with jealousy?"

"Please. Chad didn't care what I did when we were married. Why would he care now?"

"Because he always thought he owned you. You know he still does," Blair said. "And it would kill him to see you happy. He wants you pining away and miserable without him, the rotten, cheating bastard. I think you should go just to stick it to him, show him you've moved on. That you've got a career and not one man, but two to take his place."

It would be worthwhile to see Chad's face while she celebrated with Seth and Mike. Not that she had a single vindictive bone in her body. She took what she was entitled to by law in the divorce, and nothing more, much to the irritation of her attorney. She'd just wanted it to be over, wanted to forget the shame and embarrassment, the public humiliation Chad caused her with his overt cheating. But just once she would like to show him she'd made a decent life without him and that she could get another man. Maybe even two.

"I love when you grin like that," Blair said. "It's so evil. Reminds me of the old days."

Abby couldn't help it. She had actually started to visualize events, from the country club to what might happen afterward. But could she go through with it if dining and dancing led to something else with Mike, or Seth, or even, God help her, both of them? It hadn't occurred to her that they might be into that kind of action until Blair mentioned it. She was hardly a woman of the world. She didn't have experience with kinky sex like this. Not that she hadn't fantasized about it. But fantasy was one thing. Reality was something entirely different.

"I'd sell my soul for a hot night with two men like Mike Nottingham and Seth Jacobs," Callie said with a sigh. "Or even one of them. Sex has been virtually nonexistent in my life for, well, you know. A long time."

Callie stared into her margarita like a crystal ball. Abby knew she was thinking of Bobby. She slid her hand over Callie's. "You miss him."

"Yeah." Callie smiled. "It's time to move on, though. It's been long enough."

"And Bobby would kick your ass if you pined away too long," Blair added, moving her hand on top of Abby's and Callie's.

Callie's eyes glistened with unshed tears. Abby knew how much Callie had loved her husband. Losing him to cancer had been a harsh blow. But Callie was one of the toughest women she knew and had weathered it well. She'd kept on going, because that's what Bobby would have wanted her to do. But Callie was right. It had been long enough. She had to start living again.

"So I guess you're the only one getting any these days," Callie said with a grin.

Blair arched a brow. "Honey, I'm always getting some. Though I have to admit, the pickings have been rather slim lately."

"That's because you keep turning down all those marriage proposals, and the ones you do accept, you dump at the altar at the last minute. If you'd just jump on Rand McKay like you should have done fifteen years ago, your sex and love woes would be taken care of," Abby teased, knowing it would irritate Blair, but then again, Blair needed to hear it. She'd carried a torch for Rand since high school. And everyone knew it, including Rand. But for some reason, Rand was the only guy Blair refused to have anything to do with.

"Sheriff Rand McKay is not on my radar at the moment." Blair sniffed. "And frankly, he isn't my type."

Abby looked at Callie, then turned to Blair, both of them bursting into laughter. "Not your type? Not your type? Pu-leez. He is so your type. You practically drool every time he walks by."

"I do not."

"Do, too," Abby insisted, glad the subject had shifted to someone besides her.

"Okay, so maybe I do need sex. Which does not by any stretch of the imagination mean that I need Rand McKay, understand?"

"Got it," Abby said, though she and Callie exchanged another knowing glance. Oh yeah. Blair had it bad for Rand.

"I guess we all need a good fuck," Blair said. "You know what that means, don't you?"

Abby was almost afraid to ask. Blair had "that look" in her eyes. And when Blair had that look, it meant trouble. "What does that mean?"

"We need a bet."

"Oh shit," Callie whispered.

"Double oh shit," Abby added.

"Cowards. You know damn well it's what we all need. And another round." Blair shifted on the bench and searched the now crowded bar, frowning when she couldn't find their waitress. "I'll be right back. Start thinking."

After she left, Abby cast a desperate look at Callie. "I hate when she does this."

Abby nodded. "Me, too. God only knows what kind of bet she's going to come up with. I'm too old for this shit."

Nevertheless, they both giggled like they had back in high school at the thought of having to endure a bet. Though frightening, they had always been fun. Blair was usually the instigator. And she was nothing if not inventive.

When Blair returned with a slightly irritated waitress in tow, she had that gleam in her eye. "I've got it. And margaritas, too."

"You've got what?" Callie asked.

"The bet, of course."

"Aren't we a little too old for this? I mean, we're way past high school." Callie cast hopeful eyes in Abby's direction.

"Callie has a point. We can't very well toilet paper anyone's house at our age."

"For heaven's sake, that's not at all what I'm suggesting, and you know it," Blair said. "And you're right. We are past the days of egging and TPing. But the gauntlet's been thrown, and I've suggested a bet, and you know damn well you can't back out now."

Callie mumbled under her breath about some people never growing up.

Abby groaned. She needed advice and commiseration, not a damn bet. Sometimes she wondered why she bothered asking for help when all she'd get in return was more chaos in her already frenetic life. "Okay, what is it?"

"Sex."

Abby waited, but Blair didn't say anything else. "That's it? Sex?"

"Well, where's the rest of it?" Callie asked.

"There is no more, you morons. God, isn't that what we all want? One weekend of no-holds-barred, unbridled sex."

"Sounds good to me," Callie said. "But we hardly need a bet for that. The way things are right now, at least for me, we need a miracle. Where do you propose we get said sex?"

Blair wriggled in her seat. "Oh, this is where the fun comes in. Each of us takes a weekend turn. We have to enjoy one weekend of blistering hot sex. No strings, of course. It's not like you have to locate and meet the guy of your dreams or anything. You just have to fuck someone."

"That's doable," Callie said, munching on a nacho. "So what's the catch?"

Abby smiled. With Blair's bets, there was always a catch.

"The other two get to pick the guy."

"Huh?" Had Blair really just suggested what Abby thought she suggested?

"You heard me. We get to choose your man. For example, if it's

Abby's turn for her weekend of wild sexual mayhem, then Callie and I get to pick the guy who gets the honors."

"You're joking." Abby's eyes widened. "What if we don't like the man?"

Blair cast a sly smile. "If you can't trust your best friends to choose a man for you, honey, who can you trust?"

Callie looked as shocked as Abby felt. Sometimes Abby wondered if Blair had a screw loose somewhere. Then again, Blair had always been the most daring of the three of them. Abby shouldn't be surprised by this bet.

"I don't know, Blair. This is pretty risqué, even for you."

"Oh for the love of dick, Callie. We're not plotting espionage here. It's sex. One weekend of sex. Orgasms galore. With trustworthy men. And we'll monitor each other to be sure it's safe."

Abby looked at Callie and chewed her bottom lip, the words *I don't think so* hovering on her tongue. Then she thought of Chad, of all the nights she'd spent sitting at home while Chad was out fucking the latest skirt. He sure as hell hadn't been discriminating. And for the past several years Abby had worked her ass off while her libido had been wasting away, unattended.

She needed a fuck. And an orgasm or several hundred.

"I'm in."

Callie arched a brow. "Well if you're in, then I'm in."

Blair rolled her eyes. " 'Bout damn time. I was beginning to think I was going to have to buy purple hats and a bridge club membership. Christ, you two. You had me worried."

Abby laughed. "Not quite yet. I'm primed, and I'm ready."

"Good thing, Miss Abby. Because you're up first and this weekend," Blair said with a sly grin.

Abby's laugh died. "Me? First?"

"Oh yeah," Callie said. "And I think we already know who, too."

"Oh shit. I think I do, too." She'd walked right into this and had a feeling she'd just been set up. Her cheeks flamed hot with the thought of what she'd just agreed to do. Theory was one thing, reality another entirely. Could she do this? Could she cast aside the old Abby Lawson and grab what was right in front of her?

"And not just one guy, either. You've hit the mother lode, Abby. You get to fuck both Mike Nottingham and Seth Jacobs."

"Both? Oh, no way. That wasn't part of the bet."

"Too bad. They both want you, right? You said they were both interested. Yours is actually the easiest. These guys are already primed and ready for you."

"In *dating* me, not fucking me. At least I think that's what they want. Oh hell, I don't know." She tucked her hair behind her ears and stared at them both. "Help!"

"We are helping you, honey," Blair said. "They want you. It's obvious."

"Not to me it isn't."

"That's why you have us," Callie said. "To help you with your sex problems."

Abby glared at her. "So not funny. I have a serious sex problem now. Like how the hell I'm going to approach them. What am I going to say?"

"Start by accepting their offer to party down at the country club this weekend," Blair suggested. "We'll figure out the rest before then."

"We'll." Abby was always a little afraid when Blair spoke in terms of "we." Nevertheless, she'd agreed, and now she had to tell Mike and Seth that she was amenable to a little celebration Saturday night.

Now how was she going to turn a little dancing and drinking at the country club into a full-blown ménage à trois?

"So what happens if someone doesn't go through with the bet?" Abby asked.

Blair looked at the ceiling for a minute, then back at them with an evil grin. "All-expense-paid trip to Vegas for a weekend for all three of us."

Callie whistled. "That's a big bite to the budget."

"You said it," Abby said. "I don't want to lose."

"Me, either," Callie said.

"Then you'll go through with it. We all will. Game on, ladies," Blair said.

Abby took a deep breath. The bet was on.

three

abby turned off the living room light and strolled to the kitchen. She prepared the coffeemaker for the morning, inhaling the aroma of fresh coffee grounds. A cup right now sounded really good. Caffeine was a bad, bad idea this late, though.

Not only would she be performing surgery tomorrow, she'd also have to figure out how to tell Mike and Seth that she was agreeable to their little celebration. And somehow, someway, have to come up with an idea to maneuver them into a threesome before the weekend was over.

Damn Blair and her bets.

She shook her head, flipped off the kitchen light, and grabbed her glass of water, heading down the dark hallway into her bedroom. Her margarita buzz from earlier had mellowed, leaving behind a nice, relaxed state that was perfect for sleep. She stripped and slid under the cool sheets; the night was too warm for the quilt.

But instead of falling into an immediate sleep, she stared out the window at the three-quarter moon, which seemed to be perched on top of a tall oak tree, its silvery glow nearly blinding her.

Shit.

Why couldn't she sleep? She was calm, relaxed, over-margaritaed. She should be passed out by now. Instead, she was wide-awake and agitated.

And lack of consciousness was essential, dammit. The last thing she needed was to fall asleep in the operating room tomorrow morning. After all the praise from Mike and Seth this morning, she didn't want to disappoint them.

So, sleep already, Abby!

Restless, she knew a command to sleep was only going to make it worse. The crisp sheets that felt so good a few minutes ago scraped her nipples, now a form of torture.

She was aroused. And her mind whirled with visions of being the creamy middle of an Oreo cookie between Mike and Seth.

Damn. She needed to come. She wanted them both to magically materialize in her bedroom and lick her pussy until she had a mind-blowing orgasm. Or two or three. To touch, suck, and fuck her until she passed out from oblivious, satiated exhaustion.

Something, she might add, that had never happened with Chad, she thought with a loud snort. Which was why she'd accumulated a drawer full of toys over the years. Her sex companions. And she had a pretty vivid imagination, too. Her fantasies had been her lifesavers, because Chad had been all talk and no action.

Well, that wasn't exactly true. He'd seen action all right. But all his action had been with other women. He'd had a wild woman at home all the years they'd been married, only he'd never known it. He'd never once tapped into her sexuality, never once took the time to discover what she was about.

Dumb ass. She hoped he ended up with a severe case of dick rot.

Oh, fuck Chad. No, not Chad. Mike and Seth. She leaned over and reached into her nightstand, fumbling around until she found what she wanted. Her favorite lube and the thick jelly dildo. Her pussy clenched in anticipation.

Yeah, one way or the other she was going to get fucked tonight. Jamming the covers to the end of the bed with her feet, she breathed a sigh of relief, the night air cooling her heated body. But she was about to bring up the temperature a notch. She planted her feet flat on the bed and spread her legs, then poured some cherry lube on her hand, loving how slick it felt as it dribbled between her fingers.

Her hips lifted of their own volition, searching for her hand.

"Yeah, you want it, don't you?" she whispered in the darkness. "You need a cock in that pussy."

But first she wanted to warm it up a little. She pressed her hand to her sex, letting the lube slide over her naked mound, shivering as it dripped from her fingertips and slid down her slit to coat the crack of her ass. Deep in arousal, she didn't care. She'd been primed since yesterday, and between the conversations with Mike and Seth and the upcoming bet, she needed a hard ride tonight. She felt hot, wild, and nasty, and she needed more than just a quick strumming of her clit to get her off.

She swept her fingers around the knot, teasing it, not touching her magical spot that craved attention. Instead, she roamed outside her pleasure center, skimming her labia, her thighs, tormenting herself with whisper-light caresses until her nipples stood erect and she clenched her butt cheeks together. She panted, anticipation making her throat go dry. Wanting her dildo in her pussy, her fingers in her ass. Oh yes, she needed to be fucked hard and deep, needed it rough tonight.

Reaching for the dildo, she lubed the thick, jellied shaft, loving the feel of every ridge and vein, closing her eyes and imagining Mike standing next to her bed, his naked body showcased in the moonlight.

As she rubbed the dildo, she fantasized it was Mike's cock, imagined him looking down at her, bending over her to run his hands over her breasts, to pluck at her nipples until they stood upright and tingly, just waiting for Seth to crawl onto the bed and take them in his mouth.

"Yes," she hissed in a whisper. "Suck my nipples, Seth."

And there was Seth, naked and crawling toward her, his thick, muscled body pressing down on her as leaned in to kiss her, his hands claiming her breasts, cupping them, then removing his mouth to kiss her neck, drawing his tongue along the column of her throat and lower, until he reached her sensitive nipples. She arched her back, offering them to his eager lips.

She squeezed the cock in her hands as Seth took one bud between his teeth and tugged, just hard enough that she cried out. She heard Mike hiss as she rolled the shaft up, then down, slamming hard against his balls as the fevered frenzy of her arousal took over.

"Fuck me," she whimpered, spreading her legs wide.

Mike crawled onto the bed and took her ankles in his hands, spreading her legs apart. Abby placed the dildo at the entrance to her pussy lips. It was hard and hot, like his cock would be. Thick at the head, almost too big for her to take.

"But you'll take it baby, won't you?" he asked. "All of it."

"Yes."

"You want me to pound it hard in your pussy, don't you?"

"Oh, God, yes. Hard and deep, Mike. Make it hurt."

"She likes it hard, Seth. You ready to give it to her?"

"You know it."

"On your belly, Abby."

Sweet Jesus, yes. Just the way she liked it. She flipped over, using her hand to massage the sweet spot of her clit as she dragged a pillow under her and fell on top of it. She reached into the drawer for another dildo, this one slimmer with a thick base. With shaky hands she greased it up with the lube, then slipped it behind her.

"Who do you want in your ass, baby?" Mike's voice was taut with tension.

"Seth. I want Seth to fuck my ass."

Her fingers worked diligently on her clit now, fantasy mixing with reality as she spread apart the cheeks of her buttocks. She poured lube on her anus and probed there with the smaller dildo, pushing just inside with the tip. She panted at the exquisite sensations.

"It's going to hurt," Seth said. "You want it to hurt or do you want me to take it slow and easy?"

"Hurt me," she commanded, passion taking her to a frenzied pitch of near insanity. "I want it hard, Seth."

"I knew you would," he said, leaning over to lick her spine from her lower back to her neck. When he bit down on the nape of her neck, she shuddered and cried out, her fluids pouring onto the mattress.

Mike lifted her and slid underneath. His thick cock stroked her clit as he positioned himself against her pussy lips. His face was tight as he grabbed a fistful of her hair and made her focus on him. "Me first, Abby. I'm going to pound that sweet pussy of yours while Seth fucks your ass."

She loved his look of intense concentration, the way he needed her. Only her.

"Yes. Oh, yes." This is what she wanted. Both of them fucking her at the same time. She reached down and slid the thick dildo between her pussy lips and drove it deep. Her pussy squeezed the dildo, pulsing around it. God, she could come right now.

Not yet. Not yet. She wanted more. She paused, letting the contractions subside. She couldn't climax now. The fantasy wasn't over.

"You ready, Abby?"

Seth's voice, the dildo probing her ass. She pushed past the tight-muscled barrier, driving the smaller shaft into her anus, screaming as she was utterly filled with cock.

"Oh, yes! Fuck me!"

She double-fucked herself, rubbing her clit against the pillow, the sensations driving her wild as she pulled one dildo out while she powered the other deep. The quiet of the room allowed her to hear the sucking sounds of the dildos as they moved in and out of her. The sounds were wildly erotic, and she could well imagine what the reality would be like.

"You're a nasty wild thing, Abby," Mike groaned, lifting his hips to power his cock upward.

"Fucking hot, tight ass," Seth said behind her, digging his fingers into the globes of her ass. "Sweet, hot ass, Abby."

She hunched against the pillow, rubbing her clit as she felt her climax approach.

"Ohhhh, oh, God," she moaned, pushing the dildos in as far as they would go. Faster, now, even faster. Then her world shattered as she came and screamed, fluids gushing past the dildo in her pussy, pouring onto her hand as she held it in place while strong contractions shuddered through her. Sweet, unbearable pleasure crashed inside her, and she rode every sensation, held onto them, and never wanted to stop.

She collapsed, exhausted, soaked, sweating, and utterly satisfied. She panted for awhile, keeping her eyes closed and letting the fantasy play out. They'd kiss her, stroke her hair, murmur how much she meant to them, what pleasure she gave them.

God, it was fantastic.

When she could move, she got out of bed and went into the bathroom to clean herself and her toys.

Staring at the woman in the mirror, Abby couldn't believe the woman who stared back. Her hair disheveled, her eyes glassy, breathing still irregular, nipples like tight points, she looked like a total wild thing. And damn sexy, too.

Why hadn't Chad seen that in her? She had one seriously sparky libido. But he'd never even tried to discover what turned her on. Just jumped on, pounded away for a minute or two, shot his load, and promptly fell asleep. He'd never once made her come. She'd been so young, so inexperienced, she'd never thought to talk to him about what pleased her. Not that it would have made a difference. He didn't care. Never had.

"Fuck you, Chad. You missed out. But Mike and Seth won't."

More determined than ever to make this weekend work, she finally let the stress drain away. She was entitled to a little fun. No, she was entitled to a hell of a lot of fun. There were years of sexual neglect to make up for, and starting this weekend, it was her turn to party.

She turned out the bathroom light and climbed into bed, closed her eyes, and promptly passed out.

four

"i'm going to throw up."

Blair glared at Abby. "You are not. I just did your makeup, and you're about to slip on this sinful dress. If you puke on it, I'm going to slap you."

Abby choked out a laugh. "Okay, now that was funny." God, she needed that. Leave it to Blair to snap her out of her terror.

"You look beautiful," Callie said, picking up the dress they'd helped her shop for. "You're going to have those guys as hard as rocks the minute you walk through the door."

"Oh, God." Her stomach flipped, and she cast a look of desperation at her friends. "Can I really do this?"

"Course you can. You're hot stuff, babe," Blair said. "Now get into this dress, and let's see how you look."

She slipped off the robe, catching a glimpse of herself in the doorway mirror as she did. Lord. The lingerie alone made her pussy wet. A wisp of black silk thong, garter and stockings, a matching black bra that was designed only to thrust her breasts upward but didn't cover them at all. Her nipples pebbled to hard little points.

The spandex dress was black, tight, and it molded to her body like liquid pouring over her. Callie zipped her up. She couldn't breathe, but she knew it was nerves, not the clothes.

"We should go into business doing this," Blair said, offering up a smug smile.

"I agree," Callie replied. "Look, Abby."

Abby turned and faced the mirror. Clearly, her friends were geniuses. Callie had pulled her hair back and up, leaving pieces falling over her neck and against her cheek. Kind of a messy, incredibly seductive look. Blair had done her makeup in a smoky, sultry way that wasn't at all overdone but definitely brought out her eyes. They sparkled like sapphires.

The dress hugged her breasts, the bra doing the trick of pushing them nearly over the top of the bodice, which held onto them securely enough she didn't feel like they'd pop out. Tiny little straps of rhinestones were for show alone, since the bodice was snug enough to hold the dress in place. The waist crisscrossed and then flared out at the hips, the fabric swishing around her as she twirled from side to side.

She felt alluring as hell. Looked it, too. And she was never one to dress up or feel seductive. But she did tonight.

"Thank you. You are both incredible."

"We know," Blair quipped with a wink. "Now, we'd better get dressed. You go find earrings. Oh, and one bracelet. No more. And those shoes that make your legs look a mile long. I'm jealous as hell and wish I was taller. I'm going to have to wear stilettos tonight just to compete."

Abby laughed and went to her jewelry box after Blair and Callie left to get dressed.

This was like high school again, all of them gathered together to get dressed before a dance. Only this was her house, and they were long past high school, though it was a big night.

She was just glad they'd both agreed to go with her. Of course when she'd told them that Mike and Seth had invited them, too, Blair said she wouldn't miss this night for all the money in Bill Gates's bank account. And Callie was giddy with excitement.

Abby still wanted to throw up.

"Maybe I read the whole conversation wrong," she said to Blair and Callie in the car a little while later. "It's possible they just wanted to throw this shindig because they're nice and wanted to congratulate me. They probably aren't even interested in me . . . that way."

Blair turned around in her seat and arched a brow. "You're kidding me, right? How many times do we have to go over this? You're gorgeous. They're hot. They both want to fuck you. Now shut up, or I'll have Callie stop the car and I'm coming back there and slapping you."

She couldn't help it. She giggled at the visual of Blair climbing over the center console in her skintight dress and wrestling with her. And once she started giggling, she couldn't stop. Blair started to laugh, then Callie joined in. By the time they reached the front entrance of the country club, she had at least relaxed enough to stop hyperventilating.

But now they were here, and she had to actually get out of the SUV and walk in there like she knew what she was doing. Like she was some worldly woman who did this all the time.

Right. Some worldly woman. She didn't even date—hadn't had a date since . . . Chad.

"Why did I agree to this stupid bet?" Abby asked as she stepped out of the vehicle.

"Because you desperately need to get laid," Blair whispered, wrapping her shawl around her tight red dress.

"We all do," Callie added, stepping up on the other side of Abby. Abby glanced over at Callie, her one calming presence. Blair was flash and fire. Callie was serenity and common sense. Just looking at her made her feel better.

"I'm going to lose you as soon as we walk in the door tonight," Abby said, eyeing Callie's cream silk dress that clung to her generous curves like a second skin. "You look so damn beautiful."

Callie grinned. "I'm so excited to be here. Hell, honey, we all work so damn hard. This is our chance to party. And your chance to shine, to shake off the remnants of Chad and all that hard work you've put yourself through. Go strut your stuff." She pushed Abby ahead of her, and she and Blair took up right behind her.

Steeling herself, Abby sucked in a breath and stepped through the doors of the club, feeling the strength of her girls behind her.

She could do this. She would. She wanted it and needed it. If nothing else happened tonight, she was at least going to party her ass off.

Silverwood Country Club was the *it* place in town. The elite belonged here, and it showed. Elegant, tasteful, yet ritzy as hell, from the marble floors to the crystal chandeliers to the brass handles on the doors and the dark paneling on the walls. Everything spoke of money, money, money.

Abby felt out of place. She knew Chad frequented the club, but this just wasn't her thing. She wasn't a party girl. She was a sundress or blue jeans and tank top and no shoes, sit on a swing on the front porch and sip iced tea and watch the stars kind of girl. Not dress up and be someone she wasn't.

She stopped dead in her tracks and turned around.

"I can't do this."

Blair hit her with a determined look. "Yes you can."

She shook her head. "I can't. This isn't me. You know me, Blair. This isn't me."

"Abby. Look at me."

She turned to Callie. "I can't, Callie. Please. You know."

Callie nodded. "I know, baby. He hurt you. He made you believe you were worthless, but he was full of shit. You wear that dress like you were born to walk a runway in it. And you might not feel like yourself in it, but you look like a million bucks."

"But it's not me, Callie. You know it's not me. I feel like a fraud."

Callie grabbed her hands, her fingers warm and comforting. "You know what? Sometimes it's okay to play the part of the fairy princess. Just for one night."

"Abby! Just in time!"

Oh, God. Seth's voice. Her heart just about exploded out of her chest. She cast a look of abject panic at Blair and Callie, who grinned. Callie's fingers slipped away, and she backed off. Abby had no choice but to turn around.

Some friends they were, deserting her in her time of need.

Seth came toward her dressed in a dark gray suit, light gray shirt, and midnight blue silk tie. His eyes widened.

"Wow," he said with a wide grin. "You look incredible."

Instead of shaking her hand, he wrapped one strong, warm arm around her waist and pulled her against him for a hug. Oh! He was damn firm, too, his body all chiseled muscle as she instinctively grabbed for his bicep. The last guy she'd been held against had been Chad, and he didn't exactly work out. But Seth definitely worked on his body. And for the love of God he smelled so damn good her knees nearly buckled. Not cologne, either. Just . . . man.

She really needed sex. If it felt this good just to have a man wrap one arm around her, she might not live through a night of really good fucking.

When he pulled back, he gave her a look unlike any look he'd ever given her at work. "You look . . . damn, Abby. I'm speechless."

She felt the heat rise up her neck at the compliment. "Thank you. You look great, too."

"Let's go party. And who are your friends here?" He glanced away and offered up the friendly Seth Jacobs smile to Blair and Callie.

Which meant she had to find her voice. "These are my best friends, Blair Newcastle and Callie Jameson."

He shook their hands. "I'm so glad you came tonight. I'm not sure Abby would have come without you two."

"Oh, I think she would have," Callie said.

"Party's in full swing. Can I escort you lovely ladies into the ballroom?"

"Honey, you can escort me anywhere you'd like." Blair winked and slipped her arm in Seth's, nodding at Abby to do the same on Seth's other side. She did, and grabbed Callie's hand for support. They walked into the ballroom, which was wildly noisy, since a band was playing.

And dark. Good thing Seth was leading. Abby was having a hard enough time walking on the stupid high heels Blair had insisted she wear because they "made her legs look a mile long." Whatever. Her legs wouldn't look sexy when she broke one and ended up in a cast.

The ballroom, which doubled as the dining room, was packed, individual tables set up for people to enjoy dinner with their families and friends. White tablecloths, elegant china, multiple forks. Everything screamed class and money. Abby looked around to see if she knew anyone—okay, she was looking for Chad. But she didn't spot him, and she was simply too awed by her surroundings to keep searching.

"We've got a corner spot set up a little bit apart from all this," Seth said, pointing to several tables near the double doors by the balcony.

She nodded, smiled, and tried to focus on remembering how to walk in heels.

Most of the staff from the clinic had made it, greeting her with congratulatory hugs. She was really going to miss working with these people. They had helped her more than she could ever tell them. She wound her way through the crowd, making sure she stopped to individually talk to and thank every one of them. The one person she didn't see was Mike.

"Where's Mike?" she asked Seth after she'd finished visiting with the staff.

"Doing his hair, probably," Seth replied with a cocky grin.

Abby snorted. She seriously doubted Mike had to do anything other than step out of the shower and look like a god. He was probably busy doing something else. Maybe he wouldn't even come tonight. It's not like he was required to be there. And why was she obsessing over this, anyway?

She wondered if Blair and Callie would feel out of place, but by the time Seth had put a glass of champagne in her hands, her friends had wandered off, mingling with some of the staff members and laughing their assess off at a joke one of the vet techs, Dave, was telling.

Ah, yes, Dave, teller of ribald jokes. No wonder they were laughing. She should have known not to worry about her pals. They could find their own amusement.

"Hungry? There are plenty of hors d'oeuvres."

Seth's voice over her shoulder sent chills down her spine. "Not really."

"Good. Let's dance." His hand slipped around her waist, and she felt the burn of sensual heat singe straight through her clothes. He turned her around and reached for her hand, leading her onto the dance floor.

Don't fall on your ass, Abby. Kicking her shoes off in the middle of the dance floor at Silverwood Country Club would probably be unseemly. This wasn't exactly Whisker's Bar, and she wasn't in jeans.

Seth pulled her close and rested his hand at the small of her back, pressing in with an intimate gesture that put her pelvis in contact with his thigh. Her pussy responded with a twitch of recognition. Oh yeah—man. Something she hadn't been around in far too long. He twirled her around to the melody of one of her favorite slow songs. Though other couples were dancing, she felt as if everyone was watching them.

"You're nervous as hell, aren't you?" he whispered against her ear.

She tilted her head back to look at him. "Me? No. Not at all."

"Bullshit. You're stiff as a board. Relax, Abby. Nobody's watching us. This place is packed. Everyone's here for their own party. The staff is drinking and eating up the free food and drink. You're not on display."

She didn't know why she was so edgy, but Seth was right. As she scanned the room, she realized no one was paying the slightest attention to the two of them. "Sorry. You're right."

"Then lean into me, let me enjoy your company, and loosen up, babe."

God, he was sexy. His voice was soft and gentle, coaxing the tension right out of her. His hand on her back molded to her skin like a warm blanket, and she let him guide her across the dance floor as she stared into his chocolate brown eyes. She always felt so comfortable with Seth.

"Better. Your muscles aren't so tight now."

"Thanks. I feel stupid for acting so skittish."

"Don't be. It's a little nerve-racking to be here the first time. Though isn't your ex-husband a member?"

She nodded. "He never brought me here, though."

Seth shook his head. "Asshole."

She grinned. "An adequate description." She liked Seth even more now. The way he held her close, but not too close, was non-threatening, nothing untoward, not pushy at all. And their bodies fit together perfectly. He was tall, built like a piece of solid rock. Her nipples hardened, imagining what it would be like to be pressed naked against that wall of muscle, to be able to rub against him, run her hands over his body—

"Okay, you've had her long enough. My turn."

Abby's head shot up to see Mike holding out his hand. She looked to Seth, who smiled. "If I have to." Seth kissed her hand and delivered her into Mike's arms with a "Later, Abby."

"Later, Seth." She stepped into Mike's arms, and it was completely different. Gone was the respectable distance. Mike pulled her intimately into his embrace, and it was like a thousand degrees of heat enveloped her. When he wrapped his arm around her back, resting his palm against her bare skin, she felt every lick of flame along her nerve endings. Her throat constricted, her nipples pebbled, and her panties flooded with moisture. Holy hell, did he fire up her libido in a hurry.

He was dressed in a black suit, white shirt, and silver tie, his blue eyes a stark contrast to his tanned skin. She'd never been this close to him before other than passing instruments and files back and forth at work. He smelled like thunderstorms and spring rain. She wanted to lick him all over.

"Sorry I'm late. We had a complication from a surgery today, and I was dealing with that."

She struggled to find something remotely coherent to say. "Everything all right?"

"It is now. I'm just glad I made it in time. I wouldn't have wanted to miss tonight."

She looked away, searching for Seth. He was over keeping Blair and Callie company, standing in between them, laughing. Of course Blair could capture any man's attention and hold it for hours. Possibly days. And Callie was so gorgeous she could hold a man enraptured forever. And Seth was fabulous for making sure her friends didn't feel left out.

"I make you nervous, don't I?" Mike asked.

She tore her gaze away from Seth and turned it back on Mike. "Pretty much everything tonight is making me nervous. I'm a little out of my element here."

"Quit worrying about Seth when you're with me. And don't worry about me when you're with Seth. We're grown-ups. We'll figure this out."

"Whatever 'this' is."

"This is whatever you want it to be, Abby. Nothing is going to happen tonight that you don't want to happen. Just relax and have fun. It's a party with the staff and your friends. If more comes of it, so be it." He twirled her toward the open balcony doors and straight through them, then tucked her arm in his and walked her toward the balustrade. The moon was full, the stars out en masse, the summer night achingly beautiful. Sweetly scented gardenias overflowed their containers beneath her feet. She couldn't have asked for a more perfect setting.

She wanted to freeze this moment in time and not move either forward or backward. But Mike turned to her, and she knew she had to respond in kind by giving him her attention.

Something was going to happen out here. She could feel the anticipation humming through her like a vibration.

Threading his hand through her hair, Mike held her mesmerized. "If tonight turns out to be something more than a simple party, then we'll take it one step at a time."

When he leaned in, she stopped breathing.

"Okay?" he whispered, his lips hovering a fraction of an inch from hers.

"Okay."

He pressed his lips to hers, then deepened the kiss, and she damn near fell off her stiletto heels.

five

when mike leaned her over his arm, she felt like the heroine in a romance movie, and Abby finally understood what the word *swoon* meant. Holy shit, this was romantic as hell. And hot, as his tongue pressed insistently between her lips, invading the recesses of her mouth to sweep against hers. Things like this didn't happen to people like her.

Mike was almost too much for her senses, and she was already on maximum overload just being held against him. To feel his hand threading through her hair, his mouth insistent over hers, his tongue plunging in and out was like having her mouth fucked, like a tease, a promise of great sex to come. It was a good thing he was holding her, because her limbs were trembling. When was the last time she was kissed like this? Hell, she'd *never* been kissed like this! It made her want to search out Chad and kick him for all he'd lacked. She grasped Mike's arms, felt his strength, his heat, and wanted to strip him down right out here on the balcony, then explore every inch of him with her tongue.

When his other hand began to move along her leg, sliding upward toward her thigh, inching inside the hem of her dress, she shuddered. Her pussy quaked with need. Shock mixed with desire, and she didn't know whether to stop him or open her legs wider and beg him to fuck her right there.

But he lifted her upright and pulled his mouth from hers, breaking the spell. She was dizzy, disoriented, and damned turned on.

"Sorry," he said, his voice thick with desire. "Lost control for a second. We'd better stop before I end up with my fingers inside you."

She shuddered and let her eyes drift closed for a second, wrapping herself around the visual. And that would be a bad thing? Reality had been stripped away, and she was in a fantasy land right now. Of course, he would have to be the one to think logically. She breathed in and out to clear her head. She could only imagine what she must look like: her hair a mess from his caresses, her lips swollen from his kiss.

Okay, time to get a grip. She glanced down, her gaze zeroing in on his magnificent cock outlined against his pants. And holy Christ, it was huge! So much for gaining control.

"Sorry. I was kind of lost there for a second, too." She lifted her hand and tried to fix her hair.

He reached out and smoothed it for her. "You look beautiful." He blew out a breath. "Goddamn, Abby, I want to fuck you."

Her heart skipped a beat. How was she supposed to respond to that? Honestly, probably. Isn't this what she wanted? She should tell Mike that's exactly what she wanted, because she did. Her pussy was wet and aching for his fingers, his mouth, his cock on her and in her.

"Hey, did you two start without me?"

She whirled at the sound of Seth's voice. He stepped out onto the balcony with a waitress in tow. She carried a tray of champagne glasses and a bottle. Seth picked up the bottle and three glasses, then winked at the waitress. "Close the door behind you, Cin."

"You bet, Mr. Jacobs."

Seth turned to them. "So, what did I miss?" He poured champagne and handed Abby a glass. She reached for it, her hand shaking, and took a long swallow.

"Not much," Mike said. "Abby tastes good. At least her mouth does."

Oh, God. She was going to go up in flames right here on the balcony. Would the people inside notice the bonfire through the sheer curtains?

"Is that right?" Seth placed his glass on the ledge and took Abby's, handing it to Mike. He placed his palm on Abby's neck. "I think I need to taste, too. May I?"

Oh yeah. She was going to implode. Right now. But first, she was going to kiss Seth. "Yes. Definitely yes."

His kiss was softer than Mike's. At least at first. Tentative, he applied gentle pressure to her lips, then drew her closer, his fingers encircling the back of her neck, his other arm wrapping around her waist to draw her against his muscled strength. She felt his cock, hard and insistent, rocking against her sex, touching her clit. Explosions went off inside her. When his tongue hit hers, it was like a shock to her system. She whimpered against his mouth, then he groaned into hers, licking at her tongue like he was starving. The sensuality in his kiss was like water to a thirsty woman. She craved it like nothing ever before. Where Mike was abrupt fire and passion, Seth was coaxing and teasing, like climbing a slow stairway to ecstasy. These men were driving her crazy.

When he stepped back and smiled, Abby held onto the ledge for support. Seth picked up her glass and handed it to her.

"Now I feel like I caught up," he said.

"oh, shit, i'm getting turned on just watching them." Blair shifted in the corner and turned to Callie, who's amber-eyed gaze was wide with shock. They let the curtain drop.

"Girl, you and me both. I'm going to need a double vibrator shot tonight. Is Abby the luckiest woman on earth or what?"

"I want to know why she isn't fucking them both right now."

Callie rolled her eyes. "Come on, Blair. That's not Abby's style, and you know it. She's not into public sex." Callie shuddered, wishing it was her out there on the balcony with those two men. The idea of doing it in public view made her so hot she could come right there in the ballroom.

Blair pursed her lips. "Well, you're right. But I'd say our girl is well on her way to some serious ménage action tonight." Blair sighed. "Oh, to be a fly on the wall and be able to watch."

Callie felt the room close in around her, heat and her libido firing her up to a near fevered pitch. "So, you like to watch, do you?"

Blair shrugged. "I can take it or leave it. But who wouldn't want to see a play-by-play of the kind of fun Abby's going to have tonight?"

Callie would sell her soul to watch. Then again, it was a voyeur's favorite thing to do. And not even her two best friends knew her deep, dark secrets. There were some things a girl just didn't talk about, even with her friends. But she'd sure as hell fantasize about it tonight and put herself in place of Abby, standing there on that balcony. Only she wouldn't stop at just a kiss.

When it came time for fucking, Callie would do it out in full view. Because she didn't just like to watch other people having sex. She also got off on the thought of having other people watch her.

"I can't wait to get the report from Abby after this weekend," Blair said, picking up a piece of fruit from her plate. "I wonder how kinky Mike and Seth are?"

"You mean, if they're into bondage or spankings or anything like that?"

Blair's face colored a healthy blush. She shrugged. "Hey, you just never know about some people."

Callie smiled. And some people you instinctively knew what turned them on. Like Blair. Who claimed to like being in charge, who walked all over every man she'd ever been involved with. But Callie would bet a million what Blair needed was the right man to spank the dominance right out of her.

"No," Callie mused. "You just never know about some people."

"so, should we toast to tonight?" mike asked abby, raising his glass.

Toast? Oh yeah. She was toast all right. Burnt to a crisp already. "Uh, sure."

"Here's to whatever you want, Abby. However you want it," Seth said.

"I'll drink to that," Mike added.

"To both of you. Thank you for all of this. I don't even know what to say." So she took a long swallow of champagne, hoping for words that could express what she felt. Unfortunately, all she could do was revel in the sight of the two gorgeous men who'd just kissed her, who obviously both wanted her. And she had no clue what the next step should be.

She thought of Blair and Callie, what they would advise her to do at this moment, and wished they'd rush out here and hold her hand. But they weren't going to do that. It was time to stand on her own and go for what she wanted. She was an adult, a woman, and she had needs. It was time to lay it out there and see which way the wind would blow.

"Why don't you just tell us what you'd like to see happen next," Seth suggested. "We can hang out here all night. Dance and party with everyone and have a great time."

"Or we can slip away and have a private party," Mike suggested, leaning against the ledge, glancing at her out of the corner of his eye with a smoldering look that singed her insides.

Seth cleared his throat. "With either one of us, or both of us. Really Abby, the choice is yours."

"I think she's fully aware what her choices are," Mike countered. "It's up to Abby to decide what she wants. We're all adults here, and both Seth and I can handle you making a choice. If you want to be with only one of us, that's fine. Hey, if you don't want either of us, that's fine, too. So, Abby. What do you want?"

She looked at both of them, so different in so many ways, and knew she'd regret it the rest of her life if she didn't take what they were offering. "I'm going to be honest here. I've never done anything like this before." She looked down at her shoes, her dress, the persona that so wasn't her, and felt the tremble of nervousness shaking her from the inside out. If Chad saw her now, racked with indecision, he'd laugh at her.

Fuck off, Chad. Her head shot up, and she looked them both in the eye. "What I'd really like is to get out of here without too much commotion or attention and spend some time alone. With both of you. Whatever happens after that . . . well, we'll just take it a moment at a time."

Mike lifted a brow and nodded. Seth smiled and said, "Then that's what we'll do. Come on, let's go back to the party for a bit, then we'll slip out."

She sighed in relief and followed them inside, spotted Blair and Callie, and excused herself while they dragged her off to the ladies' room.

"Well?" Blair asked as soon as she was sure they were alone in there.

"I told them I wanted to go off alone with them." God, she couldn't believe she'd done it, but she had. She really was going to have a three-way with Mike and Seth.

Callie squealed. "You are going to have so much fun! And I can't wait to hear every sordid detail!"

"Take notes if you have to. You want my pen and some paper?" Blair added.

Abby rolled her eyes, grateful for her friends' teasing to diffuse some of the tension frying her nerves. "No thanks. I think I'll have vivid enough memories to last a lifetime." Her smile died, and she grabbed their hands. "I can't believe I'm doing this. *Can* I do this?" She felt queasy.

"Of course you can," Blair said. "You need this, and more important, honey, you deserve it. Now, go have some fun and fuck your brains out."

Seth watched Abby and her friends retreat to the ladies' room.

"They're going to talk about us, you know," Mike said.

"Of course they are." He looked over at Mike. "You don't think they'll try to talk her out of it, do you?"

Mike laughed. "I doubt it. I saw the grins on her friends' faces when they were peeking through the drapes while we were out on the balcony. I'd say they were instrumental in getting Abby to agree to this in the first place."

"Ah. Well, that's good." He kept his eye trained on the bathroom door as if he expected Abby to bolt out of there any second and head for the nearest exit. "How are we going to handle this, anyway?"

"Same way we've done any other woman we've shared before."

Seth frowned. "Abby's not like any other woman we've shared, Mike. You know that. She's . . . different."

"You've got a thing for her, don't you?"

"A thing?"

Mike grinned. "Yeah. A thing. And don't pretend you don't know what I'm talking about."

"I don't have a thing for her. I just don't want to see her get hurt."

"I hardly think Abby's looking at this with any romance bloom-
ing in her eyes. She's looking for some great sex, and that's it. And
she's so damn tense I'll bet she could use a couple dozen orgasms. So
we'll give them to her."

Now, that thought made him grin. Seth was looking forward to
making her come. Over and over again. "That we will."

Mike clasped him on the upper shoulder. "So quit worrying
about it. We'll be nice. And gentle. And let her lead. And she'll have
a great time. And when it's over, it's over."

"You're right. She knows what she's doing."

"Your place or mine?"

"I don't care." Women sure spent a lot of time in the bathroom
together. Were they creating a battle plan? He always wondered
what they talked about.

"Seth. You paying attention?"

"Huh? Oh. I don't care. Yours is fine."

"Okay. I'm going to say my good-byes and head to the house, get
things set up. Why don't you bring Abby?"

"I'll do that. See you in a bit." He tore his gaze from the women's
restroom door and stepped back to the party. God, he was practically
stalking her. Pathetic.

The last thing he needed was involvement with Abby. Mike was
right. When the sex was over, they'd go their separate ways.

It was better that way. She had her life and was just starting out.
He had his, and he wasn't about to get involved again.

Fun and fucking. That's all this was. And the way his cock tightened at the thought of stripping that sinfully tight dress off her body,
he was ready for both. Right now.

when seth pulled into the circular drive in front
of the sprawling ranch house, Abby had a moment of panic. Okay, so

she might have already worn deep gouges in the leather of Seth's car. And she might be near hyperventilating from her rapid breathing.

So maybe her moment of panic had been going on a little longer than just a moment.

Seth squeezed her hand, capturing her attention.

"The word *no* works really well on both Mike and me, Abby. Use it whenever you want tonight, and everything stops."

She exhaled and nodded. "I'm sorry. Like I said before, I've never done this."

He leaned over and kissed her, stealing her breath in an entirely different way. She relaxed against the seat back and gave herself up to the sensations of his lips and his tongue moving against hers, the way he cupped her neck and held her as if he were keeping her safe. Her tension melted.

"We'll make it good for you, baby," he murmured against her lips.

She shuddered, letting in all the feelings of desire, pushing away any of her second thoughts. She reached up and palmed his cheek, shuddering a sigh. "I know you will."

He came around and opened her door, helping her out of the car and escorting her to the front door, which was already open. She stepped inside, awed by the beauty of Mike's home.

The tile floor was dark and masculine, so like the man who lived there. Two Irish setters greeted her, and when Seth told them to stay, they stopped and sat obediently.

"That's Salt and Pepper," he said, introducing them.

Abby petted them both, tangling her fingers in their silken fur. "They're beautiful."

"Hey! Glad to see we didn't lose you along the road to perdition," Mike teased as he stepped into the entryway.

He'd slipped off his jacket and taken off his tie, undoing a couple buttons of his shirt. Dark hair peeked out the top of his shirt, that shadow of fur and skin making her mouth water.

"Come on and have a seat, and I'll fix us all a drink. Seth, take off
your coat and tie. You look like a stockbroker."

Seth snorted. The dogs scurried through a large door flap into
the backyard. Abby followed Mike into a spacious living room pop-
ulated with very comfortable-looking leather couches and chairs,
enough stereo equipment to blast out anyone's eardrums, and a big-
screen television mounted on one of the walls. Outside the sliding
glass door was a very well lit Olympic-sized swimming pool.

"It's beautiful here," she said, sliding onto one of the couches and
slipping off the shoes that were now making her feet throb. She resisted the urge to groan in relief.

"Thanks. What would you like to drink?"

"Something with rum would be nice. And soda."

"Got it. Seth, turn on some music."

Seth put on something slow and jazzy. Abby drew her feet up behind her and nestled comfortably in a corner of the couch, feeling
oddly serene. Whatever was going to happen would happen. And it
might even be nothing. She had a feeling even if all they did was talk
and had a cocktail or two, and then she said she wanted to go home,
it would be okay with both of them.

That was enough to make her relax.

Mike brought her drink and set it on a coaster on the glass table
next to the sofa, then took a seat in the leather chair next to her. Seth
plopped down on the middle cushion of the couch and leaned his
head back, closed his eyes, and sipped his drink.

"Has it been the longest damn week on record or what?" he asked.

"Seems that way," Mike replied, relaxing back into his chair and
stretching his legs out. "I must have done fifteen surgeries this week,
and none of them simple ones." He blew out a long, slow breath.

Abby watched them both. This all seemed so . . . normal. She
wasn't sure what she'd expected when she walked in here. Instant
ravaging, maybe? Certainly not this. She smiled and sipped her

drink, feeling more assured about the decision she'd made. They were doing this for her benefit, to relax her, and she knew it.

"What are your plans now that you're finished with school, Abby?" Seth asked.

"Mmm, not sure. Start a practice somewhere."

"Oh, break my heart. More competition," Mike teased.

"I don't think you have to worry about me," Abby said.

"Famous last words." Mike drained his glass and pointed to hers as he stood. "Another drink?"

She took another swallow of her cocktail, then placed it on the table and stood to face Mike. They'd let her do this all night, and she knew it. If something was going to happen, she was going to have to make the first move. "I think we've made enough small talk tonight, don't you?"

Though her heart was pounding, she turned to Seth and held out her hand. He took it, and she gave it a small tug to get him to stand. Facing them both, she said, "I'm warm, I'm relaxed, and I'd like to finish what the three of us started on the balcony at the club."

Now she had their attention in a way that made her mouth water. Seth arched a brow, and Mike cast her a lazy grin.

Just say it, Abby. Before you lose your nerve. This was her chance to live out every fantasy she'd ever masturbated to.

"I'd really like it if you'd both undress me."

six

mike set his glass down and approached her, his half smile making her legs quiver. Seth squeezed her hand. A sign of reassurance? He would do that, wouldn't he?

"You sure?" Seth asked.

"Yes," she whispered. It was all she was capable of voicing right now.

Mike moved to her other side and nuzzled her neck, his lips pressing down against her pulse point there. When he licked her, she shivered.

"Are you wet, Abby?" he murmured against her neck.

She nodded, her breath catching in her throat.

"Good. I want your pussy soaked and dripping down your legs."

Seth kissed the palm of her hand. "You make me hard just look-ing at you, watching how your body responds." He stepped closer, his fingertips blazing a sensual trail up her inner arm. "The way you shiver when you're touched, the way your pupils dilate so fast."

He threaded his arm around her waist, resting his fingers just above her ass. She wanted him to pull her dress up and plunge his fingers inside her. But she didn't move.

"How long has it been since you were fucked?" Seth asked.

"Several years."

"Not just fucked. Well-fucked," Mike added.

She turned to him, wanting to dive into the darkness of his eyes. "Never."

He nodded. "Thought so. That changes tonight."

Spasms of untamed desire waved through her belly, Mike's words promising more than she could ever hope for.

Seth moved his hand upward, taking his time to skim over the exposed flesh of her back. Abby watched his face, then turned to Mike, enraptured by the looks the two of them gave each other, as if they instinctively knew what to do.

"You've done this before," she said in realization.

"Yes," Seth said, then looked down at her. "Does that bother you?"

"No." And it really didn't. It probably should, but tonight she didn't care.

"We don't make a habit of it, Abby," Seth said. "It just happened a couple times before. We've known each other a lot of years."

Abby half-shifted to face Seth. "I don't care what you did before tonight. I just want you both to fuck me. And make it good."

Seth glided his fingers underneath the straps of her dress and slid them down her arms, letting them fall to her elbows. Mike moved in behind her, his body nestling against her back. He grasped the bodice of her dress and pulled it down, baring her to the waist, then unhooked her bra and tossed it aside.

Her ex-husband had never taken the time to look at her or even undress her. There had never been a slow unveiling of her skin, any interest on his part other than getting her naked and getting inside her as fast as possible. She'd hated his disinterest, as if the whole of her hadn't mattered. His only goal had been her pussy.

This slow revelation made her gasp. Mike rested his hands on her shoulders, skimming his fingers over her flesh. Seth stared at her as if he were memorizing every inch of her skin, as if he wanted to savor every second and study her. She felt flushed, her nipples hardening under his gaze. She didn't have a perfect body. She was thirty-three, and things weren't in the same places they used to be. She wasn't toned and in great shape. Yet these men made her feel beautiful.

"You're fucking gorgeous, Abby," Seth said in answer to her unspoken thoughts.

Mike cupped her breasts, his chin brushing against her hair. "I've jacked off thinking about you this past year."

She turned her head to look at him. "You have?"

He grinned down at her. "Oh yeah. I came hard thinking about all the ways I wanted to fuck you."

She couldn't believe he was telling her this. That he had fantasies about her. That he masturbated thinking about her.

"Lick and suck her nipples, Seth," Mike said, and Abby turned her attention back to Seth.

Mike held her breasts, and Seth leaned in. Abby's breath caught as Seth's lips closed around one peak, his tongue warm and wet as he licked the distended bud. Her knees nearly buckled, the sensation rocketing to her pussy. She shuddered and moaned, biting down on her lip.

His mouth was so soft, and watching him do it to her was an incredible thing. Sex with Chad had always been in the dark. And of course, foreplay wasn't in his realm of knowledge. Then again, Seth and Mike were nothing like Chad. These men had so much raw, potent sexuality there was no comparison. Her ex-husband was a moron. And she'd missed out on years of phenomenal sex.

She arched her back, willing him to take more of her nipple into his mouth. Seth dropped to his knees, grasping both breasts in his hands and licking first one nipple, then the other.

"You're shaking, Abby," Mike said. "I think you have very sensitive nipples. Does it make your pussy even wetter when Seth sucks them?"

"Yes."

He reached behind her and lifted her dress, his hand on the bare skin of her buttocks nearly driving her to the floor. But he wrapped an arm around her waist, refusing to let her fall.

"Mmm, such smooth, soft skin. And these sexy little stockings and garter. Did you dress to seduce Seth and me tonight, Abby?"

"Yes."

"Did you fantasize about fucking us?"

"Yes."

"Take her panties off, Seth."

Seth trained his gaze on her face, then slipped his hands under her dress, sliding his palms over her thighs and reaching for the strings of her thong. He dragged the panties down her legs, and she stepped out of them.

"I can smell you," Seth said. "Like a sweet, musky honey, Abby. It makes me so goddamn hot." He rubbed his thumb over her panties. "And these are soaked."

She wasn't going to be able to stand up much longer. If Mike wasn't holding onto her, she'd have collapsed. She couldn't handle this much arousal, these overwhelming sensations. And they were just playing with her right now. The really serious stuff hadn't even started yet. Her heart was racing, she was breathing in a fast, panting rhythm, and there was no way she could form a coherent sentence.

"You're doing fine, baby," Mike said in answer to her unspoken thoughts. "We know this is a new experience for you. Just relax and let us take care of you."

Take care of her? If it got any hotter than this, she was going to pass out and miss the whole experience.

"Ever known a woman like Abby, Mike?" Seth asked. "You're like this sweet, innocent little thing. But there's a fire burning inside you, Abby. A spark waiting for a flame."

"You just needed us to light you up," Mike replied, palming her buttocks and slipping his hand between them.

She couldn't help it. It had been so long since a man had touched her pussy. When she felt Mike's warm, hot hand cup her, she let out a shaky whimper.

"Shh, it's okay." He rocked his palm against her. She was soaked, knew she was flooding his hand. But she couldn't stop the sensations, the way her body responded. And she didn't want to. She wanted to come and come hard against his hand.

"Please, please touch me."

"Oh, I'm going to touch you, Abby. All. Night. Long."

She shut her eyes and gave herself up to the sensation of his fingers probing her throbbing pussy, slipping inside her with first one finger, then two. She felt the pulses as her cunt surrounded him, the sweet contractions of pleasure at the invasion.

Oh, it felt so good to feel human touch against her body again. She hadn't realized how alone and isolated she'd been the past few years, how she'd come to depend on only her own touch. How much she'd missed a man's hand against her flesh. Inside her, thrusting slowly, the sweet rush of her juices pouring forth in response.

She moved against his hand, squeezing and releasing, finding a rhythm that would give her release. So lost in her own world of self-pleasure, she almost forgot she wasn't alone.

She'd spent so much time alone. Way too long.

"Look at me, Abby."

Seth's voice, below her, called to her through this haze of ecstasy.

She lifted her lids and looked down to see him on his knees, poised between her legs.

"Spread for me."

Shuddering, she widened her legs. Mike thrust his fingers in deeper, and she let out a panting gasp.

Seth leaned in and fit his mouth over her clit, sucking the hood between his teeth, licking along the folds to capture the tiny pearl that burst with pleasure.

"Ahh, oh God," she cried, digging her nails into Mike's arm as she watched Seth's tongue bathing her with warm, wet, relentless pulses, while Mike's fingers fucked her with a steady rhythm. She couldn't take it. Though it was too soon, she couldn't hold back. She spun over the edge in seconds, tensing and arching her back, shuddering through a wild climax that seemed to come out of nowhere and caught her unaware. Mike held her, forcing his fingers past the tightening muscles of her cunt, continuing to pump her until she was right on the edge again.

But when he pulled out, she nearly cried at the feeling of emptiness. Seth stood, and she was left shaky and alone, half-naked and feeling incredibly vulnerable.

Not for long, though. Seth's mouth met hers in a tangle of passion that surprised her. Where formerly he'd been slow and tender, now he was forceful and filled with a need that matched her own. He drove one hand into her hair, wrapping his hand into the tangle of curls and pulling her head back, ravaging her mouth with relentless stabs of his tongue. She met him eagerly, fumbling for the buttons of his shirt, desperate to feel his skin against hers.

Behind her, she heard the rustle of clothing, assumed Mike was undressing. When he tugged at her skirt, she didn't even pull away from Seth's mouth. A hunger possessed her now, and all she wanted was these men inside her, in any way possible. The soft preliminaries and nice conversation were over. She wanted hard cocks inside her, and she wanted them now.

Mike resisted the impulse to rip his clothes off, but damn if Abby didn't make the task arduous. The scent of her filled the air around him, his hand covered with her come. He licked it from his fingers. Sweet, tangy, making him want to bury his face between her legs until he heard her soft cries again.

She came fast. When she let go, she really let go. His cock was painfully rigid and ready to go off just listening to her whimper and feeling her cunt tighten around his fingers.

Worthless ex-husband of hers. He'd bet a million the man had treated her like shit the entire time they were married. The guy should have his balls wound up in a rubber band until they rotted and fell off.

Ah, screw her ex, the worthless dickhead. Right now Abby was all that mattered. And getting inside her, every which way possible. He tore off his shirt and unfastened his pants, letting them slip to the floor and kicking them away. Soon he was naked and tugging down her dress, casting it on top of his clothes.

"Damn." Garters and stockings. Nothing turned him on more. Something about a woman still partially dressed made his balls quiver. He kneeled behind her and swept his hands upward from her ankles to her thighs, savoring the feel of silk against his palms, lingering where the lace met the straps of her garters. He inhaled her musky fragrance, reached between her legs to capture some of the moisture there. He could see it dripping from her, she was so fucking wet, and he could imagine how easily he could slide inside her, bury himself to the hilt.

His cock lurched, demanding it.

He stood and looked at Seth, who had just finished undressing. It was good to be such close friends with someone. Someone you trusted and knew so well. He motioned Seth to the couch with an inclination of his head. Seth nodded and smiled.

Yeah, Seth knew where Mike was headed with this.

"Abby, I want my cock in your pussy."

Abby half-turned. Her half-lidded gaze told him she was gone, drunk with passion and the need to fully experience this.

"Fuck me," she said, her voice harsher than he'd ever heard from her.

He knew there was a wildcat lurking underneath all that innocence. Barely leashed and just waiting for the right man—or men in this case—to let her out of her cage. He loved a woman whose passions met his own. And Abby was having her first taste of this kind of wildness.

Yeah, her ex was a dimwit.

Her gaze darted to his cock, her eyes widening for a second. He grasped his shaft and stroked it for her, letting her see what she was getting. She swallowed, licked her lips, and turned away from him to focus on Seth.

Seth sat on the couch and beckoned to her, his hand closing around his shaft. "Suck my cock, Abby."

Mike stepped behind her and placed his hand on the middle of her back, directing her forward. She bent from the waist and placed her hands on Seth's thighs while at the same time spreading her legs.

In this position, Mike had a perfect view of her pussy. She'd shaved it bare, the pink, puffy lips wet and swollen. His cock twitched at the delectable sight of her spread out like a feast for his mouth. He squatted, leaning in to take a long, slow swipe with his tongue, needing to taste her.

The sweetest cream. She shuddered and spilled more of it onto his tongue. Oh yeah, he could lick her like this until she came again. The temptation to take her there was strong, to linger between her legs and suck her pussy until she was begging to come. But this time, he wanted her to come on his cock.

He nestled against her buttocks, taking a moment to run his hand along the curve of her hip, savoring the position, the curve of her body. He probed between her pussy lips, her heat drawing him in.

He was big, and he knew it, so despite the urge to plunge inside her with one quick thrust, he took his time, giving it to her slow and easy and gauging her reaction by watching her. Her nails dug into Seth's thighs as she paused, her lips just a fraction of an inch from Seth's cock.

Christ, she was tight. He could tell she hadn't been used in awhile. Her pussy gripped him like a vise, squeezing and pulsing. Damn good thing he had decent control, or he'd be coming right now. Her cunt was sweet heaven, and he wanted to be in there for awhile. And the sounds she made—the soft little groans and whimpers as he eased his way in—were enough to drive a sane man crazy.

He'd had his share of women over the years, but Abby was something special.

And that surprised the hell out of him. Because Mike never thought women were special. A woman was good for a fuck, and that was it. No doubt Abby was a good fuck, but there was a lot more to this woman than just a one-night screw.

Quit thinking. Thinking only led to emotion, and emotion only led to entanglement, which was unfamiliar and unwelcome territory.

Once she'd grown accustomed to his size, once he felt her juices pouring over him and her body easing onto him, he thrust hard and buried himself the rest of the way, taking in her stunned cry with a sense of satisfaction. He'd hurt her a little, but she liked it. He could sense it in her gasping moans, the way her cream poured over his balls, and the way she fucked back against his dick.

Welcome to the Nottingham Monster, Abby.

Abby felt like she'd been impaled by a monster. A monster-sized cock in her pussy. She couldn't breathe as Mike's cock pulsed within her, filling her. It had been so damn long since she'd felt a dick inside her. A real one, anyway. There was definitely a discernible difference between a real man and a dildo. Heat swelled inside her, and he moved. God, how he moved against her. It hurt, but it felt so damn good as he rubbed her g-spot with his sizable cock.

And right in front of her eyes was another cock. Seth's. What a turn-on to see him watching her get fucked by Mike with a look of hunger in his eyes, stroking his own shaft and waiting for her to take it in her mouth. To know he wanted her so badly he was touching himself in anticipation.

She had a hunger of her own, too. She wanted a taste of him. The chance to have two cocks at the same time, to pleasure two men. She bent down and let Seth guide his cock head to her lips, sliding her tongue out to taste the cream that lingered just on the tip.

"Salty," she said in a voice too low, too sexy to be her own. She licked her lips in satisfaction.

Seth's chin dipped to his chest, and he cocked his head to the side, his half-lidded gaze incredibly exciting. Who knew that turning a man on could be so arousing to her? It wasn't like she had a ton of experience there. She paused, waiting for him to thrust his cock in her mouth.

But he didn't. Instead, he waited for her to take it, putting her in control. Oh, she liked that part. She'd never been a tease before. This was her opportunity. She swept her tongue over him again, taking her time to savor the soft, velvety texture of the satiny crest, to let her saliva flow over the shaft so she could stroke it with her hand. She enveloped his cock head between her lips, sucking it gently into her mouth. Seth groaned and pushed upward with his hips, feeding his cock to her.

Behind her, Mike gave her slow, deliberate strokes, sliding in, then back out, making it easy for her to concentrate her efforts on sucking Seth's cock. To be the recipient of such earth-shattering pleasure while at the same time giving it to someone else was almost too much to absorb at one time. But she was determined to memorize every stroke, every taste and texture. Burn it into her memory banks so she would never forget this one special night.

Because this wild woman getting fucked and simultaneously sucking a man's cock wasn't the real Abby Lawson. She was a fantasy, a daydream, and she was going to enjoy every magical moment of her fantasy world for as long as it lasted.

seven

seth thrust upward, watching his cock disappear between Abby's full lips. He looked over her at Mike, watching the taut lines of concentration on his face as his friend fucked her, imagining what it must feel like to be buried in her hot little pussy.

Soon enough he'd be tucked inside her cunt. The thought of it made his balls quiver. If he could, he'd be in both places at once. But he couldn't, so he focused on her lips. Her mouth was wet liquid heat, surrounding him, sucking him, driving him to an unbearable agony as he fought back a climax that threatened to rush forth like a geyser. He tangled his fingers in her hair, pulling the pins out and tossing them aside, freeing the soft waves to cascade along her face. That's the way he liked her, with her hair unbound and framing her face. She looked wild and untamed as her emerald green eyes met his, the fire of her arousal burning him.

She loved giving pleasure as much as she enjoyed receiving it. That didn't surprise him, considering how much he knew about her.

She savored his cock like a hungry animal, pulling it out to stare at it, lick the drops of pearly liquid gathering at the head, only to devour it once again, swallowing him all the way to the back of her throat.

He could come down her throat, and she'd take it all, swallow every pulsing drop of it. Her eagerness and enjoyment of tonight amazed him. Oh, she'd been unsure of herself at first, hesitant about this whole thing, but now she was enjoying every second of it. He liked seeing her unleashed like this, but admittedly, a part of him wanted this wildness all for himself, wanted her licking only his cock, fucking only him.

Tonight, though, was for Abby. Tonight, he had to share.

"That's it, baby," he said, lifting his hips to feed her. "Suck it deep." He made eye contact with Mike, saw the way Mike gritted his teeth, and knew he was close. Seth didn't think either of them were ready to come yet. Not until Abby had her turn again. He watched the movements of her mouth, mentally tamping down the urge to drive his shaft faster between the tight suction of her lips, then reached for her face, pulling her up.

"Enough for now."

"I want you to come," she said, her voice no more than a throaty whisper.

God, what she did to him. "I know. And I will. Later."

Mike withdrew, too, and Seth stood, pulling Abby upright. "Don't want you to get too tired or get your back in a spasm. We have all night."

He pulled her against him and kissed her, driving his tongue inside to taste where his cock had just been. She tasted like rum and like him. Her nipples rubbed against his chest, the hard points teasing his flesh. He cupped them, rubbing his thumbs over her distended nipples, forcing himself to break the contact of their kiss just so he could watch her eyes when he teased the buds. She gasped when he rolled them between his fingers. He used her response as a guide. She liked a little more pressure, a little harder pinching.

She was so responsive with her sighs, her moans, her facial expressions, telling him without words what wasn't enough and what was too much.

He was going to give her whatever she wanted. And even what she didn't yet know she wanted. But right now he wanted inside her tight little pussy, wanted to seat himself in her heat and feel her wet cunt surrounding him. He lifted one of Abby's legs, fitting it over his hip.

Mike had left the room. Seth didn't know where he'd gone. Frankly, he didn't care, wanted to take however much time he had with Abby alone. He fit his cock against her pussy, rubbing it against her clit, watching how her eyes glazed over. She twined her arms around his neck and lifted up, sliding her pussy over his shaft and impaled herself on him.

"Christ," he murmured when he felt how tight she was inside. She pulsed, gripped him, and began to move up and down over him. He held her leg, squeezed her ass with his other hand, and powered upward, wanting to bury himself deep inside her. And he loved watching her, the look on her face. She captured her bottom lip between her teeth, concentrating as if she were holding back her own orgasm as she held tight onto his shoulders and leaned back. Now he could watch the movement of her breasts, see her clit each time she lifted off him. Her pussy was swollen, wet, the aroma of her arousal permeating the air around them. Her body was bathed in the soft light of the room, flushed pink with the heat of her movements. Her hair was tousled around her face, her lips swollen from sucking and kissing him. She was panting, little gasps escaping her lips as she rode his cock. With every thrust he made, she moaned deep in the back of her throat.

"Come for me, Abby."

He wanted this time just for the two of them, without Mike in the room, wanted to have this experience alone. Selfish, he knew, but he didn't care. A sense of urgency built within him, a need to have this moment with her.

He reached between them and stroked her clit—fuck, she was so wet—he rubbed her juices over the nub with gentle motions. Her eyes widened, her mouth opened, and she had a pained look of sheer ecstasy on her face. Her nails dug into his shoulders as he powered his cock harder, faster, feeling the walls of her cunt squeezing him, her sweet liquids pouring over his balls.

"Come on, baby," he whispered. "Do it for me. Come on my cock."

She trembled, ground her pussy against his pelvis, and cried out. He felt the contractions surrounding him and held back as long as he could. He wanted to watch her face as she came. And she did, tilting her head back and screaming as she orgasmed, raking her nails across his shoulders and down his arms. He held onto her tight, then let go himself, groaning as he jettisoned hot spurts of come into her. He pulled her upright, burying his face in her neck as he shuddered through the force of his climax.

Seth opened his eyes. Mike stood in the doorway, his cock in his hand, stroking it as he watched them.

"Nice show."

Seth withdrew, and turned Abby around to face Mike. "Sorry," he said, though there was no sincerity in the word. "I couldn't wait."

Mike shrugged and pushed off from the doorway. "Don't blame you. If I had Abby to myself for a few minutes, I wouldn't have waited for you, either. Besides, I enjoy watching."

Still shaking from the aftereffects of the stunning orgasm she'd had with Seth, Abby stared warily at Mike, wondering if he was angry that he hadn't been included. She'd been so focused on Seth she hadn't even noticed he'd left the room.

But he didn't look upset, his mouth crooked in a half smile. His cock certainly didn't look offended as he walked toward her unashamedly naked and erect. He stopped in front of her, slipped his hand behind her neck, and pulled her face to his, slipping his tongue inside her mouth.

Warm, wet, possessive, as if he were claiming her away from Seth. He devoured her lips in a tantalizing kiss that made her pussy pulse with desire again. She didn't think it was possible to feel desire so soon after the climax she'd just had, but just like that, she was ready to go. When Mike pulled back, she was breathing heavily, her nipples pebbled into tight points. He caressed her cheek with the back of his hand, his blue eyes dark like an approaching storm, yet his voice was soft, as if he were keeping a tight rein on his own need.

"There's plenty of time for us to come together tonight, Abby. No jealousy here, so don't sweat it, okay?"

"Okay." She relaxed the tension in her shoulders and grasped the hand he offered.

"Let's take a little break. How about a soak in the hot tub?"

Grateful for a moment to gather her composure, she nodded. "That sounds wonderful." She craned her neck around to see if Seth was following.

"I'll be there in a minute," he said but stood at the doorway and watched as she and Mike stepped outside.

A high wooden fence surrounded Mike's yard, and there were no nearby neighbors, so it wasn't like anyone could see them. Yet, it was odd to be outside stark naked. How incredibly liberating.

The night air was still very warm, and he lived far enough out of town that the lights of the city didn't obscure the view of the stars overhead. It was truly a magical evening. The hot tub was built up on a ledge overlooking the pool, a cascading waterfall spilling over the top of the various oversize rocks into the pool below. Rather than just a basic pool/tub combo, it looked like an oasis, with palm trees, bushes, and birds of paradise adjacent to the water. A canopy of white latticed arbors filled the rest of the yard behind the pool, with dark pink bougainvillea highlighted by in-ground spotlights.

"It's beautiful out here."

"Thanks," he said, leading her up a smooth path toward the tub. "I tend to do a lot of activities outside, since most of my days are spent inside at the clinic. Took me awhile to put all this in."

"You built all this yourself?"

He shrugged as he stepped into the tub and held both her hands while she maneuvered over the edge and slipped her feet in. The water was perfect.

"Contractors helped out with the pool and tub, but I designed it all. Did all the landscaping and arbor myself."

As she settled into the water up to her neck, she kept her gaze focused on him. "I'm . . . surprised."

"Why?"

"You just don't seem the type."

He laughed. "To do what? Build anything with my hands? Do landscaping? What?"

"I don't know. I didn't mean it like that." She realized then that she'd probably just insulted him. *What I meant was you're rich, successful, and gorgeous. Surely you just work at the clinic during the day and go out at night, pick up women, and fuck your brains out. It's not like you'd do anything useful with your off time.* Ugh. Sometimes she wondered where she stored all her supposed brains.

"Oh, you just thought I was pretty and useless."

Her eyes widened, and she was about to launch into an apology when she realized he was laughing.

"I really didn't mean it as an insult. Honestly."

He stretched his arms out on the ledge outside the hot tub. "I know you didn't. Because of my looks, most people think all I do is go out and party and fuck. Hey, guys get stereotyped just as much as women do."

She'd never thought of that. People probably assumed a lot about

Mike Nottingham. She knew she had. Then again, she still felt there was much she didn't know about him, that he held back parts of himself. It wasn't like he was an open book. Maybe that was part of his appeal. Women loved to uncover a mystery, and an enigmatic man was intriguing as hell. Then again, most women probably didn't get past his gorgeous looks, mesmerizing eyes, and killer body. She was probably guilty of the same, though she'd been lucky enough to work beside him for almost a year. At least she knew a little about him beyond the physical, knew he was smart and kind and funny.

And still, she knew very little about him.

Or about Seth, for that matter.

Yet she'd already fucked both of them.

Then again, did she really need to have an extensive bio on them to have sex them? Men never cared about a woman's background before they took her to bed. Why did she care? She knew they were both responsible and successful. She knew they were honorable and trustworthy. At least so far.

The sex had been phenomenal to this point. She had nothing to complain about.

"You're smiling."

She looked up at Seth, who had managed to sneak up on her while she was lost in thought. "I am?"

"Yeah, you are. A contented smile." He slipped into the hot tub next to her. "I hope that's a sign you're having a good time."

"I am. A very good time."

"Relaxed now that you've had a little breather?" Mike asked.

She glanced over at him. "Yes. Very. Thank you both for tonight. It's been . . . beyond my wildest expectations."

Mike arched a brow. "And what are your expectations, Abby?"

"I don't have any," she blurted.

"You mean you don't have fantasies? Come on. Everyone has them."

She shrugged, feeling heat suffuse her face and knowing it didn't come from the warm water. She looked down at the frothy bubbles skimming the surface. "Maybe."

Mike tipped her chin and forced her gaze to his. "I hardly think you'd be shy with us now. I fantasize all the time."

"You do?"

"Hell yeah. Gets me through an otherwise routine day. And I know Seth has them, too, don't you?"

She looked to Seth, who nodded.

"What normal guy doesn't think about sex every free moment he has?" Seth admitted.

She laughed. "I suppose that's true. Women do, too. My friends and I talk about sex a lot." If Mike and Seth only knew about the reason she was here . . . about the bet she and Blair and Callie had made . . .

"Tell us what you've fantasized about when you think about having two men, Abby." Seth reached behind him and pulled down a fresh glass of champagne, handing it to her. She took a sip, the cool liquid a sharp contrast to the heat within the Jacuzzi.

"Oh, I don't think I can do that." A sudden attack of shyness constricted her throat. Discussing fantasies with her girlfriends was one thing. Telling her deepest, darkest nighttime desires to two men was another. She couldn't do it. No way.

"How can we make all your dreams come true if we don't know what they are?" Mike reached for one of the glasses of champagne, his gaze intent as he took a long, slow, sip.

"I . . . can't." She stared down into her glass, rimming the edge with her fingertip.

"Because you touch yourself when you think about them? Because you think no one's supposed to know about them but you?" Mike asked.

God, he was insistent. And his voice—so sexy, demanding, so incredibly arousing. She looked up at him, and it was almost painful the way he seemed to probe the inner recesses of her mind. He was too much for her. Way too much.

"Abby."

She turned her head at the sound of Seth's voice, grateful to be pulled away from the intensity of Mike's probing look.

"Don't do anything you're uncomfortable with. But honestly, I'd love to know what turns you on, what gets you hot and wet. We both would."

Something about Seth—she didn't know if it was the way he put things into words or just the way he talked to her—made her feel more comfortable about revealing parts of herself. Even her fantasies.

But not all the questions had to be answered by her, either. It was time to turn the tables a little.

"What turns *you* on, Seth?" She scooted to the other side of the hot tub so she now faced them both. "And you, Mike? I'd like to know what the two of you fantasize about. Tell me about the ménages you've experienced together."

Mike's lip curled as if he knew what she was doing. "I get turned on watching a woman's excitement. Watching you come, for example. When you were with Seth in there, riding his cock. The way you threw your head back, abandoning yourself to the sensation. When you let go like that and came . . . now, that was hot. That's what I fantasized about you. That the all-business, prim-and-proper Abby Lawson would just let loose and go wild when she was fucked." He tipped the glass and took another long swallow of his champagne, as if talking about the things that excited him were so easy for him.

She wished it were as easy for her.

"Mike and I have only done a few three-ways; mostly they just happened because we were all drunk and ended up in bed together. Nothing really planned out. Nothing like this, with you," Seth said.

Lifting a brow, she asked, "You two have a plan with me?"

Seth laughed lightly. "Not really a plan. Just a desire to please you."

"Well, you've done that."

"Oh, we've just started, Abby," Mike added, moving to the center of the tub and standing. "Have you ever had your pussy licked by two men at the same time?"

Again, her throat went dry, and she fought to swallow past the giant boulder that had suddenly appeared there. She shook her head.

"Let's dry off and go inside." Mike turned and stepped out, grabbing robes off a hook on the wall right behind the hot tub. He reached for her hand and hauled her out of the tub, slipping one of the long cotton robes over her. Seth stepped out behind her and grabbed the champagne bottle, Mike took their glasses, and they headed into the house.

Mutely, Abby followed, wondering what new adventures they had in store for her. Anticipation doubled the warmth of her body, heightening the sensation of her nipples rubbing against the soft cotton robe.

Mike led her down a dimly lit long hallway toward a set of double doors that opened into a spacious master bedroom with a monumentally large king-size bed as the focal point of the room. White plantation shutters made the room seem bright despite the lateness of the evening, and the matching white slatted bed and wardrobe made the room appear even lighter.

"How many people sleep in that thing?" she asked, staring in awe at the bed, then realized what she'd just said.

Idiot.

But Mike laughed. "No sleepovers. Just me. I sprawl."

Thank God he wasn't easily offended.

"Sorry. It's so big."

"Most women only say that about my dick," Mike teased.

Abby burst out laughing.

"Plenty of room for all three of us, then," Seth said, coming up behind her and moving the collar of the robe aside to plant a kiss between her neck and shoulder. She shivered, her nipples tightening.

Mike came toward her, untying the robe and opening it to slide his hands around her waist. "You warm enough?"

She nodded, and he pushed the robe all the way off, then took her hands in his and led her to the bed, turning her around so the back of her knees were pressed against the edge of the mattress.

"Right here. I want you to be able to watch."

Watch what?

Seth stepped up next to Mike, and then she didn't think about questions as they both dropped their robes, allowing her to drink her fill of their bodies.

Side by side, they were a study in contrasts. Mike was taller and leaner. Seth was more muscular. Mike's cock was longer, Seth's was thicker. Mike's entire aura was one of dangerous excitement, whereas Seth had a sensual allure she found incredibly appealing.

Which one would she choose? If she actually had a choice, which she knew she didn't. An interesting question, though.

They both reached for her at the same time, and she couldn't resist the tiny gasp that escaped her lips at the first touch of their hands on her breasts.

Seth paused. "Something wrong?"

"No. God, no. Touch me, please."

It was so incredibly erotic to have them both smoothing their hands over her skin, to not know where they were going to touch her next. It was a sensual examination from head to toe, an intimate exploration of every inch of her body. Seth brushed her hair aside to press a kiss to the nape of her neck, while Mike rubbed the pad of his thumb over her nipples. Seth skimmed a hand down her arm, then over her hip, and Mike traced a barely felt line down her belly with the tip of one finger.

An explosion of sensation was going off inside her. Hands, mouths, everywhere on her body, kissing her ear, licking her nipple, caressing her back, cupping her pussy. She moaned, and Mike took her mouth, plunging his tongue inside at the same time a finger—whose finger she didn't even know—slid inside her cunt, pumping with slow and deliberate strokes. She felt the flood of warm wetness slide out of her, the pulsing need of arousal as it built like a rising flame in her belly.

"Spread your legs apart, Abby," Seth whispered in her ear, then slid down her body, kneeling in front of her.

"Watch," Mike said as he pulled his mouth away from hers, then kissed his way down over her breasts, licking her nipples, her stomach, and lower, until he, too, positioned himself on his knees, shoulder to shoulder with Seth.

"Oh, God." She reached for the tall white post at one end of the bed and held onto it as Mike leaned his head between her legs, his tongue snaking out to take a long, slow lick around her distended clit. The heat and moisture as he drove along her sensitive tissues nearly buckled her, but she grasped the post and held on, tugging her bottom lip between her teeth as she watched what he did to her.

He lapped her like a kitten licking milk, drawing lazy circles around her clit. Oh yes, that was exactly how she liked it. Just as she felt the spirals of taut ecstasy surrounding her, he leaned back, and Seth moved in, his mouth covering her mound completely, sucking her clit between his teeth. The sensation was so different from what Mike had done, so erotic to see him suckling her clit like that.

She held onto the bed as a lifeline and watched these two men as they took turns licking her, bringing her ever closer to a climax she craved as desperately as an addict needed her next fix. She felt addicted right now. Needy for these sensations, for this tormenting pleasure that went on and on, this naughty, wicked scene they'd laid out for her. She felt like a queen being serviced by her men, and she loved it, reveled in it, didn't want it to ever end.

But the tightening grew, her slick, hot core melting under their tongues. She bucked against their faces as the vortex began to spin wildly out of control, whimpering out loud, no longer caring that she demanded in a loud voice what they could give her. Their faces were wet, covered with her juice, and it turned her on even more to know that it was her cream on their faces. Part of her wanted to drop to the floor to lick her own pussy juice off their lips. She felt wild and completely out of control.

Mike twisted two fingers inside her pussy, thrusting hard. She nearly wept with joy at the sensation, and nearly cried with frustration when he removed them.

"Shhh, baby, it's okay," he said, then moved his fingers behind her, parting the cheeks of her ass, moistening her anus with her own cream. Seth sucked her clit and slid his fingers inside her pussy, replacing that feeling of loss with his thick fingers as he fucked her pussy while Mike teased her anus with his fingers.

Oh! These sensations were new and wholly incredible. "What are you doing?" she whispered to Mike.

"I'm going to fuck your ass with my finger," he said, keeping his eyes focused on hers as he spread her buttocks with one hand and slid his finger past the tight barrier of her ass. Seth pumped her pussy with his fingers, lapping at her clit with easy and wickedly delightful strokes of his tongue. She cried out at the pleasure of having Mike's finger invade her ass.

This was her dream, her fantasy, this wild invasion of both her holes by these two men. "Yes, fuck me there, Mike," she urged, her anus gripping his finger as he slid it all the way in. She looked down at Seth, watched as his tongue circled around her clit, as he sucked it between his lips, saw how wet his hand was from her cream pouring over it.

"I want to come," she cried, thrusting her hips against the fingers inside her, feeling the tightening coils of need about to burst. Seth teased her with his tongue now, his movements so rapid she exploded against his mouth and screamed, digging her nails into the wood post. Her pussy and ass contracted around their fingers, liquid pouring down her legs, the complete bliss of a climax so powerful she fell back on the bed, trembling.

She lay there for the longest time, past the point of caring when they both removed their fingers and momentarily left the room. Tiny orgasmic aftershocks continued long after the rush of that initial orgasm, and she smiled.

"Wow," she whispered to no one in particular.

"I'll say."

She peeked her eyes open to see Seth standing over her, grinning. She wanted to give him back what he'd given her. Him and Mike both. God, that had to have been the most wonderful orgasm of her life. When Mike moved in beside him, she looked at both of them and knew what the term *raging hard-ons* meant. They were both painfully erect.

That scene had been totally focused on her pleasure and hers alone, something she'd never experienced before.

Not with Chad, anyway. That there were men who would put their own release aside in order to give her pleasure astounded her.

Abby had an awful lot to learn about sex.

And she was a very eager student.

eight

abby looked like a goddess, sprawled out on the bed, her body flushed with the aftereffects of her orgasm, her legs splayed open. Her breasts rose and fell with each breath, and she looked completely contented. Seth smiled down at her, wanting to kiss her and hold her in his arms, cherish her forever.

But those were emotions he wasn't ready to deal with.

As Mike reminded him, tonight was for fucking and nothing else.

And frankly, that was all he was willing to commit to. Anything more, and he'd be setting himself up for disaster again.

She certainly looked fuckable as hell, her pussy lips plump and wet and begging for a dick. His balls were so tight and drawn they were throbbing. He wanted to bury himself inside her tight little pussy and bang away until he yelled long and loud and shot a ton of come inside her.

And he knew exactly where Mike wanted to be.

"On your belly, Abby," Mike said.

She arched a brow, a satisfied smile on her face. "Aye, aye, Captain."

Mike tossed several pillows in the center of the bed and moved Abby belly-down over them. He started to climb up, but Seth put his hand on Mike's shoulder. "Hang on a second. I want to fuck her this way first."

Mike shrugged. "Fine. She can suck me. I've been dying to have those hot little lips of hers around my dick."

The thought of watching Abby suck Mike was more arousing than Seth wanted to admit. But hell, he loved watching porn, and the blow jobs always got him off. Mike's cock was huge, and he'd always enjoyed watching women suck him. Seeing Abby do it while Seth fucked her would only heighten the experience.

He arranged himself between Abby's legs, taking a moment to admire the view of Abby's backside. Spread open like this, her asshole was in perfect view, her pussy lips dark pink and glistening with her come. Mike slid onto the bed at Abby's head, spreading his legs and positioning his cock right at her mouth.

"Suck me, Abby," Mike commanded.

Seth placed his cock at the entrance to her pussy while she took Mike's cock head between her lips and drew it in. He shuddered, remembering what it felt like to have her hot mouth surrounding his dick. He slowly inched his way into her pussy, closing his eyes and groaning as the liquid heat of her cunt surrounded him.

"You're so tight, Abby. Gripping, squeezing me, pulling me in." He inched back and pushed forward, giving it to her gently while he watched her lips slowly descend over Mike's cock, saw the way her little pink tongue darted out of her mouth to lick along the side of his shaft.

He didn't know which was better, fucking her or having her suck him. One thing was certain; Abby really enjoyed sex. And there was nothing better than a woman who openly enjoyed fucking.

Once again, Abby was sandwiched and savoring two cocks. Mike's shaft slid between her lips, the texture and taste of him so much different than Seth's. She couldn't take as much of him inside her mouth as she could Seth, and Seth certainly didn't have a small cock. But Mike's was monstrously large, and she could barely fit half of it in her mouth. He was so careful with her, though, barely pumping against her lips so he wouldn't drive it too deep against the soft tissues at the back of her throat.

She studied Mike's heavy-lidded gaze as she sucked him, the way he tilted his head to the side and focused on her mouth, almost as if he were detached from the emotion of the experience. So completely different from Seth, who had seemed deeply connected, his every expression mirroring his pleasure. Seth had made contact with her eyes. Mike was watching her mouth.

Though she hated comparing the two men, she couldn't help but note the differences in their reactions to what she did to them.

Mike cupped her chin. "Abby, you ever been fucked in the ass?"

She paused while he withdrew his cock. "No."

He directed his gaze toward Seth. "Slip underneath her. I want her ass."

She shuddered at the dark promise in his voice. Seth withdrew and pulled her upright, jerking the pillows to the floor. He moved around her and slid underneath on his back, pulling Abby astride him.

"Ride my cock," Seth said, grasping her hips. "Fuck it."

The urgency in the room picked up, a thick wall of tense excitement that surrounded Abby. She shuddered and raised up, sliding down over Seth's shaft, her clit rubbing every glorious inch as he entered her. She braced her hands on either side of his shoulders and lifted, then fell, controlling the movements. Seth skimmed her breasts, grazing her nipples with his thumbs. The sensation shot straight to her clit, tight, spiraling sensations like a vortex of electrical pulses.

Behind her, Mike moved her hair aside and kissed her neck. "Lean forward on Seth, baby."

She did, and Mike kissed his way down her back, following her spine and lingering when he reached the spot where her back became her buttocks.

"You smell so good, Abby," he said. "Everywhere."

In this position, she heard Mike, felt what he was doing, but she could only see Seth, who tangled his fingers in her hair and brought her forward for a kiss. While he did, Mike spread apart her buttocks and continued to kiss his way down her body. She gasped when she felt the warm wetness of his tongue invading her anus,

Oh, God! What was he doing to her? The sensitivity there rocketed her into a wild moan against Seth's lips.

Breaking the kiss with Seth, her eyes widened, but Seth pulled her back again, devouring her mouth as Mike did wicked things to her asshole with his tongue.

Oh, God, it felt so good. Every naughty fantasy she'd ever had came to life under Mike's penetrating tongue. She even wondered if Seth felt Mike's tongue on his balls and his cock while Mike was licking her down there. Oh how naughty. The thought made her pussy clench against Seth's cock, and he groaned, sucking on her tongue and thrusting his shaft deeper into her cunt.

She could come so easily from these dual sensations, her clit dragging against Seth's pelvis with every movement. But she held back, wanting the culmination of her dark fantasies to come true. When Mike moved behind her and she felt something cool and wet coating her anus, she panted against Seth's mouth, waiting for the invasion.

"Relax, Abby," Mike said behind her. "I'll go slow."

She couldn't relax. She was excited, aroused, on the verge of orgasm and desperate to be filled with two dicks at once. She'd masturbated to this fantasy countless times, loved the idea of being double-fucked. And now it was about to become a reality.

Mike pressed his thick cock head against her anus, pushing past the tight muscles there. It burned, but she expected it to, and she pushed out, letting him slide easily past the barrier. Seth held her, caressed her hair, stopped his own movements as she adjusted to Mike's cock inside her. She waited while her body accommodated Mike's length, savoring each pulsing sensation. Mike slid every inch slowly inside her, vibrations pounding throughout her body. Her pussy gripped Seth's cock harder as Mike pushed her vaginal walls deeper around Seth. Her clit banged Seth's skin every time Mike withdrew a bit. And her ass was filled with glorious inches of Mike's cock.

This was really happening. She was really being double-fucked. God, she wished she had this on video so she could masturbate to it over and over again. It was so much better than doing it herself with dildos. Real cocks, warm, pulsing flesh, separated by only a thin barrier as they moved within her. They could almost be fucking against each other.

And that was a wild thought. She'd never even realized a male-to-male thing could turn her on so much, and yet she knew that even now, their balls were probably touching each other.

Did they realize it? Did it excite them? Oh, she hoped in some way that it did, because it excited her. The forbidden always charged her fantasies. Only tonight was her reality.

"Can you two feel each other?" she asked, needing to know.

"Yeah," Seth said, his eyes dark with passion. He lifted up, thrusting deep, and her pussy gripped him in a tight vise that made him hiss.

"Does that turn you on, Abby?" Mike asked. "The thought that we can feel each other's dicks moving inside you?"

"Yes," she answered without hesitation, bucking back against his cock. He responded by fucking her ass harder.

And then she was flying over the edge and couldn't hold it back.

"Oh, I'm coming!" She didn't know what to do to stop it, but the feeling of being filled, of knowing they were all but fucking each other, was a fantasy that sent her reeling. Her clit exploded, and she screamed, tightening around them as she writhed and clenched and fucked back against them. They both moved then, furiously pumping against her, one in, one back, their rhythm taking her from orgasm to peak again, her own moisture keeping her right with them as she continued with one aftershock after another.

It was like falling into a black hole of sensation, and she couldn't speak, just fucked them both like a wild woman, scratching at Seth's chest. Mike leaned over her, burying his cock deep in her ass, biting the nape of her neck and growling as he pistoned his cock with hard, punishing thrusts.

She didn't care. She wanted the pain, wanted to come again. When she did, her scream was even louder. She reared back this time, pushing off Seth's chest to reach back for Mike, turning her head to the side to devour his lips with her own. She must have bitten him, because she tasted blood. He growled and laughed, the sound dark and demonic. He grabbed her breasts, pinching her nipples, and then shuddered against her, cursing as he came.

Beneath her, Seth gripped her hips hard, his fingers digging into her flesh as he pushed her down on his cock. She tore her mouth from Mike's and stared down at him, at his face so lost in pleasure it nearly hurt to watch him as he came, bucking wildly against her, thrusting his hips up and thrashing underneath her.

Panting, she could barely move. She was covered in sweat, knew she looked a wreck, and had never felt so womanly, so wild, or so satiated in her entire life. Exhaustion took hold, and she hung there limply while Mike withdrew and pulled her off Seth. They took her into the shower and cleaned her up, dried her off, and tucked her into bed, but she was only vaguely aware of any of it, just grateful for the blissful darkness as the light was turned off.

A warm body nestled in on either side of her, and she smiled as she drifted off to sleep, thinking a girl could get used to this.

nine

abby woke to sunlight streaming into the room and shining on her face. And warmth.

And a very large, very empty bed.

A bed that wasn't hers. She shot straight up, momentarily disoriented. Then it all came rushing back to her, and she pushed her hair off her face.

Oh yeah. This was Mike's bed. Where she'd had really wild sex last night. With two amazing men.

She'd done it. She'd freed herself from the last vestiges of being Chad's boring, dutiful, stupid ex-wife. For the first time she felt like an independent, sexual woman. All in all, she felt pretty damn worldly now.

With a satisfied half grin, she lifted her arms over her head, stretched and yawned, then slipped off the edge and padded down the hall in search of her sex buddies.

Nobody in the kitchen, but she spotted a pot of coffee that got her eyes popping open in a hurry. And an empty cup. She poured a cup and went to the back door, where she saw Seth swimming laps in the pool.

Naked, of course. She leaned against the door and sipped her coffee, content to watch Seth's powerful body slice through the water. The morning sun reflected off the surface of the pool, casting his body in a golden glow. His taut buttocks appeared, then disappeared as he rolled from side to side. She sighed with utter contentment at the vision he presented.

She really liked this whole naked thing. Especially when two gorgeous men paraded unclothed around her.

When he reached the far edge, he dove down and disappeared. Abby waited. And waited some more. Concerned, she stepped through the open door and walked outside to the edge of the pool, peering down into the clear water.

Okay, he'd been under a really long time.

Seth bobbed up just as she was about to set down her cup and dive in after him, his head appearing right at her feet.

"Mornin', beautiful."

Relief flooded her. "I thought you had drowned."

He grinned. "I'm touched by your concern." He lifted his arms out of the water and placed them on the edge of the pool. "Were you watching me?"

"Yes. From the doorway."

"I was on the swim team in college. Don't worry, I can go down for a long time."

Go down. The words heated her core in ways that had nothing to do with swimming. She would have thought after last night's events the furthest thing from her mind would be sex. She was sore in places that hadn't been used in . . . well, ever. But it was a well-satisfied soreness.

"Come in here with me."

A morning swim did sound heavenly. "Okay."

She set her cup on a nearby table and dove in the deep end. The water was cool and refreshing, clearing away the last of the cobwebs from her mind. Seth met her in the middle of the pool, and they surfaced together.

She pushed her hair back, blinking the water out of her eyes. "Where's Mike?"

"He went to the hospital to check on the dog he operated on yesterday. He'll be back in a bit." Seth wrapped his arms around Abby's waist, drawing her against him. "But for now, we're alone."

In the water she was buoyant, so it was easy to wrap her legs around Seth's waist. Her pussy made immediate contact with one very hard dick. She grinned and twined her arms around his neck. "Yes, as a matter of fact, we are. What are you going to do about that?"

His eyes went dark, and his normally carefree and easy grin died, replaced by a look so intense it sent thick heat pooling between her legs. "I'm going to fuck you. Hard. Right here." He walked across the pool until her back hit the edge. His cock was inside her before she could take a breath.

The feel of his naked cock inside her was so wildly erotic she let out a strangled cry and surged upward. His eyes widened and then he grinned as she came apart around him, her orgasm hitting them both by surprise.

She'd never come this fast. It just wasn't in her to do so, yet she climaxed with a sharp, intense burst of pleasure that rocketed her into his arms. His mouth covered hers, his tongue plunging inside her as he thrust so hard her back scraped the pool edge. She welcomed the pain, enjoyed his groaning orgasm almost as much as her own.

They panted together for a few seconds, then Seth laughed.

"That was a quickie," he murmured against her neck.

Abby laughed and leaned back, grinning at him. "But a great quickie."

He kissed her, and this time it was sweet as he savored her lips with slow, measured kisses that felt . . . emotional. Abby's heart clenched, her stomach tumbling at the way he held her, touched her, his mouth moving over her in tender caresses.

When he pulled away, his gaze was so intense she held her breath.

"Abby, I need to say something here—"

"Have you two been fucking without me this morning?"

She jerked her head up and stared into the harsh sunlight. Mike's form was shadowed, tall and imposing against the bright light. "Hey."

"Hell yes, we were fucking without you," Seth replied, pushing away from her and pulling himself out of the water. "You didn't think I was going to wait for you, did you?" He grabbed a towel and dried himself off.

Abby wondered what Seth had been about to say to her before Mike interrupted. From the serious look on his face, it seemed as if it was something important.

"No, I guess you weren't going to wait. Hell, I wouldn't have, either," Mike said, winking at Abby.

She smiled and reached for Mike's extended hand. He hauled her out of the pool and handed her a towel.

"You look like a mermaid, all wet and freshly fucked."

She giggled. "Well, thanks." He was dressed in jeans and a polo shirt. "How's the patient?"

"Doing fine. I brought breakfast. You hungry?"

She followed him into the kitchen. "Starving. And, uh, naked. I need to take a shower and get dressed."

"Toss on one of my T-shirts for now. Top drawer of the dresser."

After a quick shower, she pulled on one of Mike's oversize T-shirts that was so big it fit her like a dress, skimming the top of her knees. When she walked back into the kitchen, Mike had set out warm croissants with jelly, juice, and another steaming cup of coffee.

Mike and Seth both looked up from the kitchen table with a look of hunger in their eyes as they watched her walk in.

Geez, her hair was a mess, damp and uncombed, and she had on one of Mike's T-shirts that was ten sizes too large for her. She was hardly a walking advertisement for sexy.

Figuring their hunger had to be for the food on the table, she grabbed a croissant and a chair and dug in. Her stomach growled a loud complaint at the delicious scents. Obviously, copious hours of sex worked up an appetite.

After she'd satisfied her appetite for food, she wondered what was going to happen next. The only clothing she had with her was the skintight dress from last night. And while she was loath to end this magical fantasy, like Cinderella, the clock had struck midnight, and the ball was over. It was time to turn back into dreary old Abby and return to the drudgery that was her normal life.

"I need a ride home," she said as she downed the last sip of orange juice.

"I can drop you off," Seth offered. "I have some paperwork at the office."

"Great."

Mike leaned back in his chair and smiled at her while he sipped his coffee. Seth did the same thing. She suddenly felt as if she were on a stage, the first act in a comedy show, and she were about to get the hook because she couldn't think of a damn thing to say.

They stared at her expectantly. But why?

Because it's chess, and it's your move, idiot.

Wow. This was awkward. How was she going to handle this? *Uhh, thanks for the great ménage, guys. Best fuck of my life.* Nah, too cold. And she felt way too warm and cozy inside to make it sound so . . . unemotional.

But what, really, did emotion have to do with it?

Sometimes the best move was just to concede defeat. Admittedly, last night was all about fantasy and role-playing. In the harsh light of morning, she was still Abby Lawson, and she had no idea how to handle two gorgeous, virile men who stared at her with expectation on their faces.

"Let me clean this up, then I'll . . . get dressed. I have so much to do at home." She bent her head to her task, swiping away the napkins and plates and remnants of breakfast, hoping to hell neither of them spoke or, God forbid, moved from their chairs.

Last night's bravado had fled. In its place, her customary sheer terror. She was so out of her league here. Tongue-tied and nervous, her hands shook as she emptied the garbage in the compactor, then rinsed the dishes and piled them in the empty dishwasher.

"Abby."

She froze at the sound of Mike's low voice behind her, not even realizing he had snuck up behind her. When he snaked an arm around her waist, she jumped and whirled around.

"Damn, woman. You're tense this morning."

Blowing an errant hair out of her face, she smiled brightly, hoping to mask her discomfort. "Sorry. Just thinking about my to-do list. I have a final paper due in a few days, and need to get started on it."

"What's wrong?"

Casting a look toward the table out of the corner of her eye, she realized Seth had left the kitchen. "Nothing's wrong." *Other than the fact your nearness makes me realize I have no idea what I'm doing.* She needed to get out of there.

"Your heart's beating like a racehorse at the end of a quarter mile. Calm down and tell me what's the matter."

She was staring at his chest, realizing her breasts were flattened against the hard planes of his pecs. No wonder he felt her heart hammering. She inhaled deeply, which only filled her senses with the crisp scent of whatever soap he used. She wanted to bury her nose in his neck, wrap her legs around him, and beg him to fuck her again, wanted to deny her reality and boring existence and live in this fantasy world forever.

Exhaling, she palmed his chest and gently pushed him back. He took the step, reading her signal. Then she looked at him, as always, immediately lost in his blue eyes. "I'm just feeling the reality of all this."

His knowing smile and nod helped. "It's okay. We had a great time last night. No strings." He cupped her neck and drew her forward for a kiss that started out gentle and friendly but quickly turned into something more. God, how she could get lost in him so easily. His magnetism was overpowering, the way he took control and led her to a dark place within her own head where this wild, untamed creature lived. In seconds she was wet, her clit pounding, her pussy aching with need for his cock. He pressed the length of his shaft against her thigh, insistent, demanding, rocking against her until she clutched his shirt and whimpered into his mouth.

"Yes," he whispered against her neck when he pulled his mouth away. "Here. Right now."

He lifted the T-shirt she wore, cupping her bare pussy with his big hand. She arched into his touch, mindless of their location and not even caring if Seth was going to walk in.

"You're so fucking wet already, Abby. You want my dick in your pussy?"

"You know I do. Fuck me." She spread her legs, chewing her bottom lip while he unzipped his jeans and jerked them partially down, freeing his dick. He cupped her buttocks with one hand and lifted her, impaling her on his cock.

She slid onto him, discarding the thought that she could be so easily taken by either of these men, that they could snap their fingers, and she was wet and ready for them. Right now she didn't give a shit. She was being fucked and loving it.

"So hot. Christ, you're tight, Abby. One of the best fucks I've ever had." His voice was gritty and dark, ratcheting up her desire tenfold. She braced her hands on the sink ledge behind her and lifted on and off his cock, letting her clit drag along the ridges of his shaft. Splintering shock waves gripped her pussy, tightening around her.

"Harder," she demanded, her gaze locked on his, watching the pained expression on his face as he squeezed her ass cheeks, his fingers digging into her flesh. He pulled back and slammed against her, striking her clit, making her cry out with pain and ecstasy. "Yes, like that. Fuck me hard."

She gritted her teeth and held on, her arms shaking, her clit swelling as the tightening spirals grew ever stronger. "I'm going to come on your cock, Mike."

He made her wild, made her feel naughty. She loved it.

"Come for me, Abby. Come on me."

"Yes. Yes, I'm coming!" Then she couldn't hold back as torrents of waves crashed inside her, flooding him with her juices. She screamed at the power of her orgasm. Mike grabbed onto her and pulled her against him, grunting as he came, burying his cock deep inside her while he shuddered and rocked through his climax.

Panting, she pushed off the sink and locked her arms onto him, licking the salty sweat from his neck until he set her feet on the ground. Still trembling, she held onto him for a few seconds, wondering what the hell had just happened to her.

God, she'd lost control. She had been about to get dressed and leave, and he whispered her name, and she fucked him.

"Seth went to take a shower. He'll be out soon. You can clean up in the other bathroom if you'd like."

She could barely meet his gaze, though he looked unaffected by what just happened, whereas she wanted to crumple to the ground and sob. "Okay. Let me just grab my clothes."

With as much nonchalance as possible, she shot him a casual smile and took off down the hallway, snatching her dress from the living room and finding her way to the guest bathroom. After a quick shower, she shimmied into the dress, finger-combed her hair, then took a few seconds to catch her breath.

A knock on the door had her whirling around, her heart pounding. *For the love of God, Abby. Get a grip.* "Yes?"

"It's Mike. Can I come in?"

"Uh, sure." She leaned against the bathroom counter, trying to appear calm and relaxed, offering him a smile as he walked in and shut the door behind him. "I'm almost ready to go."

"You can stay if you'd like. I'm not trying to run you off." He leaned against the closed door, his arms crossed in front of him. "Though I get the idea you'd like to get the hell out of here."

"No! That's not it at all! I just have a lot to do at home."

"Uh-huh."

She was failing miserably at this nonchalance thing. "I had a great time, Mike. Honestly. Thank you. It was . . . beyond my wildest fantasies. Having this night with you and Seth was—"

"I want to see you again."

She halted midsentence. "You do?"

"Yes. Go out with me tonight."

She knew her mouth was hanging open, but she honestly hadn't expected this. "With you."

"Yes."

"Tonight."

"Yes."

"Just you and me?"

He arched a brow. "Did you want another threesome?"

Now there was a million-dollar question. Did she want a threesome? Did she want to go out with Mike? Hell, at the moment her brain wasn't functioning at all. Mike had just asked her to go out. She assumed just the two of them.

What did she want?

"I need to think on this."

"Really."

"Oh! Not in the way you think. I mean, I'm honored you asked me out. Any woman would wet her pants being asked out by you, Mike. I think you know that. But honest to God, my synapses aren't firing right now. I need to go home and regroup."

He laughed. "Okay. I'll call you later."

She hoped she hadn't just insulted him. But she really didn't know what she wanted right now. She knew what she needed, though. Distance and some time to think.

Mike opened the door and let her out. Seth was waiting in the living room, tilting his head curiously when she and Mike came out of the same bathroom.

"You ready?" he asked.

"Yes." She turned to Mike. "Thank you again. For everything."

He kissed her lightly on the lips, dragging his thumb across her bottom lip afterward. "I'll call you later."

Her lip throbbed where he touched her, and she shuddered her next breath. "Okay."

Strangely, the ride back to her place with Seth was silent. And not a comfortable silence, either. She sensed he was irritated about something, but she didn't want to be the one to bring it up.

Surely he wasn't jealous that she'd spent time alone with Mike, was he?

Oh sure, Abby. You're just so incredibly desirable that both these men are now going to fight over you.

It was utterly unbelievable the amount of time she could spend in fantasy land.

When Seth pulled into her apartment complex, Abby was convinced he was simply in a hurry to dump her and be rid of her. But when she unbuckled her seat belt and grabbed the door handle, he put his hand on her arm.

"Abby, wait."

She paused, knowing he was going to say something nice, like *Thanks for a great night.*"

"Go out with me tonight."

She blinked. "What?"

"I know it's stupid, but I tried to figure out the right way to pose this question the whole way over here, without it sounding like I just wanted to fuck you again. But it's more than that. Though I do want to fuck you again," he added with a sexy grin.

Her throat constricted, and she fought for breath. Okay, this couldn't be happening to her. Mike asked her to go out with him. Seth did, too. Her brain was a muddy mess, and she didn't know what to make of all this.

Did she want to see either of them again? And what did it all mean?

"I . . . I guess that would be fine," she blurted, then realized Mike had asked her first. Was there some sort of protocol for this? Was there some reason she had just said yes to Seth but she had told Mike earlier she needed to think?

Her brain cells needed repowering. No doubt about it.

He snorted. "Well, that was enthusiastic."

She rubbed the spot between her eyebrows that throbbed with the beginnings of a headache. "I'm sorry. I think I need a nap."

"I'll call you this afternoon, and we'll figure it out. Go rest." He leaned in and pressed his lips to hers, his breath crisp and tasting like cinnamon. She wanted to stay in the car and lick his lips, dive into his embrace, invite him inside her house. Anything. She didn't want to let go. Yet she needed space, too.

Conflicted much, Abby?

She opened the door to her apartment, closed it, threw her purse on the floor, kicked off her shoes, and collapsed in the nearest chair.

She'd just agreed to go out with Seth tonight. And Mike was going to call her later for an answer on his proposal for a date tonight.

Fucking both of them was one thing. Dating both of them another thing entirely. And obviously she sucked at multiple-guy dating because she'd already screwed it up by not answering Mike first.

Now what the hell was she supposed to do?

ten

abby stared at the phone, waiting for it to ring. She still had no idea what she was going to say to Mike when he called.

She supposed to she could try the truth. She wasn't much of a liar. That was Chad's area of expertise, and he'd been damn good at it. Maybe she should call her ex-husband and ask for some lessons.

She snorted at the thought.

That would never work. Unlike Chad, she was terrible at hurting someone's feelings.

Of course, Mike would have to care about her to be hurt, right? And he didn't really care about her, so how could she offend him by turning down his offer of a date tonight?

Simple, really.

The phone rang, and she nearly fell off the arm of the couch.

"Honestly," she murmured to herself. Her pulse raced, but she forced calm into her voice as she picked up the cordless and pressed the button.

"Hey, babe."

"Hi, Mike."

"Get some rest?"

"Yeah, a little," she lied. Instead of resting, working on her paper, or doing something to eliminate her pounding headache, she'd fretted the past four hours about what to do about Mike and Seth.

"Good. So, how about tonight?"

Despite how easy she thought this was going to be, she wasn't good at letting someone down. Hell, she had no practice at it. "Seth asked me out, too," she blurted before she ended up accepting a date with both of them.

"He did, huh? And you said yes."

"How'd you know?"

"Because I know you. It's okay, Abby. We'll do it another night."

She stared outside her window, watching little kids play on the gym equipment in the park across the street while she rubbed her throbbing temple. "I feel awful about this."

She heard his soft laugh on the other end. "Why? It's no big deal. Quit worrying about it, okay?"

Guilt pounded at her stomach like a jackhammer. She'd never quit worrying about it. "Okay."

"I enjoyed fucking you last night."

His whispered voice, low and dark, sent shivers running through her. And just like that, she was wet. Her nipples tightened, and she felt the urge to place her hands between her legs and rub her clit. How did he do that to her? "I enjoyed it, too."

"Later, Abby."

The click in her ear was a shock to her system. He turned her on and left her hanging. Aroused, needy, and primed. With one fucking sentence.

Dammit.

She was so easy.

Shuddering out a sigh, she placed the phone on the table and forced herself into her work, though it was damn hard to concentrate. What she really wanted to do was call Blair or Callie for some advice. But she wasn't going to do that. It was time to make her own decisions about her life, without her friends' input.

Whatever those decisions were. It wasn't like she was in total control of what to do about Mike and Seth.

Then again, maybe she was. Maybe she really was in charge. They both asked to see her again. Why couldn't she admit it was possible they were both interested in her? Had Chad beaten down her self-esteem so badly she couldn't even admit that two fabulous men found her interesting enough to want to see her again? That this ménage thing they'd shared last night had sparked their interest enough to want to pursue her individually? That maybe there was more to their interest in her than just sex?

And what if they did? Did she want to date both of them?

God, could she handle both of them? They were so different. Talk about a study in contrasts. Seth was sensuality personified, coupled with intelligence and warmth and caring, and he made her feel safe. Mike, on the other hand, was a walking, ticking sex bomb. He made her feel reckless and wild and utterly out of control, a heady feeling she didn't mind admitting she enjoyed.

Could she choose between them if she was forced to?

Did she even have to?

She didn't want to think about it right now. Too many thoughts and conflicting emotions were trying to fight for supremacy. She didn't know how she felt.

To distract herself, she worked, focusing on the final paper that was due next week. It helped to take her mind off Seth and Mike, to concentrate on something else besides men and sex. Before she knew it, four hours had passed, and it was time to get ready for her date with Seth. Instead of calling, he'd e-mailed to suggest he pick her up at six. She saved her file and took a shower, then stood in front of her closet trying to figure out what to wear.

Shit. She'd never even asked Seth where they were going.

Damn, damn, damn. Now what was she supposed to wear? She supposed she could call him, but that would be lame. After debating a few minutes, she grabbed a flowered sundress and slipped it on with some low-heeled sandals. That would work for either semidressy or casual.

She dried her hair and left it down tonight, put on a little makeup, earrings, and a bracelet and called it good.

Tonight, she was going out as Abby Lawson, not someone else.

As the minutes ticked by and she waited for Seth to pick her up, she was actually amused by how nervous she was. A few times she stared at the phone, wanting to call Blair or Callie. Frankly, she was surprised they hadn't called her or showed up at her place, demanding every sordid detail about last night.

Then again, maybe they thought she was still with Mike and Seth.

Maybe she should still be with them. Did she make a mistake by running out on them so quickly?

No. She hadn't made a mistake. She'd done exactly what she wanted to do—had a magnificent night with two amazing men. And made a graceful exit after it was over.

Her doorbell rang, and her heart leaped, excitement pumping adrenaline through her system. Seth was here!

Smoothing her dress, she opened the door and let out a sigh of pure feminine appreciation.

He wore jeans and a dark blue polo shirt, unbuttoned, revealing a smooth expanse of his chest. She inhaled and caught the clean scent of freshly showered man. Damn, that smell was always so sexy.

"Hi," she said, moving to the side to let him in.

"Hi yourself. You look gorgeous." He stepped in and gathered her in his arms. She went willingly, realizing how much she'd missed him in the few hours they'd been apart. His lips caught hers in a warm, gentle kiss, his tongue probing softly as he moved his mouth over hers. She melted into his embrace, right there at her front door. It was like something out of a romance movie where the hero takes the heroine into his arms and kisses her senseless.

That's how she felt whenever Seth was around—senseless.

He broke the kiss and stepped back. "I guess I'd better stop that, or we may never get out of here tonight."

And that was a bad thing? "If you insist. Where are we going?"

"If you don't mind a repeat of the club, there's a fifties and sixties band playing tonight. They're doing hot dogs and hamburgers and fries. We'll eat and do some dancing."

"Oh! I love that era. It sounds fun."

"Glad you think so." He held out his hand, tilted his head down, and cast her his best smoldering Elvis look. "Let's go rock and roll, baby."

the club was definitely rocking by the time they got there. Decorated like a high school prom with streamers and balloons and a band playing all her favorite oldies songs. Seth had grabbed hot dogs and fries for both of them, and they sat at a table and ate, laughing at some of the clothes people were dressed up in. Anything from rolled up jeans to early hippie garb was the theme of the night.

She'd thought about changing clothes, but Seth wouldn't let her. He'd told her she looked comfortable and sexy, and he liked the feel of her in her dress.

How could she argue with him after he'd complimented her like that?

"Thirsty?" he asked.

"Sure."

"Beer?"

She arched a teasing brow and mockingly gasped. "What? No champagne tonight?"

He shrugged. "Doesn't go with hot dogs. And frankly, I'm a beer kind of guy."

She was falling madly in love with him. "A guy after my own heart. I'd love one."

He grinned. "I'll be right back." He disappeared into the throng of people milling about. Abby couldn't believe the number of people here. Seth had told her events like this always brought a huge crowd.

"Fancy meeting you here."

Her gaze shot up at Mike's deep voice. "Mike! What are you doing here?"

He arched a brow and pulled up a chair. "I'm a member."

"Oh. Of course. I didn't mean it like that." Flames of embarrassment licked at her face. She felt as if she'd been caught doing something she shouldn't. But he knew damn well she was going out with Seth tonight, so why should she feel guilty?

"Having fun?"

She clasped her hands in her lap and forced the guilt demons away. "So far, yes. We had hot dogs. Seth is getting us beer." And she felt stilted and nervous around him. But why?

"Good. You look beautiful. Your legs look sexy as hell in that dress." His fingers brushed the edge of her hem, just lightly grazing her skin, and she jumped.

Holy shit! Now what was she supposed to do? Her body fired up under his touch, her pussy responding with a familiar ache of wanting. And she recognized it for what it was: a purely physical response. What woman wouldn't react to attention from Mike? He was hands down one of the most dynamic, handsome, and compelling men she'd ever met. The kind of man that made a woman's head turn. The kind that made a woman look twice. No, three times. And when a man like Mike Nottingham gave you attention, you wanted to start pulling your clothes off for him. He was that charismatic.

But she was on a date with Seth! She wasn't supposed to see Mike tonight.

Now tell that to her body, which was jumping up and down in enthusiastic response to being near him.

But when his fingers began to creep inside her dress, she placed her hand over his.

"Mike, I . . . don't think that's a good idea."

He moved his hand away and shrugged. "If you say so. But I really don't think Seth will mind. We share all the time. We shared you last night."

"That was last night, buddy. Tonight, I do mind."

Seth stood at their table with two beers in his hand, looking not at all happy to see his best friend and partner.

mike was probably right. seth shouldn't care that Mike had shown up tonight, that he'd slipped his hand up Abby's dress, that he was fondling her in a way that normally would excite him just to watch.

But goddammit . . . he did care. More than he wanted to. In fact, seething anger made him place the bottles of beer carefully on the table and take a couple deep breaths before he said or did something that would cause irreparable harm to their friendship or partnership.

"You're not serious." Mike had a look of incredulity on his face that Seth found laughable. If the tables were turned, would Mike react in the same way?

No. Of course Mike wouldn't think anything of it. Mike never formed emotional attachments to women. Mike didn't care about

Abby. And that's where the difference was. Because, like it or not, Seth did.

"Mike, let's talk. Outside."

"Hey, you two. I'm sorry if I caused any—"

"You didn't do anything wrong, Abby," Seth said, keeping his attention on Mike.

Mike arched a brow. "And I did? Come on, man. You know better."

"Outside, Mike. Now."

"Sure," he said with a shrug. He scooted his chair back and looked at Abby. "I'll be right back."

No, Mike. You won't.

The sultry summer heat slapped Seth in the face as soon as he opened the door, doing nothing to assuage his lingering frustration. He dragged his fingers through his hair and turned to Mike as soon as the door closed.

"I want you to leave Abby alone."

Mike's eyes widened. "Where did this come from? Last night it was fine for both of us to play with her."

"That was last night."

"I don't think you get to make that decision, man. That's Abby's call."

The rational part of him knew that, the voice inside him telling him it wasn't his choice to make. But he wasn't exactly thinking rationally right now. "I care about her, Mike."

"So do I. Do you think I don't?"

"Why are you here tonight?"

Mike looked around the parking lot, turning his head from side to side. Anywhere but meeting Seth's gaze. He shrugged, then finally looked at him. "Nothing else to do. Thought I'd check out the party."

"You knew I was going to bring Abby here."

Rolling his eyes, Mike said, "Oh, so now I'm psychic? How the hell was I supposed to know you were going to bring her here? Should I have called you first before I came here?"

Shit. Mike was right. He didn't know Seth was bringing Abby here tonight. "This is going to be complicated."

Mike shoved his hands in his jeans and shrugged. "It doesn't have to be."

"Maybe not for you. Goddammit, Mike, I don't want you to see her!"

"But I'm going to. If she agrees. I'm sorry, Seth."

"Fine. But if I happen to see the two of you when you're out, I won't muscle in on your date."

Mike nodded. "You got me there. I'm sorry, man. You're right. I overstepped, and I shouldn't have. I'll see you at work, buddy." He held out his hand, and Seth took it.

"Thanks. I'll see you at work."

He watched Mike walk away, then went back inside. Abby looked like a deer caught in the headlights at the start of hunting season. "It's okay. He's gone."

She turned to face him. "I'm so sorry. I just didn't know what to say."

He pulled her chair closer, fitting her knees between his out-stretched legs. "It's complicated for all of us. I understand. And so does Mike." Tucking a piece of errant hair behind her ear, he said, "If I had it my way, I'd keep you all to myself."

Her eyes widened. "You would?"

"Yeah. What do you think about that?"

She grabbed her bottom lip with her teeth, then let go. "I don't know. This weekend has been a wild rush, and I don't know what to make of all of it, Seth. I don't know how to answer that just yet."

He bent in and pressed his lips to hers. "Fair enough. How about a dance?"

She tilted her head and grinned as the familiar strains of "Unchained Melody" began to play. "And they're playing my favorite love song."

"Then my timing is perfect, isn't it?" He stood and held out his hand.

Abby loved this song. Seth pulled her into his arms and against his body, his warmth erasing all the tension of a few moments ago. She had no idea what went down between Mike and him outside, but he didn't seem angry at all, so they must have worked it out. Either way, she was relieved not to be caught in the middle anymore.

Now she could enjoy her time with one man. The other one she'd worry about later.

And this particular man was a great dancer. He twirled her around the floor, dipping her, turning her, holding her tight against his muscular body, and leading her like a master.

"Where did you learn to dance?"

"My mother insisted we take lessons when we were kids. I *loathed* them at the time. But now I can see the benefits."

When his hand pressed into the small of her back, driving her toward his thigh, her eyes widened. "You're exceptionally good at it. I'm putty in your hands."

"Does that mean you'll do anything I ask?"

"Depends on what it is. You have something particular in mind?"

The band moved from one slow song to another, so they kept dancing. She liked being in Seth's arms. It felt . . . right, somehow. They fit together perfectly.

"I have lots of things in mind."

"For example?"

"Spending the evening with you alone for starters. I like this."

Despite the crowded dance floor and people bumping into them left and right, to Abby, they were the only two people in the room. Seth made her forget there was anyone else around them. "I like it, too."

"Do you know your lips part and you breathe through your mouth when you're aroused?"

She arched a brow. "I do?"

"Yeah. And you tug on your lower lip when you're thinking about something. Or you're nervous."

"I do not."

"Yeah you do. And it makes me want to take that pouty little lip between my teeth and bite it."

Desire flooded between her legs, her nipples hardening. She realized just then that her lips were parted, and she smiled.

"I want you, Abby."

He bent her over his arm, then righted her, insinuating his hard cock between her legs. She gasped at the exquisite sensation. Between her thin panties and the silk sundress, there wasn't much fabric between her clit and his erection. "Then get me out of here and fuck me," she whispered.

They were out of the club in less than two minutes. Seth tore out of the parking lot and onto the main road, nearly breaking speed records in his haste to get wherever they were going.

Abby damn near hyperventilated the entire way, her body on fire with need for him. She would have thought after last night she'd be sated, but that wasn't the case at all. It was like a dam had burst inside her, and she was flooded with the desire to fuck.

Fortunately, Seth didn't live far out of town. He pulled into a long driveway in front of a modest two-story home, shut off the ignition, and pulled Abby toward him, ravaging her mouth with a kiss that spoke of building passion. As soon as he broke the kiss, she unbuckled her seat belt and reached for the door handle, hurrying to get out of the car. There was no time to wait for chivalrous behavior like him coming around to her side. She wanted in his house and in his pants.

He fumbled with his keys in the dark, then dropped them, and they both attempted to choke back their giggles like a couple of kids trying to avoid being caught smooching at the front door. When he finally got the door open, he yanked her inside, then slammed it shut behind him, pushing her against the door and covering her body with his.

"Goddammit, I can't wait to be inside you," he murmured, his hands roaming her body. He cupped her breasts, and she moaned when his thumb found the sensitive peak of her nipple. When he moved down her rib cage, then over her hips and thighs, fisting the hem of her dress, she moaned out loud.

"Then don't," she panted against his lips. "Fuck me right here."

He raised her skirt and found her panties, jerking them down her legs.

"Shit," he said against her mouth, then bent down to pull her panties off. He stepped back long enough to unzip his jeans and push them down, releasing his cock. Swollen, thick, he rubbed his thumb over the slitted head, capturing the pearly liquid gathered there. He brought his thumb to her mouth.

"Suck it," he commanded.

She grabbed his thumb and swiped it over the crest, tasting his fluid, watching his eyes darken as she took his thumb between her lips and sucked it like a cock.

"Fuck!" He jerked her leg over his hip, then positioned his cock at the entrance of her pussy, driving inside her hard. She cried out at the pleasurable pain of his invasion.

Wet and ready for him, her pussy gripped his shaft, squeezing, pulsing around him as he reared back and plunged again, giving her exactly what she'd been craving ever since he pulled her onto the dance floor. She bit down on the pad of his thumb, then sucked it again.

"Ah, baby, that makes me crazy when you do that. It's like sucking and fucking me at the same time." He gripped her ass and squeezed it, holding her tight against the door as he slammed into her repeatedly. With every thrust his body rasped against her clit, taking her closer and closer to a building orgasm.

She pulled his thumb from her mouth and drew his head forward for a kiss, sucking his tongue as she had his thumb. He ground his lips hard against her mouth while he pounded her pussy.

Abby was mindless with pleasure, needing this maelstrom of passion as much as Seth seemed to. She'd never felt these uncontrollable urges of animalistic hunger before, but right now she wanted to ravage Seth, to mark him, to make him hers in a primitive way she couldn't explain. She tore his shirt aside and buried her teeth in the fleshy part between his neck and shoulder.

He grunted and slammed his cock harder inside her, grabbing her ass and lifting her off her feet to hammer her with thrust after thrust until she lifted her head, meeting his gaze, feeling the eruption coming.

"Yeah, baby, come on me," he said. "Come on my cock, Abby."

She kept her gaze on his, digging her nails into his shoulders. Tears filled her eyes as he stilled and ground his pelvis against her. The sensation against her clit was her undoing, and she shattered, coming in shrieking waves of pleasure. Seth watched her, and she couldn't help herself. She screamed and pounded at him, shuddering and crying as the sensations continued. He took her mouth and groaned, emptying his come inside her in one hard, final thrust.

He held onto her like that, seemingly content to brace her against his front door and carry all her weight.

"I've got to be heavy," she murmured against his neck.

"Hardly." But he finally slid her down his body, slowly, capturing her mouth in a searing kiss as he did so. "Sorry. That wasn't quite the slow, romantic seduction I had in mind."

She grinned and wrapped her arms around his neck. "Forget slow and romantic. I wanted you."

"And I wanted you. Still do." He swept her in his arms and carried her down the hall to his bedroom, kicking the partially closed door open.

He nudged the light on with his elbow. A very masculine room with dark wood furniture and a king-size bed filled the room. But what really caught her eye was the decor.

"Oh, it's a jungle theme! I love it!"

Animal prints adorned the dusky walls. Everything from elephants to giraffes to tigers. Even the gently waving ceiling fan blades were palms. Ceiling-high palm trees towered over the bed, the fan blowing them as if a soft breeze sailed through the room. She half expected to hear the sound of screeching monkeys or the roar of a lion any second.

He set her on her feet. "Went on safari several years back. Fell in love with Africa. The animals there are incredible, the people even more so."

"I can't even imagine an adventure like that. It must have been amazing."

"It was. I went with a group of vets on a care mission. Three months. It was a remarkable experience."

"I'd love to do that someday."

He grinned. "You can. You're graduating next month, and soon you'll be setting up your own practice. You can do anything you want."

She pulled her arms around herself. "I can't even fathom a life like that."

"The world is opening up for you, Abby," he said, coming up behind her and threading his arms around her waist. His breath ruffled her hair as he spoke. "Anything you can envision you can have."

It all seemed unreal and out of reach. "One day at a time." It was hard to believe she'd gotten this far.

Or that she was in Seth's bedroom, for that matter.

He turned her around to face him. "You can do anything, be anything you want to be. You have the talent and the drive."

"You have such faith in me."

He shrugged. "I just know what you're capable of."

She pressed her palm against his cheek, loving the rough texture of his beard stubble. "Thank you. That means more to me than I could ever explain." She stood on her tiptoes and grasped his neck, pulling his head to hers for a kiss.

The first flutter of his lips against hers always made her suck in a breath. It was so painfully tender, just so damn perfect it made her belly clench in anticipation. No one had ever kissed her like this, had made her gasp for breath with just a brush of lips against lips.

Not even Chad. Especially not Chad. She'd been so dumb.

And she was never going to be that dumb again. Her eyes were wide open this time.

Figuratively speaking, anyway, since right now her eyes were closed, her palms floating down Seth's chest and resting on his pecs. His heart beat a strong and steady rhythm against her hand as he thoroughly kissed her. She melted like butter against him, leaning into his hard, sturdy body.

He reached behind her and unzipped her dress. It fell to the floor, the sensual slide of silk down her body an unbearable torture of her senses. Every one of her nerve endings, every sense was alive and awake, anticipating his touch. She could almost imagine herself in the jungle with him, surrounded by animals and trees. They'd be in a tent, and he'd undress her, lingering over every inch of her skin like he was doing right now.

He kissed her shoulder as he pulled down the strap of her bra. The sensation of fabric along her skin made her shiver with anticipation.

"Strawberries. You smell like strawberries," he murmured.

She smiled and kept her eyes closed, focusing on the touch of his lips along her neck, her jaw, her mouth, where he lingered, brushing his lips back and forth across hers.

The man liked to kiss. And she loved that he took the time to explore her mouth, delving inside with his tongue, stroking her slowly, tenderly, with the same gentle strokes that he used to caress her body.

That Seth could fuck her with a wild rush of passion or make their joining an achingly slow journey was a testament to his skill as a lover. He swept her into his arms and laid her on the bed, then stood next to it while he undressed. She turned on her side and watched the slow unveiling of his well-muscled flesh, eager for him to touch her again. When he slid his jeans off, his cock sprang up, and she smiled, reaching for it.

"Let me suck it." She grabbed her lip between her teeth, waiting. He made her bold, made her ask out loud for things she'd only fantasized about before. Would he accept?

He dropped his lids halfway down in that way she found oh so sexy, then crawled onto the bed, kneeling beside her. Taking his shaft in his hand, he stroked it for her. God, that made her pussy clench, warm cream oozing from her cunt. She reached between her legs.

Just like her fantasies.

"Oh yeah," he said, approaching her head. "Touch your pussy for me, baby. I like to watch."

She wanted to make it good for him, to show him how she did it when she was alone in the dark. Planting her feet flat on the bed, she rubbed her pussy, mesmerized by the way he touched himself. He squeezed the head, then fisted the shaft, stroking leisurely at first.

"I'm hungry," she said, affecting a pout. "Feed me."

"Christ, Abby." He scooted toward her and leaned over, sliding his cock between her lips. She took him greedily into her mouth, pressing the heel of her hand against her clit.

Sucking him while masturbating was a heady experience. Her clit swelled, her pussy throbbing. She slid a finger inside her cunt. It gripped her, pulsing around the digit.

Seth fucked her mouth and she lifted her hips, mimicking his movements.

"That's so fucking hot," he said. He alternated watching her face and the movements of her hand. She was already close to another orgasm. Bringing herself there with her own hand had always been easy. Frankly, she was amazed she could do it in front of someone. But for some reason it was easy with Seth. He made it so natural for her to show him what pleased her. Because he was more focused on her pleasure than his own.

"Make yourself come for me, Abby. Show me."

He pulled his cock back, then thrust forward, holding the back of her head so he was feeding her. She plunged two fingers into her cunt and used her other hand now to pluck at her clit.

She was close now, moaning against his shaft.

"Let go, baby," he whispered. "Come on. Do it for me."

She did. Seth pulled his cock away from her mouth just as she let out a cry of triumph. A shattering climax sent waves of ecstasy spiraling through her. Seth bent down and drank in her cry with his lips, plunging his tongue inside her mouth.

She was still in the throes of her orgasm when he rolled on top of her and plunged his cock inside her.

Oh, it was heaven, feeling her pussy surround him, contracting with the aftereffects of her orgasm. He held tight to her, gripping her ass as she rode out pulses of sensation that never seemed to stop.

She wrapped her legs around him, arching upward, holding onto him, kissing him.

Loving him.

The revelation made her eyes widen. She stared into his eyes, so open and filled with his own emotion as he made love to her.

Then she squeezed her eyes shut and enveloped Seth in her embrace, feeling him shudder and shake against her as he came. He held her so tight when he climaxed, as if he were crawling inside her to become one with her.

God, she loved that about him.

No.

She couldn't, wouldn't think about love.

Not now.

Not ever.

She was just getting her life together, just beginning to explore her freedom. This was just sex. Incredible, mind-blowing sex. And she was confusing orgasms with emotion.

Wasn't she?

Or was it something altogether different? Was it the fact that he made her feel good about herself, that he took her places she'd never been before, both physically and emotionally? That he genuinely cared about her?

No. No, no, no. She wasn't ready for this. She had a new life to start. New adventures to have.

How could she be falling in love?

eleven

abby had a date with mike tonight.

Convinced that she was absolutely, positively mistaken about her emotional reaction to Seth last night, she'd accepted Mike's offer when he'd called this morning.

At first she was going to turn him down. She had papers to finish and last-minute things to do for school. She had to figure out what to do about her career. And after the wild weekend with both men, the last thing she wanted was more turmoil. Some space to think would have been nice.

But the niggling doubts about Seth had kept her up all night.

Seth had wanted her to spend the night. To sleep in his bed.

God, she'd wanted to. Wanted to nestle against him and fall asleep wrapped up in the comfort of his arms. But she'd said no, that she had things to do today.

And he'd been great about it. Said he understood. Took her home, gave her a kiss good night that curled her toes and made her wet all over again. She'd almost invited him in and asked him to stay with her.

She didn't want to let him go.

Goddammit.

But she had. And then hadn't slept all night because his scent had lingered on her, his touch and kiss a memory so vivid she'd ached all night for him.

Tonight she'd figure out if she felt the same way about Mike.

She knew what the problem was. Her sexual drought had lingered so long it was like a first rain in the desert; she was simply making up for lost time. Having the one-on-one with Seth last night had been spectacular, and she'd confused emotion for really great sex.

She'd wager tonight would be the same way.

Mike told her they were going to the casino in town. She was excited about that since she could never afford to go there on her own and had never been. She wore a black short skirt and a slinky silver halter top that she'd borrowed from Blair a few weeks ago. She'd pulled her hair up and slipped on some fake crystal earrings. Even wore her stiletto heels again.

She was dressed to kill. Or rather, to fuck.

Tingling with anticipation, she hurried to the door when Mike rang the bell. He arched a brow and whistled as he stepped in.

"Are you sure we even want to go out tonight?" he asked, eyeing every inch of her.

She laughed and twirled for him, giddy with excitement. "You like?"

He nodded. "Hell yeah. You look hot."

"Thanks." He looked pretty damn hot himself in black slacks that were tailored to fit his fine ass and a simple white shirt that hugged his body.

Whatever scent he wore, whether it was cologne or just him,

sailed into her senses like a shot to her pheromones. It screamed hot and sexy, which didn't surprise her in the least.

"You ready?"

Oh yeah. She was ready. Her body was primed to take off like a rocket.

The casino crowd was light since it was a Monday, so they wandered, stopping at tables here and there. She learned about craps and roulette, even played a few hands of blackjack, which she quickly discovered was not her game at all. The most fun she had was playing the slots because she could stay there the longest without losing all her money.

Though Mike was very generous, she refused to toss money down the drain gambling. That's why she liked playing the quarter slots. He was involved at the craps table for awhile and seemed to be amassing quite a bit of chips, so she found a quarter slot machine and dumped in a twenty. And she was winning, which amused her enough that she continued to play.

"Having fun?"

She whirled around, thinking it was Mike, and grinned. "As a matter of fact—"

It wasn't Mike. Her smile froze, then died as she looked into the dark gaze of her ex-husband, Chad.

Her heart slammed against her ribs, her pulse skittering along her nerve endings. A wash of memories, all unpleasant, rushed back to her, and suddenly she was the mousy housewife again. Tall, dark, handsome Chad, the boy of her dreams. Yeah, right. The worst mistake she'd ever made. All the excitement and fun she'd been having dissolved in an instant. Talk about a buzz kill. "What are you doing here?"

He leaned against the machine she was playing and picked at his cuticle, a habit that always annoyed her. "I'm gambling, darlin'. And you?"

I'm scrubbing the floors, jackass. What do you think I'm doing? "I'm on a date."

"Seems as if your date has deserted you, since I don't see him around."

Stay calm, Abby. He's trying to irritate you on purpose. She offered a smug smile. "Actually, I know exactly where he is."

"Which is?"

"Craps table. Right over there." She inclined her head to the outer table, where Mike was standing at the end. Mike looked up at the same instant she gazed in his direction. He winked at her, then threw the dice.

"Ah. Nottingham."

"Yes."

"I saw you the other night at the club with him."

Chad was at the club the other night? She hadn't seen him, but then again, after the first five minutes she'd been so wrapped up in Mike and Seth she wouldn't have noticed him if he'd stepped right on her toes. "Really."

"Yeah. You were with Nottingham. And Seth Jacobs."

Ah. So he had seen her. She wondered how much he'd seen. A small flame of triumph began to flicker inside her. "So I was. Funny, I didn't see you there. Then again, I was rather busy with my dates."

Chad's eyes widened. "You were there with both of them?"

She punched the button on her machine, ignoring him. "As a matter of fact, I was."

"Kind of slutty, isn't it, Abby?"

She didn't even look away from the blinking lights on the slot machine. "Kind of like the pot calling the kettle black, isn't it Chad?"

"You used to be such a good girl."

The disgust in his voice was evident, but he no longer had the power to hurt her. She finally tore her gaze away from the screen in front of her and arched a brow.

"Oh, I'm still a good girl, Chad. A very good girl."

"I can't believe how you've changed from the sweet girl I married."

She snorted. "Please. And where did that get me, Chad? I was faithful, I stayed home every night waiting for you. Where were you? Out with another woman, fucking her instead of me. Well, now I'm fucking other men instead of you." She pressed the cash out button, waited for her ticket to print, and snatched it out of the machine. "And let me tell you, I'm having the best damn sex of my life right now. All those wasted years on a minute man like you. If only I'd known what I was missing."

She waited for a comeback, but he only stared at her, his face turning red. Then she realized he was speechless. For the first time in her life, she'd rendered the bastard unable to speak. Time to zero in for the kill. "All those girls you fucked while we were married— what did they see in you, anyway?"

He looked like he wanted to strangle her. Triumphant, she waved her ticket in front of his face. "I'd love to stay and chat with you longer, Chad, but I have a life now that doesn't include you."

She walked away without looking back, sidling up to Mike and leaning against his shoulder. He threaded an arm around her waist and planted a scorching kiss on her lips.

She hoped Chad was still watching.

"I saw you talking to your ex over there," Mike said after she broke the kiss. He gathered his chips and stepped away from the table, leading her to the cashier's booth.

"He's a prick," she said, handing the cashier her ticket.

"Give you any trouble?" Mike asked, pocketing the sizable amount of bills the cashier handed him.

Abby handed him back the money she'd won in the slot machine, despite Mike's attempts to prevent her from doing so. "No trouble at all. I handled him just fine."

"I figured you could." He slipped his arm around her and walked outside. He'd parked his Navigator at the end of the parking lot. Isolated, within a semicircle of trees surrounding them, and it was dark. The second they reached his car he whirled her around and pushed her against the door, his mouth descending on hers.

Her breath left her body as he plunged his tongue inside, devouring her lips in a hungry kiss. She reached for his arms, feeling the heat, the lean muscle through his shirt. He parted her legs with his knee, insinuating his thigh between them.

Her body responded with an instantaneous explosion, her pussy moistening, her nipples tightening as they brushed against his chest. She couldn't help her reaction to him. He was damned overpowering, and she was helpless to do anything but let her body answer.

Did she want him? Hell yes. But while his hands were roaming her body, caressing her breasts, pinching her nipples, making her crazed with desire for him, part of her recognized what she was experiencing was a pure and simple physical reaction to him.

She lusted for Mike. Oh, God did she ever lust for him.

But that's all she felt. That's all she would ever feel. On some elemental level she realized that Mike Nottingham was way, way too much for her. That while he was gorgeous and desirable and exciting as hell, he wasn't the kind of man she could ever have a relationship with.

Not the kind of relationship she craved.

Not the kind of relationship she wanted.

Like the kind she wanted with Seth.

Oh, God.

Seth.

Mike moved his mouth from her lips to her neck, licking her pulse point and making goose bumps pop out all over her skin. He inserted his hand and slipped down the front of her skirt, cupping her pussy. She damn near came.

This had to stop. She felt guilty!

She palmed his chest and pressed against him, subtly at first, then a little harder.

"Mike, stop."

He rocked his palm against her clit, and she fought the sensations. She was close, so damn close she almost thought about coming, of tossing aside her convictions and letting it all loose.

But she couldn't. Goddamit, she couldn't. Damn scruples.

"Mike, please stop." She grabbed his wrist and pulled his hand out of her skirt.

He lifted his head and looked at her, a confused frown lining his brow.

And in that moment, she knew exactly why. Because she was panting, her breasts heaving against his chest, her body shaking all over. And though his cock was hard as he rocked it against her thigh, there was something in his eyes that told her he wasn't as invested in this as she was. A detachment she'd noticed before.

Something that wasn't there when she looked into Seth's eyes. With Seth there was sex, but she could look into his eyes and see clear down to his soul. When he was with her he was wholly engaged in the two of them, in the experience.

Mike felt no emotion in this. It was pure lust and nothing more. He and Abby didn't have the emotional connection she and Seth did.

"What's wrong Abby? You're so damn close I can feel you trembling."

"I know. God, I know. I'm sorry. I can't do this."

"We can go to my place if it bothers you. I wasn't thinking about the lack of privacy here."

She shook her head. "It's not that. I . . . I don't even know where to start."

Mike blew out a breath and stepped back, putting distance between them. He tilted his head to the side and studied her. "It's Seth."

Her eyes widened. "How did you know?"

"He said as much about you last night."

"He did?" She couldn't help the smile that crept onto her face. She didn't mean to, really. It just appeared. And she felt really shitty about it and tried to wipe it off, but she couldn't.

"You're people who fall in love. It's sickening the way it's written all over your face."

He was teasing her. She saw it in the half curve of his lips, the way he tilted his head a certain way.

"I'm sorry, Mike."

"Don't be." He pulled her to him and hugged her, pressing a kiss to the top of her head. He paused for a few seconds, then whispered, "I envy your ability to love."

She was going to ask him what he meant, but he pushed her back and grinned. "I'm going to drop you off at Seth's. I might have mentioned to him that you and I had a date tonight, and he's probably tearing his house apart in jealousy right now."

"You didn't."

Mike shrugged. "Hey, I'm a prick. Everyone knows that."

seth paced his living room, downing the last of the rum and staring down the wet bar, contemplating another drink.

Bad idea. He had surgery early in the morning. Besides, the alcohol hadn't even touched the irritation burning inside him all night. Screw all night—try ever since earlier today, when Mike had casually mentioned on his way out of the clinic that he was picking up Abby tonight.

Which meant she'd no more left his place last night, left his *bed* last night, than she'd gone home and agreed to a date with Mike tonight. Maybe she'd even called Mike when she'd gotten home.

Either way, he knew what it meant. She didn't care about him.

Which kind of annoyed him. Okay, it really hurt, goddammit.

And he hadn't gone into this to get hurt again. But didn't it just figure it had happened anyway? He'd closed his heart to loving a woman after his ex had stomped all over it and left a withered, dried-out stump in her wake. After that, he used women for sex and nothing more.

He'd done a pretty damn good job of it, too. Mike was a good teacher in that area, and he'd watched and learned from the master.

But somewhere along the way, he'd left the door open. And over the past year, Abby had crept in.

Now he'd have to close it again.

Maybe he'd have that second drink after all.

When the doorbell rang, he frowned. Shit. Who the hell would come over this time of night? He went to the door and looked out the peephole, shocked as hell to see Abby. He opened the door, regarding her warily.

"Hey," she said, a wash of color covering her cheeks.

"Hey yourself. I thought you were out with Mike tonight."

That color on her cheeks deepened. "I know. He told me that you knew. He just dropped me off."

"Why?"

"Can I come in, or do you want to do this out here?"

"Oh. Sorry." He moved aside to let her in. Damn, she looked hot in a tight black skirt and skimpy little halter. Her hair was partially up with little blonde tendrils escaping a jeweled clip. He clenched his fingers into a fist to keep from reaching out and touching her. "Have a seat. Would you like a drink?"

"No. Thanks." She sat on the sofa in the living room. Balanced precariously on the edge like she might fall off any second was more like it.

And she looked profoundly uncomfortable.

Which meant only one thing. She had come here to tell him she didn't want to see him anymore.

How nice of Mike to let her do this alone. Then again, maybe she'd wanted to do it without him being here. That would be Abby's way. She wouldn't want Mike to stand around smiling victoriously while she let Seth down.

"Why are you here, Abby?"

Her head shot up, her eyes wide with something akin to abject terror. "I . . . I need to tell you something."

He supposed he could be a gentleman and make it easier for her, but he wasn't feeling particularly chivalrous at the moment. Instead, he took a seat on the sofa across from hers. "Sure. Shoot."

He stretched his legs out, resting his arms on the back of the sofa. No fucking way was he going to clue her in that her dismissal bothered him. When she told him, he'd just brush it off as no big deal and send her on her way. Mike was probably waiting outside in the car.

Just say it and get it over with, Abby.

"You have something to say?"

"I'm in love with you, Seth."

He drummed his fingers on the top of the sofa, looking bored. "So?"

She arched a brow. "So?"

But as her words sank in, his fingers stilled and he leaned forward. "What did you just say?"

She swallowed, and he watched the movement of her creamy throat. "I said I'm love with you."

That wasn't at all what he'd prepared himself to hear. Not at all. Holy fucking shit!

abby watched the play of emotions crossing seth's face, resisting the urge to grin. She gathered he had been prepared for her to say something else entirely.

"You love me."

"Yes."

"Goddamn." He blinked, then jammed his fingers through his hair and looked up at her again. "You love me."

"Yes," she said, this time laughing. "I love you."

He stood and took the two steps toward her, then grabbed her hands and pulled her up.

"You love me."

She nodded.

He shook his head. "I thought . . . fuck it. It doesn't matter what I thought." He bent and pressed his lips to hers. His kiss was achingly tender, filled with so much emotion and heart it brought tears to her eyes. His fingers splayed over the bare skin of her back, drawing her closer.

She wanted to crawl right inside him.

He pulled away, his gaze dark, filled with emotions she couldn't name.

"I've been falling in love with you every day since you first came to the clinic, Abby. I didn't want to fall in love. I swore I wouldn't. And after this weekend with you and me and Mike, I wasn't sure what you wanted, but I sure as hell knew what I wanted. I wanted you. Not to share you. Never, ever to share you again."

Her heart soared with every word. "I'm a one-man woman. This weekend was the experience of a lifetime, a fantasy come true. I won't deny that I enjoyed the hell out of it. But I don't ever want to repeat it."

He grinned. "I enjoyed it, too. But I can fulfill your fantasies in a lot of different ways."

Her brows lifted. "I'll just bet you can."

"And I'll wager you have some really wild fantasies."

Somehow she knew he'd be open to exploring every single one of them with her. She couldn't wait. "As a matter of fact, I do."

His fingers blazed a slow, sensual trail along her spine, sliding into her skirt and stopping just short of the crack of her ass. "Tell me one right now."

She looked around, then smiled. "I've always had this fantasy about being bent over a sofa, with my skirt hiked up . . ."

His smile was devastating to her senses. Dark and filled with promise.

"I think we can accommodate you." He moved behind the sofa, then bent her over it.

She wiggled her ass for him, then spread her legs.

"Oh yeah. I like this fantasy of yours, Abby."

He hadn't even touched her yet, and she was soaking wet. She felt his hands at the hem of her skirt, his knuckles brushing the skin of her thighs. He raised her skirt so slowly she wanted to scream, her clit throbbing in anticipation.

What she hadn't expected was for him to pull her panties aside and slide his hot tongue right into her pussy. She shrieked and gripped the couch cushions. He lapped her cream, his tongue snaking up to encircle her clit.

The man was a marvel with his tongue, and a constant sexual surprise. He reached between her legs with his fingers to stroke her pussy, tugging her clit until she was writhing against his hand.

"Come for me, baby," he urged, coaxing an orgasm from her as easily as if he'd asked her to pass the salt. She tensed and cried out, shuddering against his probing tongue and fingers.

God, she'd been so primed for an orgasm, so pumped up and sexually charged from Mike earlier, that Seth took her over the edge in seconds. She panted, her eyes closed, thinking she should feel guilty that one man had finished what another had started.

No. The right man had finished what the wrong man had started. And that she wouldn't feel guilty about.

She was still trembling when he stood, parted her legs with his thighs, and entered her with a solid thrust, driving her against the back of the couch. She held on as he pounded her hard, giving her exactly what she'd asked for, fulfilling yet another of her deep, dark fantasies.

He fucked her relentlessly, giving her no time to even catch her breath as he pistoned his cock upward, rocking her clit against the couch until her pussy gripped him so hard he yelled her name, grabbed her hips in a punishing grip, and came in a torrent of shuddering gasps. He fell against her back, his heartbeat hammering against her.

When he withdrew, he turned her around and lifted her legs to wrap them around him. He kissed her—he seemed to love kissing her, thank God—once again tenderly, taking the clip out of her hair so he could thread his fingers through the tendrils.

She loved how he touched her.

He carried her this way to his bedroom, his pants nearly halfway down, both of them laughing as he almost tripped several times. They fell onto the bed and lay there, looking at each other.

"You love me," he said again, a silly smile on his face that she was certain mirrored her own.

"Yes. And you love me."

"I sure as hell do."

"So now what?"

He leaned up on an elbow and untied the strings of her halter. "Now we fuck again."

Laughing, she said, "I know that. I mean with us."

As he pulled the fabric down, exposing her breasts, he said, "We take it a day at a time. You have a career to start, and a life to begin. I won't stand in the way of that."

And that was one of the things she loved most about him. He recognized her need to be independent, even without her saying it. Falling in love had been the wildest part of her weekend. Unexpected, but certainly not unwanted.

She'd gotten way more out of this bet than she had planned.

She couldn't wait to tell Blair and Callie when she saw them again. But right now there was an incredibly sexy man undressing her. She reached for the buttons of his shirt and began undoing them.

"So, Seth, we've delved a lot into my fantasies. Let's talk about yours . . ."

wicked

BLAIR

one

"step out of the vehicle and spread your legs."

Blair tapped her long, just-manicured fingernails on the leather steering wheel and stared straight ahead, counting slowly to ten before she even looked out the window to acknowledge Rand McKay's existence. And there was no way in hell she'd obey his ridiculous order. It was bad enough he'd pulled her over on this deserted stretch of road, sirens blaring, when she was already late for lunch with Abby and Callie. But to tell her to get out of her car and spread her legs like a common criminal?

He could kiss her ass.

No, wait. He'd probably enjoy that. And Blair wasn't about to do anything Rand might enjoy.

"Get lost, Rand. I'm late for an appointment."

Out of the corner of her eye, she caught the slow slide of his Ray-Bans down his long, straight nose, the revelation of his steel gray eyes, the firm line of his full lips.

She would not be affected. She would not be affected. Her pebbling nipples be damned, she would *not* be affected!

"Maybe you misunderstood that siren I was wailing behind your speeding ass for the past three miles, Miss Newcastle. It means pull over and get out of the damn car. Now."

Miss Newcastle. Whatever. She'd known Rand McKay since elementary school and long before he became sheriff of Silverwood. And he only called her Miss Newcastle when he wanted to piss her off.

It worked. She was good and angry. She pulled off her sunglasses and stared him down, refusing to even unbuckle her seat belt. "Mail me a ticket. You know my address."

He bent over and leaned well-muscled, tanned forearms on the door. "Get out of the goddamned car now, Blair. Or I'll come in there and get you. And if I have to come in there and get you, I'll strip-search you right here on the road."

"You wouldn't dare."

"Try me."

With a disgusted sigh, she punched the button to release her seat belt, then flung the door open, hoping she'd toss Rand on his ass in the process. But he simply backed up with fluid ease and waited for her to exit her Mercedes. With a hard slam she shut the car door and crossed her arms in front of her.

"What the hell is your problem?" she asked, tapping her foot on the gravel.

She couldn't see Rand's eyes behind the silver of his sunglasses, but his smirk told her everything she needed to know.

"You were speeding."

"Was not."

"Eighty-five in a sixty is definitely speeding, Blair."

"So write me a ticket and let me get out of here."

"I'll need to see your driver's license and insurance verification."

"Oh, for the love of God. Like you don't have my data memorized." He knew everything about her, including her address and license number. They'd known each other forever. They'd been at each other's throats since high school. She knew Rand McKay better than any other man. The most irritating man she'd ever known. She leaned into the open window of her vehicle and took out her purse, rummaging through it for her identification.

"Is that a gun in your purse, Blair?"

"You know damn well it is."

"Put the bag down, turn around, and place your hands on the roof of your car."

She arched a brow. "Are you serious?"

"Do as I say. Now."

"Rand, you know damn well I have a—"

"Do it!"

Man, he was in a pissy mood. And normally she'd fight him on this. But she could tell he was into playing cop today, and she wasn't going to make lunch if she stood there and argued with him. This was a game. They'd played it before. If she let him have his way and he annoyed her for a few seconds, she'd be on her way. She turned around and placed her fingertips on the roof of her car.

"Spread your legs."

Which is exactly what he'd said to her when he pulled her over. Only she'd thought he was joking. "Christ, Rand. This is not funny."

"I'll have to pat you down, see what else you're hiding."

She shot him an irritated glare over her shoulder. "You see what I'm wearing? I could hardly be hiding much." Her skimpy silk skirt and tank top were all she could tolerate in the summer heat. If she wasn't meeting Blair and Callie for drinks, she wouldn't even have a bra on.

"Turn around and face your vehicle."

He kicked her legs apart and stepped behind her, the nearness of his body crowding her against her car. She breathed in the spicy scent of him, made even more powerful by the afternoon heat. What was it about this man that both infuriated her and turned her on so much?

"I'm going to report you to your superiors," she complained.

"You do that."

He started at her wrists and ran his hands up her bare arms, over her shoulder, then made his way down. He didn't need to touch her there, dammit. Her skin broke out in goose bumps when his fingertips brushed the outer swells of her breasts.

"Careful there," she warned.

"Oh, I'm being very careful."

He reached around and palmed her breasts. Her sheer silk bra couldn't hide her traitorous rising nipples, her breasts swelling eagerly into his hands.

"That is not patting me down!"

"Just checking to see if you have anything hidden in your bra."

"I do. My breasts. Now leave them alone!"

His warm breath blew against the nape of her neck, not at all cooling the sweat there. "They don't act as if they want me to leave them alone." To prove his point, he scraped his thumbs over her distended nipples. She bit back the groan that wanted to escape her throat. God, that man had talented hands. And she hadn't been touched in . . . far too long. Her clit was throbbing, her pussy wet, and her panties clung to her skin.

She wanted sex.

But she didn't want Rand. She didn't!

"Are you quite finished?" she asked, gritting her teeth.

"Not quite."

Somehow she'd make him pay for doing this to her, for forcing her to ignore her body's needs. Any other man, and she'd have her legs wrapped around him and her pussy on his dick by now.

But she would never, ever fuck Rand McKay.

Not if he was the last man on earth and she was desperately horny. She'd rather fuck a cactus.

He finally relinquished his hold on her breasts, and she exhaled, but then his hot, huge hands skimmed her rib cage, sliding up and under the tank top to touch her bare skin. She flinched.

"Something wrong?"

"Nothing." She'd be damned if she'd give him the satisfaction of knowing he affected her. She'd simply pretend irritation and nothing else. And then she'd get him fired.

His knee insinuated itself farther between her legs as his hands found her hips. When he jerked her toward him, she'd had enough.

"Rand," she warned.

But her warning fell on deaf ears. He lifted her skirt and sat her on his jeans-clad thigh, the scrape of denim against her swollen clit enough to make her gasp.

"You're wet," he whispered against her ear.

"It's hot outside. I'm sweating," she lied.

"Bullshit. I can smell you. That sweet scent is pussy, baby, not sweat."

Asshole. And his cock was hard, rubbing against her ass as he clenched her hip. She breathed in and out through her nose, trying to avoid panting. She was so aroused every fiber of her being was screaming at her to turn around and beg him to fuck her. Right there on the side of the road.

And that's just what he wanted her to do.

Never!

His hand inched along her upper leg, his fingertips traveling precariously close to her pussy. He began to rub her inner thigh now, mere inches away from her clit. If she shifted just a little, she could place the throbbing bud right in his hand. Oh, and he'd take her there. She knew he could. A few strokes, and she'd fly right over the edge. She was so damn close already. Hot, achy, her pussy quaking with need.

She hated Rand McKay right now, hated that he had this much control over her.

"Let me go, Rand. This has gone way beyond a simple body search."

"Oh, I'm searching your body all right, Blair. I'm looking for a key."

She swallowed, her throat dry. "What key?"

"They key to unlocking the fire within you, Blair. Just say the word, and I'll do it. You know I can. I'm the only one who can."

His fingers massaged the spot where her panties met her thigh, the side of his hand a fraction of an inch from her clit. Her swollen pussy lips trembled at his touch.

"You need me to take you there, baby," he said, rocking his hard cock against her. "Give up that famous Newcastle control to me, and I'll make you come like you've never come before. Let me have it, Blair."

She froze as if a sudden icy rain had begun to fall in the dead afternoon of August. Rigid, she began to push at his hand. "Let me go, Rand."

And he knew it, too. In an instant he backed away, and she smoothed down her skirt, ignoring the inferno flaming inside her, the roaring climax she'd been seconds from having.

The one she was never going to have with Rand McKay.

Forcing a calm and cool demeanor she didn't feel, she whirled around and took two steps toward him, placing a finger in the center of his wide, masculine chest. "Get this straight, Rand. You want to write me a ticket for speeding, fine. You want to haul me into the station for possession of a gun I *have* a permit to possess, do it. But don't you ever"—she accentuated the *ever* with a push of her finger against his chest—"ever touch me again."

Instead of arguing with her, he folded his arms across his well-muscled chest and smiled smugly at her. How dare he look so unaffected when she was damn near shaking all over? If it wasn't for the ridge of his erection clearly visible through his jeans, she could swear the man was cold as ice.

"When you're ready to turn over control, Blair, you know where to find me."

"When they announce the next Winter Olympics in hell, I'll do that."

Without bothering to gauge his reaction, she mustered up what dignity she had left, slipped in her car, buckled her seat belt, and drove away, blasting the air conditioner at arctic level. She was so goddamned hot she was going to self-combust. On fire with anger and unrequited passion.

She hated him. Absolutely hated him.

And she'd never wanted a man more than she wanted Rand McKay.

She always had.

rand leaned against his squad car and watched blair speed away, her tires spitting out gravel in her wake. Breaking the speeding laws again, no doubt. He owed her a ticket, too. Then again, he knew right where to find her.

And she knew where to find him. Which she would, soon enough.

For fifteen years he'd watched her go through man after man. She'd even gone as far as getting engaged to three of them but had never made it to the altar yet.

He knew why. Because none of those men could satisfy her. They didn't understand what she needed.

Rand knew exactly what she needed.

Blair Newcastle might be cool, calm, and in charge on the outside, but inside she was desperate for a man to take charge and dominate her.

He knew it, and she knew it.

He slipped into his squad car, radioed the station that he was back on patrol, and drove off, heading toward town.

His cock was still hard and aching. God almighty was he miserable right now. It was all he could do to resist taking it out and jacking off on the side of the road, releasing the tight throbbing in his balls. He lifted his fingers to his nose, inhaling Blair's sweet, musky scent that lingered on his hands.

Shit. He groaned and mentally cursed the stubborn woman. What the hell was wrong with her, anyway? Her nipples had been tight when he'd cupped her full breasts, her pussy moist when he'd brushed his fingers against her silken panties. It had been damn torture for him not to palm her heat and take her over the edge. He'd heard the soft panting gasps she thought to mask, knew she could fall with the slightest brush of his fingers against her hard little clit. She'd been primed and ready for a good hard climax. Until she'd fought her natural urges.

Though she'd hardly fought. Usually she cussed him out and slapped his hand away when they tussled. Not this time though. Arousal had seethed inside her, and she'd been moments away from giving up control to him.

But she just refused to surrender the last vestiges of it, too afraid of what might happen if she submitted to him.

They'd been dancing around each other for fifteen goddamn years. He'd never force the issue with her, because she was going to have to come to him if she wanted him to take control.

So far she hadn't. But he was a very patient man. And she *was* waffling, getting closer and closer to caving in; he could tell.

Sooner or later she'd figure out that the only man who was going to make her happy was him.

And when she did, he'd be ready for her.

debating whether or not to spread her legs in the car and massage her hard clit to orgasm right there in Callie's driveway, Blair mentally cursed Rand McKay a thousand times over and turned the ignition off with an oath of disgust, dropping her keys in her purse.

Asshole. Her body was still vibrating from his touch, the way he whispered dark promises in her ear with his deep, husky voice, enticing her toward an orgasm she was all too eager to have at his hands.

Never. Never, never, never. Once she gave up her power to a man, she'd never be in charge of her destiny again. And Rand was alpha to the core, the kind to wrestle control away from her and stomp her freedom right into the ground. He was nothing like the men she usually dated. Nothing. The men she chose were men she could manage.

Tossing thoughts of Rand into the gentle summer breeze, she walked through the unlocked front door of Callie's modest little house, announcing her arrival. "I'm here!"

"You're late!" Callie called from the kitchen.

"I know!" She grinned and wandered into the kitchen, thrilled to see a laughing Abby parked at the island counter. She threw her arms around Abby and gave her a huge hug. "Looks like you survived your wild weekend."

"She sure did," Callie said. "She's been smiling like that since she got here, but she won't tell me a damn thing."

"Hey, it's not my fault Blair's late."

"Guilty as charged," Blair said, pulling up a stool at the counter. She grabbed one of the mimosas Callie slid in her direction and took a long swallow of the cool liquid, hoping it would douse the fire burning inside her. "But it wasn't my fault. I was . . . waylaid on my drive over."

Callie arched a dark brow. "Really."

"Yeah. Rand McKay was fucking with me."

"Oooh. In a good way, I hope," Abby said, wagging her eyebrows.

"No. Just fucking with me in his normal annoying as hell way."

Abby and Callie exchanged knowing glances.

"Oh, you two quit looking at each other like that. And don't even start on me and Rand. You know damn well I'm not the least bit interested in him. He's like a pesky brother."

Callie snorted. "Yeah, right. I don't think so."

"We are not here to discuss me. I want to hear about Abby's wild weekend with Mike and Seth. How did it go?"

Abby's face flushed with the cutest blush. "It was . . . phenomenal."

Callie squealed. "I knew it!"

Blair nodded. "So did I. So, details, woman, details! At the club they were both drooling over you, and we saw you outside on the balcony with them. Dayum. What woman wouldn't have multiple orgasms over attention like that from two men?"

Abby laid her elbows on the counter and palmed her face. "I can barely even think about it now without flushing with heat. I can't even describe what that night was like other than to say it fulfilled every single fantasy I'd ever had—and then some. They were magnificent."

Blair laid her hand over Abby's. "Well, it's about time you got laid."

Abby's eyelashes fluttered down, and she clasped her hands together. "Oh, it went way beyond just sex, Blair. Way beyond."

"There's more? Come on, girl. Spill," Callie demanded.

When Abby looked back at them, her eyes were filled with tears. "I fell in love."

"You're joking," Blair said.

"No, I'm not."

Abby filled them in on what transpired over the weekend and the following week. Everything, including her individual reactions to both Mike and Seth and her run-in with Chad at the casino. By the time she'd finished, it made perfect sense to Blair. "Of course you're in love. Seth is the ideal man for you, and Mike isn't. Mike is sexually overpowering—fun to play with but not a man to have a relationship with. Seth is everything you should have had the first time around, but instead you ended up with Chad, the lying, cheating, whoring son of a bitch."

"Oh, honey. I'm so damn happy for you!" Callie hurried around the counter and enveloped Abby in a hug.

Even Blair had to admit to blinking away a few tears. Okay, she was downright thrilled for Abby. And admittedly, more than a little envious that a bet in order to have a little sex had turned into a love match for one of her best friends.

So they spent the afternoon wildly celebrating Abby's newfound love while she filled them in about what was next for her—namely graduation and starting out her new career as a veterinarian while finding her way in her relationship with Seth.

By the time they were kicked back in Callie's living room, Blair had relaxed and had a good buzz going. She propped her feet on the worn wood coffee table and laced her arms behind her head.

"So, Blair, I think it's your turn next."

She looked over at Abby, who was equally kicked back with her feet tucked under her in the wicker chair. "My turn for what?"

"The bet."

Blair arched a brow. "Oh yeah?"

"Great idea. And I have just the suggestion for man meat for you," Callie said.

Now they were talking about subject that interested her. She couldn't imagine what man Callie and Abby would have in mind for her. "Who?"

"Rand McKay," Callie replied with a smug smile.

"Rand is perfect," Abby added.

"Oh, you two are hilarious." Blair stretched and wiggled her toes. "But I don't think so."

"Unless I'm mistaken, Miss Newcastle, you were the one who thought up and set the terms of this bet," Abby said. "And those terms included that we got to choose who you fucked. Not you."

She sat up straight and gaped at them. "You're serious, aren't you?"

"Deadly," Callie said.

"I thought you were my friends."

"We are."

"Then how can you do this to me?"

Abby rolled her eyes. "We're not *doing* anything to you. We've simply chosen the man we think you should have your weekend sex fest with."

This was unbelievable. She couldn't do it. Not Rand. Anyone but Rand. Her stomach tightened at the thought. "I'll just renege on the bet."

Callie gasped. "Blair Newcastle. You have never backed out on a bet in all the years we've known you. Are you that much of a coward?"

Goddammit! Callie was right. She had never, ever failed to see a bet through. But it was Rand, for the love of God. How could she accept the terms? Why were they doing this to her when they knew how she felt about him?

"Blair," Abby said. "You might think you're keeping some deep dark secret, but not from us."

Blair's eyes widened. They could *not* know! "What are you talking about?"

"Rand McKay. You've been hot for him since high school. It's obvious to everyone who knows the two of you."

"It is not." And that wasn't her secret. It wasn't what kept her away from Rand. They had no idea what they were asking of her.

"It is, too," Callie said. "The way you two look at each other is like watching animals in heat. Honey, you were meant to be together. We're just giving fate a little push in the right direction."

"Especially since you're too bullheaded to take that step, for some reason that is completely unclear to Callie and me," Abby added.

"Fate has nothing to do with why Rand and I aren't together. We aren't together because I choose not to be with him."

"He wants you," Abby said.

"That's his fucking problem."

"Not this weekend it isn't," Callie replied, then laughed. "This weekend he gets to have you. Over and over and over again."

"This is not funny, goddammit!" She pushed off the sofa and stalked to the window where her car sat in the driveway. The car she'd leaned against while Rand ran his hands all over her body, inciting her senses to near fever pitch. If she let him touch her, she'd lose control. He'd wrest it away from her and dominate her. She couldn't give up her advantage to him. If she did, she'd never get it back.

Then again, did she really have to give up control? She was a master at wrapping men around her little finger. She'd been doing it for years, and she was damn good at it. If she worked her wiles on Rand, she'd wager he'd come crawling. He'd be so surprised she was willing to spread her legs for him, he wouldn't even notice she wasn't giving him anything she didn't really want to give. He'd dive into her pussy, so happy she was giving it up to him after all these years, he wouldn't have time to realize she was the one in total control of the situation, that she was the one calling all the shots.

He'd just think he was in charge. And by the time he figured it out, she'd have fulfilled the terms of the bet, fucked his brains out, and be on her way. Door closed.

Heart protected.

She turned away from the window and regarded her traitorous friends with a sly grin. "You know. You're absolutely right. It's about damn time I throw Rand McKay down and fuck him. I'll do it."

"You mean, you'll do *him*?" Callie asked. "After all these years, you're finally going to screw Rand?

"Yes, I'll do *him*. I'll fuck Rand McKay."

two

blair sat in her office and tapped her nails on her desk, staring out the window and pondering her epic blunder. How could she have set the terms of the bet in such a way that she was stuck having to seduce Rand McKay?

Not that there'd be much effort on her part in the seduction arena. He was primed and ready for her, and as he'd told her yesterday, all she had to do was go to him, and he'd take her on.

Arrogant prick.

It wasn't in her nature to prostrate herself in front of a man. She was the ice queen, goddammit, an image she'd spent years perfecting: untouchable, untamable, wicked, and out of control. She had a reputation as a ball buster, a woman in charge. Every woman envied her. Every man feared her.

Every man except Rand, who'd never once bought her act.

Because that's all it was. An act. And he damn well knew it.

Dickhead. How the hell he knew it was beyond her, but he did know. And that's why she had steered clear of him all these years.

Other men fell at her feet to worship her, to do anything she wanted them to. She only had to snap her fingers, and the world was her oyster. Men would stand on their heads if she asked them to.

She'd almost married a few of them. They really were nice guys. Nice, sweet, safe guys. She'd really tried to make it all the way to the altar with them. Until she came to her senses and realized how utterly bored she'd be. Because even though she only fucked men she could control, she knew she'd never be happy with a man like that.

Catch-22. Damned if she did and damned if she didn't.

Who needed to get married, anyway? She could have her pick of any man in Silverwood. She'd been wined and dined and romanced by many of them, and though she left them all, she left them with smiles on their faces and fond memories of the best sex they'd ever had. And no regrets on their part.

So she got a little lonely now and then. Lots of women spent their lives alone. She was used to getting her own way, and she wasn't about to change now. It was probably best she remained single and unattached. And completely in charge of her life.

Now she had to spend the weekend fucking a man she couldn't direct. Her logical, controlling mind dreaded it. Her body zinged with anticipation.

Traitor.

How to do it, though? She couldn't—wouldn't—walk up to him and put her fate in his hands. Oh, no, he'd enjoy that way too much. She refused to hand her power to him on a silver platter.

It had to be something more subtle, which was going to be difficult, since subtle wasn't exactly her typical method.

He knew her inside and out, so she'd have to surprise him.

Damsel in distress! That was it. Since Blair was the last woman on earth to ever play that card, he'd be surprised as hell when she played it on him. He'd be shell-shocked and scratching his head, trying to figure out her angle. By the time she wrestled him to the ground and had his pants off, it would be too late. He'd give in, and she'd have control over the situation. He'd be so damn happy to have his cock in her pussy, he wouldn't care how it got there.

She'd win, he'd lose, and she'd fulfill the terms of the bet.

Admittedly, the thought of fucking Rand had her steamy hot and anticipating a wild ride. The men she'd been screwing for the past fifteen years hadn't exactly lit all her fires. Barely enough to flicker a candle, actually. Any hot action came from her own hand or after giving a man detailed instructions and a road map to her pussy. And nine times out of ten, they still didn't get it right.

She'd just bet Rand knew his way around a woman's pussy. Blindfolded. With his hands tied behind his back.

Her nipples tightened at the remembered feel of his hands cupping her breasts, his thumbs sweeping over the taut buds with an expert touch that had her panting like a dog in heat.

She'd have to play this game very carefully. And in the game of sex, she was a master.

First thing to do was select her outfit. She turned off her computer and strolled out of her home office and into her bedroom, swinging open the door to her walk-in closet and flipping on the light.

Casting a critical eye on her femme fatale outfits, she chose one she knew would cause maximum distraction. Scandalously short, hip riding, thigh-length skirt that swirled around her legs when she walked. Belly-skimming, tight spandex top in white to show off her tan. Low-cut, with a scoop neck to accentuate her cleavage and just short enough to let her crystal belly ring peek out underneath the hem.

She took a long shower, dried her hair until the auburn tresses shone brightly and curled in soft waves around her shoulders, then dressed. She chose a pair of wedge-heeled sandals to show off her well-toned calves, then checked her appearance in the mirror.

If Rand McKay didn't get a hard-on when he saw her, he wasn't a man.

Devious plan worked out in her head, she grabbed her purse and headed out the door, calling Callie on her cell phone so her friends would know the game was on. Her intent was to wind up at Rand's house tonight, so if Abby and Callie wanted to take a peek and make sure she was fulfilling her part of the bargain, they were welcome to come on over.

She had every intention of making sure they knew exactly where she was. She'd made the bet, they'd chosen her man, and she was damn well going to fuck him.

what a long freakin' day. rand blew out a breath, anticipating a cold beer as soon as he walked through the door at home. What he hadn't anticipated was the sight of sexy, tanned legs bent over the open hood of a white Mercedes right outside the entrance to his property. He pulled the Jeep to a stop behind Blair's car and stepped out.

She didn't even bother to raise her head from underneath the hood of her car, just tapped one sandaled foot and hummed. The slight breeze blew her flowery skirt just enough to give him a glimpse of sleek, slender thighs and the lower curve of one fine ass. He swallowed past the dry lump in his throat and tamped down the lump of flesh in his jeans quickly springing to life.

Sliding next to her, he looked under the hood. "Problem?"

"No, I'm working on my tan."

She had a smart mouth. Such a pretty mouth, too. Full, pink, pouty lips he'd like to slide his dick between. Adjusting himself to accommodate his growing discomfort, he said, "Funny. So what's the problem?"

With a slow turn of her head in his direction, she tilted her sunglasses partway down her nose, revealing crystal blue eyes. "If I knew what the problem was, would I be here?"

"Scoot." He bumped her hip. "What's it not doing?"

"Running, dumb ass."

"Careful with those smart-ass replies. I'm not above tossing you over my knee right here, baring your ass, and spanking you."

Her sharp hiss of outraged breath was music to his ears. He checked the battery, which was fine. Electrical system was operational. Everything was fine, with the exception of one loose wire that Blair had obviously jerked out to make sure the car wouldn't start. And it wasn't an easy wire to see. He'd gotten lucky finding it.

Smart girl. The question was, why? Though it didn't take a rocket scientist to figure it out.

He stood and wiped his hands on his jeans. "Go start it up."

"You get it fixed?"

That was not a hopeful expression on her face. "Not sure. Give it a try."

She slid behind the wheel and cranked the engine. Of course he hadn't bothered to slip the wire back into place, so the engine didn't turn over. He could have sworn he saw a triumphant smirk on her face. "Nothing's happening."

"Hmmm," she said, managing to sound irritated and disappointed.

He leaned over the engine again, jimmying a couple of the wires for effect. A few more seconds, and he'd give her the bad news, then take over. She'd started this game. He planned to take every advantage of it. Because as far as he was concerned, Blair had thrown down the gauntlet. She had come to him. Maybe not exactly in the way he'd wanted, but when had Blair ever done anything the conventional way?

"I don't know what the problem is. Let me hook it up to my Jeep and tow it onto my property. I can take a look at it there."

"Oh, you can call me a tow truck. I'll just wait here," she said, slipping out of the car to look at him over the roof.

"Won't work. Head-on accident out on I-34. Both wreckers are on scene."

"Well damn." She chewed her bottom lip.

"You got a date?"

Her lips curled. "Honey, I've always got a date."

Yeah, right. "Get in the Jeep, Blair. You're wilting out in this heat. Start it up and back it in front of your car."

"Fine." She grabbed her purse and sauntered over to the Jeep, doing an expert job of backing it up perfectly in line with her Mercedes. In short order he had the tow line set, then slid into the driver's seat of the Jeep and drove onto the entrance of his land.

Blair stayed mute throughout the five-minute drive down the dirt road. Rand took the opportunity to ogle her barely concealed body. She'd dressed to kill in that outfit. And she was damn near killing him. Midriff-baring tight little shirt that showed off her gorgeous tits and that scandalously short skirt that barely covered her ass, revealing her long legs.

She made his dick twitch. And her appearance outside the gate of his property had been as intentional as the clothes she wore. Good thing the drive was short, because his dick was getting longer with every passing second.

And her scent permeated the cab of the Jeep. Nothing flowery or perfumy, either. No, Blair was much more subtle than that. She let her natural fragrance do the talking for her. Soap, shampoo, and the smell of a nice clean woman was all it took to drive him up the wall.

By the time he took the circular curve and parked in front of the ranch house, he was primed and ready, his dick twitching like a divining rod that had just found the mother lode of water.

Rascal, his collie, came bounding toward them from the back of the house, barking and wagging his tail.

He judged a lot of women by how they treated his dog. Rascal wasn't what you'd call a good-looking dog. Part sheepdog and Lord only knew what else, he was mostly a mess of dirt and tangled, matted hair with a long tongue just made for copious amounts of slobber.

Most women wouldn't even get out of the car 'til he shooed Rascal away. Not Blair, though. She opened the door and greeted Rascal with an enthusiastic squeal, petting him and scratching his ears. Soon she was bent down and lavishing attention all over the mangy beast, cooing and making baby sounds. And Rascal was loving every second of it.

Well, she'd passed that test. He shook his head. "Come on inside before he gets his dirty paws all over your white top."

Blair grinned at Rascal, stood, and patted the dog's head. Rascal stepped up right beside Blair and kept up with her as they headed toward the house. "Oh, I don't mind. I love dogs."

Rascal bounded up the steps ahead of them, shooting through the door as soon as Rand opened it. "We won't see him the rest of the night. He'll plop down on one of my air conditioner vents and pass out."

Blair snorted. "Can't blame him. It's damn hot out there."

"He hangs out in the barn all day where's it cool and shady. Don't let his sad look fool you." Rand realized he'd never had Blair in his house before. Hell, he rarely brought women here. Home was his refuge, his place to get away from everything and everyone. To bring a woman in here would be an invasion of his personal space, his privacy. It was a rare occurrence.

Blair, however, was different. He wanted her here, had wanted her here for years. The fact that she showed up on the edge of his property meant something to him. A first step. He'd waited a long time for this.

"You gonna fix my car?" she asked, skimming her fingertips over the polished surface of his grandma's antique end table.

"Too hot outside right now. Thought we'd relax a bit, have a beer or two, and talk. Wait for it to cool down outside."

She pulled her sunglasses off and tucked them in her purse, then laid the bag on the table and slipped into the kitchen to wash the dog goobers off her hands. "I suppose I don't have much of a choice, do I?"

"You always have a choice, Blair." He wasn't going to let her take the easy way out. If what was going to happen was what he thought was going to happen, then it was going to be her conscious decision. It didn't work any other way.

"Not always." After she dried her hands, she wandered through his living room as if she were taking inventory. Okay, so he was a bachelor, and it wasn't pretty. A few hand-me-down antique pieces here and there, but otherwise completely threadbare. He kept meaning to do something about that, but frankly, who cared? He never had before. She turned to face him. "How about that beer?"

He grabbed two bottles from the fridge, returning and handing her one.

"Sit down."

She chose the single recliner. Figured. Safer that way. God forbid she should park on the sofa. He might actually sit next to her.

"I'm sorry about your granddad," she said, and from the tone of her voice, he knew she meant it. His grandfather had passed on a month ago, though he'd been in a nursing home for two years. The last of his relatives were gone now. All that was left of his family was this house.

"Thanks."

He had to give her this: she was calm. Or a damn good actress. The tension between them, as it had always been, sizzled the air between them. There was a combustible quality about their altercations. Even the simplest conversation tended to turn down a stormy road, sexual tension crackling between them.

Even now, without her having to say a thing, her body language told him everything she didn't want him to know. Her back held ramrod straight as if the slightest shift in posture would reveal too much of what she was feeling. Her breasts rising with each sharp intake of breath—oh yeah—that meant she was well aware there was a man in the room. And he was sure as hell aware of her. Every, lickable inch of her. The way her red hair caught and held the light as it streamed in through the half-opened shutters, surrounding her face like a fiery halo. Her skin, tan and glistening with some kind of body lotion that made it sparkle and smelled like pure, springtime rain. Mixed within all that was the unmistakable musky scent of a woman primed for sex.

He took a long swallow of beer, the cool liquid rolling down his throat and at least quenching the fire there. It did nothing to cool the flame between his legs, though. Then again, nothing would. Not until he had Blair stripped, spread-eagled, and begging him to fuck her. Once those sweet words passed her lips, he'd drive his cock deep in her cunt and finally have what he'd wanted for fifteen long years.

He'd never needed a woman more than Blair. He'd always wanted Blair. And he knew damn well Blair wanted him. But she'd built this wall around herself where he was concerned. Instead, she spent her time with wimpy, useless, pansy-assed toadies who were worthless in and out of the bedroom. No wonder she never kept a man around for long. What good were they?

What Blair showed to the world and what Blair really needed were two different things. Sometimes Rand wondered if he was the only man who saw underneath that cool, controlling exterior to the frightened woman who was afraid to express her true needs.

All she had to do was say the word, and he'd open the world to her. He'd give her everything she'd ever wanted. He'd make her come over and over again.

Come on baby. You know I can give it to you. Just ask me.

Because the one thing Rand would not do is take. If Blair wanted it, she'd have to ask him for it.

Once she did, though, there'd be no going back.

if blair held this position for much longer, her back was going to go into spasms. It was like a game of chicken between them. A stare-down until one of them flinched. And she wasn't about to flinch. But Goddamit, Rand was staring at her. And not just staring at her, but devouring her with his probing, enigmatic eyes that always seemed to be able to see right through her. As if he knew all her deep, dark secrets and was just waiting for her to blurt them out.

She'd made it this far. She was inside his house, she could see the line of his erection in his jeans and knew he was hot for her. Why the hell hadn't he made a move on her yet? Did she have to do a striptease on his coffee table to get his attention? It wasn't like she showed up at his place in her sexiest outfit on a regular basis.

Grab a clue, Rand. I'm here, I'm sexy and horny as hell. Fuck me, goddammit!

But no. He continued to stare at her as if he expected her to make the first move instead. Surely she hadn't read him wrong all these years. He couldn't be like all the other men she'd dated, could he? Spineless, weak, too afraid to take what they wanted? Had she misjudged him?

Disappointment washed over her, her mood souring so fast and making her stomach ache with such a hollow emptiness it almost made her cry. How could she have been so wrong about him? The games they played, the way he teased her, touched her, tormented her all these years with promises of the best sex of her life. No way could she have been wrong about her body's reaction. No freakin' way!

But still, he sat there, while she was all but spreading her legs in front of him. Was he waiting for an engraved invitation? Her verbal permission to come over and touch her? That so wasn't like Rand, wasn't at all like the man who'd damn near fucked her by the side of the road yesterday.

If it wasn't for the bet, she'd get up and leave. Instead, she had to stay here and fuck this jackass who was beginning to annoy the hell out of her. Fine. The sooner she got it over with, the better. She stood, took a long guzzle of her beer, then swaggered over to the sofa, plopping herself down next to Rand. She tilted her head down and looked at him through lowered lashes, one of her sexiest moves.

"What is it that you want, Blair?" he asked, a slight smile curving along his generous bottom lip.

"You need me to spell it out for you?"

"I need you to tell me what you want. What you really want."

His gray gaze challenged, daring her to be the one to say the words. But Blair was an expert at this game, knew how to manipulate men better than any woman she knew. She leaned into him, pressing her breast against the solid flesh of his arm. "Why don't you tell me what you'd like to do?"

He shifted and pushed a knee in between hers, his gaze direct and intense. "I'm not the kind of man to tell you what I might like, Blair. I'm going to tell you what will happen if you stay here. I want you on your knees in front of me sucking my cock. I want to fuck that sassy little mouth of yours until I shoot a hot load of come between those beautiful lips. Then I'm going to fuck you. I'm going to tie you to my bed, your legs spread, your pretty pussy open for my view. I'm going to lick and suck your clit until you scream my name and beg me to fuck you. Then I'm going to drive my cock hard and deep inside until you're squirming underneath me and pleading to come. After that I'm going to turn you over on your belly, spread those sweet cheeks and spear my dick between them into your tight ass. I'm going to fuck you all night long, all weekend long, until you can't remember any man you've been with before, because no man has fucked you like I'm going to."

Oh holy hell. The room temperature raised ten degrees in an instant, and she'd just gone up in flames. Blair swallowed, parting her lips to breathe in great gasps of air, stunned at the images his words created. No man had ever spoken to her like that. The men she chose damn near asked permission before kissing her. Rand had gone way beyond asking permission. He'd given her a graphic outline of every wicked thing he intended to do to her.

"My patience is wearing thin, Blair. You're here, and I want you. You don't want this, now is the time to say so, because I won't be asking for a goddamn thing this weekend. I'll be taking. You stay, you're mine. Any way I want you, any time I want you."

Oh, God. He knew. Somehow, he knew what she craved, knew what she hadn't had all these years. All those men, they'd never known what kind of woman she was, what kind of needs she had. But Rand did. He was offering her everything she'd ever wanted, and everything she feared.

The one thing she wanted most of all, the one thing that scared her most: to completely submit to a man.

And not just any man, but Rand McKay.

Her body was on fire, her nipples hard and straining against the soft cotton of her top, her pussy juices coating the thin strip of panty covering her crotch. Her clit swelled, the knot throbbing with an incessant pulse. The thought of what he could do to her—what he could do for her.

He almost made her come yesterday without even touching her pussy. Without even rubbing her clit.

She'd had nothing but lousy sex for the past fifteen years.

She had a bet to uphold.

It was one weekend, not forever. The chance to throw out her inhibitions and give up control to a man. No commitment other than giving in to her deepest, darkest, most wicked desires.

Just for the weekend.

After the weekend, it was over. He had no power over her, no control, no expectation that this would last beyond the weekend.

What harm would it do to indulge in her fantasies, to experience what she already knew would be the greatest sex of her life? Quite possibly the only chance she'd have at such phenomenal sex.

It wouldn't do any harm at all. As long as she remained in control, as long as she knew that once the weekend was over, this game was over.

As long as she didn't involve her heart, then when the weekend was over, she could walk away with a smile on her face.

A big-ass wicked smile.

She raised her chin, refusing just yet to give up complete control. "You want it. Then take it, Rand."

three

rand watched the play of emotion cross blair's face as she spat out the words. Indecision, a shadow of fear. Even anger, then resolution. She held her chin in a stubborn tilt as if daring him to command her to do anything she didn't want to do.

She didn't yet understand. But before the weekend was through, she'd realize she was the one who held all the power.

He stood and looked down at her, holding his hand out. For the longest few seconds she stared at it, then slid her warm fingers in his palm. He pulled her to her feet, jerking her roughly against his chest.

"I've waited fifteen years for this," he said, then slanted his mouth across hers, breathing in the scent of cinnamon.

The first touch of his mouth to hers was wildfire. Uncontrolled, unchecked flames scorched him. He knew it was going to be like this, yet he still wasn't prepared for how goddamned hot she was, how perfect her body felt pressed alongside his. Her full breasts crushed against his chest, her hips nestled against his pelvis. He wanted to touch her and kiss her everywhere all at once.

Slow. Down. His heart pumped like a churning freight train as he moved his lips over hers, digging his fingers in the lush softness of her hair, devouring her mouth and licking at her tongue like it was the nectar of the gods. His cock was ramrod stiff and insistent on breaking free of the denim, straining his zipper. His balls ached, his fingers itching to wrap themselves around the firm globes of her sweet ass.

It wasn't until he was damn near delirious that he realized the only one spiraling out of control was him. Blair was stiff, unyielding, holding back. Though her palms were braced against his chest, her mouth responding under his, she wasn't participating. She was following his lead, but not in the way he wanted her to.

Blair was scared to let go. Which meant he was going to have to take over and force it. Take the control away from her so she wasn't acquiescing but being forced to participate. He knew the game; it was the same one they'd been playing for fifteen years. Obviously they'd have to continue to play it.

He slowed down his kiss, forced his racing pulse from its breakneck speed into something more manageable. Time to gather his wits and take over this situation before Blair turned into a steel girder in his arms.

He broke the kiss and stepped away from her. Her eyes shot open, and she stared at him, frowning.

"What?" she asked.

"On your knees."

"Excuse me?"

"You heard me." He flipped open the button on his jeans, his cock pounding in anticipation. "Get down on your knees."

She looked to his crotch, her gaze riveted on the slow slide of his zipper as he drew it down.

"You're joking."

"Do I look like I'm joking?" He drew his shirt over his head and tossed it on the sofa behind her. Her gaze never left the vee of his jeans. Not until those gorgeous baby blues took a long, leisurely look up and over his hips, stomach, chest, finally focusing on his face again. Only this time she wasn't wide-eyed with shock.

She was pissed. But beyond the frown and tight lips there was a fire in her eyes that hadn't been there before, a passion that had been lacking when she had come to him "willingly."

Okay, so she liked to be told what to do. He could sure as hell live with that. "I mean now, Blair. Do what I tell you or I'll *make* you do it."

He was going to enjoy every fucking minute of bending her to his will. And deep down, he knew Blair would, too.

Game on.

blair sucked in a heaving breath of righteous indignation. Down on her knees.

He could damn well kiss her ass if he thought she'd drop like some subject to a king and suck his cock just because he commanded it. They were kissing. Things were going fine. Then what the hell happened?

Okay, so maybe the earth wasn't moving for her, but it was okay.

And so maybe as soon as he commanded her to drop down in front of him, her clit quivered and her nipples tightened. But that didn't mean she was going to do it.

"You're not moving," he said, his voice lowering an octave.

One damn sexy octave, too.

"I don't intend to. This is stupid. I'm not playing—"

"And neither am I," he interrupted, grabbing her wrist and jerking her against him. In seconds they had switched positions, and Rand was seated on the couch with Blair belly down across his lap. "This has been a long time coming."

Her breath momentarily left her diaphragm, or she would have been screaming. Instead, all she could manage was a grunt of outrage as Rand placed one firm hand on her ass, sliding her skirt up over her hips and ripping off the tiny scrap of her thong to bare her buttocks.

"Such a fine, firm ass you have, Blair. I've been dying to get my hands on it."

She couldn't help it. She flooded with moisture as he swept his huge hand over her ass. Anticipation swelled her clit, and she tensed, waiting for it.

Needing it.

When the first swat hit her left cheek, she bit back a moan, refusing to let him know how much it excited her. But oh, it did. He knew just how hard to spank her. The sting was hot, sweet, and he followed it up by caressing the spot, sliding his hand down over her thighs and back up again, then swatted her other cheek.

She flinched, then sucked in a breath of air as he petted her ass again, his movements gentle as he slipped his hand between her legs, coming so close to her clit it drove her crazy. But he didn't touch her there. He meant to torment.

Damn, he was good.

"You've been a very bad girl, Blair," he said, his hand coming down to land on her ass again, this time striking the lower part of both cheeks with a light tap that made her pussy quiver. "I think you're going to need a lot of punishing."

Oh, she hoped so. Her body trembled under his sexy assault, anticipating his next move, craving his touch. She was starving for it.

"And your pussy is wet." He cupped her, rubbing her clit. This time, she did moan. She couldn't help it. What he was doing to her wasn't inadvertent. It was deliberate, meant to entice, to let her know who was in charge of her pleasure.

He was a goddamn master at this game.

She'd underestimated him.

She shifted, undulating against his hand, trying to move her clit closer to his palm.

He removed his hand.

Bastard.

"You'll come when I decide," he said, swatting her again. "I call the shots here, Blair. Not you."

He slid her off his lap and onto her knees on the floor, grabbing a fistful of her hair. Jerking his jeans down his hips, he pulled out his cock, stroking it near her face.

Long, thick, the crest was wide and smooth. She couldn't help herself. She licked her lips as she looked at it, her nipples tightening as she breathed in the musky scent of him. God, he was beautiful.

"Suck it."

Her pussy throbbed at his command.

"Fuck you," she replied, clenching her teeth.

He jerked her head back and smiled down at her. "Baby, you'll be doing that soon enough. Right now you're going to suck my dick."

He grasped his cock with his free hand and painted her lips with the drops of liquid pearling at the tip.

She wanted to defy him.

She wanted to suck him, to reach out and grasp his shaft with both hands and devour his flesh. But she would be giving up control to him if she surrendered to her desires, and that she wouldn't do.

With careful restraint, she opened her mouth and licked his cock head, tilting her head back to watch his face, relishing the way his eyes glazed over as she took a long, slow swipe of his silken head.

Her belly quivered as she tasted him. Salty, wild like the man. So carefully in control as he watched her, his brows tilted upward, his breathing quick and labored as she swirled her tongue over the head, wrapping her lips around him and drawing his shaft inside the heat of her mouth.

"Christ," he whispered, loosening his hold on her hair. "That's good, baby. Suck it in."

He surged forward, feeding her inch by glorious inch of his cock, his fingers tangled in her hair as she teased the swollen crest, feeling his heat slide between her lips.

What she wouldn't give to let go, to cup his balls in the palm of her hand and milk him as she swallowed his cock.

But they played a game. A game she refused to lose. The stakes were high, and no matter how intense the sensations were, she would not give in.

Still, it was oh-so-sweet, his taste, his primal scent, compelling her to release her inhibitions and give him everything.

She wanted to. Oh, how she wanted to. Her body ached for him, her need for him beyond anything she could ever admit to even her two closest friends. They wouldn't understand.

No one understood what she needed.

Only Rand knew. Because he matched the wildness within her, his muscles coiled and tight, the tension around them thick as he pumped his hips forward and slid his cock over her tongue. She suctioned him in, feeling him jerk in response as she tightened her mouth around him when he pulled back.

"Tease," he whispered. "You like that, don't you, baby? Your mouth was made to suck cock. Sweet, full lips and that hot tongue."

He had no idea what she was capable of doing to him, how much she enjoyed his pleasure, what it did to her own body. She was wet, throbbing, pulsing between her legs with the need for his hand, his tongue, his cock down there.

She pulled back and lightly dragged her teeth over his cock head, feeling him shudder. Then she couldn't resist touching him. She grabbed the base of his cock and began to stroke as she sucked, wanting what he had to give her, wanting everything.

She wanted the control, wrestling it away from him, going to the place where she was comfortable. She squeezed his shaft as she sucked the head, swiping her tongue over the fluids that escaped, using her other hand to gently palm his balls. When his cock lurched forward and speared her mouth, she knew she'd found his weakness.

"Fuck, Blair!" he groaned, tightening his hold on her hair, pumping forward to feed her more of his dick.

She had him now. No man could hold back, not even Rand. She took him deep, feeling his balls tighten under her grasp as he pushed forward, fucking her mouth with erotic movements that made her pussy cry out for attention.

She wanted his hips propelling forward in her cunt the same way, fucking her pussy the way he did her mouth. She let her lips do the work while she reached down between her legs to massage the unbearable ache, wanting to come when he did. She found her clit, knew how little it would take to get her there, knew how close he was to giving her a hot load of come. She hurried her movements on her clit, panting with need, groaning against his shaft as she sucked him, moving her mouth over him in rapid strokes now, squeezing his balls tight with one hand while strumming her clit with the other.

She was close . . . so damn close.

Come in my mouth, Rand. Come on, baby, we're both almost there.

When he pulled his cock out of her mouth and jerked her hand away from her pussy, she gasped in utter shock. He drew her to her feet, his gaze dark and angry, his breath sawing in and out with great effort.

What the hell was wrong with him? They were both seconds from one incredible dual orgasm.

"You'll come when I say so, and it won't be by your hand, Blair. You're not in charge here, remember?"

No. No way. No fucking way had he just done this to her. She couldn't even breathe, her clit was tingling, and within seconds she'd have burst into climax, and he wanted to control her orgasm?

"Are you out of your mind?"

He smiled, the half curl of his lips lethal and dangerous. "Oh, I know exactly what I'm doing. And so do you. You think you can turn the tables and control this. I warned you."

She tried to wrench her arm away, but he held tight to her wrist. She looked down at his hand and back at his face. "You're hurting me."

"No, I'm not."

"Let go."

"I told you if you agreed to this weekend, I was in charge. You're not going to call the shots, Blair. You're not going to control this. I am."

She took a quick glance at his cock. It was still rock hard and upright. And she was still throbbing and close to orgasm. Damn him. She was good at taking care of things. Why didn't he just let her pleasure them both?

"Because you need to learn to let go," he said, as if he'd read her mind.

"I don't know what you're talking about."

"You will." He pulled his jeans up over his swollen cock, then bent down and shoved his shoulder into her belly and stood, throwing her over his back.

"What the hell are you doing?" she asked as he headed out of the room.

He didn't answer, just moved with a purposeful, swift stride down a narrow hallway, stopping only long enough to open a door and enter a darkened room. She tried to lift herself off, but in this position it wasn't likely. His body was like a freakin' rock, and he had a damn good hold on her.

Until she went flying, anyway, landing with a shriek.

On something soft.

A bed.

"Asshole!" She scrambled to her knees, her intent to launch herself right off the bed and leave. But he grabbed her hands and dragged her to the head of the bed.

The room was dark despite it still being light out, and she couldn't make out much other than she was on a bed. Not much help. And he had a firm grip on her arms. No matter how much she struggled, it was like fighting a giant oak tree.

He made short work of wrestling her top off, dragging it over her head and tossing it away, then yanked her skirt down her hips and legs. She heard a jingle, then a clank, then cold steel clamped around her wrists as he tethered her to the iron bars of his bed, one wrist at a time.

"Rand, this is not funny."

"Wasn't trying to be," he said, moving down to her feet.

This time it wasn't cold steel he attached to her ankles but something a little softer—cotton rope maybe—that he tied around them as he secured her, legs spread, to the bottom of his bed. Despite her profound irritation, her nipples puckered, her clit quivering to life again.

Tied, spread-eagled, to Rand McKay's bed. In the dark, handcuffs on her wrists and rope binding her ankles.

She was at his mercy.

mercy!

His eyes adjusted to the darkness in the room, Rand watched Blair's widen with anticipation and something else. Her breath caught as he fastened the last rope to the bars on his bed, signaling her that she wasn't getting away this time. She wasn't in charge anymore. He was.

She sucked in her lower lip, her nipples hardening, and as he inhaled and light filtered in the room, he smelled it on her, saw it on her face.

Arousal.

Oh yeah. She could feign anger or indifference as much as she wanted, but her body told the truth.

He reached behind him and flipped open the shutters partway, allowing a little daylight into the room. It bathed her body, showcasing her like a golden goddess.

"I keep it dark in here when I work nights and sleep during the day. But I definitely want your body in the light. I need to see you. And you need to watch what I'm going to do to you."

She kept her lips firmly pressed together, her gaze narrowed. He allowed a smile as he walked around the bed, surveying his work, and stopped at the foot of the bed to look at her pussy spread open before him.

"You have the prettiest cunt I've ever seen, Blair. Did you spend extra time preparing it for me today?"

"Asshole. I did no such thing."

She was lying. He moved to the side of the bed and sat on the edge, lifting her foot. "And such sexy feet with your red-painted toenails. I'll bet you like to have your toes licked, too, don't you?"

She didn't answer, but she sucked in an audible breath. Yeah, she liked it, all right. He stood and discarded his clothes, moving to the head of the bed. Like a wary victim of a predator, her gaze followed his every movement.

Rand palmed his cock and stroked it, though just the thought of fucking her this way had him hard in an instant. He'd been so close to shooting his load in her mouth, down her throat, wanting to watch her throat move as she swallowed every drop of his come. It made his balls ache just thinking about how good it would have been.

But that would have put Blair in control. And that's what Blair wanted, what she was used to.

He intended to turn her world upside down this weekend, and that meant she didn't get to be in charge.

He wanted her complete and total surrender, which meant his needs had to wait.

Or maybe not. He crawled onto the bed and straddled her chest, still stroking his cock, wanting her to see it, to watch him, to know that he could do whatever he wanted.

To himself or to her.

And she could only watch.

He grasped the shaft tight, then moved forward, slipping back and brushing against his balls, letting the groan escape his lips. "Your mouth was sweet and hot on my dick, Blair. You suck cock like you were born for it."

Her lips parted on a quivering breath as she focused on the movements of his hand.

"Want to wet it for me while I stroke it? Lick the head a little? I do like your mouth."

She swallowed, then nodded, but didn't say a word. Bracing his hand on the wall over the bed, he leaned over her, sliding just the head between her lips.

Like wet hellfire, scorching him as she swirled her tongue around the crest, then wrapped her lips around him and sucked him in. His cock jerked against the roof of her mouth, and she groaned, the little hum making his balls dance in agony. He couldn't help it. He released his hold and drove in deeper, feeding her inch by inch of his dick. She took it all. Watching his cock disappear between her lips was like selling his soul to the devil herself.

God, he wanted to come in her mouth.

But not yet, and not this time.

She was going to come first. She was going to surrender.

Body and soul. He wanted it all.

"You've tasted me, now I need to taste you." He pulled his cock out of her mouth, wincing as it made a popping sound. She didn't want to give it up, damn greedy little thing. He liked that she held on so tight, that she enjoyed sucking him.

He bent over her and brushed the top of her head with his mouth, taking a deep breath. Her hair smelled like summer rain. Moving down, he kissed her forehead, her eyelids, lingering there when she opened her eyes and regarded him warily.

He kissed the top of her nose, the corner of each of her lips. Her slightly pointed chin, then hovered over her mouth, breathing in her breath, absorbing her, watching her expression change to one of anticipation.

"Tell me what you need," he said, his lips so close to hers they were almost touching.

Almost, but not quite. He wanted her to say it, needed her to say it.

"Kiss me," she finally whispered.

He did, capturing her mouth under his and taking possession, holding back the urge to ravage her. Instead, he stroked her mouth gently, sweeping his lips across hers, nipping her bottom lip, and nudging it open to slide his tongue inside.

Warm and inviting, she swept her tongue around his like an embrace, sucking at his, until their playful, tender kiss turned to something more passionate, needier, a sense of urgency enveloping them both. When she raised her hips and undulated against him, he knew what she wanted.

To fuck. Fucking would put them at least close to equal ground.

But that wasn't his plan. Regretfully, he pulled his lips from hers and seared a path down the column of her throat, dipping his tongue in the hollow there before moving lower, making a slow trek down her body.

Like an explorer, he wanted to leave nothing untouched. Every part of her was an adventure. Now that he had her trussed up so she couldn't escape, he planned to learn every inch of her body. What she liked, what she didn't like. What turned her on, what didn't, what curled her toes and what made her scream.

Oh, he was definitely going to enjoy making her scream in pleasure. He was going to earn her trust, because she was giving him a lot letting him tie her up like this. And he didn't take it lightly.

Blair was going to have the time of her life.

She was going to learn all about the fun of surrender.

four

blair gasped, her whole body tightening as rand licked a trail down her neck. His breath was hot against her ear, his whispered words evoking darkness and midnight, not late afternoon.

"How does it feel to be tied up, knowing I can do whatever I want to you, and you can't move?"

She shivered, biting back the retort hovering on the tip of her tongue. What she wanted to do was demand he let her go, to get dressed, run outside and reconnect the wires to her Mercedes, and skedaddle out of there. She didn't like this game anymore, because she no longer held the advantage.

But then she'd lose the bet.

And she hated to lose. She didn't lose.

"You're shaking, baby. Are you cold?"

He'd awakened her body to a blistering fever. She wasn't cold.

She was scared shitless because she liked this. Too much.

He raised his head and looked at her.

"No, I'm fine."

"Fine, huh?" He grinned. "I don't want you fine. Let's see what we can do about that."

He bent to her neck again, pressing soft kisses to her throat. So tender and sweet it made tears well in her eyes.

She didn't like Rand sweet. She liked him cantankerous and argumentative. Not like this, catering to her body and making her want to wrap her arms around him and beg him to put his dick inside her.

She was feeling needy.

And Rand fed her needs, moving from her neck to her breasts, gathering the globes in his hands. She lifted her head to watch him snake his tongue across one nipple, then the other, the cool air left behind making them stand up and beg for his attention.

Oh, she wanted that attention. Her nipples ached for his mouth. She wanted to beg for it but wouldn't, refused to give voice to her needs. She arched against him, the shock from the heat of his mouth searing her as he covered one nipple, gathering it between his teeth.

The sensation was incredible. She cried out as he flicked her nipple with his tongue, sucked, then nibbled with his teeth. God almighty, what was he doing to her? She felt everything he did to her all the way to her clit, the quivering, building pressure inciting her to lift upward, to feed him her breasts. She felt consumed, as if he knew every inch of her.

He devoured her, and she wanted more.

And he gave, moving to her other breast, licking, nibbling, flattening her nipple between his tongue and the roof of his mouth as if he were trying to swallow her.

She wanted him to. It was like she couldn't give him enough of herself.

He moved downward, across her rib cage, dipping his tongue in the hollow of her navel, flicking at the jewel there.

"Oh, this is so fucking sexy," he drawled as he flicked the crystals dangling at her belly button.

He looked up at her, his face bathed in the sunlight streaming into the room. His hair fell over his forehead, thick and wavy, his eyes like a dark ocean, glittering with his desires, heating her from her toes up to her head.

He smoothed his hand over the flat planes of her belly, and her muscles jerked in response. He was so close to her sex her clit was quivering, every muscle tensing in anticipation. At this moment she couldn't care less who was in charge, she simply rejoiced in being a woman.

His woman.

At least for this weekend. She wouldn't, couldn't think beyond that, beyond the pleasure of his hands on her body, the way he awoke every nerve ending in ways she'd never experienced. She wouldn't bemoan what she'd missed by keeping this man at bay all these years.

She wouldn't.

She'd just relish this moment in time, infuse her memory banks with every precious second of his hands skimming her hips, his tongue dipping into her navel and teasing the crystal jewels there, the way he caressed her flesh and coaxed every nerve ending into burning awareness.

Before moving down, between her legs, licking her inner thighs and pressing soft kisses there.

She might just die if he didn't put his tongue on her clit, if he didn't suck her, lick her, put his fingers inside her, anything to make her come. Right now. She was melting all over his sheets, wet and anxious and ready as hell for him.

Come on, Rand. Lick me. Suck my clit. Fuck me with your fingers. She wanted this so bad she couldn't stand it.

And she wanted to be untied so she could writhe all over him, grab his head between her hands, and plant her lips on his, grip his cock, and force it inside her. She lifted her hips, undulating against his questing mouth.

"Easy, baby," he said, licking along the inside of her thigh. "I know what you want."

"Then give it to me." Her voice was raspy, her breath catching on every word. She didn't even sound like herself. It was hot, sexy, even to her own ears.

"Oh, I like when you beg for it. How bad do you want it, Blair?"

She nibbled her lower lip, not wanting to give him the satisfaction of asking him to do what she knew he was going to do anyway. Eventually. Soon. He was. He had to. By God, he'd better.

"Please, Rand."

"Your wish is my command, princess."

The first touch of his tongue against her sex was a hot blast, like pressing her pussy up against a wet furnace. When he moved it upward, then back down again, she let out a long moan. And she didn't care anymore. Inhibitions flew out the window as she opened her legs as wide as they would go, giving him access to her cunt.

"Lick me," she pleaded. "Yes, like that."

Rand had a masterful tongue and knew just what to do with it. When she thought of all the men she'd had to give directions to, she let her head fall back on the pillow and cursed her years of misfortune.

She threw up the white flag, surrendered, and knew right then she was lost. Never again would a man make her feel this good, would a man know her body the way Rand did. Without instructions, without frustration, he lapped around her clit like a driver who knew exactly where the finish line was.

She bucked against his mouth, driving her pussy into his face, racing to a climax she couldn't hold back. God, she didn't want to hold it back. It was nearing, and she wanted it, craved it, wanted Rand to give it to her.

But he moved away from her clit, slowed the pace, veered off course. Her head shot off the pillow, and she gaped down to find him looking up at her with a knowing grin on his face.

She was about to call him a no good, tormenting bastard, but he slid two fingers into her cunt.

"Oh, my God."

"Fuck, baby, you're like melted butter inside," he said. "So goddamn hot and tight. I can't wait to get my dick in you."

She couldn't tear her gaze away from the movements of his fingers, from the way he was watching her.

"Do it," she whispered. "Fuck me."

He slanted a half smile at her. "Soon. My dick is hard, Blair. I need to fuck you. But first I want you to come for me. I want to suck the come from your pussy, feel you squeeze my fingers." He pulled back, then thrust his fingers inside her again. "Come on, baby. Come for me, and let me watch."

She stared, transfixed, as he planted his mouth over her clit and sucked, fucking her pussy with his fingers. Delirious sensations built, then tightened, spiraling uncontrollably ever downward.

Panting, she held on as long as she could, then released, letting her climax flow through her. Rand lapped along her clit as she came, his fingers stilling as she bucked against him and rode out what was the strongest orgasm a man had ever given her. Screams tore from her throat, her limbs shook as she struggled against the cuffs and ropes binding her, her moisture spilling in warm rivulets down her ass as she came and came in torrents that never seemed to end.

The tiny shocks reverberated through her, finally lessening enough that she fell back against the mattress, replete and exhausted but utterly exhilarated.

She was spent but energized, her pussy turning over in delightful little spasms around Rand's fingers. She lifted her head and looked down at him, his face wet. He sat up, finally removing his fingers and crawling up beside her on the bed.

"Taste," he said, lifting his fingers to her mouth.

She'd never done that before, but when he placed his fingers against her lips, she let him slide them inside, tasting her own cream. The scent was musky, the taste salty and honey sweet. He pulled his fingers away and kissed her, his face covered with her.

It was the most erotic thing she had ever experienced, tasting her own unique flavor on a man's lips. And yet not at all unpleasant. It made her tingle all over, her cunt tightening with renewed arousal. His tongue invaded, sliding against hers in a warm, velvet twist that tangled her belly in knots. She squirmed against the cuffs, wanting to reach out and take hold of him, to grab his cock and guide him into her waiting pussy.

Why wasn't he fucking her? She arched against him, thrusting her tongue against his, giving him every signal in the book save for coming right out and demanding. Yet he continued his slow, deliberate assault with his mouth, grasping her head between his hands and massaging her scalp while he kissed her.

He was doing this on purpose. She was on fire with need, and he'd reverted to simple foreplay. Kissing and touching, and she wanted fucking. The man was maddening!

When he finally broke the kiss and looked at her, she sucked in a breath at the intensity in his dark eyes. Such raw need and hunger reflected there. For her? About her? She'd never seen a man look at her that way.

Though she tried to turn her head to the side, he held her firmly between his strong hands. "Don't look away. Look at me. See how much I want you."

His cock surged between her legs, teasing her sensitized flesh. With one perfect stroke he could be inside her. Instead, he tormented, but the only thing he penetrated her with was his eyes, as if he could see inside her, knew what she was thinking.

"Stop it," she said.

"Stop what?"

"Looking at me that way."

He arched one brow. "What way?"

She hated being trussed up like this and unable to walk away. "You know perfectly well what I'm talking about. Untie me."

"No."

"My wrists hurt."

He reached up to examine her wrists. "There's no chafing. You're fine."

"I'm cramping."

"You're lying. And wet," he said, his hard shaft splitting her pussy lips and rubbing her in ways that sent sparks of pleasure deep within her cunt.

"I came, you idiot. Of course I'm wet."

He moved against her again. "You're wet because you like this."

"Do not." She felt childish saying it but couldn't help herself. She was at a serious disadvantage here and was forced to resort to whatever tactics she could think of. Which wasn't much. She was sorely lacking in battle implements.

"You want my cock in you?"

Yes! She shrugged. "I'd like to get on with this."

He laughed and bent his head down to her breasts, tickling her neck with his hair. She inhaled, absorbing the crisp scent of him, trying not to sigh in utter delight. He did crazy things to her senses.

And when he moved his way down her body again, she groaned. "What are you doing?"

"Priming you," he murmured in between kissing her skin.

"I'm already primed."

"Not nearly enough."

"Stop that. You already did that once."

He paused and looked up at her, frowning. "Once? Oh, that's not nearly enough."

Good God. What was wrong with him anyway? Weren't men typically after the jackpot? He wasn't normal, that had to be it. His cock was hard, his balls had to be throbbing mercilessly. The man needed to come. Why didn't he just fuck her?

But no. Not Rand. He was down there between her legs again, sliding his tongue all over her—"

"Oh my God."

If it was good the first time, it was even better now. His mouth covered her pussy; his tongue lapped her clit with relentless strokes. Pressure rose like a teapot under a high fire. She jerked against her bonds as he took her to the very edge of reason, swirling his tongue around her clit until she poised right at the precipice of an orgasm.

Then he stopped. She lifted her head and watched him make a lazy crawl up her body. Like a predator about to pounce. He gripped her arms, then settled his cock against the entrance to her pussy as he hovered above her.

Sunlight bathed his body, turning him into a golden god. Every muscle, taut ridged hills, every hard plane showcased like a bronzed statue as he poised over her.

She tensed, anticipating the first thrust, but still he waited, his gaze locked with hers.

"Ask for it," he said.

"What?"

"Ask for it."

Her fingers curled into her palms. She would most definitely not beg him to fuck her. He could balance on his fingertips above her until midnight if he wanted to, but she would damn well not ask him to put his cock in her.

She clamped her lips together and held them while he rocked the tip of his cock against her clit. And she couldn't squirm away, because when she tried to move, he moved with her so that he was constantly rubbing against her.

But she still refused to say it.

Eventually he'd give up. He was the one who hadn't come yet, while she'd already come. She could hold out longer. His muscles would tire as he held a half push-up above her.

He smiled down at her. God, he had a beautiful face. Rugged, tan, small lines snaking outward from the corner of each eye, a straight, long nose and a square jaw, a hint of stubble that she'd felt teasing her thighs while he'd had his face buried between her legs. She shuddered.

"You want it. Ask for it." He surged against her, right up against her clit, grinding the little nub into smithereens before pulling away and taunting her with the velvety tip again. The sensations were destroying her, making her desperate to be filled with thick, hot cock.

Still balancing on his arms, he bent down and took one nipple between his teeth, tugging sharply. The pain was exquisite but gone in a second as he bathed her nipple with his tongue. Hot, wet, and oh so tantalizing. She lifted her hips, unable to control her body's reaction when he did the same to the other nipple.

This was so unfair. Her nipples were so sensitive, and she liked a little pain with her pleasure. And he knew it. Somehow, just like everything else about her, he knew it.

Damn him.

"Ask for it," he repeated again.

Frustrated, she did. With her hips, her body, undulating against him, trying to make herself irresistible so he couldn't help himself.

Instead, he bit her nipple again, tugging with his teeth. Her clit quivered, warm cream pouring from her in response. His cock moved against her pussy lips, spreading her juices around.

"It makes you wet when I bite you. I think you like a little pain, Miss Newcastle."

No way in hell was she going to answer that. He already knew too much about her.

"Ask for it."

"I've never in my life begged a man to fuck me."

"And I'll bet you've never in your life had really good, mind-blowing sex, have you?"

Ouch.

"I'll bet you've never let your guard down, never relinquished control long enough to surrender your body to a man, let your emotions run wild and free, let a man do all the things you want him to do, have you?"

Ouch again.

"Your body is burning, Blair. Your mind is filled with the possibilities of what could be but never has been."

He bent his head and tugged at her nipple. She let out a growl as sensation flamed. He licked a fiery trail from one to the other until she arched up to meet his mouth. He moved down to capture her lips in a long, hard kiss that left her breathless.

Bastard.

"Let go, Blair. Give it up to me, and I promise you won't regret it."

He surged against her, his cock head sliding past her wet pussy lips, promising what he could deliver.

She was panting, breathless, and couldn't bear the torment one second longer. Glaring at him and hating him at this moment, but needing him more than she'd ever needed a man, she ground out the words she swore she'd never say.

"Fuck me, Rand."

thanking the gods for whatever intervention they'd provided, Rand thrust between Blair's welcoming pussy lips, burying his cock deep, allowing the satisfied groan to escape as he did.

She tilted her head back and cried out, her wrists straining against the cuffs as he powered inside her cunt.

Goddamn, he'd been waiting an eternity to be inside her. He allowed himself to drop down on top of her and slid his hands under her ass to tilt her pelvis up, aligning her even tighter against him.

Her breasts pressed against his chest, he felt every static thump of her heartbeat as he surged forward, every gripping pulse of her pussy as it squeezed his cock, every one of her staccato breaths in his ear. He wanted her arms and legs wrapped around him, wanted to feel her embrace as he pushed ever deeper inside her.

But he'd started this lesson, and he'd see it through, and that meant having her spread-eagled and unable to touch him, unable to reciprocate the strokes of his hand along her dampened skin. She couldn't move her arms and legs, could only shudder and sigh and moan underneath him as he lifted and pounded his cock against her.

She couldn't hold him, but her pussy told him everything he needed to know; the rapid thrums of her heart and the moaning pants of her breath against his cheek told him how much she enjoyed this.

It was enough for now.

"Rand," she moaned, lifting her hips, the only part of her body other than her head that was free to move.

"I like hearing you say my name baby," he said, gritting his teeth to hold on. He wanted to release inside her, to jettison the come that had been building for far too long. But he wanted her to come first. And she would. "Say it again."

"Rand." Her eyes were glittering sapphires surrounded by a sea of dark lashes. His innocent seductress who hadn't completely crossed the boundaries of surrender was begging him with her body, giving him control, asking without words to make her come.

His fingers dug into the tender globes of her ass, propelling her ever upward as he thrust harder. She whimpered and lifted, meeting every stroke.

"You wanna come, baby?" he asked, pulling back and powering down and forward again, burying his cock deep inside her.

She nodded, tossing her head back, her lips parting on a gasp.

She was his every fantasy come to life, her auburn hair spread out with her head tilted back, her full lips open and inviting as she panted while he fucked her.

"Please," she whispered.

He'd wager she didn't even know she'd said the word.

But it was the sweetest surrender.

His balls quivered in anticipation, a rush of heat scorching his insides as the liquid fire from her cunt seared him.

"Come for me, Blair. Come on my cock."

She stilled, tensed, then let out a cry that reverberated right through him. Her pussy tightened around his dick, milking him right into the throes of a climax that started at his toes and erupted from his balls. He raised up and threw his head back, emptying into her with a shudder and a groan while she bucked against him in wild abandon, still flying with her own orgasm. She was killing him, squeezing the very life and essence right out of him, and he was dying gladly inside her.

Oh, yeah. Watching her come was heaven on earth, the blush spreading across her skin, her nipples tightening, her body growing taut with tension as she released, then the way it relaxed as she came down off the high.

He withdrew, uncuffed and untied her wrists and ankles, then drew her against his chest, allowing his own heart rate and breathing to settle while enjoying the feel of wrapping her in his arms.

He could get used to having her here. But he knew they had only scratched the surface. He might have won this first skirmish with Blair, but it wasn't over yet.

The war had just begun.

five

lazy afternoons spent in bed napping were simply
decadent. Lazy afternoons spent in bed recovering from the most
magnificent orgasms of her life were simply unheard of in her world.

Having spent them with Rand was like something out of a wicked
fantasy.

He was more than she had ever hoped for, and then some.

More than she had ever feared, too.

Powerful, controlling, he knew every one of her hot buttons and
pushed them like a master puppeteer. If he'd failed at just one
of them, she would have smiled smugly and walked away knowing
that Rand, like every other man she'd been with, just simply didn't
"get" her.

He'd gotten her all right.

Too well.

She'd played right into his hands, coming apart like she had.
Where had all her self-control gone? Couldn't she have held back
just a little? Did she have to have an orgasm every time he licked her,

touched her, fucked her? One would think she'd been satisfied after the first one and could have lain there like a dead fish or something, just to let him know he wasn't in as much control as he'd like to think he was.

But oh, no. Her traitorous body had to go and respond with a resounding *Yippee! I'm coming again!* Every. Single. Time.

She sighed and tried to scoot away. But like a thief caught sneaking out with the goods, escape was impossible. He snaked an arm around her middle and pulled her back against the powerful wall of his chest.

Dammit, he made her feel safe, tucked into his body like this. It was warm and comfortable, and he was solid and strong. She felt protected, desired. Needed.

Whoa. Way too much going on in her head right now. And all the wrong things.

Rand was not the guy. He wasn't. Not for her, anyway.

"What are you thinking about?"

The deep timbre of his voice sent her nerve endings skyrocketing in a million directions.

"Nothing."

"Liar. Tell me what you're thinking about."

He cupped her breast. Didn't squeeze, like a lot of men did, just cupped it, his thumb dragging lightly over her nipple.

Her clit took notice, and bells started ringing down south.

Was she wired for Rand? Lord. One lazy little strum of his fingers, and her body took notice.

Well, dammit, she was in charge of her body. Not him. And she was going to ignore his flicking of her nipple.

"I was just thinking I was tired."

"You had a nap. An hour and a half."

An hour and a half curled in his arms. Sweet oblivion. "I'm still tired."

"No, you're not. But I'm hungry, and I'll bet you are, too. How about a shower and something to eat?"

She shrugged, but her stomach rumbled, giving her away. He laughed and released her. "Go on and shower. Towels are in the closet next to the sink. I'll start the grill, then jump in when you're finished."

Shower? In some man's bathroom? Without her makeup and blow dryer? What would she wear afterward? Did he have any idea what she looked like after a shower? She wasn't prepared for this. She padded into the bathroom and flipped on the light, grimacing at how . . . manly it all looked. Stark white single sink. Clean enough, she supposed. The shower was, too, though where was the loofah? The little purple razor? The body wash? She'd bet he didn't even have scented shampoo. He probably used something called Grizzly Peaks or Man Froth.

Ick.

She turned on the faucets, then rummaged through the linen closet, grateful to find a usable shampoo and conditioner. Thank God. And he did have nice, big soft towels. She scrubbed her makeup off, washed and rinsed, and stepped out just in time to find him standing outside the shower door stripping out of his jeans.

"Fire's blazing on the grill. Let me pop in while you're drying off."

He skirted beside her and zipped into the shower stall while she finished drying.

This was all so intimate. Something a couple that lived together would do.

And she needed her comb.

"Got a brush?" she hollered.

"Third drawer down."

She pulled it out and grabbed a wide-toothed comb to drag through the tangles in her hair.

"Don't suppose you have a blow-dryer."

"Linen closet on the floor."

Yes! She ran to the closet and dragged out the blow-dryer. Not the fanciest, but it would do. She wasn't even going to ask why he had one; she was just grateful he did. He finished his shower and stepped out, pulling a towel out of the closet and watching her dry her hair while he dried off.

And she watched him watching her.

And got hotter by the minute, especially when he wrapped the towel around his hips and grabbed a brush, then stood next to her while he brushed his hair. The towel rested low on his lean hips. She ogled the flat planes of his stomach, counted the ridged muscles there, drooled over his well-sculpted chest and arms, then mentally damned herself for staring so hard when he smiled at her in the mirror.

How dare he be so sexy? She'd just ignore him.

But dayum, he smelled good. She took a deep breath and inhaled him, resisting the urge to put the blow-dryer down, drop to her knees, and bury her face in his cock. Fortunately, he walked out of the bathroom before she could give in to her baser instincts. She turned off the dryer and followed him, checking out his fine, firm ass while he shrugged into a pair of jeans and a loose tank top.

She grabbed her skirt and top from the chair next to the bed and slipped them on. Her panties were toast, and she didn't even know where they were anyway.

Rand watched her dress.

"I like knowing you're naked under that skirt," he said, walking toward her and pulling her into his arms. He lifted her skirt and palmed her buttocks, slipping his fingers between them to tease her pussy lips. "I want to be able to play with you at will."

Her nipples rose and puckered against the stretchy fabric, alerting him to her state of arousal. He smiled down at her, fully aware of her reaction to his touch.

"I also like that you cream when I touch you. It's like this instant gush of fluid down there."

"Are you trying to embarrass me?"

He arched a brow. "Embarrass? No. I'm trying to get you to loosen up. I intend to have you this weekend, Blair. Whenever and wherever. You're going to relinquish complete control to me and learn to love it. Get used to it."

He smoothed her skirt over her buttocks, patted her ass, and walked out of the room.

Humph. Whenever and wherever, like she was some cheap whore he'd hired to be at his beck and call. She'd see about that. She was no man's plaything and especially not Rand's. And while she might thoroughly enjoy fucking him, this mind game he was playing with her wasn't going to work. She was here on a bet, and that was it.

"Blair! Come on outside," he hollered. "And bring us a bottle of red wine when you do."

She rolled her eyes, but stopped in the kitchen on her way out the back door into his yard, slipping her sandals on before she went.

He had two steaks on the grill, along with vegetables on skewers and potatoes in foil. She handed him the bottle of red wine, which he opened and set aside to breathe for a moment.

"Anything you need me to do?" she asked.

"Yeah. Sit down and relax. You look tense," he said, grinning at her.

Rascal bounded over for a pat on the head and a scratching of the ears. Blair busied herself playing with the dog while Rand cooked. It was very . . . domestic and made her squirm uncomfortably.

Sunset had breached the dense treetops on Rand's property, obliterating the opressive heat a little. It was still going to be a warm night, with hardly a breeze to offer relief. She watched Rand as he cooked, picturing him in the expansive yard with a couple kids, more dogs, and a lot of noise. A few swing sets, toys all over, maybe a swimming pool and a hot tub.

All he needed was a woman to share it with.

Not that she was that woman.

Nope, not her. That kind of life wasn't her deal at all. She was forever single, happy and carefree. The whole fantasy of family and kids and acreage and a ranch house like Rand owned was someone else's dream, not hers.

Someday he'd find a nice, sweet woman to settle down with and give him that dream.

So why did the thought make her stomach hurt?

And why did she picture herself in the middle of this backyard, up to her waist in the pool, and laughing with kids or wrestling with dogs?

It wasn't her! She was a forever-single vixen, a career woman in charge of her own destiny, in utter control of her own life. And nowhere in that life was there a ranch house, a couple of kids, a dog, and a swimming pool.

"You're doing it again."

She looked up to find Rand sliding a plate in front of her.

"Doing what?"

He slid into the chair next to her and poured a glass of wine for each of them. "You're lost in thought. What were you thinking about?"

Attributing the flush on her face to the heat outside, she grabbed a napkin and faced the plate of food that had suddenly lost its appeal. "Nothing."

"Secrets again." He started to eat but studied her, talking in between mouthfuls. "Maybe I'll just try to guess."

Never in a million years would he figure it out.

"Aren't you wondering what I'm going to do with you after dinner?"

"No."

"You should." He slanted her a sly smile and resumed eating.

And she started thinking while she ate. What *was* he going to do with her after dinner? By the time they finished eating and cleared away the dishes, she had imagined several scenarios. Thank God he didn't have any chandeliers in his house.

"Figure it out yet?" he asked as they loaded the last of the dishes into the dishwasher.

Again, more domestic stuff. Comfortable things that she found easy and relaxing doing with him. It gave her the willies. She'd never done dishes with a man before.

"Figure what out?"

"What the plan is?"

"No. But I assume you're going to tell me eventually, so I see no point in wasting brain cells trying to decipher what's going on in your warped mind."

He threw his head back and laughed, then refilled their wine-glasses and led them out onto the front porch. "Warped, huh?"

The breeze was better out here, the sun finally having set. They sat in a white wooden porch swing. Swaying gently back and forth with him pushing off with his feet, she relaxed and curled her feet up under her and sipped her wine, staring out at the clear night.

Out here in the country, the stars were clearly visible, something she never got to see in the crowded, brightly lit city.

"You're lulling me into a false sense of security," she said.

"Huh?"

"This is just weird." She didn't know how else to explain it. "Wicked sex, then dinner, wine, and now swinging on the front porch? What the hell is up with this scenario, Rand? Let's just get on with it."

He finished his wine and set it on the small table next to the swing. "You got a timetable or something?"

Yes. I need to get the hell out of here before I start enjoying myself too much. "No."

"Then chill, Blair. Quit being in such a hurry. We have all night. You even had a nap. Let your stomach settle a little bit and just enjoy the night."

She'd hardly eaten a thing, so there wasn't much to settle. She was as anxious and as unsettled as she could be. Anxiety skittered along her nerve endings. She wasn't relaxed at all, despite the few glasses of wine she'd consumed. Thoughts of barbecues, backyards, swimming pools, and kids had screwed with her head. She needed to get through this weekend of wild debauchery with one thought in mind: fucking. Wicked fucking with Rand and fulfilling the terms of the bet. That was it.

Sex, sex, and more sex. Now, that she could handle. And then obliterate it from her memories forever. Come Monday, her relationship with Rand would go back to the way it had been for the past fifteen years: antagonistic and distant.

He slipped his arm behind her and toyed with her hair, massaging her scalp, gently pulling at the tendrils.

Damn, she loved when a man played with her hair. It gave her goose bumps, turned her on. Her nipples hardened. She tilted her head into his hand for more. When her pulled a little harder, she shuddered, annoyed when her clit tingled.

She was putty in his hands, damn him. He knew all the right buttons to push.

He wound her hair around his fist and tugged, drawing her neck back, then pressed his lips against her throat. Her pulse pounded, her heart slamming against her chest. Whatever cool breeze she'd felt had evaporated under the assault of heat burning her from the inside out. He scorched a trail along her neck and jaw, then captured her mouth in a fiery kiss that exploded when he parted her lips and slid his tongue inside.

Slow and easy, velvety strokes along her tongue, he explored the inner recesses of her mouth like he had all night to do this. And still, he held onto her hair, holding her head, mastering her. She thrilled to his control, the way he guided his tongue along hers, first gentle, then more insistent, pressing his lips more firmly against hers. He moved his body over hers, skimming her waist with his free hand and sliding his fingers under her shirt, lifting it over her breasts. He bent down and took her nipple between his teeth, nibbling light and easy. She clenched her teeth and lifted her hips in response, wanting him to do the same thing to her clit. There was enough light to watch him lick and bite her nipples, to see the way his tongue rolled over them, making them stand up, wet with his saliva, exposed to the air and begging for more attention.

She shivered, but she sure as hell wasn't cold. It was the way he looked at her when he lifted his head, the hunger and passion she saw reflected in his eyes. He kept his gaze focused on hers while he popped the button on his jeans and drew the zipper down, drawing his cock out. He fisted it, stroking it, making her mouth water for a taste.

"Suck me, Blair."

Still holding onto her hair, he pushed her head toward his lap. Eager to take his cock in her mouth, she enveloped the head between her lips, licking at the fine drops of fluid gathered there, rewarded by his groan of delight.

He might think he was in control, but in this she was the master. She flicked her tongue over the crest, then suctioned her mouth around him, sliding downward, inch by agonizing inch. He surged upward, feeding her, digging his fingers in her hair again as he moaned his pleasure and leaned back against the swing.

She dug her nails into his denim-clad thighs, her pussy wet with her own desire and eager to impale herself on his cock. A wicked hunger consumed her, a need to pleasure him, to drag him with her to heights of unbearable need.

"Oh, yeah," he murmured. "Take it deep, Blair. Swallow it."

She no longer wanted to defy him. What was the point, when giving him pleasure would only heighten her own? He pushed forward, and she took him deep, all the way to her throat, swallowing him, constricting around him until he lifted off the swing and dug his fingers into her hair, pulling her off his cock.

"Goddamn!" he said, jerking her head back and pulling her upright. He covered her mouth with his and ravaged it, fucking her mouth with his tongue. Hard and insistent, with a ravaging passion that left her lips bruised, her pussy swelling and aching with the need to be filled.

She whimpered against his mouth, and he pulled his lips away, dragging her astride him, facing him.

"Fuck me," he commanded.

She thrilled to the harsh tone in his voice and impaled herself on his cock, tilting her head back and moaning at the sheer pleasure of being filled with his thick shaft.

"Yes," she murmured, grasping his shoulders and lifting, then sank down on him, driving him balls deep into her pussy.

She established the rhythm, riding him with slow strokes, every brush of her clit against his pelvis like a shock of lightning to her cunt.

"I like you like this. Fucking you with your clothes on. It's nasty. I like you a little nasty, Blair. Fuck me harder."

She complied, lifting and slamming down hard against him.

"Yeah, drop down on my balls. Goddamn, that's good."

He grabbed her buttocks and began to raise her up and down over his shaft. She lifted her skirt so she could watch the movements of his cock in and out of her pussy.

"Touch your clit for me, baby. Make yourself come."

She reached between her legs and massaged her clit, knowing he had a perfect view of his cock disappearing between her pussy lips, of her hand rubbing her clit.

"Damn, that's pretty," he said, his gaze glued to that spot where they were joined.

His cock swelled, her contractions growing stronger as she gripped him in a tight vise that signaled she was close. She strummed her clit faster, racing toward her climax, watching his eyes darken, his lips part as he panted with her.

"I'm going to come," she whispered, her breath sawing out of her lungs in painful bursts. She arched her back and ground her pussy against him.

His eyes were a dark storm, his lips parted, his half-lidded gaze so goddamn sexy she couldn't stand it.

"Come on my cock, Blair. Milk the come out of me and take me with you."

She gripped his shoulder with one hand and furiously rubbed her clit as the sensations seared her insides. Then it came, a sizzling peak that made her scream. She held onto his gaze as she came, felt him erupt at the same time, thrusting and jerking against her as he shot a hot load of come in her.

They rocked the swing in a wild arc as they rode out their orgasms, then crashed together. Blair fell forward and clasped onto Rand's shoulder, shuddering as the aftershocks of her orgasm continued to rock through her. He stroked her hair, her back, his motions gentling as they came down from the fury.

Nestled in his embrace like this, Blair realized she had never felt more herself with a man than she did with Rand.

And that scared her more than any relationship she'd ever run from.

He scooped her up and carried her into the bedroom, undressed her, and pulled her against him. His cock was still hard.

He didn't speak to her, just slid his cock inside her and stroked her, slowly, without words, making sweet, gentle love to her. He caressed her breasts, kissed the nape of her neck, his hands wandering everywhere on her body, finally settling at her clit.

It was slow and unhurried, as if he had all the time and patience in the world.

She didn't even think she could come again, and when she did, it was a surprise, her cries of completion a sweet surprise as she flew into a climax that left her shaking and near tears.

He didn't even come this time, just left his cock inside her and rocked against her for awhile, holding her, his cock finally softening until he stopped moving. Always holding her, touching her, kissing her.

It was the sweetest damn moment she'd ever experienced.

She'd loved Rand McKay for fifteen years. Tonight had only made it worse. Her heart was breaking in two.

She had to get out of here in the morning.

the sun peeked in through the half-open shades. Rascal was barking at something. It was time to get up.

Rand searched for Blair's warmth, figuring a few more minutes wouldn't hurt.

He reached across the bed, but she wasn't there.

Yawning, he slid out of bed and peeked in the bathroom. No sign of her.

He went into the kitchen. She wasn't there either.

By the time he walked out the front door, his suspicions were confirmed. Her car wasn't there.

Blair was gone.

Irritation boiled within him. Goddamn it. He stormed into his bedroom and jammed his legs into his jeans, started coffee, and fed Rascal, then tapped his fingers on the counter, waiting for the coffee, to finish.

By the time he'd downed a couple cups of the strong brew, he was awake enough that his anger had passed. And he wasn't at all surprised that Blair had hightailed it out of there. He understood her better than she understood herself.

Blair was afraid of what happened between them, because she enjoyed it. He'd cracked her shell. He knew it, and she knew it.

If she didn't care, she'd have stayed. And that was a good thing. It meant she did care. She'd taken the first step and come to him after all these years. What they'd shared had been special, and he wasn't about to lose her.

Now he just had to figure out what to do next.

He looked around the kitchen, picked up his coffee, and walked into the living room, smiling as the thought occurred to him.

He had a plan. A perfect plan.

six

blair blew out a breath and headed to the table where Abby and Callie awaited her. The two of them were practically squirming in their seats, anticipatory grins plastered to their faces as she approached.

Honest to God. She wished she'd never started this stupid bet.

"Well?" Callie asked before Blair had even planted her butt to the seat in the booth at Torinos.

Blair signaled the waitress for a margarita and grabbed a chip from the basket in front of her. "Well what?"

"Don't play coy with us," Abby said, her eyes sparkling with excitement. "You know what. Tell us."

"It was fine." She bit into the chip and started chewing.

"Fine?" Callie looked at Abby and back at Blair. "You can do better than that. We want details."

The waitress set a margarita in front of Blair. She took a couple long sips for encouragement, then said, "I went to his place. I fucked his brains out. Rinse, repeat. I went home."

Abby frowned. "And?"

"And what?"

"That's it?"

"That's it."

"There's gotta be more, honey," Callie said. "You are a fountain of sexual information. We usually hear in graphic detail about every conquest. You *never* clam up like this."

Dammit. "Fine. It was hot. Beyond hot. It was the best sex I've ever had. Are you happy now?" She grabbed a handful of chips and stuffed her mouth to keep from saying any more.

"Dayum. I knew it," Callie said.

"He was fabulous, wasn't he?" Abby asked.

"Yeah," she managed with a mouthful of chips.

"So did you stay the weekend with him?"

She polished off the margarita. "No. I went home after one night."

Callie's eyes widened. "Why?"

Blair shrugged.

"You'd better start talking, or I'm going to call Rand for the details," Abby threatened.

Blair's head shot up. "Don't you dare!"

"Then tell us what the hell happened! Because if you don't, I swear to God I will go to Rand and get his side of the story."

Blair gaped at Abby. She'd never known her friend to be so fierce before. And she really did need to talk this out, and who better to listen than her two best friends? If she couldn't trust them, who could she trust?

"Okay, but not here. I can't talk about this here."

"My place," Callie said, grabbing her purse and signaling the waitress for the check.

An hour later they were settled in Callie's living room, shoes off and comfortable with a pitcher of homemade margaritas and salty snacks spreads out all over the coffee table. Abby and Callie stared at her expectantly.

She'd never told anyone about her secret desires before, not even her two friends. It was now or never, though, and she needed counsel.

"Y'all probably aren't going to believe this, because I've always been the domineering and controlling type, but in the bedroom I'm a complete and total submissive."

"Tell me something I don't know," Callie said with a soft smile.

Blair's jaw dropped. "You knew?"

"I did. Don't know about Abby."

Abby shook her head, her eyes wide. "Color me clueless. You? Submissive? I had no idea."

Okay, that wasn't as bad as she thought it was going to be. She looked at Callie. "How did you know?"

"A few things you've said over the years. Plus I know Rand, I know his type. He's totally dominant. And he melts your butter in a big way."

Her pussy clenched just thinking about all the ways. "That he does."

"Now that much I did know," Abby said. "So why aren't you still over there?"

"Because he scares me. And my reaction to him scares me."

"Why?" Callie asked, leaning back against the sofa.

Blair tucked her feet under her and focused on her margarita glass, feeling ashamed for what she was about to admit. "I watched my father control every movement my mother made. How much money she spent. Who her friends were, where she spent her time. She couldn't even go the grocery store without him timing her and then accusing her of cheating on him. And no matter what she did it wasn't good enough. She didn't get up on time, she didn't walk right, she didn't dress right. By the time I was old enough to move out on my own she was nothing more than a robot following his commands. She lived a miserable existence her entire life because of a domineering man. She had no backbone, no self-esteem, and not enough self-worth to walk out on him. He tried to do the same thing to me, but I bucked him every chance I could, refusing to allow him to bend me to his will.

"I vowed I would never, ever fall in love with a man like that, that I would never involve myself with a strong-willed, controlling, domineering man."

The room grew silent, and Blair was afraid to look at Abby and Callie, afraid they'd judge her mother's failings and somehow find her lacking, too.

Instead, her two friends flanked her on either side of the sofa, and she was sandwiched between them in a fierce hug that made her eyes sting with tears.

"You aren't responsible for your father's behavior or your mother's lack of a spine," Callie said after she pulled back and looked at her.

Tears shined in Callie's amber eyes. And sadness.

"Don't cry for my mother. She was weak. I'm not."

"I know you're not."

Abby squeezed her hand. "And Rand is nothing like your father."

Blair nodded. "The logical part of me knows that. The emotional part of me runs like hell every time he comes near me and always has. It's what kept me from him all these years, what has drawn me to wimpy men instead of the alpha, take-charge man like Rand is."

She shuddered her next breath. "I've loved Rand McKay since I became aware of the sexual differences between men and women. He's funny, honorable, intelligent, gentle, and has a core strength that turns my knees to jelly. I knew then what he was, and what I was. I knew he could give me what I needed. Because I am sexually submissive. In every other aspect of my life I'm strong, capable, in control. In the bedroom I like to submit. And it scares me that if I surrender to him there, he might want me to surrender everywhere else. I just . . . can't."

"Have you told him about your fears?" Callie asked.

She shook her head. "No."

"You should."

"I won't take that chance. I know it's cowardly of me, but I can't risk losing my soul to a man who'll want to dominate every breath I take."

"You can trust him," Abby said. "I feel it in my heart. He's one of the good guys. And I think he's been waiting for you his whole life."

She inhaled, fear making her tremble. "That scares me, too. That I can't be what he wants me to be."

"I've never seen you this way," Callie said. "You're one of the strongest women I know. Nothing scares you."

"This does. He does. How I feel about him does. Everything about the two of us together scares me. I can't be with him."

"So you're going to walk away rather than figuring out if you and Rand could work together," Abby said.

Blair looked at her and nodded. "Yes."

"You might be walking away from the greatest love of your life."

A sharp, knifelike pain twisted in her belly. "I might."

She had a feeling she already had.

"we have a new client."

Blair looked up from her desk in her office and smiled at her assistant, Mary. "That's great."

"Maybe it is, and maybe it isn't." Mary worried her bottom lip and clutched the piece of paper in her hand.

"Let me see it."

"You're not going to like this."

Blair rolled her eyes. Her interior decorating business was her baby, her life's blood. She lived for new clients. She held out her hand. "Hand it over, Mary."

Mary slid the paper across Blair's desk. Blair scanned the request, then frowned.

What the hell was he thinking? Another game, another way to manipulate her? Oh, no. This was not going to happen. "Assign it to Sue Ellen."

"He specifically requested you do the work."

"I see that. I'm not doing it. I'm too busy."

"Your calendar is clear. And it's a big job. He said the entire house."

"I don't care. I'm not doing it."

"He said you either do the job or no deal."

She shrugged and turned to her computer. "Then I guess it's no deal."

"We can't afford to turn away business, Blair."

Dammit, she was right. Goddamn Rand for backing her into a corner like this. Exactly the reason she would never explore a relationship with him.

Manipulation, pure and simple. Just like her father. It was all about control.

She tapped her fingers on the desk and contemplated. The project was huge and would infuse some needed capital into the business. She really couldn't afford to turn it down, but she hated to submit to Rand's ultimatum.

"Fine. I'll do it. Notify Rand I'll meet him at his place tonight at seven o'clock."

Mary let out a breath. "Great! This is going to be a killer project. I'm so glad you changed your mind, Blair. It's going to be wonderful for business!"

And devastating in so many other ways.

rand leaned against the porch pillar and watched Blair pull up in the driveway. Rascal bounded out to greet her, barking and wagging his tail.

He knew the feeling. His pulse jacked up just looking at her as she slid out of her car wearing a tight pink skirt with a matching short jacket. Her sunglasses masked her eyes, but the grim set to her lips told him she wasn't happy to be there.

Not that he expected her to be. In fact, he'd wager she was downright pissed about his ultimatum.

"Blair," he said as she walked up the stairs.

"Rand."

"Thanks for coming."

"Uh-huh. Shall we get started?"

"Sure." He opened the screen door for her, and she stepped inside, her back stiff and straight.

Oh yeah. She was mad as a swatted hornet. He grinned.

"You indicated you wanted the entire house redone?" she asked, glancing around the room and jotting notes on a clipboard.

"Yeah."

"I'll make a few notes and be right back. I assume it's all right if I move around your house."

"You've been here already, Blair. I don't have a problem with you wandering around anywhere you want to."

"Take a seat then," she said, not even looking at him. "I'll be right back."

He flopped on the couch and propped his feet on the coffee table while she roamed from the living room to the small dining area and into the four bedrooms. He wondered if she remembered what they did in the bedroom the other night.

He sure as hell did. Couldn't sleep the past couple nights either. Laid awake jacking off, her scent clinging to his sheets and pillowcases.

Goddamit, he wanted her in his bed again. And not just for one night or two, either. He wanted forever. God, he could imagine how she'd react if he told her that. But he knew her fears, and he had to handle this delicately. If he pushed too hard, he'd lose her. So he had to play this cool. Very cool.

He picked up an auto magazine and flipped through it while she wandered through the house, then set it down when she returned, noticing she sat in the chair next to the sofa. Keeping her distance, was she?

Flipping the paper over in her clipboard, she cast him a direct look. "I assume you have specific ideas on redesign."

"Not really."

Her perfectly sculpted brows arched upward. "Excuse me?"

He leaned back and placed his arms over the back of the couch. "I have no clue."

"Then how am I supposed to redesign the interior of your home?"

"That's your area of expertise, Blair. I'm a lawman, not a designer."

"But this is your house."

"I trust your judgment."

"I could turn your entire house into a pink, frilly nightmare."

He laughed. "You could. But you won't. You're too ethical for that."

She sighed. "You're right. How am I supposed to know what you want, Rand?"

"It's easy. You know me. And this place is a mix and mess of furniture that doesn't match. Other than a couple antiques that belonged to my grandparents, everything goes. I want to settle down, raise a family someday, so all I'm looking for is something functional."

"Really."

She tapped her pen against the clipboard. He fought back a smile. "Yeah. Really."

"So you want to redecorate to parade the prospective brides around in something a little fancier than what you have now."

Oh, she was getting pissed. He wished he could laugh. "Not fancy. I'm a simple man. I just want it nice."

"Define *nice*."

He loved the way her bottom lip twitched when she was annoyed. He wanted to grab it with his teeth and pull her against him. His cock ached. Damn, he wanted her in the worst way. But he wasn't going to have her. Not tonight, anyway. "Decorate it in a way that would please you if you lived here."

"Fine. I'll make sure the litany of brides-to-be approve."

"Great."

"You'll need to move out for a couple weeks."

"I can stay down at the jail. There's a bedroom and shower there."

She stood and smoothed her skirt, pulling a sheet off the clipboard. "I'll need you to list and tag the items that are staying. Someone from my office will call you in the morning to notify you what day we'll start."

"I hope it'll be soon?"

She pursed her lips and studied him. "Have a candidate in mind for Mrs. McKay already?"

"You might say that."

She had trouble disguising her surprise at his comment. "I'll do my best to hurry things along for you, then. Wouldn't want to keep the impending bride waiting."

"Thanks. I appreciate it."

With a sharp inhale through her nose, since her lips were cemented shut in a tight line, she scooped up her things and stalked to the front door, practically pushing the screen off its hinges as she slammed through it on her way out.

Oh yeah. She was damn mad now.

He had her right where he wanted her. Furious, jealous, and confused.

God, he loved her.

redecorate. parade of brides-to-be. blair drummed her fingernails on her desk and tore through her catalogs, wishing she could redecorate Rand's house like a sultan's harem. Jewel-colored pillows, hanging swags, draping silks in every color of the rainbow. It would serve him right if she did.

Too bad she had professional scruples.

Asshole. Prick. Degenerate. Dickhead. She hated him. Hated, hated, hated him. With a passion that made her blood boil.

How dare he be so nice, so professional, so accommodating.

So utterly and completely unpredictable. She'd fully expected him to have a detailed outline of every piece of furniture he wanted and where, every color, every fabric, allowing her no leeway whatsoever. Instead, he blew her away by telling her to do whatever she wanted.

Her father had allowed her to redecorate one room in their house once. Right after she'd graduated from college. She'd made suggestions, but nothing she'd offered had been good enough for him. He'd changed everything. And his choices had been hideous, but of course he had to have control. Her mother hadn't said a word. So typical. Blair hadn't bothered to argue with him. It was his dime, after all. He'd wanted Early American ugly, and that's what he'd gotten. The colors were dark, not a feminine touch at all. And it was their master bedroom. By the time Blair had finished, there had been nothing left of her mother in that bedroom.

Except her mother.

And her mom had pronounced it just lovely, had praised Blair for her work and told her father that his taste was wonderful.

Sickening.

But Rand, instead of doing what Blair's father had done, had just given her free rein over his entire house. Had told her to decorate it the way she would if she lived there.

Except she wasn't going to be decorating it for herself. She was going to be decorating it for some other woman. He'd just fucked her, while he was obviously already entertaining the idea of marrying someone else.

Son of a bitch. How could she have let her heart get involved in one night of glorious fucking? Because it sure as hell hurt at the thought of Rand marrying another woman, of some other woman having that backyard with those kids and dogs and that swimming pool.

Stupid fantasies, anyway. It had been a bet. And she'd done her part and fulfilled it. Now it was over. She and Rand were over.

And when she finished this project, she never had to think about him, see him, or speak to him again.

But she would do a good job on his house. She would design it as if she was the woman who was going to move in there, as if she was the woman who was going to have his children and create a life with him.

She'd show him he could trust her with his faith in her.

Because she was a professional who was damn good at her job.

Not because she cared about him.

seven

the house turned out perfect. blair's stomach squeezed with both excited anticipation and bittersweet regret. She could live in this house, could be comfortable and happy here.

It was gorgeous, a place she would consider every woman's dream, yet a house a man could enjoy living in.

And Rand was due any minute. She cruised through every room to make sure nothing was out of place, then ran to the front porch when she heard him drive up, her stomach twisting in knots.

She was never nervous about presenting her finished product to clients, but she was today. Nevertheless, she smoothed her skirt and presented a calm, professional demeanor, leaning against the door as he came up the stairs.

And tried not to drool as he hooked his thumbs in the belt loops of his jeans and stopped at the front step, resting his hip against the porch railing, whistling.

She'd done the front porch, too. Not much, of course, but enough that he'd notice. Or she'd hoped he'd notice. She'd left the porch swing, because she really liked that. Added extra-wide wicker chairs with cushions, a few hanging plants with colorful blooms, and a couple cement floor plant stands that greeted him as he walked up the stairs. They'd painted the porch, too, so it gleamed a bright white now.

"Damn. This is nice," he said, tilting his head back and resting his palm against the butt of his pistol in his hip holster.

"It just brightens up the front porch a little."

Her throat had gone completely dry. She hoped he couldn't tell she was shaking. Honestly, why was she so nervous?

"I'll take you on a tour of your new place, if you're interested," she said with a casual shrug.

"Sure. I can't wait to see it."

Rand didn't know who was more nervous, him or Blair. She might be trying her best to hide it, but he saw it in the furtive glances she threw his way while she acted nonchalant and shrugged her way into a near fit.

For two damn weeks he'd been cooling his heels at his office, dying to sneak out here and see what she was doing, but holding true to his word and staying away. It took enormous willpower and lots of jacking off.

He missed her. Missed being around her, missed her scent, her smile, even missed annoying her. He really liked annoying her. He liked her riled up and angry, all miffed at him with righteous anger. Her face glowed when she was pissed off, her eyes sparkling with passion.

He missed touching her. Kissing her. Fucking her.

His cock ached for her.

His heart ached for her.

He was a fucking mess. He hoped to God this worked.

"If there's anything you don't like," she started, blocking the door before he could enter, "we'll of course fix it."

"Let me inside, Blair," he said softly. "I'm sure it's fine."

"I don't want it to be fine. I want you to love it."

Now there was a revelation. And as soon as the words spilled from her lips, he could tell from her wide-eyed look that she regretted saying them.

"I already love it. It has your touch."

"Whatever. The whole team worked on it, not just me." She moved out of his way, and he stepped inside.

Wow. It was a completely different house. Gone was the threadbare old furniture that didn't match. Everything was gone. And nothing looked the same. Yet the minute he walked in he felt . . . comfortable.

It wasn't stuffy or pretentious or, God forbid, too girly. Yet it wasn't overly masculine, either. Neutral-colored fabric couches sat perpendicular to the fireplace along with a couple really comfortable-looking thick leather chairs with ottomans. The rest of the living room was bare save for a couple pale wood tables next to the furniture to place drinks and magazines on. The lamps were modern but not funky. The room was practical and useful, yet cozy enough for a woman to enjoy, with a nice rug in front of all the furniture. He could envision kids with toys spread out on that rug enjoying a fire in the winter while he and Blair read the paper and drank coffee.

He walked into the kitchen and found his grandmother's old trestle table, which had been refinished. It still retained its old charm, still held the old nicks and scratches, just looked . . . better. Not as old and beat-up and junky. Now it really looked antique, but kind of cool.

"There were no chairs with this table, so I . . . the staff scouted a few sales and found several that closely matched," she said.

Six chairs, to be exact. And they didn't match perfectly. Which he loved, because his grandma's chairs hadn't matched, either. Hell, he didn't remember where they'd all gone to. Relatives' homes here and there, no doubt. But he liked that the sturdy wood chairs didn't look brand-new; they blended in with the rest of the kitchen.

The cabinetry was pine. Sturdy, dark to match Grandma's table. The countertops had been replaced in a dark granite that was cool as hell, the sink changed to a double one in a shiny chrome. It was modern yet old at the same time. It looked like a country kitchen, but any woman would squeal with delight to cook in there, with its huge refrigerator and double open and island stove.

He was speechless. And damned impressed with Blair's talent.

"If you'll follow me down the hall," Blair said, "I'll show you the bedrooms."

He knew he hadn't said a word yet, that Blair was probably going crazy with worry, but honest to God he didn't quite know what to say.

"We left three of the rooms undecorated at your request, assuming you'll want to someday make them into nurseries and children's rooms," she said, her voice ending on a squeak. She had to clear her throat as she moved down the hall.

He smiled at that. "Uh-huh."

"Now for the master bedroom." She half-turned to him as she pushed the door to his bedroom open, then moved out of his way as she flipped on the light. "I hope you like it."

There could be a cardboard box and a towel on the floor. As long as Blair was in there with him, he'd like it.

It didn't have a cardboard box. Instead, the iron bed had a scrolling pattern at the headboard and footboard. Flowers and hearts that a woman would find appealing. What he liked was the matching iron canopy. Strong and sturdy construction, too. His imagination soared into overdrive, imagining Blair trussed up in a standing position, her wrists tied to the top of the iron canopy, her legs bound and spread, her pussy at mouth height.

Goddamn. Fixated on that bed, he didn't even notice what else was in the room, though he was certain it was nice. Fuck, he didn't care.

"Did you want to see the rest of the room?"

"No." He stared at the bed.

"Um, does it meet with your approval?"

He turned to her, not even bothering to hide his erection, now straining hot and thick against the zipper of his jeans. "Does it meet with yours?"

She hinted at a smile. "Of course it does. I designed it."

"Good. Undress."

"Excuse me?"

"You heard me. Take your clothes off."

Her look went from shock to anger in an instant. "Are you out of your mind?"

"No."

"Look, Rand, I agreed to this job because it's good for business. You wanted your place redesigned, fine. I did it. You haven't even said whether you like it or not. Well, the job is done. Whoever you plan to marry is going to love it. You know it, and I know it. I'm leaving. You'll get my final bill in the mail. Our association is finished."

"Our association isn't finished by a long shot, Blair."

Her gaze narrowed. "You are so goddamned arrogant! How dare you assume that just because we've had this lurking sexual tension between us, just because we had one night of really hot sex, that I'm going to strip and fuck you because you order me to, then be content while you carry some other woman over the threshold of the house I designed for her!"

She pivoted, but before she could walk away, he said, "You're that woman, Blair."

She stalled, then turned back to him. "What?"

"You're the woman I want to carry through the front door. White dress and all. You're the woman I wanted this house redesigned for. You're the woman I've loved and wanted since we were fifteen years old and you started teasing me. You're the woman I love, Blair. I always have."

Blair had never in her entire life been at a loss for words. Always a snappy comeback, a sharp retort, she was a master at putting men in their places.

Rand had left her speechless for the first time in her life.

"You love me?"

"Yes. I love you." He approached her, his body lithe and taut, his cock unashamedly rigid against his jeans. And then he did something that brought tears to her eyes. He dropped down to one knee in front of her. This dominant, infuriating, alpha male went to his knees.

"Marry me, Blair. I love you. I love your strength, your intelligence and sense of humor. I love the life you've built for yourself despite where you came from—and yes, I know all about where you came from."

"You do?"

"Yeah. I'm not your father, and you're nothing like your mother. You are one kick-ass career woman who takes shit from no man."

She smiled at that. It was the best compliment he could have ever given her.

"I don't want to rule your life, baby. I wouldn't love the woman you've become if you were my doormat. I love that you stand up to me and give back whatever I dole out." He reached for her hand. "I want you in this house with me. I want you in this bed with me every night, fulfilling both our fantasies. Then I want to have babies and build a future together."

She'd been wrong. Oh so wrong about everything. She'd judged Rand unfairly for years, comparing him to her father. Yes, he was dominant and arrogant and self-assured and controlling. But he was nothing like her father. Nothing at all.

He wanted her to be an independent, take-charge woman in every aspect of her life except one. The one place where she wanted him to control her, where she wanted, needed his dominance.

Sexually.

"I don't know what to say."

He grinned. "Say what you feel."

She shuddered a breath. "I've been scared of you my whole life. Because of my dad, and what he did to my mom. I knew what kind of man you were, and I swore I'd never be the kind of woman my mother was."

Tired of looking down at him, she dropped to the ground and sat. Rand sat with her and cradled her hands in his.

"Go on," he said.

"After my first few sexual experiences, I came away empty. I deliberately chose guys I could control, because I was afraid to be with someone who was too dominant. The men I chose left me unfulfilled, though, and I knew then I was a sexual submissive, that I wanted to be dominated in the bedroom."

"Bet that really scared you, given your family history."

She nodded. "But I was determined to stay away from men who were like my father. And I lumped you in that category. You were strong, self-sufficient, arrogant, and powerful. I couldn't control you. You made my heart thump like a wild beast in my chest, and you made my toes curl. You made my panties wet whenever you walked by or talked to me. For years it was you I fantasized about when I masturbated. With every man I fucked it was your face in my mind, your hands all over me."

Part of her couldn't believe she'd just admitted that to him. The other part of her felt free and unafraid that she had. Because she knew Rand wouldn't use it against her, wouldn't think her weak because of it.

"That's hot, babe," he said, reaching out to caress her neck. "Thank you."

Her skin flushed at his touch, her nipples tight and achy.

She finally drew a deep breath and spilled her dark secret. "I've loved you from the first time my heart knew what love was, but it scared the shit out of me, Rand. I've never wanted a man more than I've wanted you. All these years, all those guys, all I ever really wanted was you. The only man I've ever surrendered to was you." Her body, her soul, and her heart. She'd just handed it all to him. And as she did, she realized that she wasn't afraid anymore.

Her heart swelled with the love she'd been too afraid to show him.

"I love you, Rand." She pushed to her knees and hitched up her skirt, then straddled his lap. Winding her arms around his neck, she smiled at him, her heart swelling so much she felt it might burst through her chest. So this was love. Giddy, disgustingly sweet. She didn't care how stupid it was. She felt fabulous. "I love you."

He slid his hands around her waist and pulled her against him. "Does this mean your answer is yes?"

She waited for the inevitable clutch of fear, the urge to run. It didn't come rushing toward her. The path before her was clear for the first time in her life.

"Yes. Oh, hell, yes, I'll marry you." She leaned in and pressed her lips to his, breathing in his scent, tasting the coffee and peppermint on his lips before she slid her tongue inside his mouth to claim him as her man. Hers. Forever.

She was now a one-man woman. Maybe she always had been.

He scooped his hands under her butt and stood, lifting her and placing her on her feet.

"Now, Ms. Newcastle," he said with a stern voice and an arched brow, "I believe I said something about you stripping."

She shivered at his authoritative tone, more than ready to do whatever he wanted. No barriers this time, no fear. She belonged to him and was his to command. But she could also tease him a little while doing his bidding. First she made painfully slow work of shrugging out of her jacket, folding it ever so neatly before turning to place it on the chair of the vanity across from the bed. When she turned back to him, she smiled.

"Don't be all day about it, Blair."

"These are very expensive clothes, Rand. I have to be careful with them." She undid the buttons on her blouse. One by one. Slow and easy, keeping eye contact with him. Watching every breath he took, the way his nostrils flared, the way his gaze moved down the row of buttons with her fingers. The heat of his eyes singed every inch of skin as she undressed for him. Taking this much time to remove her clothes was excruciating. She wanted to rip them off and get naked so he would touch her. But she wanted to tease him, to make him anticipate.

Or maybe she just wanted to dare him to take her. So far he was showing amazing restraint as she finished the last button on her blouse and spread it apart, letting it slide off her shoulders and skim down her arms. It floated to the floor. She left her bra alone and reached for the side button of her skirt.

"You're not moving fast enough. How expensive is that skirt?"

"Oh. Very."

In a flash he had her in his arms. The button on her skirt went flying, the zipper tearing as he lost the last of his restraint. She gasped as he made short work of yanking the skirt down and ripping her panties off.

"I'll replace it."

Like she cared.

He held her against his chest and with one hand reached behind her to undo the clasp on her bra, then stepped back, drawing the straps down her arms as he did. His gaze roamed over her naked flesh, her body reacting in the same way it would as if he touched her. Her lips parted, and she fought for air as she tried to anticipate what he had in store for her.

"Let's try out this new bed," he said, drawing her hand in his and motioning her to the bed with the other. "Get up there and put your hands on the canopy."

She knew he'd like that part of the bed. He held her hand while she climbed onto the mattress, then grasped the top rail of the canopy. Oh, she'd measured everything, made sure she could comfortably reach the top rail. Not that she expected to ever have the pleasure of using it, but she knew Rand's desires and figured some woman would.

Yeah. Her. She was that woman. Standing on her bed, gripping her canopy. She shivered in anticipation as she looked down at Rand.

He removed his gun holster, unbuckled his belt, slipping it through the loops of his jeans and holding it in the palm of his hands. She smiled down at him, wondering if he'd spank her with it.

Did she want him to? She grabbed her bottom lip with her teeth and watched intently as he laid the belt on the chair in the corner between the nightstand and dresser.

"No, baby," he said as he turned back to her. "If I smack that fine ass of yours, it's going to be with my hand. I want to feel your skin heat up with every swat."

She inhaled sharply and kept her thoughts to herself, watching as he peeled his shirt off, revealing his bronzed chest, then went to work on his jeans. Like her, he tormented her with a slow revelation of his golden body. Impatient, she wanted him to hurry and undress. But he took his damn sweet time, flipping the button open on his jeans, then drawing the zipper down, pausing to look up at her as his knuckles brushed his hard-on.

God, that was hot. She wanted to touch him, to undress him, to unveil his cock and engulf it with her mouth. She swallowed and stayed silent, her palms beginning to sweat as she held onto the canopy rail.

"Good girl," he said, shucking his jeans to the floor and casting them aside. He walked toward the bed, and she tensed, every part of her taut and ready for his touch.

"Spread your legs."

The extra-firm mattress made it easy to stand on. She gripped the top of the canopy and widened her stance, wanting to make sure he saw everything between her legs he wanted to see.

"Now, that's a goddamn picture," he said, tilting his head to study her. "I'd love to have a photograph of you like this. Do you have any idea how beautiful you are?"

She always felt beautiful when he looked at her. Her skin flushed from his perusal, her nipples thrusting forward, eager for his mouth to capture each one. Moisture gathered between her pussy lips, a quivering excitement pulsing at her clit.

Please, please touch me.

Like a mind reader, he reached between her legs, teasing her inner thighs with the tips of his fingers, keeping his gaze focused on her face.

When she designed the bed, she knew her height, and his, and configured the entire setup so that if she were standing on this bed and he standing on the floor, his mouth would be at the right level to her—

"Oh, my." Yes, that was absolutely perfect.

He'd grasped her buttocks and drew her pussy against his mouth, his tongue swirling over her needy clit. She wanted to thread her fingers into his hair, to pull him even closer, but she held onto the bar of the canopy and thrust her hips against his face, feeding him.

He pulled away and looked up at her. "You like this?"

"Yes."

"Then let me hear you."

She'd never been very verbal before. Then again, what man before Rand had given her reason to be?

He looked at her and snaked his tongue out to swirl around her clit, lifting her legs off the bed and onto his shoulders. He ate her pussy this way, his mouth clamping down on her clit to suck at it, hard.

"Oh, God, Rand! Yes!" she cried, not even realizing she'd said the words aloud until he hummed his satisfaction against her sex, which only served to drive her arousal up another notch. The heat and wetness of his mouth coupled with his tongue flicking madly around her clit, his chin fucking her pussy, saliva dripping down the crack of her ass—it was too much. She came, bucking wildly against him and screaming, glad he lived out in the middle of nowhere, because she sure as hell would have brought any nearby neighbors running in their direction with her loud wails.

But damn, she couldn't help it. The climax racked her from the inside out, crashing waves of intense contractions that curled her toes and left her shattered and shaking.

"Let go, baby," he whispered.

She did, collapsing onto her knees and drawing in gulps of air to settle herself. Rand crawled onto the bed and grasped her hands, rubbing them to restart her circulation.

"I'm fine."

"I'll say," he teased, then let go of her hands to thread his fingers in her hair. He drew her into a kiss, sliding his tongue in her mouth. The kiss was raw, passionate, his tongue diving, his lips demanding and needy.

He pushed her back onto the bed, moving them onto the center of the mattress and covering her body with his. She welcomed his possession, entwining her legs with his, arching to meet his cock. He slid inside her with one quick thrust, making her gasp with the sweet invasion.

Rand pulled back to look at her, unable to quite believe yet that Blair was his, that she'd agreed to marry him, to live here with him. Her pussy pulsed around him, milking him with tight contractions.

"Baby," he murmured against her throat, closing his eyes and living just in this moment in time. He reared back and surged against her, burying deep, needing these few seconds of just bonding with her.

She tangled her fingers in his hair and raised her hips, wrapping her legs around him to draw him closer. "Rand," she whispered back. "I love you."

For as long as he lived he'd never tire of hearing those words whispered from her lips. He never realized how much he wanted to possess her until she said yes. Now, he vowed to give her everything she wanted.

Especially here, where she'd been denied pleasure for so long.

He gripped her wrists and raised them over her head, holding them together with one hand while he raised himself off her, staring at her breasts, watching the nipples pucker under his gaze.

"You hot for me, baby?" he asked.

"Yes."

"Tell me what you want."

"Lick my nipples," she whispered.

"Like this?" He bent down and glided his tongue over one taut peak, feeling her shudder underneath him, her pussy gripping his cock in wild spasms.

"Yes," she said.

"Or like this?" He surrounded the bud with his teeth and tugged, then flicked it with his tongue, finally capturing the entire nipple and sucking it into the heat of his mouth.

"Rand!" She pulled at his hair, hard, writhing underneath him. He surged forward, pumping his cock faster as he nipped and bit and licked at her other nipple until her cream poured from her cunt.

When he looked up at her again, her eyes were glassy, unfocused, as if she were drugged or dazed. She was panting, lifting her hips, and raking her nails along his shoulders and upper back as he powered his cock hard inside her.

His woman was out of control.

Just where he wanted her. Right at the peak and ready to explode. Her pussy gripped him so hard he could barely pull away from her, but he did, withdrawing and pulling her off the bed for a moment. He threw the coverlet to the end of the bed, then pushed her forward again.

"On your hands and knees, Blair."

As she crawled onto the bed, he stood at the side and watched her, her pussy wide open, dripping wet, and ready for his invasion.

Oh, he wanted back in there, but he wanted something else, too. That tiny puckered hole above her pussy beckoned to him. He'd possessed her, but not completely. And he had to have her completely.

"I'm going to take some of that ass today, Blair. You ready for it?"

eight

was there anything she wouldn't allow rand to have? She doubted it. Now, on her hands and knees, her pussy and ass spread out before him, the thought of him fucking her tight back door only excited her even more. His cock spearing her there, taking possession of her in a way no man ever had—she wanted to reach between her legs and rub her clit to orgasm right now just thinking about him filling her ass with his thick cock.

"Yes, Rand, I'm ready for it."

She'd give him anything and everything he wanted.

"You ever let a man in your ass?"

The tight strain in his voice only fueled her own excitement. "No, Rand."

He stood at the side of the bed while she was on her hands and knees, her feet dangling over the side. He touched her legs, massaging her calves as he smoothed his hands up her thighs, then caressed her buttocks before delivering a very light swat to her ass.

"How come no man ever fucked that tight ass, baby?"

She shrugged. "Didn't want them to."

"But you're gonna let me, aren't you?"

"Yes."

"You ever fuck yourself in the ass with a toy or something?"

God, his questions. They both embarrassed and inflamed her with the need to come. "Yes, I have."

He smacked her ass again, the sting making her undulate against his hand. He caressed her butt cheek, the smooth movements of his hand the exact opposite of the hard swat of a few seconds ago. When he slid his fingers in her cunt, she pushed back against them, needing his cock to fill her pussy again.

"Tell me about it," he said, withdrawing his fingers and replacing them with his cock. He slammed into her cunt, hard. She threw her head back and moaned, then ground her ass against his pelvis.

"I sometimes fuck myself with my fingers and stick a dildo in my ass," she admitted, wondering if he'd accept all her wicked thoughts.

"Goddamn," he whispered. "And what are you fantasizing about when you do that?"

"Two men taking me."

He smacked her ass, and she moaned.

"Do you want to be double-fucked, baby?"

Animal urges coursed inside her, the need to really let loose with Rand like she'd never done with a man before. "No. But I sure as hell like thinking about it when I'm getting off."

"Stay put."

Like she'd even think about going anywhere. He withdrew and went into the bathroom. She craned her neck to see what he was doing. He returned shortly with a bottle of lubricant and a towel.

"Turn around and look straight ahead," he ordered. "And spread your legs wider. I want to see that ass."

She shivered, her clit throbbing. Oh, she wanted to touch it, to rub it until she came. The need was so strong, but she waited, knowing Rand wanted to control their play. The tension was sweet and torturous as she wondered what he was going to do and when. Not being able to watch him heightened the experience.

She felt the slow trickle of something warm along her ass. The lubricant. He dripped it down her asshole, then rubbed her anus with the tip of his finger. She couldn't help it, she whimpered. The nerve endings there were so sensitive. She'd often played with her own anus while she masturbated, but oh, it was nothing like having Rand touch her there.

"Sweet little ass," he murmured, sliding his finger past the tight-muscled barrier, penetrating her until white-hot sensation gripped her. She squeezed, feeling the ripple of ecstasy all the way to her clit. When he thrust his cock into her pussy and buried his finger in her ass, she about died, grunting in pleasure.

"Rand," was all she could say in response to the sensation of being filled with his cock, of having his finger in her ass.

"Tight. So tight," he said, withdrawing his finger a little, only to slide it back in until he was buried to the last knuckle. "Can you take my cock in there, Blair?"

"Yes."

"Tell me you want it, baby."

She pushed against his finger, against his cock. "Fuck my ass, Rand. Hurry."

He removed his finger, pouring more lubricant against her anus. She lifted her ass, anticipating, needing his invasion.

"You ready for me?"

"Yes," she said, her voice so breathless it didn't even sound like her own. "Please."

"Oh I like it when you beg for my cock, baby."

She felt the thick head probing at her anus, the initial push so tight it made her wonder if he'd fit inside her tight channel.

"This is going to hurt. I'm big."

"I know. Fuck me."

He smoothed his hand over her buttocks as he pushed his way in. Slow and gentle, despite her eager attempts to get him to shove hard and quick. It burned. It hurt. It was glorious, filling her with thick cock, invading her where no man had been.

Blair felt like a virgin, giving something to Rand that she'd given to no man before. His gentle strokes along her back and buttocks were so sweet they brought tears to her eyes.

But then he pushed, hard, shoving inside her and burying himself to the hilt.

"God," he said. "So tight."

She heard him suck in a breath, then he withdrew and pushed forward again.

"You okay?"

The pain subsided, replaced only with a heady pleasure, a need to come while he rode her ass, a need to feel him possess her completely. "I'm fine. Fuck me hard."

He groaned. "Touch your pussy for me, Blair. Make yourself come."

Finally. She reached between her legs and thrummed her clit, the nub distended and aching with building pressure. With every stroke of her fingers, the vortex swirled around her in blinding sensation, tightening, taking her closer to climax.

Rand picked up the pace, powering harder with each stroke, his balls slapping her pussy as he fucked her ass. He gripped her hips, his fingers digging into her flesh as he gave it to her hard now.

"I'm going to come in your ass, Blair. Hard and hot. You ready for me?"

Her fingers moved faster over her clit, so close she could barely speak. She moaned, ground her ass against him, and cried out, shaking all over as she came. She felt the contractions in her ass, gripping, milking his cock as she rode wave after wave of an incredible climax while Rand shuddered and tensed against her, then spent hot jets of come inside her.

He leaned over and moved her hair out of the way, kissing the damp tendrils at the back of her neck while she gasped underneath him, trying to catch her breath. He snaked an arm around her middle to support her. God, her arms were shaking.

"Shower?" he whispered in her ear.

She laughed. "Great idea."

He lifted her off the bed and carried her into the bathroom, depositing her into the shower. She'd had that remodeled to, with multiple jets on three sides. They had some fun with that after Rand had washed her from head to toe, playing for a long time and shooting each other with water before finally shutting it off.

He dried her with a large towel, then carried her to bed, ordering her to stay put while he took off down the hall.

He'd been gone awhile, and Blair wondered where he'd gone. Finally, he returned, balancing a tray with two glasses of iced tea and strawberries and chocolate syrup. She sat up in bed and smoothed the covers down while he set the tray in the center of the bed between them.

"Oh, yummy. I love strawberries." She started to grab one, but he lightly tapped her hand.

"Uh-uh. Let me." He picked one up, dipped it in the chocolate sauce, and slid it between her lips. She licked the chocolate off, then bit down, enjoying the sweet flavor bursting in her mouth.

"Oh. That's heaven."

Rand leaned forward and brushed his lips across hers, sliding his tongue to lick along hers. Her stomach tumbled in warmth and renewed desire.

"You taste sweet."

"You're the bedroom dominant. Shouldn't I be feeding you?" she asked when he fed her another bite.

He shook his head. "Doesn't work that way. At least not in my mind. I'm an equal opportunity kind of guy. You'll be doing enough servicing of me in the bedroom," he said with a wicked gleam.

"Devil."

"Wicked woman."

He popped another strawberry in her mouth, then followed it up with a kiss. She sighed in utter contentment and smiled at the man she loved.

If only she'd known what she'd been missing all these years, she'd have given up control a long time ago.

wanton

CALLIE

one

jack fellows was hot. hot, hot, hot. dayum hot.

And totally and completely out of Callie Jameson's league. Not even on the same planet.

She sighed as she poured a coffee refill for one of her regular customers, offering up the famous Jameson smile. Her coffee shop was her livelihood, her life's blood. She loved this place, had started with nothing and now had a decent, if modest, business going. And that's what she needed to concentrate on.

Not fantasizing about sex with a guy she saw once a day Monday through Friday. She served him coffee, they exchanged a couple sentences, and that was it.

In the business world, he was executive and she was service. And never the twain shall meet. Especially in the bedroom.

"Mornin' gorgeous," Jack said as he stepped up to the counter.

Thank God her skin was dark enough to hide the blush. Really, how old was she, anyway? She should be long past the blushing stage. "Mornin' yourself, Jack. The usual?"

He arched a dark brow and studied the menu. "I think I'm in the mood for something different today."

How about a nice coffee-shop owner, widow, under thirty-five, hasn't had sex in far too long, and extremely needy. God, she was pathetic. Like Mr. White Bread Executive would ever in a million years entertain the idea. "Take your time. Looks like you're the end of my morning rush."

He did a quick pivot to look behind him, then turned back to her. "Guess I'm running late this morning. Had a long night at the office finishing up some business."

So did she. Wrapping up inventory. She cleaned the counters while she waited. Oh, she could have easily walked away and had one of the other girls wait on Jack. But hell, a woman had to have one thrill out of a routine day, didn't she?

"How about a black-and-white this morning?"

She couldn't help it. She snorted. Talk about hitting the mark. "Sure. Coming right up." Black-and-white. Good God.

"You think I made a bad choice?" he asked.

She propped her arms up on the high countertop. "I think you made a fantastic choice, Jack."

He paid, she gave him the change, and stepped to the other end of the counter to hand him the coffee.

"It's going to be hot today," he said.

Hell, she was already hot, though it had nothing to do with the weather and more to do with the six foot four, tanned, chiseled centerfold man in front of her. What she wouldn't give to see him out of his impeccable business suit. She bet he dressed down just fine. Worn jeans, sleeveless shirts showing off broad shoulders and bulging biceps. Her mouth watered, and her pussy clenched. Too bad she couldn't masturbate at work. But tonight at home, Jack would be the man of her dreams. Then again, he often was. If only he knew how often she came thinking about fucking him, about climbing onto his dick and riding him until they both got off.

Yeah, it was going to be hot today, all right.

"I heard we had a big heat wave coming. Guess I'll be hanging out by the pool at the country club today," she replied with a wink.

"Now you're teasing me."

"You're so perceptive, Jack."

"Anytime you want to lounge by the pool at the country club, you just give me a holler. I'll be happy to take you."

Then he shocked the hell out of her by pulling out his business card and a pen, jotting a number on the back, and sliding it across the counter. "I'd love to take a dip with you sometime, Callie. Or anywhere else for that matter. Why don't you give me a call if you're interested, and we can plan something?"

Speechless, she stared down at the card and back up at him.

"Have a good one, Callie." He turned and walked toward the door, nodding at Blair, who just happened to be walking in at that moment. Blair did a complete turnaround before heading toward the counter, then took one look at Callie's expression and arched a brow.

"You can close your mouth now, Callie."

Callie blinked, stared down at the business card Jack had left, and pocketed it. "What are you doing here?"

Blair batted her lashes at Callie. "Nice to see you, too."

"Sorry. I didn't mean it that way."

"And I'm here because I have a client meeting downtown, and I want coffee, darlin'. Why else would I be here? But now that I am, tell me who that gorgeous hunk of dick on two legs was?"

"Jack Fellows." She stared out the door.

"Who is he? How well do you know him, and how come you've never told Abby or me about him before?"

"He works around here," Callie said, trying to shake off Jack's mesmerizing effect. "Comes in for coffee every morning. Don't know him other than as a client. And that's why I've never told you or Abby about him. There's nothing to tell."

"Uh-huh." Blair tapped the counter with her fingernails and pursed her lips.

"Don't even think about it. There's nothing going on between Jack and me."

"He sure had a helluva grin when he walked out of here."

Callie shrugged and walked out from behind the counter with two cups of coffee, handing one to Blair and motioning her to a booth near the window at the front of the shop. "He always smiles."

"Not like that. That was an *I've got a date with a hot woman* smile."

"Oh, it was not." She thought about the business card in her pocket, about Jack's suggestion to take her to the country club pool. Was he serious? The club? Her? And him? That had to be some mistake. She replayed the conversation over in her mind, certain she had just heard him wrong.

"So, does he?"

Callie frowned. "Does he what?"

"Have a date with a hot woman."

"I dunno. He might. But it's not with me."

"Dammit. Why not?"

She laughed at Blair's consternation. "Because. We're not at all the same type."

"Type my ass. You were drooling all over the counter, Cal. I know the look of a woman in lust. You've got it bad for this Jack Fellows."

"Do not. He's a customer. He's good-looking. I can appreciate a fine-looking man, can't I?"

Blair studied her. "Of course you can, honey." She took a quick glance at her watch and an equally fast gulp of her coffee. "And you're damn lucky I have an appointment. We still on for lunch tomorrow?"

"You bet. I want details on you and Rand."

Blair stood and grabbed her purse, then bent down and kissed Callie's cheek. "And you'll get them. Have I got things to tell you and Abby. Later, babe."

News from Blair about Rand, huh? Callie finished her coffee, then went back to work, her mind filled with Blair and Rand and trying not to think about Jack and the business card tucked into her pocket. It wasn't until after she closed up shop and went home and started to undress that she remembered the card.

She pulled it out of her pocket and read the front. Attorney for one of the top law firms in Silverwood. Impressive. And now she knew they were like oil and water. He was big money and country clubs. She was modest middle class and mortgaged to the hilt, struggling to keep her business afloat.

If it hadn't been for the life insurance on her late husband, Bobby, she wouldn't even have the shop. She smiled at the thought of Bobby. The years had dimmed the fresh pain of his loss, leaving only bittersweet memories. While she fixed a sandwich and ate it, she remembered the good times, the plans they'd made for their future.

Plans that had stalled when Bobby was diagnosed with cancer. Plans that had evaporated when the cancer spread and took him so damn fast. One minute they'd been hit by the diagnosis. Six months later, he was gone.

Too fast. Too soon. Much too soon.

God, those first few months she hadn't wanted to live without him, didn't think she could survive without the love of her life. They'd been together since high school, bound for marriage and forever. Everyone had known it. She and Bobby had known it from day one. It was the sweetest love ever. They had been friends from the moment they met until the moment he died.

And even now, she felt like his light still shined down on her, leading the way.

He'd told her those last few weeks that he wanted her to live on, not to pine away for him forever. To find another man to make her happy. At the time she hadn't wanted to listen to such nonsense. Bobby was her love, her soul mate, her best friend. Whenever he was near, there was warmth. Maybe not passion, but always contentment. And that had been more than good enough for her. She couldn't imagine any other man fulfilling her the way her husband had.

Now five years had passed. Five long years without companionship, without a man in her life.

Without sex.

She missed sex, missed cuddling up afterward. Masturbation got her off, but it wasn't the same. She needed a cock inside her. A hot, living cock attached to a real man. Her pussy clenched as she thought of what it would feel like to have a man moving on top of her, his strong body thrusting in and out of her cunt, his lips claiming hers, his tongue sweeping inside her mouth. A rush of heat enveloped her and she stood, walking to her front window for a little air.

It was hot, hardly any breeze. She stepped outside on the porch and sat on the chair. No moon tonight. No activity in the neighborhood either.

Her body pulsed with need and she closed her eyes, wishing for Jack to step up on her porch and grab her, plant his mouth on hers, and fuck her right there. A tingle of excitement curled her toes and shot between her legs, moistening her pussy.

She shouldn't. She really shouldn't. But the thrill of the forbidden had always been her downfall. She stood and ran inside, shutting off the light in the living room so the porch would be dark, then returned to her outside chair. She'd tossed on an old sundress after work. The street was empty. It was late. No one else was outside. She could do this fast and no one would see her. Maybe no one would see her, but what if they did? The thought sent a rush of tingling pleasure to her clit.

She spread her legs and moved her hands to her thighs, letting them rest there for a few seconds while she contemplated. Anticipation, the excitement of knowing she was going to do it, but not just yet. Her fingertips brushed the hem of her sundress, then she began to pull it toward her hips, a fraction of an inch at a time. Though it was hot outside, the air hitting her skin was like a shock to her heated body, driving her arousal. Sweat pooled between her breasts, her lips parting and her breathing labored as she realized she could get caught.

Someone could drive by and see her. A neighbor could look out their window and possibly catch a glimpse of her lifting her dress.

How exciting!

Soon, her panties were visible. But oh, she wanted more. She lifted her hips and pulled her panties down to her thighs, revealing her pussy. She was panting now, her pussy throbbing. She knew she would come fast once she touched it. But she was waiting. This was the naughty part, the wanton, forbidden, nasty part of herself that even Bobby hadn't known about.

She slid her hand over her belly, bunching the skirt of her dress in her fist before forcing herself to relax. Her heart pounded, whether from excitement or the possibility of someone catching her in the act she wasn't sure. Now she was past the point of caring. Let them come to the porch, line up, and watch. She wanted an audience.

"See me touch myself," she whispered to the darkness. "Watch me make myself come."

She reached between her legs, finding the curls damp, loving the silken softness of her own pubic hair. She toyed with the curls before moving farther down, knowing she had held back as long as she could. She lifted her hips and plunged two fingers inside her sopping-wet cunt, biting back the moan that escaped her lips as she drove her palm against her clit, undulating against the exquisite sensations that she knew would send her over the edge all too quickly.

"Fuck me," she whispered to her imaginary lover. "Fuck me hard and fast."

There, outside and in the darkness where anyone could poten-tially see her, she fucked her pussy with her fingers. The street was so quiet she could hear the sounds of her fingers thrusting in and out of her wet pussy, could hear the harsh intake of her breath, the moans she couldn't quite hold back as she tormented herself with re-lentless strokes. Her palm slid back and forth over her swollen clit, making her lift her hips to meet her own hand.

"I'm going to come," she whispered, eyes widening as the pulses shot through her. She gritted her teeth to hold back the screams, wave after wave of unbearable pleasure crashing over her. She gripped the arm of the chair and shook with violent tremors, bury-ing her fingers in her cunt until the storm subsided.

When it was over, she withdrew her fingers, pulled up her pant-ies, and smoothed her skirt over her thighs, looking out over the street and shaking her head.

She stayed in the chair and caught her breath, feeling like she'd just woken from some kind of bizarre dream. It was like she lost touch with reality. What if someone had come by? Would she have been able to stop? Or would she have sat there, her fingers buried in her pussy, continuing to strum her clit to orgasm?

Shaking off her thoughts, she rose and went inside, locked the door, and shut the curtains, hoping like hell no one had seen her de-viant behavior.

"Honest, Callie, what the hell is wrong with you?"

She was such a pervert.

jack closed his briefcase and clicked off the light on his desk at his home office, then rubbed his tired eyes. What a goddamn long day. He glanced at the clock and rolled his eyes.

After eleven. He'd left work at eight tonight, come straight home after a short side trip to the fast-food drive-through, headed straight for his desk, and continued to work. God, he needed a few days off. A week or two would be even better. Making partner was supposed to be less grueling, not more. But the work continued to pile on with no apparent letup. Weren't the grunts the ones who were supposed to put in these long hours? He stretched and leaned back in his chair, swiveling around to take a look at the swimming pool at the club across the street.

He'd been lucky to get this house. On the golf course, right near the clubhouse and pool. He smiled as he stared at the pool, remembering his invitation to Callie this morning. She'd looked so surprised, her warm amber eyes widening in shock. But why? Surely a woman as beautiful as her was deluged by offers. He was probably just one of a handful of men hitting on her.

Okay, maybe he wasn't hitting on her, but he sure as hell liked stopping for coffee every morning and seeing her. Her soft, honeyed voice and welcoming smile were a calm in the storm of his life. And it didn't hurt that she was gorgeous, either. Fashion model beautiful, with skin the color of light caramel, curly black hair, and those unusual, mesmerizing eyes. Most days he wanted to linger, to ask her to step around the counter and sit with him just so he could get to know her better. Instead, he was always in a rush, but those few minutes he spent talking to her were the best part of his day.

He knew they were flirting, noticed the way her gaze lingered on him when she thought he wasn't looking. A guy couldn't miss a beautiful woman watching him. If he hadn't been so damned busy these past few months, he'd have asked her out sooner. She even moved outside the counter sometimes when he took the time to sit at one of the tables and read the paper before he headed into the office. She'd clean the tables and pick up a few things, giving him a chance to watch her.

She made his dick hard, with her curvy body and sweet, rounded ass. Even in her loose-fitting coffee shop uniform he could tell she had a body he wanted to get his hands on. A real body, not the waify, ghostly women that frequented his normal social circles. Callie was all woman, and he wanted her in the worst way. He just needed to take that first step by asking her out, like today by mentioning the invitation to the pool.

Actually, he still hadn't asked her out. He'd tossed his business card and phone number at her as if he'd expected her to do the calling.

"Dumb ass," he whispered to himself. "Should have asked for her number. Some gentleman you are."

He wanted her. Wanted to see her outside the coffee shop. He needed a life besides working fifteen hours a day. It was time to redirect some of his projects to the associates and work on his social life.

It was time to go after Callie.

two

"engaged! oh, my god, blair!" callie leaped from the sofa and threw her arms around her friend.

"I can't believe it!" Abby said, doing the same.

They enveloped Blair in a huge group hug.

"It's true," Blair said, blinking back tears and laughing. "I can hardly believe it myself, but Rand and I are getting married."

After the squealing celebration, they settled back in the living room at Callie's house, and Blair filled them in on the details of what transpired between her and Rand. By the time she was finished, Callie had tears in her eyes.

"That man really loves you, Blair. I think he always has."

Blair grinned. "Yeah, he does. And I love him, too. God, it's so incredible to be able to say that about someone. For the first time in my life, I'm in love."

"Took you long enough," Abby said.

"Yeah, yeah, I know. I'm a little stubborn."

Callie laughed. "A little?"

"Okay, a lot. But that's in the past now. Rand and I are moving forward at a fast clip and making up for all the years of lost time."

Callie grasped Blair's hand and squeezed. "I'm glad. You deserve this."

"Thank you. So do you. Which brings up the topic of our luncheon today."

Callie swallowed. "Uh-oh. It's my turn, isn't it?"

Abby grinned. "Yep. Sure is."

"Okay, ladies, what have you got for me?" Callie leaned back in the chair, not sure whether she was eager or terrified. Since she didn't date and hadn't since Bobby died, she had no idea who Blair and Abby had chosen for her. Maybe they wouldn't be able to find a guy for her at all, and she'd escape having to fulfill her part of the bet.

Yeah, right. Like her two friends would let that happen. No way would she get out of her sex-filled weekend. They'd find someone for her, of that she was certain.

"Blair has a great idea," Abby said, pulling her knees up to her chest and grinning.

"Uh-oh. Am I going to like this?"

"Probably not," Blair said, examining one of her perfectly manicured nails. "But you're going to do it anyway."

Callie sighed. "Okay, hit me with it. Who's the guy?"

"Jack Fellows."

Callie's blood went cold. "No."

Blair's lips curled in a wicked smile. "Oh, yes."

"I don't even know him."

"Sure you do. Blair says he's a regular at the coffee shop."

"For coffee, not for me." Callie gripped the arms of the chair. "I honestly don't know much about him."

"Well, I do," Blair said. "I took the liberty of doing a little investigating. He works at Walters and Little, one of the biggest law firms in Silverwood. He's a partner and very close to making senior part-ner. A real go-getter and hasn't lost a case yet. He bought a house last year at Silverwood Lakes, is a member of the club, and on the board of directors."

"Do you know what color underwear he wears? Boxers or briefs?" Callie asked. "God, Blair, what don't you know about him?"

"Not sure on the underwear, but given enough time and a little skulking, bet I could find out." Blair grinned.

"You know Blair," Abby said, rolling her eyes at Callie. "She knows how to get information."

"I'll say." Callie had to admit, she was impressed with what Blair managed to find out about Jack. She was also a little embarrassed that Blair had gone digging. It was like an invasion of privacy.

"It's all public record, if you're worried," Blair said. "He's written up in the society section of the paper a lot."

"Oh." That, at least, made her feel a little better about what she'd discovered.

"Now, for this weekend, the country club is sponsoring a benefit dinner and dance for the new hospital. Since Jack's on the board, he'll be there. And so will you."

"Me? I don't go to the country club."

"This weekend you will. Seth got us all tickets," Abby said.

Callie looked at Abby and Blair, not sure what to say. Jack? She was supposed to fuck Jack? How would she even introduce the topic? They exchanged pleasantries at the coffee shop, and that was it.

Then she remembered his business card and his invitation. Maybe there was something there, some interest on his part. He did seem to flirt with her a lot, but she thought he was just being nice. Jack was rich, successful, a powerful man in the community. What would he want with her?

"Well?" Blair asked.

Callie shrugged. *Why not?* "I'll go. We'll see what happens. I don't think he'll even give me the time of day, especially at the club and at an event like that. The socialites will be hanging on him in droves."

Abby laughed. "Those skinny little bitches have nothing on you, honey. With that body and your sultry, exotic looks, you'll stand out like Cinderella at the ball. One look at you, and no other woman will exist in Jack's eyes."

"Abby's right," Blair said. "Especially after we take you shopping for a new dress, new shoes, get your hair and makeup done, ooh la la. His dick will be hard and pointing straight at you."

Callie couldn't help it. She laughed at the thought. "Uh-huh. We'll see, ladies, we'll see."

But she did like the idea of looking attractive for Jack, of thinking she might be able to catch his eye outside the coffee shop. Maybe he wouldn't even recognize her without her uniform and apron. She smiled at the thought of dusty, dirt-smudged Cinderella being transformed for the ball.

Oh, sure. Like that was going to happen. She might wear a dress and wear her hair up, but she'd still be the same old Callie. And if he didn't take the bait, it wasn't her fault, right? She wouldn't be any worse off than she was now, living alone in her house and enjoying her fantasies.

Nothing ventured, nothing gained.

At least they had a fun night planned for Saturday. Better than staying home and watching television.

spending saturday night at a charity ball wasn't exactly Jack's idea of a good time. Nevertheless, it was for a good cause, and it was his duty. He hated wearing a tux, though, would much rather be in shorts and a sleeveless shirt, or even better, lounging by the pool outside and enjoying a swim instead of stuck in an air-conditioned ballroom with three hundred other people.

Good cause, remember? Money. Auction. Fund-raiser. That's why he was here. It was only one night, and besides, at least there was an open bar. Which was right where he was headed, for a cold bottle of beer. He smiled at the bartender, slid a tip in the jar, and took a long, cold swallow before turning around and surveying the packed ballroom.

And cringed as two women, dressed to the nines, slinked their way toward him with perfect smiles plastered on their faces.

Kimberly Blaise and Virginia Marquette. Socialites. Social-climingettes. One brunette, the other blonde, though he doubted the hair color was original. Or anything else about their bodies. They'd wanted in his pants, or more appropriately, in his wallet, ever since he made partner at the firm. Them and several other single women at the club. Membership must come with a list of eligible bachelors and their financial statements. He plastered on a polite smile.

"Evening, ladies."

"Jack," Kimberly purred. "You look good enough to eat."

Obvious much? "You look lovely tonight, Kim. You, too, Ginny."

"Thank you, darling," Virginia said, placing her palm over his chest. "You will be saving a few dances for us tonight, now won't you?"

Not if he could help it. "Uh, sure."

"Are you two already monopolizing Jack?"

Charlotte Daniels. Great. He felt like he'd just stepped on a beehive. God save him. Fortunately, they were all so busy jockeying for position they didn't even notice he wasn't paying any attention to them. Which meant he could survey the crowd, think about his next case, sports, whatever.

His gaze caught a group who'd just walked in the door. Recognition struck when he spotted a dark-haired, golden-skinned gorgeous woman in a bronze strapless dress that showed off the color of her skin to perfection.

Something was familiar about her, but he couldn't quite figure it out. Not until she and her group moved closer, under the lights.

And she smiled.

Holy shit! It was Callie. Her hair was down around her shoulders, riotous curls all over the place, framing her beautiful face. And her smile lit up the entire room. Her gaze flitted around like she was looking for someone. She was with two other women who seemed to be escorted, but so far she didn't seem to be with anyone. Maybe she was meeting her date here.

Just his luck.

"Jack? Jack, are you listening to me?"

At the whiny pitch of Charlotte's voice, he turned his attention back to the group of women surrounding him. Listening to them? Hell, no, he hadn't been listening to them. He'd been mesmerized the moment smokin' Cinderella had walked into the ball. "Uh, please excuse me, ladies. I have some business to attend to."

Date or no date, he could at least be polite and say hello.

"Jack! Where are you headed in a such a hurry?"

"Jack. You haven't even stopped to see me yet."

Christ. Two more of Silverwood's socialites. Was he on radar or something? He glanced around their overly coiffed heads to see if he could track Callie, but he'd lost sight of her.

Dammit!

callie craned her neck around the room, knowing she shouldn't be looking for Jack but unable to help herself. At least she wasn't here alone, hadn't been tossed in the front door by her friends and left to fend for herself. They were here, too, along with their men. Abby had brought Seth Jacobs, and Blair had brought Rand McKay.

It was so strange seeing her two best friends paired up, happy as could be with the men they loved. Satisfying as hell to see them both so settled, but still strange.

And she was alone. Not that it bothered her. She was used to it. Okay, maybe she felt a twinge of jealousy that she was here alone, but it passed just as fast as it hit her. Especially after Blair and Abby went to all the trouble to take her shopping and helped her pick out this incredible dress that she absolutely could not afford, that Blair had insisted on paying for, and Abby had done her hair in wildly loose curls, even though Callie had vehemently denied having anything but disgusting tight, kinky curls.

She had to admit, when they were finished putting her together, she looked like one hot babe. The bronze dress complemented her coloring perfectly, bringing out her skin tone and making her eyes flash.

Yeah, she looked hot tonight, all right. But next to all the women here dressed in designer clothes, their bodies perfect, their hair perfect, their social graces perfect, she felt less than, well, perfect.

She was educated and owned her own business, a respected member of the community. She owned a home in a nice neighborhood, paid her taxes, and led an ordinary life. Okay, so she had a few private perversions, but no one knew about those. Other than that, she was normal. Average.

The people here were all wealthy, from high society, and didn't run in the same circles as she did. They were the blue bloods of Silverwood and she was just . . . average.

That word again. Nothing to make her stand heads above the rest of the women.

She spotted a group of them circling a man in the center of the dance floor.

Her heart thudded as she realized who that man was.

Jack. Looking spectacular in a tux, as if he'd been born to dress so fine. If she thought he'd look edible dressed down, he was even more so dressed up.

And surrounded by some of the most beautiful women she'd ever seen. Well-endowed, designer-clothed, made-up to perfection, these women looked like they could step out of a limo and onto the red carpet at any awards show and act like they belonged there.

Dayum.

Not a chance she'd ever get close to Jack tonight. She might look better than she'd ever looked before, but would Jack even notice her? Would she even get to talk to him?

"This place is packed," she whispered over Blair's shoulder as they arrived at their table and grabbed chairs.

Blair nodded and turned to her. "You're still the most beautiful woman in the room."

Callie snorted. "Please. You in your red dress and those shoes I wouldn't dare wear. And Abby with that tight, skimpy little black number. Girl, the two of you put me to shame."

"Honey, I'd kill for your skin," Abby said next to her. "That sweet honey color. So perfect. If I wasn't heterosexual, I'd be all over you."

Callie tilted her head back and laughed.

Seth leaned across Abby and said, "If you two are planning some girl-on-girl action, I'm sure Rand and I would love to watch."

"Seth!" Abby said, feigning shock, but she was laughing, too.

Rand leaned past Blair on the other side. "It'll take me less than a half hour to go buy a video camera."

"Asshole," Blair said, shaking her head. But her lips curled upward. "Men are such pigs."

"That's why you love us," Rand said, kissing her neck.

Blair giggled.

Callie was so damn happy for both her friends. Someday she'd find that kind of happiness again.

Maybe.

"So, where's the hot guy you're supposed to meet up with tonight?" Rand asked. "Hope you get as lucky in your bet as Blair did with hers."

Callie gasped. "You told him?"

Blair shrugged. "Of course I did. Abby told Seth."

"I feel so used," Rand drawled. "I hope she uses me again like that."

"Me, too," Seth said. "Nothing like being used as a sex object by a gorgeous woman. You ladies should write a book about it. I'm sure more research will be required."

Callie shook her head. "Honestly. What men won't do to get laid."

"Well, now, that's an interesting topic."

Oh, God. Jack. Callie scrunched her eyes closed, not sure if she ever wanted to turn around. But she did. She stood and turned, her heart stopping at her first close-up look at a tux-clad Jack, who looked utterly delectable in black and white. His tanned skin against the white collar made her mouth water.

"Jack! What a surprise to see you here."

"I hope I'm not interrupting," he said, taking her hand between both of his. "I thought I spotted you from across the room and wanted to say hello."

"I'm glad you did. Please, let me introduce you to my friends."

She made the introductions, then invited Jack to sit with them, certain he'd beg off so he could hang with the collection of beauties currently shooting daggers in her direction. Much to her surprise, he pulled up the chair Blair vacated by scooting over.

"I'd love to join you," he said, sliding his beer onto the white-clothed table.

"Are you sure? It looks like there's a horde of angry women over there."

Jack looked over his shoulder. "Oh. Them. They're just interested in marrying my wallet. The single Silverwood socialites are out in force tonight and looking for any eligible bachelor."

Callie smiled. "Well, that would be you, wouldn't it?"

"Yeah, but I'm not interested in them. You look gorgeous."

How could he not be interested in them? But she beamed under his praise. "Thank you. A lot more made up than my typical coffee shop look."

"I don't know. You look beautiful there, too."

Holy shit, he was good at this complimenting thing. She hadn't had a man pay attention to her in far too long. And such a fine-looking man like Jack, too. Was she drooling? This was just unreal. He was sitting at their table, signaling the waiter to bring a bottle of champagne, chatting away with Rand and Seth as if they were old friends, and charming the panties right off Blair and Abby.

He'd already charmed her panties off. Had been doing that daily for the past year and a half, even though they'd never had a deep discussion about . . . well, anything, actually. She knew virtually nothing about this man, other than he was tan, with blue eyes, and had the chiseled features of an aristocrat. He was tall, athletic, with broad shoulders that she longed to run her hands over, and she'd wager he was solid muscle underneath that luxurious tux.

She knew where he worked and that he was a partner in a law firm, but she didn't even know what type of legal field he worked in.

"What kind of law do you practice?" she asked. They were alone at the table, since Abby and Seth were off mingling and Blair and Rand were raiding the hors d'oeuvres table.

"Corporate, mainly. Our clients are some of the biggest companies here in Silverwood, as well as throughout the state of Oklahoma and in Texas, Colorado, Kansas, and we're branching out into Louisiana, Missouri, and Illinois."

She raised her brows. "Impressive. So, you're growing."

He nodded. "Yeah, opening up a few branch offices in some of the other states."

"Any chance you'll be relocating?" She hoped not.

"No way. I'm firmly entrenched here."

"Good." Dammit, why did she say that?

"Well, thanks for the compliment, darlin'. I'd miss seeing you every morning, too."

"You'd just miss my coffee."

"I don't go there for the coffee, Callie."

He'd casually rested his arm over the back of her chair, the heat from his body transferring to hers, warming her from her toes to the top of her head.

"You don't?"

"No. I go there to see you."

"You do?" *Brilliant conversationalist, Cal.*

"Yeah. I do. Thought you'd figured that out by now."

Well, color her utterly clueless. She had no idea. What planet had she been living on?

"So am I seeing things one-sided? Should I go back where I came from and leave you alone?"

"Oh, God no!" she blurted, then felt the heat rise to her cheeks. "I mean, I'm flattered. Damn, Jack, I'm embarrassed as hell. I had no idea."

"Why?" He raised his hand and toyed with her hair, winding his fingers in the wild curls. Her skin tingled all over. "Is it such a big surprise that I find you attractive?"

Um, hell yes. "We don't exactly . . . mesh, you know."

His half smile melted her. "We don't?"

"No."

"In what way don't we mesh?"

"You're a corporate lawyer. I own a coffee shop."

"So? You could be a client of mine."

She snorted, then covered her mouth. "Sorry. That's just too damn funny."

He rolled his eyes. "You're not taking this seriously."

"No, Jack, you're not taking this seriously." She half-turned in her chair to face him. "We don't travel in the same social circles. You live here at the club. I live across town in middle-classville. I'm biracial, you're whiter than a whiteout in a Denver snowstorm. I'm mortgaged to the hilt between my home and my business, and you probably make more money in a year than I'll earn in my entire lifetime. So don't tell me we mesh."

"Do you find me attractive, Callie?"

"What?"

"Answer the question. Are you attracted to me?"

Such an unfair question. "Well, yes."

"Good. Because I'm sure as hell attracted to you. Your litany of excuses don't mean a damn thing to me. Now, let's dance."

three

callie gaped at jack, openmouthed and honest-to-God in shock. He pushed back his chair and stood, holding his hand out. She stared at his hand for a moment, then slid her palm against his, feeling the light tingle of electricity pass between them.

Oh yeah. Chemistry. Undeniably charged and elemental, there was no doubt about it. They had it, and it was strong. Did that really mean the rest of it didn't matter? How could it not, when there were so many barriers between them?

Then again, it was only the bet. And only this weekend. Why the hell did she care if there were barriers? It wasn't like she was looking for a relationship with him. She was supposed to fuck him. And judging from the spark between them and the way he was looking at her right now, she could virtually guarantee that was going to happen.

So quit worrying about all those things you have no business worrying about, and start flirting your ass off, woman. She was hot for some good fucking, and for the love of God, she knew Jack would be the one to give it to her. One absolutely insane weekend where she could act the part of the wanton, free-spirited woman and fuck her brains out. Oh, it had been so, so long. She needed this.

"What are you thinking about?" he asked, wrapping his arm around her back and tugging her closer against his solid chest.

Yeah, he was a hardbody, all right. Just as she'd suspected.

"I was thinking that I was worrying about stupid things instead of just enjoying myself with one very hot-looking man," she replied, deciding to cast aside all her worries and carry out the terms of the bet while also fulfilling herself in a very satisfying way. She rested her hand on his shoulder, then smoothed it down his back just a little, loving the feel of his body under her questing palm and wishing the tux jacket wasn't in her way.

He glided her around the dance floor to the strains of a slow melody, his body so easy to follow. He moved with the grace of a man comfortable in his own skin. "You dance pretty good."

"For a white guy?" he teased.

She snickered. "Wasn't even going to go there."

"You didn't have to. I knew what you were thinking."

If he knew what she was thinking, they wouldn't be dancing. What she was thinking was how he'd look stripped out of that tux and naked, his cock hard and him coming after her. She was ready to spread her legs. Her pussy was damp, her nipples tingling, and she thanked the style of the dress for allowing her to be turned on without him knowing it.

"Hungry?" he asked.

She damn near choked. Yeah, she was hungry. "Not really. You?"

"Not at all. But this place is packed. How about some fresh air?"

"I'd love to get away from this crowd."

"Good. Let's take a walk outside. I'll show you the grounds." He tucked her hand in the crook of his arm and led her through the throng of dancers and onto the carpet.

They were met with a wall of gorgeous women, arms crossed,

breasts nearly spilling over the tops of their designer dresses, and all looking mightily pissed off.

"Jack, we've been waiting for you," one luscious brunette said, affecting a pout that just screamed, *Come with me, and a blow job is in your future.*

"Yes, Jack, you left us so abruptly," a blonde said, batting her eyelashes. Those lashes had to be fake. No one had lashes that long or thick. Then again, judging from the looks of her boobs, nose, and chin, *fake* seemed to fit her. Didn't women wear their real parts anymore?

"Sorry, ladies, but my date is here, and I couldn't possibly tear myself away from her."

His date? She was his date? Since when?

Jack smiled and brushed past the scary-looking front line. Callie gulped back the dry lump in her throat, happy she had him there to run interference.

Despite the warmth outside, she sucked in a breath of air as Jack pushed through the double doors and into the gardens. She'd never been more relieved to make an escape from a party, since between her own nervousness and the beauty brigade, she'd felt like she was suffocating.

"Better?" he asked, leading them through the maze of high hedges.

"Definitely. Thank you. I'm not much for large crowds."

"Me, either. I hate these events. Only reason I go is because I'm on the board and required to be here."

Walking with him, her arm in his, was so easy. She thought it would be uncomfortable, but it wasn't. They strolled through the gardens, and Jack led them to a secluded bench in front of a flowing fountain.

"Let's sit and talk for awhile," he suggested, taking a seat and pulling her down next to him.

The night sky was clear, a light breeze cooling the oppressive heat of the day. It was perfect here. And no one else was around, giving them complete privacy.

"We never get to talk at your shop," he said, shifting so he was facing her. "This is my chance to get to know you better."

And her chance to get to know him, too. "I'm glad we have a few minutes alone. I've been wanting to learn more about you." Funny, she found herself shy around him now. Then again, why wouldn't she be? How long had it been since she'd been alone with a man? And the last man she'd been alone with had been her husband, the one and only man she'd ever dated. It wasn't like she had tons of experience with men. Fantasies, yes. Wild, wanton, out-of-control fantasies. But reality? In that she was lacking.

He smiled. "I'll tell you everything you want to know. I'm thirty-five, born and raised here in Silverwood. My family are farmers, uneducated, but always wanted the best for me. I went to college and law school on a scholarship and whatever student loans I could get my hands on and have been working for the same law firm since graduation. I have zero social life—correction—have had zero social life for the past nine years since I've been climbing my way up the ladder to partnership. It's been all work and no play for me."

She laughed. "You complaining?"

"Hell no. It's what I wanted. Career first has always been my goal."

"And now?"

"Now I've made myself a success, worked my ass off to get here, so I'm ready to relax a little."

Admittedly, she was impressed. A self-made man, one who made no apologies for his goal of success. She admired that. "Congratulations for making it to the top."

He shrugged. "Senior partnership is the top, but they tell me that's pretty close to being in the bag. I'm not worried."

"Confident, are you?"

"A little," he said with a grin. "So, tell me about you."

"I'm thirty-three, have a house in midtown. Married my high school sweetheart, who died five years ago of cancer."

His smile died, and he reached for her hand. "I'm so sorry, Callie. I didn't know."

"It's okay. I loved Bobby. He was a wonderful man. But he wanted me to go on living and not die with him. So I have been. I bought the coffee shop, started small and worked my way up. I work hard at it, don't make millions, but enough to pay the mortgage on the house and buy groceries. It's a good life."

"And you do this all by yourself?"

"Yeah."

"No kids?"

"No. We were going to have them, just ran out of time."

"I'm sorry."

This time she squeezed his hands. "Hey, it's okay. Bobby is part of my past now. I don't dwell on him anymore. I'm trying to start a new life finally. Have some new experiences, new adventures."

"I'd like to be part of that."

She sucked in a long breath. "I'd like that, too."

Whoa, that had been difficult. And at the same time, effortless. Being with Jack was like sitting with an old friend. Talking to him about Bobby had been easier than she'd thought it would be.

"Everything that happens to us in our past shapes our future, who we are, what we become. We never really lose it," he said, standing and holding out his hand. "Let's walk a little more."

They passed the fountains and moved into the hedge maze on the far side. She liked this. A little spooky in the dark, but kind of sexy, knowing they were all alone out here. He put his arm around her bare shoulder and held her close against his side as they walked. Oh yeah, she liked the feel and heat of his body against hers. Too long.

Much too long since she'd felt a man against her, since she inhaled the crisp, clean scent of soap on a man's skin, felt a man's hand holding hers. She inhaled to stave off the tears.

"You doing okay over there?" he asked as they strolled through the maze.

"Fine."

"You went quiet on me."

"Sorry. Just enjoying the night." She looked up at him. "And the company."

He paused and turned to her, cupping her cheeks in his hands.

She stopped breathing, trying to remember the last time she'd been kissed, because he sure as hell was going to kiss her. Years. Centuries. Too long to remember what it felt like to have a man's mouth on hers.

Oh, God, he was going to kiss her. Every nerve ending in her body stood poised and ready, and she knew lightning was going to strike.

"Callie. I've been wanting to do this for a long time." He bent and brushed his lips against hers, the movement so soft and achingly tender she almost moaned. Then he pressed his mouth to hers, and there it was again: that electrical charge that tingled her clit as if he were flicking it with his tongue.

Dayum. She did moan this time, her eyelids flitting closed so she could focus on every sensation. He pulled her into his arms and wrapped her into an embrace, fitting his mouth over hers and taking over, sliding his tongue inside and sweeping against hers.

Possession. That's what it was. He was taking her, claiming her. Oh, baby, and was she ever ready to give it up. Everything, whatever he wanted, was his for the taking. Right here, as a matter of fact. Just the thought of it made her go wet between her legs, her clit quivering with need. She pressed against his leg, and he pushed it between hers, allowing her clit to make contact with his thigh. She whimpered, he groaned, and she damn near flooded his leg.

Then gentle, getting-to-know-you, calm kisses gave way to something more primal, elemental, as they began to touch each other, their kisses becoming harder, more passionate. She didn't care where they were or who might see them. She needed to feel Jack's hands on her, needed to touch him, to explore his body. God, she wanted to get naked with him, but that wasn't possible out here.

She smoothed her hands over his shoulders and down his arms, her mouth leaving his to explore his jaw, his neck, breathing in the crisp, musky scent of him. He moved his hand over her back and down, palming her ass and pushing her against his hard-on.

His rigid length rocked against her sex, making her quest to explore him even more desperate. She leaned back, searched his face, supremely satisfied by the raw desire she saw in his eyes.

"I want you, Callie. Goddamn, I want you right here."

She'd never heard sweeter words spoken. Bobby had never wanted to do anything like this, preferring his sex indoors and in their bedroom. Oh, she loved him and capitulated, but a part of her had always missed satisfying her baser cravings. She'd never even told Bobby about her secret fantasies.

Now, maybe she'd finally be able to tap into them. Hallelujah!

Until she heard whispers and laughter. She froze. Jack closed his eyes for a second, then shook his head.

"Son of a bitch," he whispered.

She smiled, laying her head on his chest while she tried to gather her wits. Someone else was in the gardens just ahead.

"Guess we're not alone anymore," she said, tilting her head back to search Jack's face.

"Guess not. Goddammit, I'm sorry, Callie."

She laughed. "It's okay." Though disappointed, she was heartened to know he wasn't afraid to take her right there in the gardens. And he would have if they hadn't been interrupted. Her body still thrummed with sexual vibrations, and that was a heady enough feeling for now. She'd have her moment with Jack soon.

"I need to walk this off," he said, adjusting the crotch of his tux.

She smirked and walked alongside him through the maze, listening to the sounds of a couple at the other end. Whispers, mostly. And deep, sensual laughter.

"What do you think they're doing out there?" she whispered.

"Not sure. Let's sneak up on them and find out." He grabbed her hand, and they tiptoed to the end of the maze of bushes.

Tucked inside a quiet, dark corner was a small, white gazebo. Thickly laced lattice on three sides offered privacy from anyone wanting to know what was going on inside, but from the sounds the couple made, Callie had a pretty good idea. Her heart thumped a mad rhythm as Jack pulled her to the right side of the bushes. She realized from that vantage point they could see the man and woman seated on the bench in the gazebo.

The woman's long, blonde hair cascaded down her naked back, the top of her dress pulled down to her waist. She couldn't see the man's face, only a thick head of dark hair. His mouth was latched around one of the woman's nipples, his fingers plucking at the other.

Raw desire shot through Callie, her deepest, darkest fantasy come to life right in front of her eyes. She gasped, a sudden urge to lift her dress and massage her pussy nearly overwhelming. But she remembered she wasn't alone. Jack was with her, seeing what she saw.

Would he jerk her away from the scene, embarrassed on her behalf? Or would he do what she secretly, fervently prayed? Would he stand there and watch?

She tilted her head back and met his inquisitive gaze.

Jack caught Callie's sharp intake of breath, wondering if she was appalled at what was going on in the gazebo. But when he saw her

eyes, her parted lips, the way her breasts rose and fell with her panting breaths, he knew. She was turned on by what she saw.

"You want to watch." He stated it, didn't ask. Knew he didn't
even need to ask.

She nodded, turning her head to stare at the couple in the gazebo.

Goddamn. Callie was a voyeur. His cock rushed with arousal,
hardening, throbbing with the need to slide inside her cunt and fuck
her while they watched the other couple.

As if Callie wasn't already the most beautiful woman in his eyes,
his estimation of her had just risen even more. A woman who shared
his love of adventure? Not only would she have fucked him in the
maze, she also wanted to stay there and watch the other couple
have sex.

Christ, was it his lucky day or what? The woman of his dreams
had the same sexual fantasies as him. What more could a man want
in a woman?

He positioned her in front of him, giving her an ample view of
the goings-on inside the gazebo. His cock brushed against the full
curve of her buttocks, and he didn't even try to hide his hard-on. Instead, he brushed forward, rocking against her, wrapping his arm
around her waist to pull her against him.

He could hear her breathing. Deep inhalations as she laid her
head against his chest. Oh, yeah. She was really hot now. The
woman in the gazebo had dropped to her knees to unbuckle the guy's
belt, taking her sweet time unzipping his pants. When she took his
cock out, Jack was impressed. Well-endowed son of a bitch, too. The
woman wrapped her lips around the head, stroking the shaft as she
sucked him.

Jack smoothed his hands over Callie's shoulders, running his fingers down her arms. "You're a voyeur, Callie."

"Yes."

"I like to watch, too."

She didn't look at him. "You do?"

"Yeah. I love watching people fuck. Makes my dick hard." He couldn't believe they had made such a fast leap in their relationship. His first thought when they had come upon the couple in the gazebo was to be a gentleman and steer Callie away. Then she'd gasped, and instinct told him it hadn't been a gasp of shock or outrage but one of excitement. He was glad his instincts had been right.

"When I was fifteen I walked in on another girl having sex in the gym with her boyfriend. Instead of running out, I stood there and watched," she said. "It made my pussy wet, right there on the spot. My clit was tingling so bad I knew I had to get off right away. I hid in the locker room doorway and masturbated while they fucked. I came when they came. And then I masturbated about that scene over and over again for months. It was the hottest thing I'd ever seen."

"Goddamn, Callie." He couldn't believe she'd told him that. He loved her refreshing honesty. She wasn't coy or playing innocent with him. He'd never met a woman like her. "In high school my buddies and I used to chip in and rent a motel room with girls and fuck all night long. Since there was only one room, we all stood around and watched. I found out pretty fast that I really got off on voyeurism. I'd jack off more to watching other people fuck than to the memory of any girl I fucked."

He figured he owed her a revelation since she'd been so honest with him.

She shuddered, and he tightened his grip around her waist.

"Jack," she whispered, her voice a whimpering plea. Having her back turned to him, not being able to read her expression, meant he had to rely on the feel of her body, the sounds she made, to tell him what she wanted. And he knew.

"Yeah, baby. I know what you need. You want it out here?"

"Yes. Oh, yeah, I want it right here."

He caressed her arms, smoothing his palms over her shoulders, leaning into her neck to inhale her fragrance. She wore no perfume, but he caught the scent of something sweet. Vanilla, maybe. He licked the smooth column of her neck, and she tilted her head to the side to give him access, not once turning her attention away from the couple in the gazebo.

Though he could tell Callie was tuned in to every one of his movements, she was also visually entranced by the other couple. He didn't mind at all. Watching the way the scene turned her on was a heady experience. He'd never met a woman like her, so completely uninhibited, the way she clutched the side of his thighs, digging her nails into the fabric of his tux.

Damn, he wanted to be naked with her, wanted to feel the sharp scrape of her nails along his bare skin. He'd bet she was a wildcat when aroused.

The woman in the gazebo was really going to town on her man's dick now, making long, fast movements with her mouth, taking the length of his shaft and nearly swallowing it before leaning back until only the head remained grasped between her greedy lips.

"She gives good head," Jack said in Callie's ear.

"Yes."

"You like sucking cock, Callie?"

"Yes. It's been a long time."

His balls quivered at the thought of being the first man to feel her full lips since her husband. But not now. Now he wanted to pleasure her, to make sure she got off while she watched the scene in front of her. He had a feeling he was the first man she'd been with since her husband died, and she hadn't had an experience like this before.

He reached around and rested his fingers lightly on her collarbone, feeling her heart beat a rapid rhythm against his palm. The swell of her breast crested upward against his hand with every breath she took, tantalizing him, tempting him. He inched his hands down over her breasts.

Full, firm, hot to the touch through the fabric of her dress, she arched her back, pushing the full globes into his hands.

"Yes, Jack, touch me. Please, touch me."

He slipped his hand down the bodice of her dress, finding one very hard nipple. When he circled it between his finger and thumb and began to pluck it gently, she made these crazy little sounds in the back of her throat. Moans, whimpers, and panting to keep herself from crying out and alerting the couple in the gazebo.

Concentrating on her, he buried his face in her hair. "Tell me what they're doing."

"She's standing now," Callie said, her voice coming out in a breathy whisper as Jack continued to pull and pluck at her nipples. "He's lifting the hem of her dress."

Jack withdrew his hand and caressed Callie's rib cage, traveling a slow path over the curve of her hip.

"She's turned away from him now and bending from the waist while he lifts the dress over her back."

"Mmm," he said, finding the hem of Callie's dress and fisting it in his hand. He felt the muscles of Callie's thigh tense. "Is she wearing panties?"

"No."

He laughed. "Maybe she was expecting to be fucked tonight."

"Maybe. He's dropped his pants now. Moving into position behind her. She's spreading her legs."

Callie spread her legs a little wider. Jack started to raise the hem of Callie's dress, inch by inch, teasing her by doing it slowly. He could hear her breathing now, fast, panting. Admittedly, his own was racing right along there, too, his cock so damn hard he could thump it against a stone statue in the garden with no ill effects. God he wanted to do what that guy in the gazebo was doing. He wanted to bend Callie over and sink his cock deep into her cunt, feel her hot, wet pussy close around him, grip him, then fuck her until they both came hard.

Instead, he raised her skirt up over her hips. "What about you, Callie? You wearing panties tonight?"

"Yes."

He smiled, teasing the skin of her inner thigh, feeling the brush of silk and lace against the side of his hand.

"Jack," she whispered.

"You want me to touch your pussy, honey?"

"Yes," she hissed.

He moved to her side now, catching a glimpse of bronze-colored silk and lace panties, cut high on her hips. He dragged the panties down around her thighs, baring her pussy to the night.

She moaned.

"You like knowing your pussy is exposed?"

"Yes."

"Want me to touch it?"

"Yes."

He wanted to get down on his knees in front of her, bury his face in her cunt, and lick her until she screamed. But he wanted to watch with her, to take this scene to culmination, to be the voyeur alongside her. He teased the inside of her thigh again, running his finger along the side of her pussy lips, turned to her, and smiled.

"Watch them, Callie. Watch them fuck while I make you come."

He cupped her pussy and she gasped, arching her hips against his hand. He tangled his fingers in the silken curls of her sex, wishing he had all the time in the world to explore her.

Later, he'd delve into all her secrets. Right now she was wet and pouring all over his hand, her clit was extended and swollen, and he'd bet no man had made her come in years.

He was going to make her come.

He turned to the couple in the gazebo. As Callie said, the man was fucking her from behind, his cock buried deep in the woman's pussy. The scene before him was hot, the woman gripping the back of the bench while the man thrust hard and fast against her buttocks, his long cock withdrawing only to slam against her again.

Jack explored Callie's pussy lips, teasing every inch of her with his touch, finally sliding two fingers into her cunt.

"Oh, Jack," she said, whimpering as he slid his fingers fully inside her.

Damn, she was hot inside. Her body gripped him in a tight vise, squeezing, contractions closing around his fingers. He moved to her side so he could work her with his other hand, using three fingers to strum her clit.

"Oh, God," she said, turning to look at him. "I haven't . . . it's been so long."

He nodded. "Come for me, Callie."

She glanced away and watched as the man and woman in the gazebo went into frenzied fucking. They were close. She was, too, grabbing his wrist and forcing his fingers deeper and harder into her cunt. The woman in the gazebo tensed and threw her head back, the man shuddering against her. Callie looked at Jack again, her eyes glazed with passion.

"I'm going to come, Jack!" she whispered, then held tight to his hand as she shuddered and flooded his fingers, trembling against him, rocking her pelvis against his palm as waves of climax crashed against her.

The look on her face was the most beautiful thing he'd ever seen. So open and honest, she gave him everything. He leaned in and took her mouth, letting her cry out against his lips as she rode out her orgasm until she finally rested her head against his shoulder.

And still, he didn't want to withdraw from her pussy, enjoying the tiny aftershocks squeezing his fingers. But he did, kissed her lips, and licked her sweet juices from his fingers.

Goddamn, he needed to fuck this woman and soon. He tilted her toward him and planted his lips on hers, kissing her with a firm desperation.

He wanted to absorb her, to take her right here.

Was she an exhibitionist as well as a voyeur? Would she fuck him in the gardens tonight? He hoped so, because he sure as hell couldn't wait much longer to have her.

four

jack stole callie's breath with his kiss, his mouth making a slow plunder of her senses that made her brain turn to mush. His hands roamed over her body, every hot touch only inflaming her more. And her panties were still located somewhere between her thighs and her knees.

She couldn't believe he'd given her an orgasm right here in the maze. Touched her pussy, fucked it with his fingers until she'd climaxed all over his hand. Had she lost her freakin' mind? No, she hadn't. Or maybe she had. She didn't care, because tonight she was living out her long-held fantasies.

The couple in the gazebo righted their clothes, kissed, then snuck out. Jack pulled her against the hedge, hiding them from sight of the couple hurrying by. She smiled up at him, wondering what he thought of her. Too wanton and uninhibited, maybe?

No, she doubted that from the look of hunger on his face, the way his hands continued to roam over her back, the way he breathed in and out in short, quick spurts.

His cock rested against her hip, still hard. She'd gotten off, but he hadn't. And she wanted him inside her, outside, here at the club just like the other couple had done. Could she even suggest that to him? What if he said no?

Oh, get over it, Callie. He'd just fucked her pussy with his fingers, his cock was hard as steel, and he had no qualms at all about nearly fucking her earlier before they'd heard voices. So why hold back now? This was her fantasy weekend, right? So she should go for it.

"Jack," she said, grabbing the lapels of his coat. "Did you enjoy watching that couple?"

He grinned. "I love watching other people have sex, Callie."

"Do you also enjoy having sex in outdoor places? With the thought that someone might catch you?" There. She'd said it. Now she'd see if her hunch was right about him. God, she hoped it was.

He reached up and caressed his hair. "You wanna fuck here? Outside?"

"That wasn't my question."

"You're asking if I'm into exhibitionism."

"Are you?"

"Are *you*?"

Damn, he was making this difficult. "I asked you first."

He laughed. "Yes. I'm a voyeur and an exhibitionist. You want to have sex in the great outdoors, Callie, I'm all for it."

Her mind screamed a resounding *Yes!* at his answer. He was her perfect match in so many ways she couldn't believe it. "Then in answer to your question, I'm also an exhibitionist. It excites me to think that someone could catch us fucking. It makes my pussy hot at the thought people could be watching."

His gaze went dark at her admission. He looked around, then grabbed her hand. "I know the perfect place."

He led her back where they came from, through the maze and toward the main building. No one was outside. Not yet, anyway. He was heading toward the double doors, but instead of going inside, he swerved around the corner to the side of the building, no more than twenty-five feet away from where they'd exited the party.

Before she could ask where they were going, he pulled her around and slammed her up against the brick wall of the building, lifted her dress, and tore her panties aside, then covered her mouth with his. Her gasp of surprise was absorbed by his lips, his tongue entering her mouth at the same time his cock plunged inside her.

She had no time to react, to think, other than to swim in the glorious sensations of his cock sinking to the hilt inside her pussy. He withdrew, then thrust again, banging against her with force and determination.

Oh, God, this was so exciting. The doors opened around the corner, and it was possible someone would round the corner and find them. Jack didn't even pause, just kept fucking her. She swept her arms inside his coat, searching for the skin of his abdomen, wanting the contact of his body against her hands. Taut, muscular, his belly flinched under her questing hands, but he never once wavered, continuing to pound her pussy with relentless strokes, his body slamming her clit each time.

The excitement of the forbidden, the chance they could be caught, coupled with Jack's ramming thrusts against her clit were too much. She wrapped her arms up and under his shirt, digging her nails into his back, and arched her hips, tightening as she came.

He groaned and flooded her with come, shuddering as he pressed full-length against her, holding her tight against the wall of the building. If someone walked around the corner right now while they were grinding together in climax, nothing could tear her away from Jack. Nothing.

Panting and exhilarated, she couldn't move a muscle, just laid her forehead on his shoulder. Once again, it was like living an out-of-body experience. What if someone had actually walked by? She remembered hearing the door open and close a few times, but at the time she just didn't care.

She tilted her head back and searched Jack's face. He was smiling at her. "You're a wild thing," he said, brushing his lips against hers.

She sighed into his mouth. At least he didn't have any regrets. Not yet, anyway. Of course, they hadn't been caught. That helped.

They cleaned up with the assistance of Jack's handkerchief. Thank God for one of those. She excused herself on the way in and freshened up in the ladies' room, then went in search of Abby and Blair. She didn't have to search long, since they grabbed her on her way to the table and escorted her out the front doors and into the lobby of the club.

"Well?" Blair asked.

"Your hair is mussed and your lips are swollen," Abby said, studying her. "And you have that look."

"What look?"

"That just-fucked smile on your face. Oh my God. Did you two do it outside?"

Callie tried not to laugh. She really loved her friends. Instead, she lifted a shoulder. "I might have."

Blair nodded and grinned. "You did. You slut."

Now she did laugh, because that was a compliment, coming from Blair. "Gee thanks."

Abby linked her arm in Callie's and drew her off to the side of the lobby and away from anyone who might hear them. "Are you going to give us details?"

No way. She couldn't even wrap her own head around what had happened out there, let alone share it with anyone yet.

Anyone but Jack.

She looked around to see if anyone had entered the lobby. No one but the three of them. "I can't. Not right now. You understand?"

Abby looked at Blair. "She wants to be with Jack."

"We're monopolizing," Blair said.

Abby nodded. "Get going. We'll wait. But we want details after the weekend."

Callie grinned. "Love you guys."

She turned and was about to head back to the ballroom when Jack pushed through the doors. He spotted her, grinned, and headed her way.

"Thought you'd run off."

She shook her head. "No, got waylaid."

"Ah, so I see. Couldn't wait for the blow-by-blow?"

Blair brushed by him and shrugged. "Hey, we're nosy. But Callie won't give, so I guess we'll have to be patient. Y'all have fun." She winked at Callie, and she and Abby headed back into the ballroom.

Callie turned to Jack. "Sorry. They dragged me away."

He laughed. "That's what I'm about to do. Go get your things, and let's get out of here."

Sounded like a really good idea to her. She slipped back into the ballroom and grabbed her purse, winked a quick good-bye to Abby and Blair, then met Jack out front.

No car, since he lived so close to the club. He grabbed her hand, and they strolled down the wide street. Quiet, with quaint lampposts embedded in the sidewalks instead of glaring overhead streetlights, they walked along the middle of the road, and Callie had a chance to check out the neighborhood.

Nice space in between houses allowing for privacy. Tall redwood fences between each house, too.

"No one can see from one house to the other," he said as though reading her mind. They rounded the walk toward his house, an enormous, at least by Callie's standards, single-story home. It had cream-colored brick with a dark brown tile roof and a wide, full-length, covered porch. Callie found it absolutely charming. She loved the porch. Open and yet private enough a couple could sit outside and—

Jack pulled her toward him and covered her lips with his. Heat enveloped her, an instant rush of wet desire pooling between her legs as he wound his arms around her and pressed his hips against hers.

The rigid length of his erection rocked against her pelvis. She loved that he could get hard again for her, right there on the front porch. When he walked with her, his lips still connected to hers, and the back of her legs hit the ledge of the porch wall, she moaned against his mouth.

Yes, she wanted him to fuck her right here.

He dragged his lips from hers, his gaze a mix of stormy blue and gray.

"There's going to be fireworks outside tonight. The crowds should be milling about soon."

"Really?" Her heart pounded, her body throbbing with the need to feel his hot cock inside her.

"Yeah."

True to his statement, she heard the sounds of laughter and conversation and turned to see the crowd from the club pouring out all the doors.

"The park behind the club will be shooting off the fireworks. Everyone heads out into the streets to watch. We can see from here."

And people could see them. "What are you saying, Jack?"

He pulled her toward him and wrapped his arm around her waist, his cock nestled against her ass. She heard the zipper of his pants draw down, his hips undulating against hers, then he lifted the back of her dress and jerked her panties over her hips and thighs. She shimmied a bit until they fell to her ankles, then kicked them off.

"I'm saying I'm going to fuck you while we watch the fireworks."

Her pussy clenched in excitement. Callie gripped the brick column next to her for support, spreading her legs a bit to give him access.

"You want that, Callie?"

He swept her hair to the side, the warmth of his breath tickling the back of her neck. "Yes," she whispered. "I want you in me."

The first boom of fireworks exploding from the launching point in the park made her jump. Jack tightened his hold on her, kicked her legs apart with his knee. The loud applause drowned out her gasp as his cock thrust inside her, hot and thick, sliding with ease inside her wet cunt.

"Damn, honey, you're sopping wet down there. Does it make you hot to know all these people could turn around and see me fucking you?"

"Yes," she panted, clutching the column. Her legs were shaking as she surveyed the crowds. Another explosion of fireworks brightened the night sky, lit up the porch, putting a spotlight over them. Anyone who wanted to look in their direction, who scrutinized the couple watching fireworks from the porch, could see what they were doing. Her dress was raised over her ass in the back, her legs spread, Jack's thrusting motions propelling her hips forward.

Oh yes, anyone looking could tell she was being fucked from behind. A rush of fluid escaped her pussy, delirious excitement obliterating her reality once again. Now she felt only the pleasure, the forbidden, the anticipation of someone discovering them.

The sky was awash with exploding colors, every thunderous boom pounding through her body as Jack powered inside her to the same rhythm. The crowd screamed with every burst, and so did Callie, not bothering to squelch her voice as Jack drove hard and relentless, digging his fingers into her hips.

He grabbed a fistful of her hair and pulled her back against him. "I'm going to come in you," he said, his voice tight, harsh with tension as he thrust deep. "You ready?"

She was as ready to burst as the finale of exploding fireworks above them, the cacophony of sounds drowning out her screaming "Yes!" But her body gave the answer, gripping his cock in a tight vise as she climaxed, gripping him in a squeezing spasm as she came. He jerked her head back and took her mouth, hot jets of come spurting inside her as he ground his lips against hers, his tongue stroking hers in a frenzied rhythm, finally settling as they shuddered and slowed.

Jack pulled out and turned her around, his kiss gentling, his hands roaming over her body in soft, pleasurable strokes. Callie panted against him, then breathed again, murmuring moans of sated pleasure as he held her against him and caressed her back.

By now, the fireworks had ended, and the crowds began to dissipate.

Had anyone seen them fucking? She didn't know.

Frankly, she didn't care. She knew the possibility of discovery existed, and that was enough to heighten her excitement. That Jack also got off on the exhibition was a plus she hadn't ever expected but planned to capitalize on for as long as she could.

"Maybe you'd like to see the rest of my house now," he said with a wry smile, kissing the top of her head.

"Sure."

He palmed open the door and pushed the light on, standing aside while Callie walked in.

"Before you ask, no, I had nothing to do with the decorating or furnishings. I had it all done for me. Didn't have time to do anything other than fall into bed at night after the move, so I had other people take care of the details."

She *was* going to ask, because the place was impeccably decorated and perfect for either a man or a woman. He led her through the house and flipped on lights in every room. The walls were a pale sand, the furnishings elegant and modern, some leather, some upholstered in bright, bold earth tones. He had wood floors polished to perfection, not a thing out of place on the tables in either the living room, dining room, or kitchen, which was enormous, bright, and with state-of-the-art appliances.

"Wow," was all she could manage.

"Looks nice because I'm never here," he said. "Plus I have a cleaning crew come in and obliterate the dust demons and mold monsters every week."

She snorted.

"There are four bedrooms. Two of them are empty except for boxes and other storage. One is my office, the other the master bedroom." He led her down the hall, pointing in all the rooms as they walked by. All of them were spacious, the square footage of his home at least twice the size of her modest little house. Then again, what did she expect? They were on nearly opposite ends of the economic scale.

The master bedroom was an absolute dream, wide open, elegant, with a floor-to-ceiling bay window in front of the bed overlooking a patio spa. She headed out the doors and onto the patio, running her fingertips over the edge of the hot tub. She peeked out through the tightly woven lattice that reminded her of the gazebo at the club. The lattice covered three sides, leaving one side open, but, of course, the fenced backyard afforded enough privacy.

"Can't see much through there, can you?"

Jack had stepped up behind her, his fingers sliding over hers. He leaned over and flipped on the button, and the hot tub jets fired up. Callie stepped back as water bubbled to the surface of the spa, bumping into Jack as she did. She pivoted and looked at him.

Arousal blended his eyes a dark, stormy color. Kind of a mix of blue and gray, his heavy-lidded gaze raked over her body.

Bobby had been a once or twice a week sex kind of guy. She'd loved him with all her heart, but he hadn't been an overly passionate

man. Caring, yes. Loving, absolutely. But not big in the sex depart-
ment. That Jack had fucked her twice and given her three orgasms
already astounded her. That he wanted her so soon again was ex-
traordinary.

"It's actually too hot outside for the spa, but how about a shower?"

"I didn't bring any other clothes with me."

He cast her a sideways glance, then said, "You'll look great in one
of my shirts."

The thought of wearing his clothes next to her skin made her
nipples tighten. "Then let's do it," she said with a grin, pulling the
straps of her dress down her arms.

Jack shucked his jacket, then his tie, hurrying through the buttons on his shirt while watching Callie peel the dress from her body.

He hadn't seen her naked yet. They'd had sex three times, and he
hadn't seen her naked yet. She drew the dress down over her breasts,
then her waist, revealing full breasts, a slender waist just made for a
man's hands, and curvy hips that he remembered gripping as he
pounded his cock inside her. She had long legs, too. A perfect body. A
woman's body, not at all like those women who hounded him at the
club with their stick-thin bodies fed by the latest diet craze, the ones
who brutalized their constitutions with personal trainers in order to
resemble the latest fashion model. He couldn't stand looking at them.

Callie, on the other hand, he could ogle all night long. Had, in
fact, been looking at her for a very long time. Her skin was warm
honey, soft as butter, and he couldn't wait to feel her full-on naked
next to him. He slid his shirt off, then unbuckled his pants and
dropped them to the floor, kicking them aside.

Her look of wide-eyed appreciation as she scanned his body was
good for his ego. There was nothing more exciting to a man than a
woman who liked looking at him.

"Dayum," she whispered.

He inhaled a sharp breath and stepped toward her, gathering her in his arms. "You keep looking at me like that, and we'll never make it to the shower."

"Oh, like I care."

Admittedly, the thought occurred to him to just grab her and throw her on the bed, but after what they'd done for the past several hours, a refreshing shower was needed. He took her hand and led her into the bathroom and turned on the jets, letting his hands roam over her smooth skin as the water warmed. They stepped into the shower stall.

"Wow," Callie said, turning around to gape at the jets pouring from three sides. "This is amazing."

She lifted her arms, and he adjusted the spray so the multiple jets sent out a pulsing massage, then stepped back to just watch her as she closed her eyes and let the water pour over her. She was a goddess, her hair soaking wet and falling over her eyes, her makeup melting down her cheeks, and she didn't even care. There was a gritty realness to her that he found incredibly appealing.

When she opened her eyes and found him staring at her, she smiled.

"I probably look like a raccoon now."

He laughed and wiped away the mascara smudges from under her eyes. "You look beautiful. I like that you don't fuss over letting me see you with your makeup running in your eyes."

She shrugged. "I'm wet. Not much I can do about it."

He grabbed the soap and washed her body, his hands gliding over her shoulders and back, fingers pressing into her muscles. She had such strength in her body, no doubt because she actually worked for a living, something else the women of the club lacked. They spent all their time being pampered and taken care of. They wouldn't know an honest day's work if it bit them in their bony asses. Callie knew, though, and he admired what she'd done with her life. A lot of women who'd lost their husbands and their hopes for the future would have given up. She hadn't. She'd moved forward and done it all on her own and had made a success of herself.

She moved back against him, the full cheeks of her ass brushing against his cock. It stirred to life, and he shook his head.

"Something's going on back there," she said, shaking her ass against his ever-growing erection.

"Really."

"Yes. I can definitely feel something."

He let her take the lead, not really expecting her to want sex again, thinking she might be too sore after three times tonight. But she leaned forward, planting her palms against the glass wall of the shower, spread her legs, and cast him a look over her shoulder that made his cock twitch.

Okay, obviously she either wasn't too sore or she just didn't care.

"You going to fuck me or stare at my ass all night?"

He cocked a half smile. "I'm debating. Both are great choices."

"Then do both. Stare at my ass while you're fucking me. I want to come again."

Goddamn. Her honesty tore him up inside. He spread her ass cheeks and speared her cunt with his cock, sliding into her wet heat slow and easy, hoping he didn't hurt her.

Hurt her, right. She pushed back against him with forceful intent, slamming her pussy against his cock.

"Hard," she said, her head bent down and her palms flat against the glass wall. "Fuck me hard." With one hand she reached between her legs to fondle her clit. "I need to come again, Jack."

He caught onto her sense of urgency and pumped his cock deep, giving her what she needed. Whatever she wanted, he'd be damn glad to provide, especially if his cock was involved.

His palms slid down the glass as she rocked backward in wild abandon. All he could do was hold on while her pussy gripped his shaft and she gyrated her ass against him. Callie was in charge here, and he let her have his dick, gripping the door of the shower as a brace and lifting his hips to bury his cock deep into her slick cunt.

"Yes, like that," she said, her throaty whisper just about to do him in. His balls tightened, and he knew he was going to shoot a hot load inside her, but he gritted his teeth and held on, wanting her to go first.

It didn't take long. Her pussy gripped him like a vise and she tensed, tossing her hair back over her shoulder. She began to shudder, then screamed.

"I'm coming, Jack! Oh, God, I'm coming so hard!"

So was he then, letting go and pumping against her, gripping her hips tight and shooting come deep, as the waves of her climax milked his cock with solid pulses until he thought his legs might give out from the sheer pleasure of it.

"Dear, God, I'm exhausted," she said as they finally settled. She pulled away and turned to him, wrapping her arms around his neck and planting her lips over his mouth. Her kisses were soft, sweeping against his lips in such gentle slow motions that he finally began to feel the exhaustion of the night.

He turned off the shower and stepped out, reached for two towels, and handed her one. They dried off, and Callie dried her hair until it fell in soft, curling waves. As she moved around his bathroom, he heard her sigh several times. Deep, contented sighs.

He liked the sound. But she was tired. So was he. He led her to his bed, and they climbed in. Jack realized he'd never once had a woman in his bed before. Not to spend the night anyway.

Having Callie here felt right. He pulled her against him, and she threw her leg over his hip and rested her head on his shoulder. Within minutes, she was asleep.

Yeah, it felt right. Perfect. He could get used to having her around.

One night with her, and he was already comfortable with her in his bed, staying the night. Scary thought, but hey, when it was right, it was right.

And Callie was the right woman for him.

five

"a sex club?" callie's eyes widened.

"Yeah. You ever been to one?"

She shook her head, not sure what to make of Jack's proposal. After sleeping in his arms last night, they'd gotten up, had breakfast, and she'd put on her dress, then Jack drove her home so she could change clothes and pack a few things. They'd spent the day tooling around Silverwood, had a picnic lunch at Rosewood Park pavilion and even played on the swings. Now they were back at his place, hiding out from the late afternoon heat.

And Jack had just suggested they go to a sex club. "No, I've never been to one. I didn't even know Silverwood had those kinds of places." God, she sounded so conservative. "What do they do there?"

"They have sex, babe. What do you think they do there?"

They were sitting in the living room having a cocktail. Callie took a long gulp of the chilled wine, shocked to her toes to discover there was a sex club in town. Talk about living a sheltered life. And now she felt naive. "Well I guess they do have sex, that's why they call it a sex club. I mean specifically. I've got this visual of leather and whips and chains secured to the wall."

He snorted. "Not quite like that. It's not a bondage club, Callie. It's a sex club. Think of it as a nightclub. Music, dancing, people milling about. They just go a little further than that. There are multiple rooms where sexual activity occurs beyond the main room where everyone mingles. And anyone who's interested can go to these rooms and do whatever they want to do."

Curious, she arched a brow. "Whatever?"

"Yeah. You interested?"

Interested? Definitely. A little nervous? Beyond that. But after what they'd done last night, how could she turn down a sex club? She didn't want Jack to think she wasn't adventurous, so she nodded. "Of course. I'd love to. What time do we go?"

by nine o'clock callie was almost hyperventilating. She'd dressed in a short skirt and body-hugging top, spiky heels, and put her hair up. She felt sexy, wanton, and ready to rock and roll.

That she was beyond nervous just meant she was excited. It had nothing to do with being completely out of her element. She trusted Jack, she really did, even though she had no idea what kind of place this sex club was.

The club looked rather unassuming from the outside. A plain, two-story building with a neon sign that said Come As You Are on the front, it looked like a bar or a nightclub. The only indicator of privacy were the two burly guards at the roped-off double-doored entrance.

Jack gave his name, and one of the guys checked his clipboard, nodded, then opened the doors for them. Okay, so was he a regular here, or did he just call ahead for reservations? She knew nothing about this kind of thing. And she wasn't about to ask. Callie held her breath as Jack grabbed her hand, and they walked inside.

They entered a big room, kind of like the ballroom at the club, with intimate tables for two and four. Two bars were set up on either side of the room with a dance floor in the middle. It was dark, with a sexy, smoky atmosphere and music playing in the background, but not so loud that people couldn't talk over it.

At first guess Callie would estimate about fifty people wandering around. Pretty good-sized crowd. She'd expected everyone to stop and stare at them as they came in. No one did. There were some couples, a few singles, and everyone milling about with drinks in their hands, talking in groups, and completely ignoring her and Jack's entrance.

Not being a spectacle helped ease her nervousness. A little. Still, she clung to Jack's hand, part of her worried some guy was going to come along and drag her away to a private room. Though even thinking that made her feel stupid. Jack would never let that happen.

"Want a drink?" Jack asked.

She nodded, swallowing through the desert in her throat. "Love one."

They stepped up to the bar and Jack bought them both cocktails. She latched onto hers and took a couple quick gulps of the rum and coke, then forced herself to slow down. Falling down drunk wouldn't help her tonight. Why the hell was she so scared? Nothing bad wasn't going to happen to her tonight. She trusted Jack. She had to keep reminding herself of that.

There was music playing. Contemporary dance music. Several couples were out in the middle of the floor moving with the beat of a fast song, heedless of anyone but each other. That was cool. And the way the women were dressed—clingy, some nearly transparent outfits, others with skirts so short the rounded bottoms of their butt cheeks were visible. Men had their hands all over the women, grabbing their asses while they danced, the couples rubbing their crotches together.

Apparently anything goes tonight. She loved watching the way the couples gyrated on the dance floor, their gazes locked together, ignoring the other people watching them. Did they get off knowing people were staring? Callie would, felt the tingle of excitement down her spine at the thought of her and Jack getting down on the dance floor while others watched. Would he touch her that intimately, rub his cock against her pussy, drive his thigh between her legs? Her pussy dampened at the mental visual.

"Like watching?"

She slanted a smile at Jack. "You know I do."

"That's why I brought you tonight. Thought you might enjoy the sights. It gets better."

"You've been here before?"

He drained his glass and set it on the table "Couple times."

"Alone or did you bring someone?" Dammit. She shouldn't have asked that. It was none of her business.

"Once with a couple buddies of mine. Once alone, just to observe. I like to watch, too, you know."

Good. She didn't know why, but she liked knowing he hadn't brought another woman here before.

"So what happens tonight?"

He slipped an arm around her waist. "Anything we want to happen. Let's go exploring."

"Okay."

Jack led her through the room. Callie tried not to, but she couldn't help gaping at all the people, not really knowing whether to smile, nod, strike up conversation, or just pretend she didn't even see them kissing and groping each other at the tables. They were doing a hell of a lot more than just holding hands. There was kissing at one table. At another a woman had her hand in a man's crotch, rubbing his cock through his pants. Another woman at the same table had her partner's fly unzipped and was going down on his dick. At another table, one man massaged a woman's breasts through her silk blouse.

A few people looked up as she and Jack walked by. One guy gave her the look. The one guys sometimes give a woman, where they look you up and down from head to toe like you're a piece of meat. Callie didn't care for that guy and hoped Jack didn't want to have anything to do with him.

The sexual activity in the room was heating up. And Callie was growing more nervous, because it seemed like she and Jack were the only ones not doing anything hot and heavy. Then again, he was probably feeding off her signals, and right now she was stiff as a board.

What the hell was wrong with her, anyway? This was a voyeur's paradise. Some wanton woman she was.

Okay, it was time to come clean with Jack, because until she did, neither of them were going to be able to enjoy the night.

She paused, placed her hand on his chest, and said, "I need to talk to you."

He tilted his head, then nodded. "Sure."

She took his hand and led him outside the room to a quiet hallway. No one else was around, so she had to spill this fast before someone came by. "I'm a voyeur and an exhibitionist. I like to watch, and I enjoy having sex in public. I'm not into orgies."

She tensed, waiting for his reaction.

He frowned, then his eyes widened and he shook his head. "Oh, no, babe! This place isn't like that at all. Did you think I brought you here for some kind of swapping party?"

She shrugged. "I didn't know."

"Shit." He dragged his hand through his hair. "Not at all. That's not what these parties are about."

Okay, now she felt stupid. She looked down at the floor and wished she'd kept her mouth shut, feeling unsophisticated and naïve.

"Callie, look at me."

With great reluctance she did and read only concern on his face.

He picked up her hands in his. "I'm sorry, Callie. I didn't explain this very well, did I? The sex club is very open and inviting, and there *are* orgies for those who want to participate in them. But the only reason I brought you here was to watch, not to participate. It's a great place for a voyeur, because there's so much to see."

"Oh." Of course. Why didn't she think of that?

"I don't share what's mine."

Her gaze shot to his. "What?"

"I won't mind fucking you knowing other people might watch. It gets me hot knowing some other guy is thinking how gorgeous and sexy you are. But no one, and I mean no one, will touch you. You're mine, and I don't share my woman. Got it?"

His woman. He'd called her his woman. She thrilled to his words, though she wasn't sure what they really meant. Was she his woman? Hesitating to broach the subject any further, she said, "I like the sound of that."

"Nothing will happen tonight that you don't want to happen. I only brought you here to watch, thought you'd enjoy it. If all we do is wander around and ogle, that'll be fine. And if you're uncomfortable, we can leave right now."

"I'm not uncomfortable, Jack." Now that she knew what wasn't going to be expected of her, she relaxed, mentally kicking herself for even thinking for a second that Jack would put her in any kind of awkward or precarious position. So much for having faith in him. She should have known better. "I'm sorry I even hesitated, or thought what might be going on here, or what your expectations were."

He reached up to trace his thumb over her bottom lip. She shivered in reaction to his touch, her body warming with liquid heat. "It's my fault for not explaining it to you in detail before we came here. I'm an asshole."

She laughed. "You are not."

"You want to get out of here?"

"No. I want to see what everyone's doing."

He frowned. "You sure?"

"Yes." And she really meant it this time. Excitement drilled down deep, the idea of watching other people fuck sparking anticipation of the night to come. "Lead the way."

"Let me show you what goes on in some of the upstairs rooms," he said, tucking her hand in his arm and leading her up the stairs.

Upstairs led to another big room, a sitting area of sorts. Couples mingled there, too, making out and some talking. There were two women seated on a love seat, with a third woman on the floor alternating between snacking on their pussies. Callie paused, watching them. She'd never seen a woman go down on another woman before. Her heart began to pump wildly against her chest as she watched how a woman licked another woman's pussy, the slow way she lapped up and down the women's slits, how she gently slid her fingers into one woman's cunt and finger-fucked her while she sucked the other woman's clit.

"You want to stay and watch that?" Jack asked.

"No, we can move on." There was too much to see to linger in one place. Callie was curious about what was going on in the other rooms.

Jack led them past that area and down a wide, thickly carpeted hallway. He stopped at the first door and turned the knob, letting Callie enter first.

It was another big room, with stairs leading down to a two-way mirror. There were a half-dozen people on their side of the mirror, watching what was happening on the other side.

"This is one of the rooms for voyeurs," he whispered behind her as he closed the door and laid his palm on the small of her back, directing her into the room. "Go on in and find a spot where we can watch."

Pinpricks of excitement tingled down her spine as she caught a glimpse of the activity on the other side of the mirror. She walked down the stairs and toward the mirror, paused in front of it, unable to take her eyes off the activity on the other side of the mirror. She barely even noticed the other people in the room with her and Jack.

On the other side of the mirror was a huge open area like a great room, mattresses spread out on the floor. There had to be two dozen people in that room, some completely naked, some half-clothed, all writhing together in various sexual acts.

Callie's throat went dry at the visual in front of her. Jack stepped behind her and fit his body against hers, wrapping his arm possessively around her middle. She inhaled sharply at the contact of his body against her and clutched his arm, needing his touch.

The scene was breath-stealing erotic, the room closing in on her. She didn't know where to look. Two men had a woman on one of the mattresses, one feeding her his thick cock and the other plunging his shaft between her wide, spread legs. Apparently sound was being piped into Callie's side of the room, because she could hear every moan, every groan, even the slapping of a dick thrusting into a wet pussy.

She turned to the other people on her side of the room. A couple women were in there alone, both touching themselves through their clothes. Oh, God, the women were masturbating as they watched the action. A man and woman were in there too, his hands all over her breasts, her hand down the front of his pants.

Callie began to pant, the turn-on from the visuals on both sides of the mirror so exciting she could barely catch a breath.

"You enjoying this?"

Jack's voice, his hot breath against the nape of her neck, only added to her excitement.

"Yes. Oh my God, Jack, yes."

"You want me to touch you? Here, with these other people in the room watching?"

If he didn't touch her she was going to do it herself. And then an explosion of arousal surged between her legs, an excitement she'd never felt before flooding her panties with wicked need.

Oh! The thought of doing that for him, of tapping into his voyeuristic tendencies, was even more arousing to her than having him get her off while she watched the others. "No. I want to do it, Jack. I want you to watch me make myself come."

He hissed in the darkness, then withdrew his arm. "Do it."

She turned around and leaned against the railing. Jack backed up, his face half-shadowed in the darkness of the room. Knowing he was there watching but not being able to clearly see him only added to the excitement. He was the voyeur now, and she was the exhibitionist, putting on a show for him. That others in the room could watch her didn't matter. This was for Jack.

Her breasts ached, heavy and hot, her nipples tingling as she reached up and spread her fingers over them, palming the globes. She caressed them through her top, teasing herself until she couldn't stand it any longer. Then she ran her hands down over her ribs, lifting the silky top to slide her fingers underneath, pulling it up and over her breasts, revealing them.

The air hit them with a shock, her nipples hardening, puckering, crying out for her touch. She rolled them between her fingers, plucking them, moaning as the sensations shot between her legs. "It makes my pussy tingle when I pull at my nipples like this."

She saw Jack reach down between his legs to palm his crotch, rubbing his cock.

"You make my dick so goddamn hard, Callie."

She knew what she wanted, then. But would he do it for her, would he give her what she wanted? "Unzip your pants for me, Jack. Let me see it."

Fingers plucking at her nipples, she zeroed in on that spot between his legs, anticipation making her lick her lips. When she heard the sound of his zipper, she nearly cried out with joy. He stepped forward into the light then, letting her see his cock as he drew it out of his pants. Long, thick, the wide head stretched smooth with his angry erection. She met his heated gaze and smiled.

Her legs trembled as she reached down and lifted her skirt, doing a slow tease with the fabric as she raised it up her thighs. Jack's pinpoint gaze on her movements only added to her breath-stealing, aroused state. She could barely get through the motions, wanting to do it fast, but knowing this agonized, tempting tease would make it good for both of them.

When she revealed her panties to him, she said, "They're wet."

"Touch yourself," he demanded, fisting his cock and stroking it with a lazy, slow motion.

Oh, he was toying with her, too. She wanted to see him come, wanted to watch it spurt from his shaft. She wanted to taste it, wanted to feel it on her tongue. God, she wanted everything, and right now. Her heart pounded so hard she could hear the blood roaring in her ears. Forcing calm, she traced the outline of her panties against her inner thigh, then laid her palm over her sex, closed her eyes, and moaned at the sheer ecstasy of the sensation. Her clit tingled, aching for her to rub it and rub it hard, but she resisted.

"God, Callie, you're making me crazy."

No more than she was driving herself mad. She was so wet her panties were soaked now. She drew the panties down, keeping her movements slow and deliberate, like a striptease, undulating her hips toward Jack as she thrust her cunt at him, letting him see what he could not touch. The scent of her own arousal filled the air, a sweet, sultry musk. She left her panties around her knees, her gaze trained on Jack's movements, watching him tighten his grip around his cock. Tension coiled around her middle as she trickled her fingertips over the curls of her mound, walking them down around her clit, twirling them through the fine, silken hairs. Her clit danced with anticipation, wanting it, needing her touch so badly she could cry out with frustration.

What she was doing to herself! When she finally laid her palm flat against her sex, she cried out, her eyes widening as she buried two fingers in her pussy at the same time her hand made contact with her clit.

"Fuck."

Jack's harsh word made her pussy clamp down around her fingers. He began to stroke faster now as she pumped her fingers inside her cunt, fucking herself in matching rhythm to his gripping thrusts on his own shaft. She was arching her pussy against her hand now, reaching out to him.

The crest of his cock head slid through the tight fist of his hand, angry and purple, tiny pearls of liquid oozing forth from the slit with each thrust. She licked her lips, her throat raw from panting, as she watched the agony spread across his taut features, knew he felt the same way she did: unbearably aroused, on the verge of a blistering orgasm that she simply couldn't hold back any longer.

A cacophony of sound surrounded her: moans of delight and climax behind her as the people in the room behind the mirror fucked and came, the people in the room with her—whatever they were doing, she didn't know, didn't care, but she heard their breathing, some of them moaning. It only added to her delirium.

And Jack, his breathing harsh, sweat beading on his brow as he tunneled his cock between his tight fist, pistoning it with fierce, rapid thrusts as she strummed her clit in a maddening rhythm.

"I'm going to come," she whispered, the sensations like an uncontrollable vortex spinning inside her.

"Fuck. Yes. Come for me, baby," he said through gritted teeth, stepping closer to her, jacking his cock with fast, hard thrusts of his hand.

She focused on his cock and let go, shaking and whimpering as she came on her own hand, shuddering as the crescendo pounded inside her, all through her. Jack pulled her hand away at that moment, nudged her legs apart, and slid inside her pussy. Her eyes widened and she cried out in pleasure as he filled her while she was climaxing.

"Oh my God!" she cried, the waves of orgasm tripling in intensity as he thrust and retreated and pounded again, grabbing onto her climax and lifting her right into another one. She clutched his shoulders as he rode her hard, capturing her lips as he came with a groan, spilling inside her with a wild shudder, his tongue sliding over hers in hungry possession.

It wasn't until they caught their breath, until the racking spasms had calmed and finally ceased, that Callie realized she hadn't even paid attention to the other people around them, hadn't noticed whether they'd been watching or not, hadn't looked to them to see what they'd been doing the entire time she and Jack had been engaged in their play.

She didn't even care if they'd watched, if they'd gotten off on what she and Jack had done.

He kissed her again, withdrew ,and helped her right her clothing.

"You okay?" he asked.

She nodded and smiled. "Oh yeah. More than okay."

And she had been worried about tonight? What the hell had been wrong with her? She trusted Jack. She trusted her heart and her instincts where he was concerned. When she was with him she felt warm, safe, and cared for.

She was falling crazy in love with him. Damn. How had that happened? Well, she knew how it had happened. He was gorgeous, successful, kind, generous, good to her, fun to be with, and shared the same interests. He catered to her sexually like . . . well, even more so than Bobby ever had. When she was with him, she felt whole.

She was having the best sex of her life with this man. Her heart was happy for the first time in a very long time. She might never let him go.

Ever.

six

"jack. you got a minute?"

Jack looked up from his desk and nodded surprised to see Bob in the office on a Sunday. Jack had popped in to do an hour's worth of work, thinking he'd have the place to himself. Guess not. But he always had a minute for Robert Walters, one of the senior partners in the firm. "Sure, Bob. Come on in."

In his early sixties with no plans to retire anytime soon, Bob was still fit and still a go-getter, still at the top of his game in the legal field. Every one of the partners aspired to be just like him. The man was dynamic, successful, and well-respected, if a little bit stuffy and conservative, but Jack had always worked well with him.

"You did a great job with the hospital benefit the other night," Bob said, taking a seat across from Jack's desk.

"Thanks. They raised a ton of money. Even surpassed the goal."

"That should make our client happy," Bob said with a grin.

Jack smiled and leaned back in his chair. "Well, that's what we like to do. Make our clients happy."

"Though you didn't make any of our club ladies happy by blow-ing them off that night."

Ah, word traveled fast in Silverwood social circles. "Well, I was busy that night. And I had a date."

Bob arched a brow. "Anyone I know?"

As if Bob hadn't already gotten the details of who Jack had been with that night. "No, I don't think so."

"Is she a club member?"

"No idea. I didn't check her membership card before I asked her out."

Bob's gaze narrowed. "I don't think I need to remind you how important it is that you find a woman within your social circle, Jack. As a potential senior partner in this firm, I trust you will choose wisely in that area. There are many women from the appropriate families who would be a fine fit for you."

He so wasn't having this conversation. He grabbed a pencil and clenched it tight in his fist. "I'll keep that in mind, Bob."

Bob stood and nodded. "Anyway, good job on the benefit. As al-ways, we know we can count on you to do the right thing."

Bob left the office and shut the door. Jack broke the pencil in half, then flung it into his trash can.

What. The. Fuck. Had Bob really just come into his office and told him his choice of date for the benefit had been socially unac-ceptable? They didn't even know Callie, yet they had already passed judgment on her because she wasn't a member of the club, wasn't from their social circle.

Anger seethed in his gut like a hot poker had stabbed him. They knew nothing about her. She came from the same background as him, so what made him acceptable and her not? Bullshit double stan-dard was what it was. And he wouldn't tolerate it.

They could dictate his work but never his private life.

He loved Callie. What he did with his private life was none of their goddamn business.

Whoa.

He loved Callie. He'd been lonely for so long he couldn't believe he'd found a woman like her. Kind, generous, with a beautiful heart, a hot body, and a wanton sex drive that made him crazy. She was nothing like the gold-digging women he was used to escorting around town. How did he get so lucky to find a treasure like her? And she shared his voyeuristic and exhibitionist tendencies. The more he dated her, the more he realized she was exactly what he wanted in his life, how lacking his existence had been before he'd met her. No wonder he looked forward to stopping in her shop in the morning for coffee. She'd been the brightest spot in his day for a very long time.

Isn't that what love was all about? He grinned as he replayed that thought over and over in his head. Yeah, he was in love with her. She was perfect for him.

The senior partners could take that and shove it up their asses.

He'd do whatever he wanted with his life. Maybe it was time to make some serious changes.

"i thought we might take in a movie tonight."

Callie looked up from the sink in her kitchen where she was washing up the last of the dinner dishes. Jack had barbecued chicken kabobs and she was doing the cleanup. They'd had another wonderful night together. Callie couldn't believe how lucky she'd been finding someone like Jack. She kept wondering where the flaw was in this relationship, but so far she hadn't found one. They meshed perfectly, came from very similar backgrounds, had the same values, and they sure had the same sex drive.

It was perfect. Scary perfect.

"A movie?" she asked.

"Yeah. You game?"

Movie. Game. Somehow she got the idea they weren't just going to be watching a movie. She grinned. "Sure. I love movies. Drive-in or theater?"

He arched one dark brow. "Now, there's a thought. I haven't been to a drive-in since I was a teenager."

She laughed. "Me either. But it's hot as blazes outside. I vote for a theater."

"Dark in there, ya know."

"We could sit in the back row and make out . . . or something."

"Or something," he added with a sly grin.

they decided on the last movie of the night. less crowded. In fact, they arrived a little late, and the previews were already showing. The theater was dark. Only a half-dozen couples came to see the film, which had been out for awhile. And they did choose the very back row, stadium seating, which meant they were sitting high up. And no one else sat up there with them.

"This film has won several awards," Callie whispered as they settled in their seats. "It's supposed to be really good."

"I'm looking forward to it."

By thirty minutes into the film Callie was wincing. The film was terrible. And she had chosen the movie. She kept glancing over at Jack, knowing he was bored out of his mind, but he was being very nice, his gaze directed at the screen, seemingly absorbed in the movie.

Absorbed, ha! He was probably sleeping with his eyes open.

Ugh. The movie sucked. They should have gone for the action

movie Jack wanted to see. It had to have been better than this pile of crap they were stuck watching.

She'd have to make it up to him. Somehow.

She looked down at the other people in the theater, then behind her, then at Jack, and an idea hit her. A really nasty one, one that made her clit swell against her jeans.

Oh that would be naughty, wouldn't it? But then, wasn't the thought of being caught half the fun? She shifted in her seat and casually draped her hand on Jack's thigh. He turned his gaze to her and smiled, then resumed watching the movie.

She moved her hand a little farther over, inching her fingers upward. Jack kept his gaze focused on the screen, but his lips curled into a wry grin.

Callie's pussy quivered. She leaned over and placed her hand on his cock and began to rub. Her body heated, her nipples beading against her thin tank top. Jack didn't look at her, but his breathing began to increase.

And his cock began to harden. In fact, it got hard fast, soon outlined against his jeans.

Sweet. She loved knowing she could get such a swift reaction from him. She rubbed her hand against him for awhile longer, totally unfocused on the movie now, then popped the button on his jeans. He leaned back in the chair. She drew the zipper down. He lifted his hips. She tugged his jeans partway down so she could pull out his cock.

Her clit throbbed now, rubbing against the seam of her jeans. Goddamn, she wanted to climb on that dick and ride him until they both had shuddering orgasms. But what she wanted even more was to suck him until he shot come down her throat.

She stroked his length, enjoying the power of him in her hands, the heat and steely strength of his cock as she gripped it and began to stroke. Slow at first, grasping it lightly and smoothing her hand over the ridges, circling the wide crest with her fingers and spiraling downward until her fist rested on his balls.

Though the noise from the movie was loud, she tuned it out, focused only on Jack's breathing, the sounds as he inhaled and exhaled. She watched his cock, his balls, mesmerized by the pearly liquid that beaded at the tip of his shaft. Oh, she wanted to taste that. She repositioned so she was on her knees on her chair, then bent over him and swiped the head of his cock, thrilled at his sharp intake of breath when her tongue glided over the smooth crest to capture his precome with her tongue.

"Baby," he whispered in the darkness, his hand cupping the back of her neck. She shivered, engrossed in pleasuring him, knowing he was watching around them to make sure no one noticed them.

Or maybe he didn't even care. She hoped he didn't, because she didn't. Her panties were damp with her own excitement; she knew that Jack would take care of her needs later. Right now, this was all about him, about catering to his desires. She cupped his cock head between her lips and lightly scraped her teeth over the sensitive tissue, then closed her mouth over him and leaned down, taking him in.

He groaned, low in his throat, his fingers tightening in her hair, grasping hold of the tendrils as she sucked him deep, then withdrew, then forward again, then withdrew, establishing a rhythm. She cupped his balls, cradling them in her hands and giving them a gentle squeeze as she rolled her tongue over his cock head. He arched his hips and drove his cock against her throat.

He was close, his balls taut against her hand, his body tensing. She sucked harder, wrapping her fingers around the base of his cock and squeezing his shaft as she licked the crest.

She had no idea that fucking him with her mouth like this could be so intensely exciting, could make her want to come with such a wild, primal hunger, but it did. Seeing him grip the arms of the seat with his hands, his knuckles whitening as he tensed and pumped his hips to propel his cock against her mouth was so incredibly arousing she went liquid inside.

She hummed against his cock, needing his orgasm almost as much as she needed her own. With a loud groan he erupted against her tongue, spurting hot jets of come against the roof of her mouth. She closed her lips around him and took him deep, swallowing the salty fluid until he had no more to give her, until he gave a last shudder, then relaxed against her.

Satisfied and smiling, she wiped her mouth, kissed him, then sat back and let him readjust his clothing while she took a sip of soda, her body flaming with need.

He grabbed her hand and stood. "I hope you've had enough of this horrible movie, because I need to take you out of here and fuck you until you scream."

She grinned. "Movie? What movie?"

He laced his fingers within hers and hauled her out of the theater in record time. She practically had to run to keep up with him. His face was grim. He wasn't smiling.

Jack was a man on a mission.

Since she was the mission, she didn't mind the single-minded look of utter concentration on his face. Anticipation tingled down her spine.

By the time they reached the crowded parking lot, she was out of breath. He opened the door to his SUV, and she slid inside, started to buckle her seat belt, while he went around to the driver's side. When he got in, he looked at her.

"Don't bother with the seat belt."

"Huh?"

"Climb in back, take your pants off, and lay down on the seat."

"Here?" She looked around. Wall-to-wall cars, people coming and going. Her pussy flared with excitement.

"Now, Callie. Goddamit I don't have much patience."

Her belly quivered. She climbed into the backseat and shifted enough to unsnap and unzip her jeans, then slid them down. Jack turned to watch her, his eyes smoky dark.

"Not fast enough. Hurry up."

Her heart began to pound, her blood racing as she scurried out of her pants and tossed them into the back of the SUV. Down to her panties, she waited.

"Those, too. Unless you want me to rip them to shreds."

Dayum. Her clit throbbed with a pulsing ache, wondering what Jack was planning. She drew her panties down over her hips and legs and cast them aside, too.

"Now lay down."

She laid on the seat. He crawled over the seat and kneeled on the floor next to her.

"Raise your knees to your chest, and spread your legs apart."

She did, struggling to find her breath. Her throat was dry. Were people walking by? The windows of the SUV were tinted, but could people see in?

"Spread 'em, Callie. Now."

She did, inching her legs apart a little. Jack wound his arms around her thighs and drew them farther apart.

"I could smell your pussy in the movie theater while you were sucking me. You were hot then, weren't you?" he asked, drawing his head down between her legs.

"Yes."

"Did it turn you on to blow me?"

"Yes." Blood roared in her ears. His hot breath tickled her thighs. She might faint.

"I'm going to eat your pussy here in the backseat of my car. I want you to scream when you come, Callie. I want everyone to hear you come."

"Oh, God, Jack." Could she do that? Knowing someone might walk by?

The first touch of his tongue to her pussy made her shriek. Hot, wet, he lapped the swollen slit, licking up the juices that poured from her. She arched up against his mouth, dying at the sensations. He moved his mouth from her clit all the way over her pussy, licking, sucking, rolling his tongue over the swollen bud, then teasing her by moving away from it and sliding it into her cunt to tongue fuck her over and over again until she thought she might die.

Then he started over again, swirling his tongue over her clit, taking her so close to climax that she clutched his head and began to pull his head down, holding him there, refusing to let him move his beautiful mouth.

"Suck me, Jack," she cried, bucking her hips upward. "Make me come! Right there, oh yes, right there!"

Then it was happening, and she couldn't hold back the screams of ecstasy as she climaxed, flooding his mouth with hot cream. She held his mouth over her pussy as she undulated against the sweet waves of orgasm, shuddering and whimpering so loud she knew anyone walking by would know exactly what was going on.

She didn't care. She was in heaven. Blissful, torturous heaven.

When she came down from the ultimate high, she let go, certain she was smothering him. He raised up and kissed her thigh, moving up her body, shucking his jeans in the process and thrusting his cock inside her. She wrapped her legs around him, driving him to the hilt inside her pussy.

"Tight," he murmured before taking her mouth. She tasted her come, licked it from his lips before diving inside his mouth with her tongue to lick the velvet softness of his.

He braced himself with one hand on the window and pounded his cock against her, renewing her desire again, taking her higher and higher with every stroke against her clit.

"Fuck me, Jack," she urged, squeezing his ass with her heels as she lifted against him, digging her nails into his back. He growled and buried his face in her neck, powering hard thrusts against her until she splintered and cried out again, this time taking him with her. He groaned, took her mouth, coming with hard, shuddering spasms against her.

She stroked his sweat-soaked back, her fingers gliding over his muscled skin, kissing his neck and tasting the salt there, too. She licked him, and he laughed.

"I'm sweating on you," he murmured.

"I don't care."

"I don't think I can move."

"I don't care."

"That movie really sucked."

She laughed. "I don't care."

callie couldn't help it. she smiled all day at work on Monday. Jack stopped by as usual, only this time it was different. They were different together. Oh, he wasn't about to embarrass her at work, so he ordered his coffee like any other customer, but it was still . . . different. He smiled different, acted different, and so did she. She giggled. Giggled! It was syrupy sweet. She was appalled at herself.

Her employees laughed at her, but they were also thrilled for her, and so in awe that she'd managed to land someone like Jack Fellows. She still couldn't quite believe it was real. She felt like Cinderella.

They were supposed to see each other tonight, though Jack said he had to work late and would come over to her place around eight.

She closed up the shop at two like she always did, finishing up the bank deposit paperwork. As usual, she was the last person in the shop but had already locked the doors. When someone knocked, she looked up and shook her head, pointing to the CLOSED sign.

"May I speak with you please, Miss Jameson?" An older gentlemen spoke through the glass door. "I'm with Jack Fellows's law firm."

Curious, Callie unlocked the door and motioned the man inside.

"Thank you." He smiled and held out his hand. "I'm Bob Walters, one of the senior partners at the law firm where Jack works."

Callie smiled and shook his hand. "Very nice to meet you, Mr. Walters. Please, have a seat."

"Thank you. And call me Bob." He sat at the table and folded his hands.

"Would you like some coffee? I've already closed everything up, but I'd be happy to make some."

"No, that's quite all right, but thank you."

Okay, so why was someone from Jack's firm here, and how did he know her name? Curiosity was killing her. She didn't know whether to hope or dread what this man was about to say.

"Miss Jameson, you're ruining Jack's career."

Her heart dropped to her feet. Well, there was her answer. "Excuse me?"

"Let me be perfectly honest. Jack is an up-and-comer with the firm. He has a very bright future. But he also works for a high-profile company, one with prominent social stature in Silverwood. Society and its connections and influences is vital, especially to someone who is about to become a senior partner."

"I'm confused, Mr. Walters. I don't understand why you've come here or what you're trying to say."

"What I'm trying to say is that I was in the movie theater with you and Jack last night. I know exactly what you two were doing in the back row."

Oh, God. Oh, God. The senior partner of Jack's firm was in the movie theater? Shit! What had she done? Flames of embarrassment licked up her neck. She looked down at the paperwork on the table, too ashamed to even look the man in the eye.

"As you can imagine, we cannot entertain that kind of depravity at Walters and Little. If word of what kind of sexual activities Jack is engaged in got out, his career would be ruined."

Tears pooled in Callie's eyes. She blinked hard, forcing them back. "I understand." She would not do anything to hurt Jack's career. She looked up at the man, trying to muster up whatever shreds of dignity remained. "What do you want me to do?"

"End your relationship with Jack. Let him find a . . . different kind of woman. One who won't embarrass him." Bob placed his hand over Callie's. "If you care at all for him, you'll do what's best for him and for his career. He's worked long and hard for his success, and he's almost reached the top. Don't make the mistake of standing in his way now."

She shook her head, forcing the nausea away. "I would never do that."

Bob nodded. "Good girl. I knew you cared for him. I could see that." He stood. "I'm sorry to do this, but I only want the best for Jack. He's like a son to me."

She walked to the door and unlocked it, her throat raw. She couldn't even speak; she just let the man out, locked the door, and pulled the night shade down. Then she fell into the chair and collapsed, letting the racking sobs overtake her.

Oh, God, what had she been thinking? She'd almost ruined Jack's life with her sexual perversions. Swiping at the tears, she stood and grabbed a towel, cleaned her face, then grabbed the bank deposit, determined to do the right thing.

No way would she stand in the way of Jack and his career. What they had was fun, but fun was one thing, and a man's career was another. She might love him, but she wasn't the right woman for him.

Tonight, she'd tell him it was over. It was the right thing to do. Because she did love him, she'd let him go.

She should have known better than to think she and Jack could ever be together.

She should have stayed on her own side of town and kept her sexual fantasies to herself.

jack hoped he wasn't too late as he knocked on Callie's door. Anticipation knotted inside him. God, he'd missed her today. She'd been all he could think about since he'd seen her bright smile this morning for coffee, saw the blush tingeing her cheeks when their fingers had brushed as she'd handed his cup over.

And now he felt like a teenager as he stood at her door waiting for her to open it.

So this was love. He grinned, feeling stupid and happy at the same time.

But his smile froze when he saw the look on her face when she opened the door.

"Callie, what's wrong?"

She looked awful, her eyes swollen, her expression so sad she looked as if someone had died.

"We need to talk. Come in."

He stepped inside and she shut the door, but she didn't invite him further into her house.

Uh-oh. Something was up. When he reached for her, she pulled away. "Callie, what's the matter?"

She wrapped her arms around herself. "I don't want to see you anymore."

His heart skipped a beat. "What?"

"The weekend we had was fun and all, but I really don't want to continue this."

Okay, something wasn't right here. "You can't be serious."

"I am."

He dragged his hand through his hair, confused as hell. "This doesn't make any sense."

Callie shrugged. "Look, Jack. I'm busy with my career, and you're busy with yours. I had a nice time this weekend, but you really can't expect me to behave that way every day, can you? I mean let's be realistic here. The public sex was hot and all, but it's not my everyday life. For a one-time fling, great. But that was it."

One-time fling? What the fuck? Hurt knifed hot in his stomach, leaving him at a loss for words. He couldn't believe this was the same Callie he'd just spent the weekend with. Something was off, but he couldn't figure it out.

"Tell me what's really going on, Callie. This isn't you."

Her gaze narrowed. "Isn't it? You really don't know me at all, Jack. You know nothing about me. We had a fun fuck, but that was it. You were a bet I made with my friends. A weekend of wanton sex. I fulfilled the terms of the bet, and now it's over."

"A bet?"

"Yes. We've been making bets since we were in high school. It was a game. A silly little game."

"I see."

He couldn't breathe. This wasn't happening. He'd been thinking forever with Callie, and all the while she'd been thinking weekend fuck. A bet. He was a goddamn bet. Shit. How could he have been so off base?

"Look, Jack, I'm sorry if I led you on in any way. I didn't mean to. I had fun. But really, I'm tired and I have to get up early for work." She opened the door and looked at him expectantly. "If you don't mind . . ."

He looked at the open door, then back at her. "Wow. I was really off base about you. About us. I'm sorry, Callie." He turned and walked out the door, wincing at the sound of it closing behind him.

He turned and watched as the lights went out in Callie's house, but as he climbed into his car and drummed his fingers on the steering wheel, he shook his head.

His instincts had never been wrong. They'd seen him through years of college and numerous cases at work. Instinct told him now that Callie had been lying.

Something was off about her performance back there. And that's what it had just been: a performance.

Callie was many things, but a cold, heartless bitch wasn't one of them.

She was warm, caring, generous.

He wanted that Callie back, and he was going to find out what the hell had happened to cause her turnaround.

callie stood at the window and watched jack get into his car, then just sit there.

"Drive away, Jack. Just drive away."

Her heart ached so much she was afraid she was going to die from the pain. It was like losing Bobby all over again, that heart-wrenching, stabbing feeling of loss.

The hurt in Jack's eyes as she'd flung her noncaring attitude at him had torn her apart. She'd never felt so callous before. God, it hurt. She wanted to open her door and run out to his car, throw her arms around him, and tell him she was lying, that the weekend they'd spend together had meant everything to her. That she was sorry for hurting him, that she hadn't meant anything she'd just said.

But if she did that, she'd ruin his life. Everything he'd worked so hard to achieve.

Finally, he drove away.

She sank to the floor and sobbed.

seven

jack searched the restaurant for two familiar faces, finally locating Blair and Abby at a corner booth. He maneuvered his way through the crowd and slipped in the empty side of the booth.

"I appreciate you both agreeing to meet with me."

Blair shrugged. "No problem. What's up?"

"I was hoping you could tell me. What's up with Callie, that is."

Abby frowned. "What do you mean?"

He relayed what happened the other night, feeling strangely comforted when both women's eyes widened.

"That's not like Callie at all," Abby said.

"She doesn't have a mean bone in her body," Blair added. "And about the bet? She'd never throw it out to you like that. No way."

"Have you spoken to her at all about the weekend we spent together and what happened afterward?"

Blair shook her head. "She's been strangely unavailable. Says she's busy. Which is really unusual for her."

"I think she's avoiding talking to us. We know she's upset, she said it didn't work out for the two of you, but we thought it was the whole social status thing," Abby said.

"Social status?" Jack asked.

"She was worried about you two being so different socioeconom- ically," Blair explained.

Jack shook his head. "That's bullshit. And we talked about it. I told her my roots. I grew up on a farm, for the love of God. We come from the same type of background, so that wasn't an issue for her."

"Hmm, then you're right. That can't be it," Blair said, tapping her nails on the table.

"Maybe it had something to do with that guy from your firm stopping by her shop the other day," Abby said.

Jack's gaze shot to Abby. "What guy?"

"She didn't say. Only that one of the senior partners of your firm came by after she'd closed up shop, and that she didn't care very much for him. Some Walters guy. Monday, I think."

And Monday night was when she'd had her little good-bye talk with him. "Ah. I see."

"What?" Blair asked.

"I think I have an idea what might have happened."

"Does it have something to do with that guy from your firm?" Abby asked.

"I think it has everything to do with that guy from my firm." He reached for Abby and Blair's hands. "Thank you, ladies. I appreciate the information. Now I have to go talk to someone and hopefully get this cleared up with Callie."

"You do that," Blair said. "Because I don't think she's very happy right now."

"Well I'm sure as hell not happy without her. I want her back."

"That's what we like to hear." Abby squeezed his hand.

Jack left the restaurant and hopped in his car, trying not to let fury overtake him. The last thing he needed was a car wreck. He forced himself to calm down while he drove, but it was damned difficult. He had an idea, a really good idea, of what had transpired between Callie and Bob.

It was really too damn bad that murder was illegal, because it was first and foremost on his mind right now.

Even though it was late, he knew Bob would still be at the office. Bob was always at the office. Jack practiced breathing in through his nose and out through his mouth while he rode the elevator to the penthouse offices, then found Bob exactly where he knew he'd be: in his office, working. He must have one understanding wife.

He didn't even bother to knock, instead stepped in and said, "Bob, I need to know what the hell you said to Callie."

Bob swiveled around in his chair and smiled. "I saw the two of you in the movie theater the other night."

Bob was there? Ah, that explained some things. "I see. And?"

"So I told Ms. Jameson I saw the two of you and what you did. I said what you should have said to her. I told her to get lost."

Blind spots sparked in front of Jack's eyes. He didn't think he'd ever been this angry before.

Stay calm. Don't kill him. Oh, but he really wanted to. "What the fuck did you think gave you the right to go to her and say anything?"

"Because you weren't going to do it, and I will do anything I have to do to protect this firm."

Jack clenched his fists at his sides. He so wanted to hit the smug bastard right now. "Callie is no threat to the firm."

"Isn't she? We have a reputation to uphold, and we can't have sexually perverted partners in our firm. I like you, Jack. You have a killer instinct, and you're going to make a phenomenal senior partner. But it won't be with that depraved woman at your side. Now, you're going to find a socially acceptable woman and marry her, and have normal sex with that woman, and that's all I'm going to say on the subject."

"You can't dictate my private life, Bob."

Bob smirked. "Can't I? How fast do you think your career will sink once word gets out about your predilections for public sex?"

"You wouldn't do that."

Bob arched a brow. "Wouldn't I? You know me, Jack. I'll do whatever it takes to get what I want. And what I want is you in this firm as senior partner. And without that Jameson woman at your side. You continue to see her, that rather unpleasant information about you goes public."

"You can't prove it."

"I won't have to. All it takes is my word of what I saw in that movie theater. Once a background investigation is started, I'm sure we'll be able to uncover many sordid little secrets about you."

He could not fucking believe this was happening. "And to think I used to respect you."

"I don't care if you respect me or not, Jack. As long as you continue to make this firm millions of dollars a year, you can hate my guts. Now, if you'll excuse me, I have work to do."

"This isn't over, Bob."

Bob smiled, his lips curling in an ugly grin. "Yes, my son, it is."

Jack pivoted and left the office before he decided to do something he regretted. Like smashing his fist right through the son of a bitch's face. As he rode the elevator back down to the parking garage, he had to satisfy himself with imagined visuals of Bob's shattered nose and blood spattered all over his legal brief. Not quite as satisfying as the real thing, but it would have to do for now.

Bob thought he had won. But he was wrong. It wasn't over. Not by a long shot. He might think he had the last word, but Jack was a shark in this business, too, and he knew a few things. Things Bob wasn't aware he knew.

All he needed now was proof. In a few days, he'd be back in Bob's office, and this time, the senior partner wouldn't be smiling.

Bob had just challenged the wrong guy.

one week later jack was back in bob's office, a thick envelope in his hand. He tossed it on Bob's desk.

Bob looked up at him. "What's this?"

"You can open it if you'd like, but I'll tell you right now what's in it. First is my letter of resignation, effective immediately. Second is a packet of pictures of you engaged in a little oral sex with your mistress."

Bob gasped.

"Oh, yeah, Bob, did you think I didn't know about you and Janet? I've known for a long time about your three-times-a-week trysts with that hot little number. The pictures are nice. I'm sure your wife would love to know about them. Or, shall we say, her attorney would love to know about these pictures. And yes, they're just copies. I have the originals. Maybe you'd better start minding your own perversions instead of worrying about what everyone else is doing."

Bob tore open the envelope and pulled out the photos, his face going pale. He looked up at Jack. "What do you want?"

"You breathe one word of my personal life anywhere to anyone, and these pictures will not only be delivered to your home but to every other competing law firm and newspaper and legal publication in town. You take me down, I take you down."

Bob's face was turning now, going from stark white to an ugly mottled shade of red. "You dirty son of a bitch."

Jack shrugged. "Hey, I learned from the best, Bob."

"I'll have you disbarred for this."

Jack laughed. "You aren't going to do a goddamn thing to me. You leave me alone, and I'm going to leave you alone. And you leave

Callie alone, too." He placed his palms down hard on Bob's desk. So hard, in fact, that Bob pushed back, fear showing on his sweating face.

"If I find out you've gone anywhere near her, I will personally come up here and beat the living shit out of you. I grew up on a farm, Bob. Remember my roots? I'm not a lily white rich boy. I can get my hands dirty when I need to, and don't you ever forget that. And I know where to hide the bodies."

Bob's eyes widened, but before he could speak, Jack leaned in and said, "Don't you *ever* challenge me again."

He pushed back from Bob's desk and started to walk out, then stopped, paused, and turned around. "Oh, and by the way. I'm opening up my own firm, where I'll be competing with this so-called topnotch firm of yours. Get ready for it, Bob, because I'm about to go head-to-head with you. And, frankly, I think I'm better than you."

He turned and walked out, feeling better tonight than he had in the past week.

One major project down, one to go.

It was time to see Callie.

callie sat out on her front porch and tried to enjoy the summer breeze that drew in the scent of gardenias from her garden and ruffled the hem of her sundress. But no matter how hard she tried, she couldn't take any pleasure from the things that used to make her smile.

Then again, for the past week she'd taken no pleasure from anything at all.

Since the night she'd thrown Jack out of her house, she'd lived like a robot, doing her job during the day and coming home at night, wandering listlessly around her house until bedtime, then lying there staring at the ceiling, unable to sleep. She didn't even want to see Abby and Blair, couldn't bring herself to tell them what she'd done to Jack.

God, she missed him so much, mourned him like she'd mourned Bobby. Oh, she knew it wasn't the same. Bobby had died. He'd been her husband, her soul mate, the man she'd lived with for years. Jack had been a fling, a weekend thing, and nothing more. He still lived, and her life should just go on. It was an experiment, a bet, a dalliance that simply hadn't worked out.

So why did it hurt so damn much? Why did she feel like there was a hole in her stomach, a gnawing ache that wouldn't go away?

Because even though she and Jack had only been together one weekend, they'd been working at this a lot longer. They were destined to be together, and she'd let his asshole boss dictate that they should break up.

What was wrong with her, anyway? Did she think so little of herself that she bowed down to the dictates of some bigwig corporate lawyer just because he thought she wasn't good enough for Jack? Why hadn't she trusted in Jack enough to at least tell him what that Bob Walters guy had said? Why hadn't she left it up to Jack to decide if she wasn't good enough for him?

Why couldn't she decide if she was good enough for Jack? Where had her backbone gone, the grit and determination that had withstood the death of Bobby, the start-up of her own company? Why hadn't she stood up to Bob Walters? Why hadn't she gone toe-to-toe with him and argued that she *was* good enough for Jack?

Fuck Bob Walters. Or rather, Bob Walters could go fuck himself. That's what was wrong with her. She'd made the wrong damn decision. She'd let someone else decide for her, and it wasn't the right decision. She owed it to Jack to tell him the truth.

And then she owed it to him to tell him how she felt about him. If he walked away after that, then at least she'd know it was honest.

She stood and went inside to grab her phone, hesitating for only a second before dialing Jack's cell phone number. He picked it up on the first ring.

"Jack?"

"Callie?"

Her heart slammed against her ribs at the sound of his voice. Would he even want to talk to her? "I need to see you."

"Is that right?"

"Yes. I need to explain about the other night. The things I said to you . . . the reasons for them . . . oh, this is so hard to say by phone."

"Then why don't you say them in person?"

She whirled around, nearly jumping out of her skin at the sight of him standing in her doorway with the phone at his ear. She hung up her phone. "You're here."

He smiled and pocketed his phone. "Was on my way to see you, actually."

"You were?" She smoothed her sweaty palms down the side of her sundress.

"Yeah."

"Why?"

"Because I have a lot of things to tell you." He stepped into her house and closed the door.

She moved toward him. "I have things to tell you, too."

"You do?"

"Yes. About the night I threw you out of my house. I lied."

They were only inches apart now. She inhaled his scent, nearly crying because she missed his smell. She wanted to reach out for him, to jump into his arms and wrap her legs around him and just breathe him in.

"You did?"

"Yes. One of your senior partners came to see me and told me I shouldn't date you anymore. He was in the movie theater the night you and I were there. He saw us, said we were perverted and you continuing to see me could jeopardize your future with the firm."

"I know."

"Then he said—you know?"

"I figured it out after I went to talk to Blair and Abby."

"You talked to Blair and Abby?"

"After you threw me out. I knew something wasn't right. That's just not you, Callie. You don't act that way."

He knew her. He really did know her. Tears welled in her eyes, and she blinked them back. "I'm sorry, Jack. I'm so sorry I said all those hateful things to you. They hurt me as much as they hurt you."

He cupped her cheek, and she nearly died at the warmth and love she felt in his touch. "I know they hurt you, baby. I know he hurt you, too. But that son of a bitch isn't going to come anywhere near you, or me, again."

Her eyes widened. "What did you do?"

"I quit the firm."

"What?" She grasped his hand. "Why?"

"Because I won't be blackmailed. Besides, what we do isn't perverted, Callie. It's our business and no one else's. It doesn't hurt anyone, and it sure as hell doesn't affect my work performance. Besides, Bob Walters has been boinking his secretary for the past five years."

"No!"

Jack nodded. "Yeah, and I got the pictures to prove it. Dumped those on his desk tonight after he threatened to go public with *my* so-called perversions if I didn't toe the line and do exactly what he said."

Callie's legs were shaking. "I can't believe he threatened you like that." She looked up at him. "You got pictures of him with his secretary?"

He grinned. "Sure did. He won't be bothering us again. Ever. Not if he wants to hold onto all his money and doesn't want a messy, expensive divorce."

"Oh, my." Still, she somehow felt responsible for all this. "You quit your job because of me."

"No, Callie. I quit my job because the senior partner is an asshole. It has nothing to do with you."

"Yes it does. It's because of me, because of what we did, what we do."

"Hey." He pulled her against him, winding his arms around her back. "What we do is fun and doesn't hurt anyone. It's thrilling, sexually stimulating, and hotter than hell. There's not a damn thing wrong with it, so don't you feel ashamed or embarrassed. What Bob is doing with his secretary is depraved. What two consenting single adults do with each other is perfectly acceptable."

She nodded. "You're right. Still, I hate that you lost your job over this."

"I'm not. Come with me. I have something to show you."

He drove her downtown and parked on the street, then walked a short distance, entering a building under construction. A modest four-story office complex, it was a short walk from her shop.

"Where are we going?" she asked.

"My new office."

She wrinkled her nose under the smell of sawdust and paint as they walked the floor plan of his new space. Bright and airy, it was small, with an open reception area and three offices.

"I'm going to start small, but I expect to grow really fast."

"You started your own company."

He nodded, grinning. "Already have two clients that have jumped firms to follow me. Hired a secretary and have an associate coming on board Monday. I'll work from home until the offices are done, but I'm up and running officially."

She squeezed his hand. "I'm so proud of you, Jack."

"Hey, this was the kick in the ass I needed. I don't really think I was ever meant to be anyone's flunky. I've had adrenaline pumping ever since I made the decision to quit the firm and start my own business. Now I can do things my way. The right way."

"And you'll be a huge success at it."

"Just like you've been a huge success at starting your own business from scratch."

She beamed at his praise. "Thank you. I'd like to think so."

"I know so. Now, would you like to help me christen my new office space?"

The breeze flapped the plastic wall barriers against the wood, and Callie shook her head.

"Here?"

"Hell yeah. My dick's getting hard just thinking about fucking you here."

Her nipples tightened. She'd missed him, missed the excitement of having him in her life. Without him, she felt empty. With him, every day was an adventure. "Where?"

He looked around, then took her hand and headed to the corner office. "My office. Let's look out on downtown while I fuck you."

There was a worktable right in the corner and some clean paint drapes. Jack opened up the drapes and spread them across the table, then palmed his cock through his jeans. "I'm already hard for you, Callie. I need my cock inside you now."

His sense of urgency spurred her desire, the breeze blowing in and flipping up her dress. She moved to the table and lay belly down over it, turning her head to look at him. "Fuck me, Jack."

She turned away and looked out over the scenic downtown, anticipation moistening her as she felt Jack step behind her, heard the rasp of his zipper. He reached under her dress and flipped it over her back, then she felt warm lips on the skin of her lower back.

"Such beautiful skin, Callie," he said. "Like the softest honey, you just melt under my hand."

He cupped her pussy. She moaned and did just as he said, melting all over his hand right through her panties. He reached for the strings at her hips and drew the panties down and off, baring her cunt, then kissed his way down between her legs, burying his mouth there and sliding his tongue into her pussy.

Her legs tensed as he licked the length of her, swirling his tongue over her distended clit. The pleasure this man gave her was unlike anything she'd ever known. Forbidden, wanton, more than she could ever desire, he took her on a wild journey that inflamed her senses and intoxicated her. When she was just at the brink of orgasm, he stopped, stood up, and leaned over to kiss her. She licked her juices from his lips, sucking on his tongue as he entered her from behind.

He grasped her wrists and pounded her while she looked out at all the office buildings downtown, wondering if anyone was in their office looking out their window at them. She creamed just thinking about being watched.

"Fuck me harder, Jack."

He powered deep, so hard the workbench scooted across the floor. His balls slapped against her clit, driving her closer and closer to a climax.

"Come for me, Callie," he said, his voice gritty and dark against her ear. "Come on my cock."

He ground against her and reached down to massage her clit. That sent her over the edge. She dug her nails into the her palms and let out a cry as she came, bucking hard against him and sending him into his own orgasm. He flooded her pussy with come and shoved deep, groaning against her neck and sinking his teeth into her nape. She shuddered at the intimacy of him marking her that way.

They were both sweating. And panting. When Jack raised up, the cool breeze from outside wafted over her damp skin. He pulled her upright and turned her around, planting his mouth on hers to kiss her. Rather than a kiss filled with passion, it was a soft, gentle kiss, filled with emotion, with feeling, with what she hoped was love, because that's what she poured into it, grabbing onto his shoulders and showing him without words how she felt about him.

When they broke apart, she laid her head on his shoulder and let him stroke her back, feeling so incredibly complete she didn't want to move, afraid the fairy tale would be shattered if she said a word.

"Think we'll ever make love in a bed?"

She snorted. Talk about the intrusion of reality. She lifted her head and smiled. "I don't know. I guess we could try it."

He grasped her hand, and they headed for the stairs. "Would be different, that's for sure."

"I'll have to think about it. I'm not sure if I'm up for anything that kinky yet."

He laughed as they headed down to the street. "You're right. We should take it slow. We'll start on the porch again and work our way inside."

When they passed by her shop, she paused, looked at him, then back at the shop, then back at him, arching a brow.

"Well, we haven't properly christened your shop yet," he said.

She grinned and dug for her keys.

epilogue

"i'm in love," callie said, slipping into the booth across from Blair and Abby.

Blair and Abby exchanged eye rolls, then Blair looked at her and said, "Tell us something we don't know."

Callie grinned. "I mean seriously and completely and head over heels in love with Jack."

Abby signaled the waitress to bring a margarita for Callie. "Did you not hear Blair? It's written all over your grinning face, you twit. Of course you're in love with Jack."

"So you two got things settled, I take it?" Blair asked, grabbing for a chip from the basket.

"Yes, we did. And he's starting his own law business. Which is just a short walk from the coffee shop."

"Fantastic."

"He wants me to move in with him."

Blair arched a brow. "Damn. That's a whirlwind courtship."

"He loves me. I love him. We have a future together." She palmed her own cheeks and took a deep breath. "God, I can't believe this is all happening so fast."

Abby shrugged. "If it's right and it's meant to be, then it is. You can't fight fate. Look at what happened with Seth and me. I never expected to fall in love after that weekend, but it happened. And it was quick for me, too."

"So true," Callie said. "Look at all of us. Not too long ago we were lamenting being single with no man in our lives. Now all three of us are hooked up and in love."

"And I'm getting married. I mean really getting married this time," Blair said, shaking her head. "To Rand, of all people."

"Just don't put us in foofy, lime green dresses for the wedding," Callie teased.

Blair rolled her eyes. "I think you know me better than that. Slinky, sexy, and designer all the way for my babes."

"I can't believe how much has changed for all of us," Abby said. "I'm starting up a new practice and have a man I love in my life now. Callie's in love. Blair's in love with Rand. Finally," she added with a teasing wink.

"Unbelievable, when you think about it," Callie said.

"And we owe it all to your idea for the bet, Blair," Abby added.

Blair grinned. "That was one hell of a bet, wasn't it?"

The waitress brought Callie's margarita, and she lifted it high and said, "A toast. To the best damn bet Blair ever made."

"To the bet!" they all said in unison.